Fighting
Redemption

KATE McCARTHY

Fighting Redemption

Copyright © Kate McCarthy 2013

ISBN-13: 978-0-9875261-5-1
ISBN-10: 0987526154

This is a work of fiction. Names, characters, businesses, places, events and incidents are either the products of the author's imagination or used in a fictitious manner. Any resemblance to actual persons, living or dead, or actual events is purely coincidental.

Please note that Kate McCarthy is an Australian author and Australian English spelling and slang have been used in this book.

Editing by Maxann Dobson, The Polished Pen.
www.polished-pen.com/

Cover Art courtesy of Damonza
http://damonza.com

Interior Design by Angela McLaurin, Fictional Formats
https://www.facebook.com/FictionalFormats

Table of Contents

There are things that we don't want to happen but have to accept,
things we don't want to know but have to learn,
and people we can't live without but have to let go.

Author's Note

Fighting Redemption, while a fictional story,
deals with the subject of the war in Afghanistan and
how it impacts the lives of soldiers and those who are left behind.
The utmost care has been taken to write this story with respect for
those who serve or have served their country
and the families that love them.

Special Acknowledgement

To the former and current soldiers of the Australian Army
who have assisted me with ensuring the accuracy of the following
fictional events, thank you so very much.

Dedication

To my daughter and son.
I'll love you longer than the stars that live in the sky.

Prologue

Not wishing to invite attention or conversation, she stood alone, adrift from the crowd—vulnerable. Dressed casually in fitted jeans and an emerald green cardigan, she was tall and a little on the slim side. Her tousled blonde waves were tied in a careless knot at the nape of her neck as though she hadn't given it a second thought, yet the effect was effortlessly beautiful. Shivering from the cold, she wrapped her arms around her body, hands moving up and down to keep warm. Green eyes remained focused on one thing, her watchful gaze never deviating from its direction. Some followed her line of sight and smiled indulgently. One man, after seeing what caught her attention, changed his mind about approaching her.

All of a sudden she smiled, wide, vibrant. The way it lit up her face drew the attention of those around her. It was like you'd been given the gift of seeing the sun radiate brilliant rays through dark clouds. It changed her demeanour completely and was enough to take your breath away. Her arms unfolded, the golden flecks in her eyes sparkling with life, and she appeared less isolated and more approachable. It made you wish it was you she was smiling at. That you were the one she needed to light up her entire soul from the inside out.

"Mummy, mummy!" yelled a little boy.

People turned at his shout seeing a toddler starting to lose his baby fat and heading towards lean, his windblown, dark brown hair curling softly over his ears. His cheeks were rosy from the cold, and his brown eyes were filled with delight as he ran towards the beautiful, solitary woman. You wouldn't have picked the resemblance until she smiled. Her profile and the same delight in her eyes told you how much they belonged together.

"Hey, my baby." She laughed, leaning down to catch him as he jumped into her arms.

"Tell me again, Mummy," he demanded as she stood back up, the little boy happily settled on her hip, his place in her arms firmly and familiarly established.

"Again, sweetie?"

He wriggled impatiently. "Pease, Mummy. Wanna hear 'bout Daddy."

"Okay," she agreed.

She shifted over to a nearby seat and sat down, the little boy settling on her lap. Patiently while he fidgeted and squirmed before getting comfortable, she took the time to tuck a loose wave behind her ear and breathe deeply to calm the racing of her heart.

"Ready?"

At his nod her smile dimmed, turning from indulgent to bittersweet, and a light sheen of tears stung her eyes. She closed them for a brief moment, composing herself, before blinking them back open to begin the tale.

"Your daddy was an SAS soldier with the Australian Army. Now these soldiers aren't just your ordinary, everyday soldiers. These are the toughest, strongest men that ever lived. They—"

He interrupted with the same question he'd asked the last time she told her tale. "Stronger than SEALS right, mummy?"

"Yes, honey. The very best," she replied at the interruption. This time, she expanded a little further. "Not just strong of body, though, sweetheart, but strong of mind ..." she pointed to her temple "... and strong of heart." She pointed to her heart. "But your father always said that being a soldier is never just about strength. It's also about knowing what you want, how hard you're willing to work for it, and what you're willing to sacrifice for it." She choked over the last words and faltered.

The little boy placed a chubby hand on her cheek. "You 'kay, Mummy?"

She swallowed the sadness that formed a lump in her throat and forced a smile for her son. "Yes, little man, Mummy is okay. In fact, Mummy is going to be just fine." She ran a loving fingertip down the soft, precious skin of his cheek. "Your father wanted to be an SAS soldier so much. More than he even wanted to breathe."

"What's breathe, Mummy?"

"See this?" She drew in a deep breath and exhaled noisily into his hair so he giggled. "That's breathing. Breathing helps keep your heart beating, sweetheart."

His big, dark eyes peered up at her intently, and her heart ached. "Did Daddy's heart beat too, Mummy?"

She swallowed another lump at the memory of the words forever etched into her heart. "Your daddy once told me that his heart only beat for one thing."

"What was that?"

"I'll tell you."

She began the rest of the story ...

Chapter One

Approximately 5 years earlier
Forward Operating Base (FOB) Khost
Eastern Afghanistan

"Yo, Kendall!" Jake called out.

Ryan turned and gave him the finger. Jake hadn't shut up the entire afternoon. He'd been trying to tune him out, but Jake was a relentless bastard. Always had been.

Jake shook his head in mock disgust. "That all you got, mate?"

Ryan chuckled and turned back, continuing behind their Troop Commander, Paul "Monty" Montgomery, as he set the pace along the Pakistani border. Monty was enough to inspire confidence in any soldier—fit and experienced with uncanny instincts. He'd proven himself numerous times under fire. Relying on Monty to make split-second decisions—whether to fire or hold ground, push forward or retreat—was reassuring as fuck.

Twenty-five long days they'd been in the field now, finishing up their final patrol before heading back to base. Their SAS team was tasked with reconnaissance. Gathering intelligence on the Taliban in the mountains of Eastern Afghanistan was notoriously dangerous.

The air was dry and hot, and the mountains rocky and a pain in the ass to navigate under the cover of night. And the dust—fuck, he was over it. It got in his hair, his clothes, and even his ass crack, making the trek that much more uncomfortable.

"Is that all I got?" Ryan raised his brows at Jake as they kept up the punishing pace. "It'll hold you for now."

"I need more than that to hold me. I need a drink and something to fucking eat."

Ryan's stomach grumbled in reply, rolling over with a loud, queasy thump. Rations had been depleted two days ago, and he'd been pushing away visions of thick steaks and hot chips ever since. "Don't talk about food."

"How much further 'til we hit our extraction zone, Monty?" Jake called out quietly.

"Two k's," Monty replied without allowing his focus on their surroundings to waver. Despite the talk, the hunger, and the exhaustion, his entire team remained alert and vigilant. The thought of an action being the cause of an injury or death was their worst nightmare—simply unthinkable. But that shit happened, and when it did, Ryan was just that much more determined to keep being a soldier. They all had more to fight for than a war—they were fighting for those they'd lost too.

"I can handle that," Jake replied. "Not so sure about Kendall here. He's looking a bit weak and tired. Maybe we need to stop so he can have a nanna nap."

With a back aching from the heavy weight of his pack, Ryan turned and rolled his dark brown eyes at Jake.

Jake grinned in reply, his teeth white against the filthy camouflage covering his face. Jake was a good looking sonofabitch—

choppy blond hair, green eyes, and a movie star smile. It fooled most because he was a tough, determined bastard with more drive in his pinky finger than any other asshole that made it through SAS selection. Jake could out-run, out-shoot, and out-lift all of them. He was only one of a handful that made it through the hell that was SAS selection.

"Good one, asshole," Ryan muttered. "Why don't you quit eyeballing my ass and keep your mind to the fucking terrain."

After a few moments of peace, a loud thunk broke the silence and a quiet "fuck" was muttered. They turned and laughs rang out at their team sniper, Chris Galloway, on his hands and knees, palms no doubt bleeding from the sharp rocks. He stood and dusted his hands on his Army issue fatigues.

"Go fuck yourselves," he said with a rueful grin.

"Christ. No talk about fucking. I'm horny," Kyle moaned.

"You're a sick bastard, Brooks," Jake told Kyle.

Kyle grinned and grabbed his crotch. "No sicker than you."

Ryan tuned them out for a while, concentrating on keeping his feet moving, until Jake's voice filled the silence again. "Gonna Skype Fin when we get back. You should say hello to her, Kendall. You never do."

The old familiar ache at the mention of Jake's sister taunted him, and he shoved it away. "Why the fuck would I want to do that? You Skype enough for all of us combined ..." he shook his head "... chattering like a fucking girl."

Ryan had no intention of talking to Finlay Tanner, and he was desperate to keep it that way. Six impossibly long years had passed since he walked out of her life. Despite not having seen her since, Ryan thought of her constantly, the ache of missing her hurting a little more each day. The never ending loneliness he felt had been his choice, and he forced himself to live with it. Being a soldier like his grandfather had been Ryan's dream for as long as he could remember. Like blinking or breathing, it was just there, living inside him, giving his body a reason to function. He couldn't let anything stand in the way of it. Yet Fin almost had, without him even realising it until it was almost too late.

Jake interrupted his thoughts. "Too bad. I'll drag you there if I have to. Maybe Fin might be able to get a smile out of you, considering my jokes are wasted on your sorry ass."

"I can smile." Ryan turned and bared his teeth, locking his thoughts of Fin into the box of precious memories tucked inside him—an almost impossible feat with Jake being her older brother. They looked so much alike, down to sharing the same cheeky sparkle of life in their matching green eyes. "Besides, I told you to quit eyeballing my ass. Next thing you'll be getting a boner over it."

"Fuck. I'm trying to get you to smile, not get all impressed over my monster dick."

"Jesus, your sister is fucking hot. I'd do more than Skype her," Kyle called out from the back of the pack with a grin.

Ryan opened his mouth, ready to tell Kyle to keep his hands to himself, but Jake beat him to it.

"Fuck you, Brooks," Jake called back. "My sister is too smart for your fat, ugly ass, and if you ever got anywhere near her, I'd chop your tiny fucking dick off."

Kyle Brooks, made up of nothing but rock solid muscle, laughed. "Tiny? You'd need a magnifying glass to see yours. And I wish it was fucking."

"Keep it in your pants," Connor, the final member of their six man team, told him. Connor was their patrol signaller and went by "Tex" to the troops because he'd been born in Texas. Tex had moved to Australia when he was five to live with his aunt and uncle after his parents, both Australian expats, died in a car accident.

Eventually they reached their extraction point, and hearing the *woomph, woomph, woomph* of the Black Hawk helicopter, Ryan set off a small smoke grenade to reveal their position.

Once inside the big camouflaged beast, the chopper lifted off and he held on, his stomach lurching as they launched hard right into the sky. The wind fluttered his short, dark hair, and he lifted his head, revelling in the rush of the ride.

On their way back to base, Ryan's thoughts once again returned to Fin and the day he'd met her.

He'd been ten years old and even at that age his dream of being a soldier had already taken hold. Life at home was a nightmare he couldn't wait to escape from. His parents fought constantly, and he was always getting caught in the crossfire. His dad was an asshole and a drunk. Most kids his age got grounded, but Ryan wasn't that lucky. He got the belt, and if his dad was drunk enough, he got a fist. He did his best to hide it—the bruising, the fractures, and the painful welts—because he had a plan. He was going to get out and see places. He would become someone that would make a difference. At school he'd been popular, excelling at sports and grades. None of it came easy. Ryan wanted to close himself off from the world, yet he persevered, working hard at all of it, slowly building his escape.

Then Fin stumbled into his life, and he almost lost focus. It had been the first day of the school year. Ryan and his friends were congregated in front of the school, leaning against the red brick building or sitting by the top of the stairs, unwilling to give up their last moments of freedom by going inside.

A young girl, blonde hair tumbling over her shoulders in messy waves, approached the stairs and caught Ryan's eye. Having never seen her before, he watched curiously. Her steps were awkward, timid even. His eyes fell to her hands. The knuckles were white where they gripped the shoulder straps of her bag. She took the first step on the stairs, stumbled over her shoelace, and fell to her knees.

Teasing laughter rang out behind him as her hands planted hard on the steps to catch her fall. She lifted her head, wide green eyes looking right at him. His chest tightened at the sweet vulnerability in her face. Something about her had him wanting to reach out and hide her behind his back, like the world would have to get through him before anything could touch her.

"Shut up," Ryan growled over his shoulder to his friends and made his way down the stairs to help her.

Reaching the second step from the bottom, he held out a hand, palm up, and waited. Her eyes moved from Ryan's face to his hand before reaching out and taking it in hers. Her hand was tiny, disappearing when his fingers closed around it.

"Th-thank you," she stammered as he helped her to her feet.

"Maybe you should keep your shoelaces tied in the future," he told her sharply, hiding his confusion behind a frown. The immediate attachment he felt left him unsettled.

"Fin!" The girl turned and around the corner came a boy who looked just like her, except taller. His eyes fell on their joined hands, his brows drawn. "What's going on?" Ryan let go hastily as the blond boy turned his focus on him. "Who the hell are you?"

Ryan folded his arms as he stepped back, distancing himself from the both of them. "I was just helping her. She fell up the stairs."

"Seriously?" The boy rolled his eyes and nudged her shoulder. "School hasn't even started yet. Are you okay?"

"Sorry," she mumbled, averting her face. A lock of hair fell into her eyes, and Ryan watched as she tucked it behind her ear, revealing her flushed cheeks.

"Thanks, dude," he said. "I'm Jake." He jerked his thumb at the younger girl. "This is my sister Finlay."

"You're new?"

"Yup. Just moved here from Sydney."

Ryan nodded. "I'm Ryan."

The school bell rang, shrilling its warning to get inside. Not wishing to make new friends, Ryan turned and started up the stairs, anxious to leave the pair.

Jake quickly fell into step beside him, already appearing comfortable in Ryan's company. Glancing sideways at Ryan, he asked, "What grade are you in?"

"Five," Ryan replied curtly, picking up the pace. Jake kept up alongside him, and feeling stupid for being rude, Ryan asked, "You?"

Jake grinned. "Same. Fin here..." he nodded at where she followed quietly behind the two of them "...starts grade three."

Loud and quick to laugh, Jake was hard to ignore. They became fast friends before Ryan even realised it was happening. When they talked about the future, he found himself trusting Jake enough to talk about his dream. Impressed and excited, Jake shared it with him— both of them making a vow to one day join the Army together.

The beatings didn't go away though, and there was only so much you could hide from your best friend. A game of basketball in the driveway revealed a set of bruised ribs when they were twelve. Jake had a hand shoved in Ryan's chest as he leaped for the basket. Doing his best to block the shot, Ryan shoved back and they both went crashing to the ground. Jake's elbow caught him hard, and Ryan curled into a ball, stifling the cry of pain.

"Dude, what the fuck?"

His stomach rolling, Ryan blinked, focusing on Jake's face peering down at him.

"You okay?"

Frowning, Jake's eyes fell to where Ryan cradled his ribs, as though trying to keep the pain from getting loose. Grabbing the hem of Ryan's shirt, he shoved it upwards and his eyes went wide.

"You can't say anything," Ryan whispered, not looking at him.

"Who did this?"

They sat there in the driveway, the sun fading warmly in the humid afternoon as Ryan told Jake what happened to his family. He kept it brief, holding onto the basketball and twirling it in his hands as he spoke.

From that day on, Ryan spent most of his time at the Tanners'. Their home in Cottesloe became his refuge—the one place he never felt worthless, only welcome ... and safe. Ryan would stay over often. While everyone slept, he could let the hurt he hid so well rise to the surface. The tears he kept back would spill over, falling silently down his face and soaking the pillow.

Jake, it seemed, had it all. Ryan tried not to let jealousy eat him up because Jake was sharing it with him. Mike and Julie Tanner became like parents to him. Mike was tall and broad, fit from years of playing rugby at national level. He settled into a career of physiotherapy, but he got both Jake and Ryan into the sport. He would ferry them both to and from rugby training, sometimes staying to help out. Jake and Fin got their green eyes from their father, but their blond hair came from Julie. She worked as a personal assistant, but she still found time to get involved in team administration: sorting sign-ups, uniforms, and coordinating schedules.

Spending most of his time at the Tanners' meant growing up with Fin. Fin was quiet and not quick to make friends like Jake was.

She was the person who sat back until she had you figured out. Ryan knew the moment she was comfortable in his company. The lowering of her eyes around him stopped. Instead, he watched them fill with light and laughter, revealing a personality beneath that was just like Jake's, only softer. It was a side she didn't show many people, and he felt special being the one to see it.

Fin would spend time hanging out with them. Jake would get irritated with her tagging along all the time, but Ryan didn't mind. He liked having her nearby where he could watch out for her, or just simply watch her. He was fascinated at seeing the way her brain ticked over, absorbing life with her smart, analytical mind. Fin seemed to have swallowed the world encyclopaedia, spitting out facts at random moments and making him laugh. She saw things in a way he never could—with an open heart and a smile.

Eventually, Fin found her group of friends. They would sit around in her room on weekends, playing boy band music that made him and Jake gag. In retaliation, Jake would turn their own music up until the walls started thumping. It usually ended with Mike yelling up the stairs to *"turn that bloody crap off."*

If their music wasn't painful enough, the giggles started. With Jake and him lazing on the couch in the living room watching television, the girls would walk by and break out in squeals of laughter before dashing quickly away. Jake would roll his eyes and ignore them, but Ryan always had a smile for Fin. He liked that her eyes would brighten when she smiled back. It warmed the coldest part of him, the part buried so deep it rarely saw the light of day.

When he was fourteen, Fin started coming to rugby matches. She would bring her study books and sit so quietly you'd forget she was there. But Ryan never forgot. Prickles of awareness would tingle down his spine whenever she was close. When he glanced her way from the rugby field, she was watching him, and a pretty flush began accompanying the bright smiles she gave him.

He was sixteen when he realised the tightening in his chest when he looked at Fin was not how you would feel towards a sister. One simple word echoed in his head when he thought of her. *Mine.* That urge to protect didn't just grow hotter and brighter, it burned him like a possessive punch to the gut, and at their weekend rugby match it caught fire.

Fin was sitting quietly, her study books spread out as she did her thing. In the middle of the game, Ryan caught two boys his age knocking the books off the table. If he had a second, he would've taken it to admire her. It seemed his Fin had a voice. She stood up, shouting as she jabbed a finger at the one closest. He got in her space, tugging a lock of her pretty hair. Ryan saw bright, burning red—every protective instinct in his young body firing like a rocket. With dark eyes blazing, he passed the ball, ran right off the field, and started swinging.

Although missing what happened, Jake immediately had Ryan's back. Joining in the fight, wild punches were thrown until they were all pulled apart. The match had to be halted, and in the end, Ryan's team had to forfeit the game.

Ryan disappeared that afternoon, needing to distance himself from the Tanners and not knowing how. He couldn't think of Fin as his. He couldn't feel that way. Ryan had to focus on fighting his way out of this town. How could he do that if Fin owned his heart?

Staying away didn't work. Ryan was too entrenched in their lives. So he watched Fin grow older. Her slight frame grew taller and filled out a little. Her hair, usually tied off her face, was left to hang in thick golden sheets down her back. He would find his eyes dropping to her mouth constantly, his heart thumping as he imagined leaning in and kissing her.

By eighteen Ryan ached constantly with the need to touch her. He could barely meet her eyes anymore for fear of her seeing the craving in his. It didn't help when Fin and her posse of friends sprawled under the sun in the backyard. Stripped down to bikinis, they would giggle and chatter lazily as they watched Ryan, Jake, and their friends play cricket. Ryan would wish they were playing rugby instead. That way he could at least tackle his friends when he caught them looking Fin's way.

Then the day Ryan feared came all too soon. Fin got asked out on her first date.

The five of them were sitting down at the table eating dinner when she told them. Ryan's jaw clenched at the news. He stared blindly at his dinner plate, his appetite suddenly disappearing. The urge to push away from the table so he could hurt in private overwhelmed him.

"No," Mike replied firmly.

Ryan closed his eyes, relief rushing through him.

"But, Dad—"

"You're only sixteen," Mike pointed out with a shake of his head. "That's too young for dating."

Fin looked at Julie. "Mum—"

"Honey," she said softly. "How about you give it another year before you think about that, okay?"

Another year? Ryan could live with that. Another year and he would be gone. He wouldn't have to stand by and watch Fin give to someone else what should be his. The thought of someone else kissing her and touching her made him feel sick.

With dinner finished Fin pushed away from the table. Ryan watched her stride through the living room and out to the backyard.

Jake looked at him across the table and nodded upstairs. "Ghost Recon rematch?"

"Sure." Ryan's eyes fell on Fin sitting cross-legged outside in the grass, and he felt a tug at his heart. With Jake already at the stairs, he said, "Be up in sec, okay?"

"Okay," Jake called out, disappearing towards his room.

With Mike and Julie chattering quietly in the kitchen, Ryan made his way outside. Fin looked up at his approach and he sat down at her side.

"Are you okay?"

She nodded silently, plucking at the fat blades of grass Jake had mowed that very morning.

"Who asked you out?"

Fin shrugged. "Does it matter?"

Of course it mattered. No one would ever be good enough for her, not even him, and despite Ryan wanting to be, it wasn't ever going to happen. He swallowed the sudden burst of anger before he choked on it. "I guess not," he lied.

"Ryan?"

"Mmm?"

"All my friends are starting to date, but I ... I'm not sure if I'm ready for that um ... stuff yet. I can't bring myself to care too much about it." She looked sideways at him, her cheeks flushing. "Does that make me weird?"

"No," he replied quickly, his fists unclenching at her words.

Why was she telling *him*? He was the last person she should be talking to about this stuff. Ryan wasn't a virgin. Neither was Jake. They both had their fair share of girls chasing them. Sex was good, but for him it was never more than that. Ryan could let himself go physically, but emotionally he was never in the moment. Knowing that Fin would be subjected to guys that felt the same way made his blood run cold.

He plucked at the same blades of grass and tossed them at her. She looked up from beneath her long, pretty lashes, firing a grin his way that tripped his heart.

"What *do* you care about?" he asked.

She tossed some blades of grass back his way, chuckling softly as he brushed it out of his hair, bits of green falling in his lap. "Promise not to laugh?"

He crossed his heart silently and waited.

"I want to be a scientist."

Ryan's chest expanded with pride. Fin was so smart. She could do anything she wanted. "Why would I laugh at that?"

"Because my best friend Rachael did." She bit down on her lip but they twitched a little. "She thinks I'm so clumsy I'll blow up a lab or something."

He laughed then. Fin *was* clumsy. Crashing her way around a lab was highly possible.

Fin punched his shoulder.

"Ouch." He winced, pretending it hurt, and rubbed his shoulder. "What sort of scientist anyway?"

"Environmental or marine. I'm not sure. Maybe I'll study both."

Ryan grinned. "You're a nerd."

An utterly beautiful, adorable, clumsy nerd.

She straightened her shoulders and returned his grin. "I am a nerd and proud of it, so there."

"Fin."

"What?"

Ryan shook his head, swallowing the lump rising in his throat. He was so close to kissing that grin off her lips he couldn't stand it.

"Nothing."

Fin fell back on the grass, her hair fanning out around her. Her eyes on the stars, she asked, "What about you, Ryan?"

"What about me?" he quipped.

"What do *you* care about?"

Ryan stretched out beside her and found his hand reaching for hers; it was so tiny and smooth in his. The warmth of it sent flutters through his stomach. He squeezed her hand, fighting the sensation.

"Being in the Army. Being a soldier."

You.

"That's it?"

"Yep. That's it."

"I already know that. Tell me something new."

Ryan glanced across at her, finding her eyes on him. "There is nothing new. I want to get out, Fin. I need to. I can't live at that place for much longer. I'm tired of the fighting and the yelling, the alcohol and the ..."

"He hits you."

Ryan closed his eyes, hating that she knew—hoping she didn't see him as someone weak and helpless for putting up with it. He would never tell her why his family fell apart and why his father turned into such a lousy drunk. He couldn't stand her knowing and looking at him differently.

"I want to be SAS," he replied eventually, deliberately ignoring her statement. "The best there is. There are countries full of people unable to fight for themselves. I want to be there to do it for them in the only way that can make a difference."

Rolling to her side, she cupped his cheek with her hand. "Ryan," she whispered. His heart pounded as her eyes searched his face. Unable to summon any restraint, he turned his head and pressed a soft kiss against her palm, feeling her shiver at the intimate touch.

After a beat of silence, his eyes lost in hers, Ryan came to his senses and pulled back.

"I better get back inside," he stammered, and scrambling to his feet, left her sitting there by herself.

After that he was careful about being alone with her, but then Fin turned seventeen and she got her first date. Jake and Ryan were nineteen by then and rarely home on a weekend, but they were both home that Saturday night to see Ian come collect her. The guy had been in the year below them at school. He was tall and outgoing, with broad shoulders and a wide chest from playing rugby. From what Ryan knew of him, he was actually a nice guy, but that didn't stop the urge Ryan felt to pound him into the ground.

That one date turned into another, and another, until Ian was over at the Tanners' almost as much as he was. Ryan felt sick seeing Ian kiss her, wrap his arms around her waist, make her smile like he used to do. It was Ian causing a flush to fill her cheeks in a way that was no longer awkward, but charming and sexy.

Ryan wanted to punch him. Hard. Over and over. That was how he knew it was time to leave.

Two weeks later, he packed his belongings and stole his way into Fin's room. She wasn't there, so he stretched out on her bed, hands tucked behind his head, eyes trained on the ceiling, and waited.

It was midnight when she came through the door, giggling as she read a message on her phone. Finished, she tossed it on her bedside table and froze when she caught him lying there in the dark.

He heard her breath catch. "Ryan?"

The lamp by her bed switched on, coating the room in a warm, cozy glow. Fin was illuminated, her skin golden in the soft light, her cheeks flushed with happiness.

"What are you ..." She trailed off after meeting his eyes. He knew what she saw. He couldn't hold any of it back—regret, heartache, and loss for something that had never been his.

"You're leaving," she choked out.

Ryan couldn't speak. He watched her stride to the open window, its sheer white curtains billowing. Staring out into the night, she wiped away tears that spilled over and ran down her cheeks.

He blinked, his own eyes burning. "I'm sorry," he said eventually.

Fin turned and walked across the room. Sinking to the edge of the bed, she stared down at her hands. "When?"

Ryan unlocked his hands from behind his head and reached for her, pulling her down beside him. She stretched out, tucking her head under his chin. Closing his eyes, he breathed her in, allowing his arms to wrap around her. "In the morning."

Fin's hand fisted in his shirt as she let out a sob.

"I have to do this," he whispered hoarsely. He trailed his fingers through her hair and touched his lips to her forehead.

She started to wipe away the tears on her face, and Ryan took hold of her hand, stilling her. "You understand, don't you, Fin, why I have to do this?"

Ryan needed to know that she understood he wasn't leaving her, he was leaving his past, and trying to build a new future with the Army.

"I do." She choked again and buried her face in his neck, sobs breaking free.

"Don't," he whispered thickly. "Please don't cry. You have such a big future ahead of you. You're going to do big things with your life. Don't let anyone stop you from being who you need to be, okay?"

Fin nodded into his neck.

Ryan pushed back so he could look her in the eye. He wouldn't be there to watch over her anymore, so he needed to know she would look out for herself. "Promise me, Fin."

"I promise."

Satisfied, he reached out and switched off the lamp. Thrust into sudden darkness, Ryan laced his fingers in hers and held her close. When her tears dried up, she drifted off into a deep slumber. In the early hours of the morning, he pressed a soft kiss to her cheek, and disentangling himself, he left the room. Having already said his goodbyes to Mike and Julie earlier in the evening, Ryan clicked the door shut softly behind him and left the house, careful not to look back.

That was the last he saw of Finlay Tanner.

A month later Jake joined him on the other side of the country. After three years of hard work in the Army, they went through the SAS selection. Ryan found himself thriving under the mental and physical challenge. Sometimes a mere five percent made it through the three weeks. The Regiment had standards—high ones. Ones that wouldn't be compromised no matter how low their numbers got.

Nine months before the selection course, the screening process began. Jake and Ryan trained for months—lifting weights, donning packs that weighed into the tens of kilos, and running miles over mountainous rocky terrain. Together they built endurance, mental strength, and a powerful physique, making them a formidable team.

Nearing the end of selection, Ryan was exhausted and almost sure he wasn't going to survive it. He could see his dream slipping through his fingers, and he was so utterly beaten down, he almost couldn't give a shit.

Then Jake came up beside him, his eyes lighting up in a wide grin, and said, "Don't let this shit beat you, Kendall. Dig deep and show these cunts how it's done."

So he did, and after losing a massive ten kilograms over the three weeks, they made it through together.

After extensive training operations, their first deployment into Afghanistan arrived. Ryan didn't sleep once during the entire trip over. Blood fired in his veins, and his heart beat so hard and so fast he thought it would thump out of his chest.

The Commanding Officer briefed the entire team honestly. Saying "conditions were extremely dangerous and casualties were to be expected." That "you will be forced in a split second to determine a pregnant woman from a suicide bomber, traverse fields covered with IEDs that will blow you apart in seconds" and finished with "some of you *will* be killed."

But none of his team had even been injured, and now here he was on his second deployment, right where he belonged.

"Ryan!"

He blinked.

"Ryan!"

Coming back from the past, he realised the Black Hawk had landed back at base and everyone was leaping out.

After a team debrief and hot shower, Ryan was walking past the computer room and heard Jake's shout of laughter. He paused, closing his eyes when he heard Fin's laugh ring out in return.

They were returning to Australia in two weeks. Maybe it wouldn't hurt to go home and see her. Just this once.

Chapter Two

Two weeks later
Fremantle, Western Australia

Morning light swirled inside Fin's bedroom, highlighting the floating dust from another week of not getting housework done. She yawned and stretched noisily, trying to shove the image of Ryan from her mind.

Six years of nothing and the hurt was still a dull ache. What if something happened to him and she never saw him again? The ache throbbed a little harder at the thought. Fin never expected him to keep in regular contact, but the fact that he didn't, hurt. Did he never think of her?

Ryan had been the first new friend she'd made after moving from Sydney when her dad was relocated for work. The image of him standing there holding out his hand when she'd stumbled on the steps at school was something she would never forget. The early morning sun swirling behind him had made his brown hair gleam. Thick, dark eyelashes surrounded eyes so deep in colour they appeared almost black. Her eyes fell to his hand. It looked warm and inviting—his skin a colour that always looked tanned no matter what the season.

Jake and Ryan had become fast friends, and Ryan was always staying over more often than not. So much that Mum and Dad even set up two beds in Jake's room—one on either side. Between both sat two desks against the wall so they could study together. But Jake and Fin had never been to Ryan's house. The invitation was never extended, and it wasn't until she was fourteen that she realised why.

Late one night she'd left her room in just a singlet and panties, intent on getting a glass of water because she couldn't sleep.

The bathroom door opened and Ryan stepped out, hair dripping wet, a towel slung casually around his lean hips.

Fin froze, her breath catching in her throat. He was already getting tall—his lean muscular frame slowly filling out after years of sport. Water dripped down his chest and over prominent bruises lining his shoulder.

"Fin," he muttered.

She looked up, flushing when his eyes wandered down her legs, slowly trailing up her body and landing on her chest, and then she saw his face.

"Ryan." A hand came to her mouth. "Your eye."

It was bruised and swollen. A split in his brow was bleeding and looked like it needed stitches.

Turning, he averted his face.

"Go back to bed, Fin," he mumbled and gave her his back.

Fin's eyes fell to the fading yellow and purple marks over his shoulder blade, and her breath hitched in horror. His lean muscles bunched and flexed as he began walking down the hallway.

"Wait!" Fin called softly. Reaching out, she took hold of his arm before he could disappear into Jake's room.

Ryan paused, half turning towards her. "What?"

His face was shadowed, but she could still see the pain in his eyes and his chest rising and falling a little more rapidly.

"Who did this?"

Ryan turned to face her, meeting her eyes. His jaw was tight, his face impassive. "It's nothing."

"It's not nothing," she replied. "Who hurt you?"

He chuckled, but it didn't sound happy. "You should see the other guy."

Fin frowned. "What other guy?"

Ryan shrugged his arm free. "It's not a big deal, Fin, okay? Don't make more of it than it is."

"If it's not a big deal then why won't you tell me what happened?"

He sighed deeply and took hold of her hand, dragging her into her own room and shutting the door behind them.

Fin whirled around, suddenly breathless. Ryan was alone with her in her room and wearing nothing but a towel. She hoped it didn't fall off. She wasn't really prepared to see what was underneath. Fin and her friends had seen pictures, and she couldn't lie, it was more than a little scary.

"This is not a good idea," he mumbled under his breath.

Fin pointed towards her bed. "Sit down."

"Fin—"

"Sit," she commanded.

Shrugging as though it was no big deal, Ryan shuffled tiredly towards her bed. Turning around, he sat.

"Don't move," she added. Disappearing out the door, she returned with the first aid kit.

Ryan arched his brow. "Doctor Tanner, I presume?"

She giggled as she set the kit on the bed and flipped the lid. "Shush."

Taking out a packet of butterfly tape, she peeled one open. Standing over him, she leaned down and stuck one edge down. Her stomach rolled a little as she held the small cut together and stuck down the other side.

Her face close to his, she whispered, "You should go to the doctor, Ryan."

"Fin …" He breathed as she patted gently at the tape. He reached out, his hand circling her wrist, making her pause.

Her gaze dropped from his brow to his eyes. "What?"

Ryan caressed her skin, sliding his hand up her forearm until he cupped her face. The look in his eyes had her pulse racing. "Thank you."

"For what?"

He leaned in a little and she held her breath. "For caring."

It wasn't until he let go and left the room that she realised he never told her what happened.

The following afternoon Fin stole into Jake's room where he sat studying at his desk.

She crawled her way onto his bed and after bunching his pillow comfortably beneath her, she came straight out and asked, "What happened to Ryan yesterday?"

Jake turned his head and looked at her. His expression was blank as his pen hovered over the page. "Nothing."

"I saw the bruises, Jake," Fin told him when he went back to scribbling notes. "Did you two have a fight?"

Intent on the page in front of him, he replied, "It's none of your business."

"Fine. I'll ask Ryan then." She started to sit up from the bed and

Jake dropped his pen with a huff.

"No, Fin. Don't." Jake spun in his chair and faced her, running a hand through his choppy blond hair. "Why do you think he's always here and never at home? His dad's an asshole and a lousy drunk."

"His dad did that?" Fin whispered, shock making her stomach roll.

Jake nodded, the movement sharp and angry. "Don't say anything, okay?"

"That's why Ryan's here all the time, isn't it? Because this isn't the first time it's happened."

"No, it's not."

"Why doesn't he say anything?"

"Leave it alone," Jake growled and turned back to his books. "A couple more years or so and we'll be joining the Army, and then he doesn't have to be there anymore."

Deep down Fin held hope that Ryan would change his mind about leaving. She didn't want him to go, but she knew now why he had to. Fin would want to leave too, move as far away from here as she could possibly get.

As Jake asked, she tried not to say anything, but it slipped out one night when she was sixteen. A guy in her year at school had blushed and stammered his way through asking her to the movies. Her head filled only with Ryan, her immediate reaction had been to say no. If she was going to date anyone, she wanted it to be him. But Ryan was leaving, so she told him maybe. They were at the dinner table when she blurted it out in front of everyone.

"No," her dad replied.

Her gaze shifted to Ryan. His face had paled, his eyes falling to his dinner plate. He didn't want her to date? The mixture of relief and regret confused her, and pushing away from the table, she strode outside. Sitting out in the yard, she picked at the grass. Her pulse raced when Ryan came out and sat down next to her, both of them flinging bits of grass at each other as they talked quietly.

"I want to get out, Fin," he told her. "I need to. I can't live at that place for much longer. I'm tired of the fighting and the yelling, the alcohol and the ..."

"He hits you."

Ryan closed his eyes and her heart ached. Instead of acknowledging her words, he kept talking, but his voice held a world of hurt. Not knowing what else to do, she rolled over and cupped his face in her hand.

"Ryan," she whispered.

He turned his head, pressing a soft kiss against her palm. She shivered. The way Ryan was looking at her stole her breath.

As though waking up, he shook his head, pulling away. Scrambling to his feet, he walked inside leaving Fin alone. She sat there in the dark, crickets chirping, the smell of jasmine sweet in the warm air, and she cried.

Eventually she turned seventeen and reached the age her parents decreed as the magical dating number. Ryan had withdrawn from her over the past year, so when Ian asked her out, she didn't allow herself to hesitate.

Ian was in the year above her at school, and hot. Tall and blond with flirty blue eyes, he was muscular, outgoing, and funny. Fin surprised herself by having a good time. When Ian walked her to her door, she pushed down thoughts of Ryan being her first kiss and gave it to Ian.

Taking hold of her hands, Ian leaned forward and pressed his lips to hers. He opened her mouth under his and slid his tongue inside, and the touch sent a punch of heat through her body. Fin wound her arms around his neck and his came around her waist, pulling her close.

Embarrassed at the thought her parents could possibly be watching, she broke away.

"Can I ring you?" he asked breathlessly.

She licked her lips and his eyes fell on her mouth. "Okay," she replied with a smile.

After two months of dating Ian, she had him over to watch a movie while her parents were out at a function. She had no idea what was playing out on the television. Ian had her beneath him on the couch, his weight pushing her into the cushions as they made out until the credits rolled.

His touch became firmer and more insistent. She flushed at the foreign feeling of his big, warm hands travelling underneath her shirt and up the bare skin of her torso.

Hesitant, he pulled back to look at her. "Fin ... is this okay?"

For a brief moment, she'd wanted to say no—your eyes are too blue instead of a brown so dark it bordered on black, and your hair is blond, not dark and silky. *Leaving*, she reminded herself. *Ryan was leaving.*

She couldn't wait for something that wasn't going to happen. She liked Ian. Her parents liked Ian. He had dreams of his own and they didn't involve fighting someone else's war—he was going to be a police officer.

Ian pulled back at her pause, and Jake and Ryan chose that moment to return home early. Fin's lips were swollen and her hair mussed. As she quickly adjusted her shirt, it was obvious what they'd been up to.

"Ian," Jake said coldly. "Think it's about time you left, mate."

Ian ignored Jake and looked at her. "Do you want me to leave?"

Her eyes slid to where Ryan leaned against the doorframe. His stance was casual, yet his knuckles were white. His dark eyes focused on Ian's hand where it was tucked intimately on her hip.

Anger welled in her chest at feeling guilty. How dare Ryan feel that way? He had no right.

"No, I don't want you to leave," she said irritably, her eyes returning to Ian, "but it *is* getting late." Fin stood up and held out her hand. He took it in his and gave it a squeeze as he followed behind her. Fin threw Jake a dirty look as she led Ian out the front door, shutting it sharply behind the both of them.

"Sorry," she told him, rolling her eyes as they stood on the front porch. "Brothers."

"Don't apologise." He pulled her close, running his tongue over his lips. "Just kiss me again."

Fin leaned in, touching her mouth to his, enjoying the way he hugged her close like she was something precious. When he left she stood on the porch as he walked down the drive and got in his car. She waved as he drove off and slipped inside, moving hastily towards the stairs.

"Fin!" Jake called out from the couch.

She paused, one foot on the step, and tilted her head to meet her brother's eyes.

"I don't want him here with you when no one's home."

Fin flushed, embarrassed at being caught fooling around. "You're not Dad, Jake, so knock it off."

Ryan walked out of the kitchen holding two beers in his hand. She met his eyes for a brief moment before he looked away and continued into the living room.

"No, I'm not, but have some goddamn self-respect, okay?"

Fin gasped, hurt.

"Christ, Jake." Frowning, Ryan put the beers down on the coffee table and gave Jake a smack on the back of his head.

"Shit," Jake muttered. "Fin, I—"

But Fin was already running up towards her room, utterly mortified. Stripping off to a tank top and panties, she crawled into bed and buried her face in the pillow. She could still smell Ian on her skin, and it was oddly comforting.

"Fin?" Jake whispered, opening her door slightly and peeking in.

Fin wasn't in any mood to talk. She pretended to be sleeping when he crept into the room, fighting to keep her breathing even when he sat down on the edge of her bed.

"I'm sorry." Jake brushed the hair off her face. "I didn't mean that how it sounded," he said softly. "You're just so smart and beautiful. You're better than him. You're better than anyone I've ever known. I'm so proud of you."

Two months later, Fin and Ian were becoming almost inseparable. She'd met his parents, had even stayed over a few times in their guest room. Ian would sneak in during the night. Climbing in next to her, he would pull her close, running his hands over her body and underneath her shirt, cupping her breasts in his palms as they kissed. Eventually they roamed down her back, slipping beneath the elastic of her panties, Ian groaning as he gripped her ass.

Two weeks later on a Saturday night, it was Ian's parents that were out. He led her to his room at the back of his house. It was neat and clean. Never having seen it that way before except the first time she'd visited, she knew, and her heart thumped with nerves.

Ian grinned, taking her hands and pulling her towards him. His eyes fell on her mouth. "I want you, Fin."

She bit her lip, pausing for a moment, and said, "I want you too, Ian."

Fin heard his breath catch. "Are you sure?"

She nodded.

Gripping the neckline of his shirt, Ian tugged it off and her eyes fell on the tanned, muscled chest bared before her.

With a shaky hand, she reached up and placed her palms on his chest. Ian groaned when she skimmed them slowly downwards, shuddering when she reached the waistband of his jeans and tugged gently. Feeling more confident at his response, she smiled up at him from beneath her lashes.

Grabbing her hips, he pulled her towards him and kissed her. His hands lifted the hem of her shirt, and breaking the kiss, he peeled it off. Her long, messy waves tumbled over her naked shoulders and down her back. Trailing his fingers up her ribs, he cupped her breasts in his palms, his thumbs brushing along the lacy edges of her bra.

Ian tugged softly at the strap. "Can I take this off?"

Fin inhaled deeply and nodded.

He reached around, and fumbling, managed to undo the clasp and slide it down her arms. Her bra dropped to the floor, and she flushed, averting her eyes from his gaze.

"You're blushing, Fin." He tucked his thumb and forefinger under her chin and tilted her head so she was looking at him. "Don't be shy. You're so beautiful."

"So are you," she whispered softly.

He ducked his head and found her lips, his tongue delving inside her mouth until she forgot about being embarrassed and about where her hands were supposed to be. Instinct took over and soon they stood naked before each other.

"I've never ..." Fin trailed off as she ran her eyes down his body. It was the first time she'd seen a guy naked, and remembering the pictures she giggled over with her friends, she realised the real life

31

version wasn't any less scary.

"Me either," he whispered.

Ian pulled her close, running his hands lightly down her back until he was holding her ass in his hands. He was so hard she could feel it pressing against her belly.

With shaky hands she reached down and circled him, surprised at the heat and silky smooth skin. He jolted at her touch, and she snatched her hands away, mumbling an apology.

"No, it's okay," he said hoarsely. "I just don't want to ... to, you know, too soon."

Fin giggled and then Ian was chuckling and pulling her towards the bed. Soon she lay beneath him, forcing herself to relax her body as he touched her. His hands found their way between her thighs, and she closed her eyes at the invasion, her body aching and tingling at the touch.

"Ian," she whispered.

"Does it hurt?"

"No. I ... it feels good," she moaned.

"You feel good," he replied, his mouth and tongue swirling maddeningly around her nipple, his fingers leaving her wanting more. "All soft and wet and hot. Can I ..." he trailed off.

"Yes," Fin replied, breathless. "Please."

He sat up and reached for a condom. Fin didn't know whether to avert her eyes or help. She pushed up on her shoulders. "Should I—"

"No, I got it, baby."

Then he was pressing her back down, the pillow soft behind her head as he slowly pushed his way inside her body.

She tensed.

"Just relax," he whispered in her ear.

She nodded and felt him slide all the way inside.

Burying his head in her neck, he shuddered. "You feel so good," he moaned.

After a moment Ian drew back, bracing his hands on either side of her. His eyes holding hers with an intimacy that was new as he began a gentle thrust.

Fin closed her eyes and whispered, "Don't stop."

When she wrapped her legs around him, he paused, drawing a deep shaky breath into his lungs.

Her eyes flew open. "Are you okay?"

Ian nodded. "I just need a minute. I want this to feel good for you too."

It did feel good, but it was over quickly.

"I'm sorry," he mumbled into her neck and pressed a kiss against her ear. "I'll make it better next time. Promise."

Afterwards, she showered for the first time with another person. They laughed as they fought over the soap and ran slippery hands over each other. With hot water pounding over their skin, they learned what made the other giggle or moan.

After flicking off the taps, Ian helped dry her off before leading her back to his bed. He kissed his way down her body, his mouth finding its way between her thighs. Soon she was breathless and falling over the edge with mind numbing pleasure.

Grinning, he crawled up her body and she could feel him hard again and pressing against her belly. "Stay a bit longer," he whispered, trailing his lips up her neck.

"I can't. It's midnight. I have to get back."

Ian nodded into her neck. "Okay."

Pulling into the driveway of her house, she pressed a quick kiss against his lips and ducked from his car towards the house.

Breathless, Fin waved at her parents before running up the stairs and to her room, unable to wipe the grin from her lips. Her phone buzzed, a message from Ian telling her that he couldn't wait to see her in the morning. She giggled softly, tossing her phone on the bedside table, and that was when she saw him. Ryan was lying on her bed in the dark.

Fin's breath caught in shock.

"Ryan?"

Her eyes adjusted to the dark. His hands were tucked behind his head, eyes trained on the ceiling, surrounded by masses of pink and white lace sheets. They'd been so pretty, she couldn't resist buying them when she went shopping with Rachael just over a month ago. Now when she looked at them, all she would ever see was Ryan.

"What are you—"

She halted her words because suddenly she knew. Ryan was leaving. Her heart, so recently buoyed by her night with Ian, cracked wide open.

A month later she waved goodbye to Jake, and she hadn't been the same since. Fin finished school and after another six months of dating, she broke up with Ian when he moved to Sydney for university.

Fin stayed behind, completing her studies in environmental and marine science at the local university where she roomed with Rachael. Both girls were beautiful in their own right and dates were never hard to come by, despite Fin's tendency to wear simple clothes like tank tops and sweatpants. Her heart just wasn't in it to make the effort.

"My God. For once would you wear something that doesn't make my eyes bleed," Rachael told her as Fin dressed for another day of uni lectures. She blinked her huge brown eyes at Fin with exaggeration. With Rachael's dark hair styled in a Mia Farrow pixie cut, it only made them look even bigger.

Fin laughed and did a bootie dance in Rachael's face after yanking on her sweatpants.

Rachael groaned and tossed a cushion at her. "That was so not attractive."

Fin puckered her lips at her friend. "You love me."

"You're lucky I do," Rachael replied with a raise of her perfectly arched brows. "You know," she added, "I reckon Ian would have stuck around if you'd tried hard enough."

Fin, stuffing textbooks into her bag, paused and looked at Rachael. "Tried hard enough? Are you serious?"

Rachael flopped backwards onto her bed. "Yes. You never gave him a real chance, Fin. Honestly, the only time I've seen your eyes light up around a guy was when…"

Fin slung her bag onto her back. "When what?"

"When Ryan was around," Rachael mumbled.

Three years and she hadn't heard a word from Ryan. Anything she *did* know was all second hand information from Jake. They were finishing up SAS selection or would be soon. She wasn't sure.

Fin frowned at Rachael. "Don't mention his name."

"Fine. Are you going out with that guy tonight? What's his name—Marlin?"

"Marlin?" Fin laughed. "Martin. And maybe," she replied, hoisting her bag over her shoulder.

"Good. I'll pick you out something to wear," Rachael yelled as Fin strode out the door, shutting it loudly behind her.

Later that afternoon Jake rang to tell her they made it through. Ryan had done exactly what he'd set out to do and soon they would be fighting in Afghanistan. That night she let Rachael dress her. In a slinky black dress, smoky eyes, and slick red lips, she didn't recognise herself in the mirror.

Good.

Blowing off her date with Martin, she went out with Rachael and a group of friends and drank well into the night.

Hands grabbed her hips as she leaned over the bar to order another round of drinks.

"Baby," came the voice in her ear.

"Ian!" She spun around. "You're back."

He stood there, bigger, older, and still as hot as she remembered. Paying for the drinks, she turned back to face him again. "You look good."

Heavy lidded eyes roamed over her. "You look hot. I almost didn't recognise you."

Fin flushed, looking down at her dress. "I don't usually dress like this."

"I like it." Sliding an arm around her waist, he leaned in, his eyes on her lips. "I missed you."

Her eyes searched his face. "Me too. I missed you too, Ian."

Ian's eyes crinkled in a grin, and her heart lifted a little. "Wanna get out of here?"

Fin looked over at her friends. Rachael was giving her an obvious thumbs up. Her other friends were laughing and whooping, catching male attention and appearing to love every minute of it.

Taking a deep breath, she looked at him. "Okay."

And just like that, they picked up where they left off.

That was two years ago. Fin graduated and Ian worked with the Perth City Police. He was pushing for them to move in together, yet Fin resisted. She valued her independence. She had a great job with the Department of Environment and Conservation. She also owned a restored cottage in Fremantle. She'd bought it with Jake when he came to visit before being sent on his first tour to Afghanistan.

Now they were back on their second deployment and Fin was thankful she was busy with work to take her mind off the worry. She'd completed an Antarctic research expedition last year and would be off for another one in two weeks. Ian wasn't happy about it and she was waiting for the ultimatum. The sad part was she knew what she'd choose.

The phone rang, pulling her from her memories.

"Hello."

"Hi, baby."

"Ian," she breathed softly and rolled out of bed, planting her feet on the solid timber floors. The same floors Jake had spent weeks sanding and refinishing during his return. The cottage was in the perfect spot, close to the beach and family. Single-story, painted beige with white trim, lush green lawns, and a back yard with a big timber deck covered with a large shade sail. A vegetable patch traversed the left side of the lawn, which gave her fits with the painstaking maintenance it required. Yet Fin persevered, hating to fail at anything.

A mammoth, smushed face Himalayan cat came trotting in as Fin stood up and shrugged on a short cotton robe. She tripped over him as she left the bedroom and slammed into the hallway wall face first.

"Dammit, Crookshanks," she muttered irritably and rubbed at what felt like a painful, burgeoning lump on her forehead. "Why can't you sleep in like normal cats?"

"Meow, meow," he replied impatiently, looking more cranky than normal this morning. Fin had had Crookshanks since moving into the cottage, naming him after Hermione's cat from her beloved Harry Potter books. What was not to love about a magical world where one could fly about on a broom without pillaging the world of resources in order to do so? Solving wars between worlds with just a flick of the wand.

"Tripping over again, Fin?" Ian said down the phone with a sigh.

"Just the cat," she muttered, watching him trot ahead of her down the hallway and into the kitchen, checking behind him repeatedly to make sure she was hot on his heels.

"Jeff, Ray, and Becca are having a barbecue over by the beach today. Let's go, okay?"

Fin cringed as she reached for her cat's Fancy Feast Royale. "Actually, I have to go into work."

"Dammit, Fin." He was obviously irritated and Fin paused to rest her hip up against the kitchen bench. "You're leaving for six months soon. Don't they get enough of your time?"

"I'm sorry. There's just so much to do …" she trailed off as Crookshanks head-butted her leg.

"Well, I'm going anyway then."

"That's good," she replied, bending over to spoon food into the cat bowl on the floor by the fridge. "You should go. Tell them I said hi, okay?"

Ian exhaled loudly into the phone. "Fin …"

Shoved out of the way by her cat, Fin stood and rinsed the spoon in the sink. "Hmm?"

"Nothing. I'll see you tonight?"

"I'll give you a call," she told him.

"Yeah, sure, okay," he replied and hung up.

"Well that went well," she muttered to the cat and tossed the spoon into the sink with a clatter. Turning around, she realised she was talking to herself; Crookshanks was already gone.

Later that afternoon, Fin was sitting at her desk at the DEC putting the finishing touches to some reports for the research project when her phone buzzed, startling her out of a paperwork coma. Seeing Jake's name on the display, she picked it up with a frown.

"Hello?" she answered cautiously.

"Fin!" came the shout down the line.

Fin frowned, wondering why Jake was ringing on her mobile. He only ever rang the house phone when he was away.

"Jake?"

"Wow, are you quick this morning or what? I thought you were the smarts of the family."

"But—"

"I'm home!"

"You are? Like Australia home? Or home, home?"

"Home, home, Fin. I'm looking into Crookshanks' evil mastermind eyes as we speak."

Fin's heart leaped in excitement. The urge to throw all her paperwork to the wind and rush home was overwhelming. She grinned like a maniac instead. "Oh my God, Jake. I can't wait to see you! Does Mum know? And Dad? What about—"

"Whoa, whoa, Fin. Don't tell anyone we're home early. We both want a couple of days to get some sleep before the entire family descends, okay? Please?"

Fin nodded, adding an "of course" when she realised he couldn't actually see her nodding. She was used to talking to him on Skype. Then her brow furrowed. "Wait a minute ... We?"

"Yeah, me and Ryan. He's staying here in the guest room. That's okay, right? You're gonna be gone most of the time we're here, honey, so I didn't think it would be a bother."

Fin spun around wildly in her swivel chair at his words, knocking a stapler flying. It whacked the wall divider between her and Paul, a fellow researcher. He bobbed his head up like a meerkat at the clang, and she smothered a laugh. She shook her head at him, and he bobbed back down with an eye roll when he spotted the stapler on the floor.

"Fin?"

"Yeah, that's like umm, cool. Okay."

There was a pause. "Are you okay? You sound odd. You're not getting sick, are you?"

She hadn't been, but the thought of seeing Ryan again after six long years had her stomach churning. She exhaled deeply. Why was Ryan suddenly deciding to re-enter her life now?

"No. I'm fine." She cleared her throat and checked her watch. "I can't get out of here until after five. I have so much to get through. I'm sorry. Do you want me to pick something up for dinner on my way home?"

There was a pause where she could hear Jake conferring with Ryan. She didn't hear what Ryan said, only catching the murmur of a deep voice that sent shivers down her spine.

Jake came back on the line. "Okay. That would be great."

"Alright. Message me what you want me to pick up. Jake?"

"Yeah?"

"Can't wait to see you."

"You too," he replied softly. She went to hang up when he called out, "Oh, was Crookshanks fed this morning? The evil ball of fluff keeps head-butting my leg and I don't believe it's because he missed me."

"Yes he was so don't let him fool you. Just shoo him outside."

"Okay. See ya, Fin."

"Bye, Jake."

Fin hung up the phone and spun her chair back around, flinging the phone on her desk and staring blindly at the paperwork in front of her. How was she going to concentrate now?

Chapter Three

Heart pounding, Fin stumbled through the front door weighted under by an armful of paperwork and dinner. After hearing from Jake, focusing on her reports had been a lost cause. She would have to work through Sunday now. She winced at the thought, realising that would irritate Ian even more. She hadn't had a chance to call him yet and cancel on tonight.

Kicking the door shut behind her with the shiny, four inch heel of her shoe, Jake wandered out from the kitchen.

The files slid from her arms, scattering carelessly to the floor.

"Jake," she breathed, tears burning her eyes.

He grinned at her. "Hey, Fin."

Her eyes roamed over him quickly. In two long years he was bigger than she thought possible—his shoulders wider, his hair lighter, his eyes brighter.

Jake opened his arms, and dropping her bags to the floor, she rushed down the hall and flung herself into them, burying her face in his chest. Picking her up, he spun her around.

"Missed you so much," she mumbled into his shirt when she was set back on her feet.

Jake pressed a kiss to the top of her head. "Not as much as I missed you."

"Rubbish." Fin pulled back, her lips twitching as she wiped at her tears with shaky hands. "It's all just one big party, isn't it? That's why you joined the SAS."

He laughed down at her. "Of course. Sex, drugs, and rock 'n' roll."

The smile died on her lips. "Two weeks and I'll be leaving for Antarctica for six months. You'll be gone again when I get back, won't you?"

Jake nodded, his jaw tight, and her heart sank.

"I wish I wasn't going now."

"Don't say that." He forced a grin. "You're saving the earth, one whale at a time. They need you."

Fin pressed her lips together, her eyes on her feet. "I know."

"Look at me." Fin closed her eyes for a moment, swallowing tears, and looked at Jake. "Don't forget about your own dreams, honey."

She sniffed and arched a brow. "Would I do that?"

His smile came a little easier. "Of course not. You're a Tanner. Nothing gets in our way."

Dropping his arms, Jake stepped into the kitchen and opened the fridge.

Her brows flew up as she caught sight of the contents. "Did you get enough beer?" she asked, watching him pull one from the fully stocked shelves.

Jake offered it to her with a wink. "Enough for a couple of days."

"No thanks," she replied with as shudder. Beer made her feel bloated and tired. "I'll have a wine though."

He set the beer on the kitchen counter and reached for a glass from the cupboards above.

Fin looked around the living area, searching out Ryan and not seeing him. "I thought Ryan was with you?"

"He's in the shower," Jake told her as he poured out a red wine.

Trying to ignore the flutters filling her stomach, she returned to the hallway to collect the dinner and files she'd dumped on the floor.

Showered and dressed, Ryan rubbed a towel at his hair haphazardly. Hearing voices coming from the kitchen, he hung it neatly on the rack and leaned his knuckles down on the bathroom vanity, frowning into the sink.

What the hell are you doing staying here, Ryan?

It wasn't the first time he'd questioned his own motives, but he couldn't seem to find an answer. He missed her. It was that simple and that complicated.

Looking up, he saw nothing in the mirror except tired eyes and the ghosts of those he'd killed in the line of duty. He rubbed a hand across his face as though to wipe it all away and left the bathroom.

Back in the hallway, his eyes fell on the scattered files littering the floor. He crouched down and started pulling them together.

"Ryan."

He froze for a moment, time standing still when he turned and saw Fin in the hallway. Her blonde hair was a tousled mess, reading glasses were caught in the neckline of her pretty top, and her legs— so damn long—were on display in a short, black skirt. His eyes skimmed the length of her before falling to her full pink lips.

She was utterly beautiful and it was like a punch to the gut. Despite tears filling her eyes, she smiled the smile that haunted his sleep at night, and seeing it right before his eyes left him breathless.

Fuck, he swore to himself and dragged his eyes away from her mouth.

"Fin," he murmured. He stood slowly as she reached his side. Her eyes went wide as they followed him.

"You okay?" he asked.

Was I okay?

Fin eyed the stranger in her hallway, realising she wasn't okay at all. The person that left her bedroom six years ago had been a boy. The man that stood before her had dark eyes that should have been familiar, but they were hard now, and intense. Framed in long black lashes, they were studying her face, darkening when they came to rest on her mouth.

Despite Ryan being dressed casually in a fitted white shirt and navy blue cargo pants, his stance was imposing and powerful. His biceps were heavily muscled with thick veins, and tattoos ran the entire length of his right arm. The entrance hall was crowded by the bulk of his wide shoulders.

She drew a burning breath into her lungs.

"I missed you, Ryan," she said thickly.

Those hard, dark eyes of his softened, reminding her of who he used to be. "I missed you too."

"It's been six years."

Ryan nodded again, staring at her, and replied softly, "I know."

A beat of time passed, and then another, until Jake called out from the kitchen. "Fin, are you going to bring that food in here or do I have to serve up Crookshanks for dinner? I'm starving."

Flustered, Fin picked up her bags. "Hungry?"

He smiled slowly. "Always."

Ryan followed her into the kitchen and took hold of the beer Jake held out to him. "Thanks."

She picked up her wine and leaned against the counter as Jake pulled out plates. Ryan stepped into the room and suddenly the quaint cottage kitchen felt tiny.

"So … Tell me about Afghanistan?" she asked. Jake wasn't able to tell her much during their Skype chats, and she wanted to know everything. She needed the distraction because her fingers were aching to touch Ryan, wanting to make sure he was real and not an illusion.

"It's hot," Jake replied.

"And dusty," Ryan added.

"The bunks on base are small," Jake told her as he carried their dinner to the table.

"Jake's learning to play the guitar."

Fin raised her brows at Jake as they all sat down at the dining table. "Really?"

Jake grinned. "Yep."

Ryan looked at her across the table. "And it's killing us. Your cat could play better than he does."

Jake leaned over the table and punched Ryan in the arm with a laugh. "Ryan's lazy," Jake told her as they started eating. "He falls asleep during all our training exercises."

Ryan, taking a sip of his beer, almost spat it out. "Fuck off. That was you!" Ryan looked at Fin, laughter in his eyes. "One morning

Jake was sleeping like the dead and missed training. He was sleeping on a camp bed so we carried him out to the mess hall. Eventually he woke up, looking around at everyone eating breakfast and watching him snore like a freight train."

"I woke to a standing ovation," Jake boasted.

"And baked beans down your pants."

Fin burst out laughing, and as they one upped each other with stories through dinner, her laughter almost turned to tears. How had she ever managed without them?

"So, what's going on with you?" Ryan asked as they stood washing and drying dishes at the sink.

Jake, reclining on the couch with his feet on the coffee table, called out, "Fin's a caped climate change crusader now, aren't you, Fin?" He pointed the remote at the television and began channel flicking.

"I work at the Department of Environment and Conservation now," she told him and her lips twitched, "but I save my Supergirl suit for special occasions."

Ryan chuckled. "You've been there for over two years now?"

Her mouth fell open. "You know?"

"I know."

Of course he knew. Jake never tired of talking about her, and Ryan never tired of hearing it. He heard every detail of her life from Jake, and it obviously hadn't been enough because here he was.

Fin hung the tea towel over the rack on the oven door. "So I guess you know I'm headed for Antarctica in two weeks?"

Ryan should have felt relieved. Two weeks with Fin was going to be hard enough knowing he had to keep his distance, but he was worried about her being in Antarctica. What if she got caught in a snow storm, or fell down a deep crevice? Shit. He was acting like an irrational twat. Ryan gave himself a mental shake and forced a grin. "I always said you were going to do big things with your life."

"You did," she agreed.

Ryan took hold of her hand and pulled her a little closer. She looked up at him and his heart hammered in his chest when her green eyes fixed on his. "I'm proud of you, you know."

Fin licked her lips. "You are?"

His eyes fell to her mouth and all the blood in his body began heading in one, single-minded direction. He cursed under his breath. Two weeks of this? What had he been thinking?

Ryan let go and stepped back. Clearing his throat, he said, "I think I'll head to bed."

"You don't want a coffee or anything first?"

"No. I'm good, thanks."

He turned to leave.

"Ryan, wait!"

He paused.

"I need to make up the bed in the guest room for you."

"No," he said firmly. "I can do it. Jake showed me where the sheets are."

"Yes, but there's a whole bunch of different sizes in there," she pointed out. "It won't take a minute."

He backed up. "You don't have to do that."

"Do mine too, Fin!" Jake called out.

"Do your own," she retorted as she left the kitchen for the laundry at the back of the house.

"Why does Ryan get his done and I don't?"

She came back out under a pile of sheets, quilts, and pillows. "Because Ryan is a guest."

"Ryan isn't a guest, he's family." Jake turned on the couch and looked over his shoulder. "Right, Kendall?"

Ryan looked at the man that was his brother in every sense of the word but blood. "Right."

With the linens piled high, Fin walked blindly into the guest room and cracked her shin hard on the timber bed frame.

"Ouch," she yelped, her stomach pitching from the sharp burst of pain.

Ryan yanked the sheets from her arms. She watched them sail across the room and land on the bed. Pillows flew everywhere. She looked at Ryan.

He was frowning. "Are you okay?"

She gritted her teeth, waiting for the twinge to pass. "Fine."

Taking hold of her shoulders, Ryan directed her towards the bed. "Sit," he ordered.

Reminded of how she'd taped his split brow, she sat. "Doctor Kendall, I presume?"

He chuckled. Crouching down, he gripped the smooth skin of her calf in his hands, lifting it up to rest on his knee for a closer inspection.

She sucked in a breath.

"Hurts?"

Yes. Your touch is warm and your palms are rough, and it hurts to have you so close when you don't want me.

"A little."

Ryan trailed his fingertips over the red, burgeoning lump on her shin until it felt like an intimate caress.

She shivered and he looked up at her, heat blazing from his eyes. "Fin," he said hoarsely.

"Mmm?"

He stared at her for moment. His lips curved into a smile, and the hard edges on his face softened, making him almost beautiful. "I think you'll live."

She tried to remain casual, but his hand was still caressing her leg. "You have a very capable bedside manner, Doctor Kendall."

"Fin? What the hell is going on here?"

Ryan snatched his hands away hastily, the smile sliding from his face as they both turned towards the door. He stood as Ian stalked into the room.

Fin cleared her throat, her stomach sinking because she realised she forgot to ring Ian. "Ian. You remember Ryan, don't you?"

Ryan held out his hand.

Ian looked at it, then at Ryan.

Fin gritted her teeth at the tension in the air.

"I do," he eventually said, his voice flat and unhappy as he shook Ryan's hand. Letting go, he added, "I didn't know you and Jake were home."

Ian turned to Fin expectantly.

"Jake and Ryan just got—"

"Fin," he cut her off. "Can we talk?"

Fin stood up, glancing at the unmade bed. "Sure, uh …"

"I can do this, Fin," Ryan said and nodded at the door. "You go."

"If you can't find anything, Ryan, just let me know," she told him before following Ian out the door.

Walking into her bedroom, he shut the door behind them and folded his arms. "You didn't ring."

"I'm sorry. I meant to, but Jake's return was an unexpected surprise." Her eyes filled. "I haven't seen him for two years, Ian. I … we got caught up talking. I missed him so much."

Ian unfolded his arms and walked towards Fin until he was in her space. His hand came up and cupped her cheek. "Okay. I get that, I do, but … I feel like you're not invested in us. You're about to leave for another six months and I don't want you to go."

Ian leaned in and touched his lips softly to hers.

"Ian," she whispered. "This is important to me."

"You're important to me."

Her voice rose a little. "So what I want doesn't count?"

Ian dropped his hand. "It's a job, Fin. I'm tired of coming second best to everything else in your life. Christ, even Ryan …"

"Ryan what?"

"Nothing," he ground out. Ian walked around her and sat on the bed, rubbing at the back of his neck wearily. Fin walked towards him and he reached out and took hold of her hips. Pulling her in, he pressed a kiss against her belly. "Should I stay?"

Fin looked down at him, trailing a hand through his choppy blond hair. "Don't you have work in the morning?"

Ian's jaw tightened. "I don't care about work."

Fin took a step back. "Okay. I'll just go check in with Jake and come back. Can I get you anything?"

Ian was already peeling off his shirt, exposing the wide, tanned chest he worked hard at keeping in shape for his job. "Just you."

Fin paused at the door, looking back over her shoulder. "Be back in a minute."

Walking down the hall, she saw Ryan's door was shut. She closed her eyes for a moment, but all she could see was him lying in that bed. She wanted to walk in there, peel off all her clothes, and have him sink himself inside her until she couldn't breathe from it.

Damn you, Ryan. Why did you have to come back now?

Remembering Ian was waiting, she continued down the hall, rubbing her forehead as her emotions twisted into painful knots.

Reaching the back deck, she found Jake reclining on a cushioned deck chair, coffee in hand as he stared at the stars.

She sighed, sitting down beside him, and picked up the hot tea he'd made her.

"How does it feel being home?"

"It's hard," he admitted.

Fin frowned. "Hard?"

"Hard to adjust to normal life," he expanded. "What we've seen and done is so far beyond normal that it's like being home isn't my life anymore."

"What have you seen?"

Jake exhaled loudly. "Children—so many of them—hungry, missing limbs, dirty, and begging in the village streets. We've trekked through mountains for days on end and miles of dust. We've watched people die." He looked at her. "I've killed people, Fin," he told her thickly, "and then you come home and everyone is going about their everyday lives—shopping and working, being impatient or unkind, and I want to shout at them all to wake up and see how lucky they are."

Blinded by tears, Fin reached out and took his hand. "I love you, Jake."

He squeezed it. "Love you too, Fin."

"Tell me something good."

So he did, his voice deep and soothing. Her eyelids felt heavy and over an hour later Jake was nudging her awake.

"Shit," she muttered.

"What?" Jake asked as they shuffled tiredly towards to their respective rooms.

"Nothing."

"Is it Ian?" They paused outside her bedroom door. "What's going on with the two of you?" he asked quietly.

Fin rubbed her brow. "I don't know what's going on."

"Do I need to punch him?"

"No!"

Jake wrapped his hand around the back of her neck and pulled her towards him, planting a kiss on her forehead. "Just say the word."

He drew back and she arched a brow at him. "Violence isn't the answer."

Jake frowned, pressing his lips together for a moment. "Sometimes it's the only thing that gets through."

Chapter Four

Ryan swung his legs over the bed in the early morning and planted his feet on the floor. Sliding on shorts, a loose sleeveless shirt, and his running shoes, he yawned, scratching the back of his head as he made his way to the kitchen.

Jake was already there filling a bottle of water. "Made it out of bed, huh?"

A noise came from behind them before he could reply. They both turned. Ian was there in uniform, gun belt slung around his waist.

Fuck. How could he have forgotten about Ian? Ryan wondered if he was still a nice guy because that urge to pound him into the ground hadn't dulled. In fact, the way Ian spoke to Fin in his room last night had Ryan grinding his teeth in irritation.

Jake, usually outgoing with a smile for anyone, gave him a short nod and said coolly, "Ian."

Ian patted his pockets before spying his keys on the breakfast table. "Morning guys," he replied, picking them up and jingling them in his hands. "Good to see you back."

Jake screwed the cap back on his drink. "Good to be back."

Ian nodded over his shoulder towards the front door. "Gotta

get to work. Might see you guys tonight? Fin mentioned something about a family dinner."

After the door shut behind Ian, Jake looked at Ryan, his expression flat.

"Nice guy," Ryan commented, thinking anything but.

"You think so too, huh?" Jake replied.

Later that morning after their workout and shower, Jake fell asleep on the couch. Feeling at a loss with nothing but time on his hands, Ryan wandered down the hall towards Fin's room. She was sitting at a little study nook in the corner, laptop open with one foot resting on her chair. She was wearing a tank top and a little pair of shorts. Leaning up against the doorframe, he couldn't tear his eyes away from those long, delectable legs.

As though sensing his presence, she turned in her chair. He forced his eyes upwards, catching a sexy flush fill her cheeks at his blatant perusal.

"Morning, Ryan." She took off her black framed reading glasses and tossed them on the desk.

"Morning, Fin," he replied.

Against his better judgement, Ryan pushed away from the door and walked farther into the room. Fin hadn't changed at all and neither had his desire for her. His heart kicked over when she met his eyes. He knew everything he was feeling right now was written all over him, but he couldn't seem to shut it off.

Her eyelids fluttered closed and she whispered, "Why now?"

Ryan took a deep breath. "I don't know," he replied honestly.

He shouldn't still be feeling this way after so many years. Why was he doing this to her, and to himself? It was better for everyone if he stayed away like he was supposed to.

"I'm sorry. I shouldn't have come. I'll go stay at the barracks."

He turned to leave.

"Ryan!" she called out. Scrambling out of the chair, she grabbed his arm as he was halfway out the door.

"Fin," he warned, looking down at her hand pointedly.

She took a step closer and he breathed her in, her scent like jasmine on a hot summer's day. He was surprised when he looked into her eyes and saw anger burning hotly in their depths.

"Six years, Ryan. Do you know how hurt I was, each day passing by and getting nothing—not even a note or an email? I didn't just lose you. I lost my brother too. Both of you left me, and I was okay with that. I understood that this was what you needed to do, so I moved on. I built a life that doesn't include you. That was what *I* had to do." She paused and raised a shaky hand to cup his cheek. "I'd have given you my entire heart if you'd only asked, but it's not yours now. It's not yours."

Ryan closed his eyes, agony for losing what was never his rose in his chest until he felt strangled by it. He placed his hand over hers, holding it there until she tugged it away.

"You're right," Fin told him. "You should stay on the barracks … but I don't want you to. Damn you, Ryan," she whispered fiercely. "I don't want you to."

Ryan used his bulk to crowd her against the wall until there was no room for her to move. Leaning one hand against the wall, he grabbed her hip with the other. Her breathing rose rapidly and he leaned in, ducking his head until their mouths hovered a mere breath apart.

"Why can't I force myself to leave?" He rested his forehead against hers and closed his eyes. "I hurt too. For six years I fought every day not to think of you, and I lost, because every day you were all I could see. You were the best thing in my life—so sweet and innocent, and so goddamn tempting." His hand strayed from her hip and slid down to grip her ass. He swallowed the groan. "I stayed away so you could move on."

Fin reached up and planted both hands on his chest, shoving him away. Ryan took a step back, his hands falling to his sides.

"So let me. Nothing's changed for us. I'm leaving in two weeks, you're going back to Afghanistan, and Ian ..."

His jaw clenched but he nodded, angry at himself for thinking that staying here had ever been a good idea. "Christ, Fin. I fucked up by coming here, didn't I?"

Tears filled her eyes. "Just ... don't go, okay? Stay. Jake wouldn't understand you moving to the barracks."

"I'll let you get back to your work," Ryan muttered. "I'll be back later for dinner."

Later that night Fin dressed up a little—wearing her pretty, cream dress with the lace bodice and flirty skirt—because it was Jake and Ryan's welcome home dinner. *I'm not dressing up for Ryan,* she told herself. *Mum would expect everyone to make an effort, that's all.*

Irritated, Fin stood in front of the bathroom mirror, fussing at her hair. She was trying to tame the tousled mess into some kind of updo, but it wasn't happening.

"Dammit," she muttered. Why couldn't she ever manage anything more complicated than a ponytail? She shoved the useless hairpins back in the drawer and snapped it shut angrily, leaving her hair to tumble wildly down her back.

Sitting down on the edge of the bath, she took a deep breath and sighed. Her anger levels had been high today—anger at Ian for pressuring her, anger at the timing of her expedition, anger at Ryan for being everything she wanted and couldn't have, and anger at herself because she couldn't move on.

Why did life have to be so complicated?

"Fin!" A fist rapped smartly on the bathroom door. "Hurry up. We're already late."

"You guys go on ahead," she called out to Jake, standing up and smoothing a hand down her dress. She picked up her earrings and started putting them on. "Ian's picking me up anyway, so I'll just meet you there."

There was a pause. "Are you sure?"

Fin felt a rush of love for Jake at hearing the concern in his voice. How did she ever get so lucky to have a brother like him? It only made the loss all the greater when he left along with Ryan.

"Positive," she told him and rubbed her lips together, checking her lipstick.

"Okay, honey. See you there then."

The front door opened and closed and after a moment, she left the bathroom and slipped her shoes on. Her phone buzzed a message that told her Ian was five minutes away. Crookshanks head-butted her leg as she poured him out some biscuits. She gave his water bowl a quick clean and refill, and after a quick scratch behind his ear, she grabbed her bag and keys, locking the door behind her, and walked down the little paved pathway at the front of her house to wait.

He drove down her street a minute later, his Subaru growling angrily as he down-shifted gears and pulled to the kerb.

She slid inside the car.

"Seatbelt," he muttered before she even had a chance to put her bag down.

Determined to turn her crappy day around, Fin swallowed her irritation and smiled at Ian. "You look nice," she told him as she clicked the belt into place, because he did. The light grey pants were smart, and his pale blue shirt matched his eyes.

"Thanks." He gave her a quick once over before gunning the engine and accelerating down the street. "Been shopping with Rachael again? That looks new."

"It is and I don't know why I bothered. It's hardly something I'll be able to wear in Antarctica."

His jaw clenched at the mention of her upcoming expedition, and she sighed audibly.

Ian glanced across at her before checking his mirrors and changing lanes. "What?"

"Nothing."

He changed gears and looked at her again. "No, it's not nothing. Why do women always say that," he muttered irritably.

Facing her window, Fin closed her eyes and counted to ten. "I'm just tired, Ian. That's all," she lied.

They were all seated at the dining table when Fin and Ian walked in—Mike and Julie, Jake's Uncle David and Aunt Emily, and their cousins Heath and Laura. Jake sat to Ryan's left and Rachael across from him, next to the two empty seats for Fin and Ian.

Ryan looked up from the outdoor table and his breath caught. Her hair tumbled over her shoulders, gleaming in the soft flicker of fairy lights. The dress she wore fluttered around her tanned thighs. He imagined his hands sliding up the smooth skin beneath her skirt and repressed the shudder as he grew hard.

A light sweat broke out on his brow as he fought to get himself under control. He picked up his beer and took a deep swallow in an effort to cool off.

Ian walked a step behind her. His hand was curled around her hip, guiding her outside where they sat. Ryan watched it slide down until it hovered over the same sweet spot he'd grabbed earlier today. His hand clenched around his beer as he shifted his gaze from Ian's hand to Fin. Her eyes were on him and they were pained.

After greeting everyone at the table, Ian leaned in, saying something in her ear as he pulled her chair out for her. Looking up at him, she frowned and replied with something that had Ian clenching his fists.

Jake, watching them too, turned back to Ryan and muttered, "I don't know what's going on with those two, but Ian's really pissing me off right now."

Ryan cursed under his breath. He hoped it wasn't anything to do with what happened between Fin and him this morning. He shouldn't have touched her, but it was too late for that now. He only wanted to do it again.

He made it through dinner, barely. He kept his focus mostly on Mike as they talked, thankful that Jake was driving as he downed beer after beer until he lost count.

Rachael turned to Fin and said, "I think we need another round of drinks."

Ryan skimmed his eyes down the length of the table and arched a brow. Everyone had a full glass.

"Ouch," Fin mumbled after a thump came from underneath the

table. She frowned at Rachael.

Rachael narrowed her eyes in some form of silent female communication and they disappeared inside.

"I'll go help," Laura said and standing up, followed them in.

"Women's summit," Jake muttered.

Ryan glanced through the window into the kitchen, seeing the three of them talking in a huddle. "What's going on?"

Jake picked up his beer. "I'm sure we'll find out eventually."

"Oh my God, Fin," Rachael hissed and grabbed a napkin off the bench. She started fanning herself with it. "The tension out there is thick enough to give me an eye twitch. Look," she said, pointing at her eye. "Can you see it? It's annoying the crap out of me."

"No, I can't see it," Fin replied, peering at Rachael's eye. "Is the tension that obvious?" She sighed. "Ian and I fought the whole way over in the car."

"I wasn't talking about Ian. I meant you and Ryan," Rachael said.

"I don't know what you're talking about," she lied.

Laura sauntered into the kitchen, wine glass in hand, her pale blue maxi dress billowing as she walked. "What are we talking about?"

"The tension between Fin and Ryan."

"Oooh, do tell." Laura ran a hand through her shoulder length blonde hair and pinned her hazel eyes on Fin. "I remember coming to stay at your place plenty of times before we moved here from Adelaide. Ryan was always there. So was the tension."

Rachael pointed at Laura. "Exactly."

Fin looked between the two of them, folding her arms. "There's no tension."

"Fin, you do know we're not talking about hostile tension, don't you? Ryan's been downing beer after beer all night. I can't wait to see if he can stand up. And the way he looks at you when he thinks no one's watching?" Rachael started fanning herself again. "God. I've been waiting for you to catch fire."

"Rubbish," she snapped, flushing as she remembered this morning and the heat that filled her body when Ryan crowded her into the wall. Rachael and Laura's eyes were wide with disbelief. "Maybe just a little tension." Fin moaned and pressed her hands to her cheeks. "Okay. Look. Let's be real about this."

"Fuck real," Rachael muttered. "Get to the details."

"There *are* no details. Jake and Ryan only arrived yesterday morning," she pointed out.

"And?" Laura waved her arm for her to keep going.

"And this morning we may have had a moment."

"Yes!" Rachael hissed and did a fist pump, almost sloshing wine out of the glass she held in her other hand.

"But I can assure you both that *nothing* happened. And as I was going to say, nothing can happen. He's fighting a war, I'm off to Antarctica in two weeks, and in case you both happened to forget, I have Ian!"

"Do you?" came the steely voice from behind them.

Fin closed her eyes, her heart sinking. Turning around, she faced Ian standing in the entryway to the kitchen. His hands were tucked casually into his pockets, but his eyes were hard and his body was tense.

"Rachael, Laura, can you give us a minute?" she said softly. They both looked at her, reluctant to leave. "Please."

Ian held her eyes as they both left the room. When the back door slid shut behind them, he folded his arms and asked, "What happened between you and Ryan?"

"Ian. It was nothing. We—"

"Don't bullshit me, Fin!" he shouted.

"Please don't be angry," she pleaded softly. "Nothing happened."

Ian stared at the floor for a moment, one hand on his hip, the other wrapped around the back of his neck. "I've seen how he looks at you—right from the beginning. And the worst part is that I've seen how you look at him. God. That first time between us, I've never felt more in love in all my life, but all this time it's been him for you, hasn't it?"

"I'm sorry," she whispered.

"Fuck sorry!" Ian yelled, his fists clenching angrily. He grabbed a glass off the kitchen counter and smashed it against the cupboards behind her. She flinched as the fragments splintered across the kitchen tiles. "Tell me you love me," he choked out.

Tears spilled over and ran down her face. "I love you."

He stood there, chest heaving. "I don't believe you."

The back door flew open and Ryan came charging in. His eyes were on Ian, and they were so dark and cold, she shivered.

Ryan looked up when Rachael and Laura walked back to their seats having left Ian and Fin alone. When Ian's raised voice was heard, the table fell silent and all eyes went to the window.

Ryan stood suddenly, his chair skating backwards, his body tense.

When Ian threw a glass and it shattered against the cupboards behind Fin, red was a bright, burning haze that obliterated everything around him.

"Fuck," Jake muttered beside him, but Ryan was already running for the door. He slid it open, fists clenched, and stormed inside.

Ian turned, nostrils flaring. "You."

But Ryan didn't stop. He came fast at Ian and cocking back his fist, slammed it with a satisfying crack into Ian's jaw.

He vaguely heard someone shouting at him, but he tuned it out. Instead, he took a step forward as Ian staggered backwards. Then, head down, Ian charged, knocking Ryan off his feet. They both went down, Ryan landing hard on the small timber table beside the couch and cracking his head. The table splintered beneath him, sending him to the floor with a thud. When Ian landed above him, they rolled until Ryan had him pinned on the ground. Grabbing the neckline of Ian's shirt, he pulled back his fist and slammed it in Ian's face. His knuckles burned from the contact as Ian's head snapped back. Ryan pulled his fist back, ready to do it again, but Ian reached up and grabbed him in a headlock. He grabbed at Ian's shoulders, ready to flip him over, but arms locked around his waist and yanked him backwards.

"Enough!" Mike yelled.

Ryan shrugged off Mike's hold, his chest heaving as he nailed Ian with a savage glare.

"Fuck that," Jake growled, and moving swiftly, grabbed Ian and hauled him to his feet, ready to throw his own punch.

"Jake!" Mike shouted. "Both of you."

Ryan's shirt had ridden up in the tussle, and he tugged it down before looking at Fin. She was standing next to Rachael, her face pale, her hand to her mouth.

"Fin," he murmured.

Ian wiped a trickle of blood from his mouth with the back of his hand and pointed at Ryan. "You stay the hell away from, Fin."

"What the fuck is going on here?" Mike growled.

Ian looked at Mike. "Maybe you should be asking Ryan that, Mike."

Mike looked between Ian and Ryan and shook his head. "Ian, I think it's probably best for now if you left."

Ryan's eyes narrowed on Ian when he looked at Fin.

He nodded at Mike. "Okay."

Without sparing a glance at Fin, Ian turned and strode out the door, shutting it behind him with a soft click.

Chapter Five

The drive home with Jake and Ryan was silent and tense. Jake's knuckles were white on the steering wheel, his lips a tight line. Fin wasn't sure how many beers Ryan had drunk because his head was tilted back in his seat, his eyes closed as Jake drove through the dark streets.

Fin sat in the back, staring out the window. Trying to turn her crappy day around hadn't gone as planned. How the hell had a simple welcome home dinner spiralled into such disaster?

After an eternity of strained silence, Jake pulled into the driveway of the cottage. Fin fumbled for the door handle in her haste to leave the car. Keys already in hand, she unlocked the front door, went straight for her room, and shut the door behind her. Once inside, she moaned a sigh of relief.

Using the mirror on the back of her wardrobe door, she plucked out some wipes and took her make up off. Within minutes she was changed into a tank top and panties and sliding her way into bed. Her phone buzzed a message from a Rachael. *What happened with you and Ian? Did you break up?*

I don't know, she replied. *He was pretty mad.*

Her phone buzzed again. *No shit. He threw a glass at you, Fin. I'm glad Ryan punched him.*

Fin sighed as she tapped out a response. *Is that what everyone thinks? He threw it at the cupboard, not at me.*

I think you should break up with him, came Rachael's response.

Should she? She always told herself she valued her independence and her work. Did she value Ian more? She wasn't sure. Maybe if she made more of an effort this wouldn't have happened.

Flipping onto her stomach, Fin pushed up on her elbows and tapped out a reply. *He's not to blame. I'm the one that keeps pushing him away.*

Maybe you need to look at why, Rachael replied.

Shaking her head, Fin put her phone back on her bedside table. Lying back down, she cuddled her pillow. Ryan had always been the first one to defend her when they were growing up. That hadn't changed. But neither had anything else.

Resolving to do everything in her power to move on, Fin reached for her phone again. She would ring Ian, and she would make an effort to be who he needed her to be.

A soft knock came at her door.

Before she could say anything, it opened slightly and Jake whispered, "It's just me, Fin. Can I come in?"

Ignoring the irrational disappointment that it wasn't Ryan at her door, she mumbled, "Sure," and put the phone back on the table.

Fin rolled to her side as Jake climbed on her bed and stretched out on his back. He turned his head to look at her and sighed deeply. "What the fuck was that?"

She rubbed at her brow. "Things haven't been going so well with Ian and me lately." Jake raised his brows. "He wants us to move in together."

"First of all—no fucking way. Second—how does that end up

with him throwing a fucking glass at you?"

"Ian didn't throw it at me," she defended him. "He threw it at the cupboard behind me."

"Why?"

Fin buried her head in the pillow, shifting her face slightly so she could breathe. "He thinks there's something going on between Ryan and me," she mumbled.

"Is there?" Jake frowned, his eyes searching her face in the soft darkness. "Because even if there was, that's no excuse to throw a fucking glass at your face," he growled.

"No!"

After a pause, Jake nodded and said, "I don't like Ian. Maybe he used to be a nice guy, but I don't like the way he treats you."

"You don't have to like him," she said, her voice muffled by the pillow. She rolled over and stared at the ceiling. "I'm going to ring him in the morning and see if we can work this out. Ian and I … We have a lot of history."

"So do you and Ryan."

Fin's brow furrowed in confusion. "What's that supposed to mean?"

Jake rolled to his side and sat up, putting his feet over the edge of the bed. He looked at her over his shoulder. "You two have always been friends. I thought the Army would be good for him, and it is, but he's not letting go, Fin. Maybe you're the one who can help him do that." Jake stood up and moved to the door.

"How can I possibly help him do that?"

Jake shrugged. "You could try being friends again."

"But he's the one who left!" she burst out. "Six years have gone by, Jake, and he didn't contact me once."

"Did you get in touch with him either?"

"He didn't want me to," she told him.

"Sometimes it's not about what you want, but what you need."

Jake opened her bedroom door and stepped out.

"Jake—"

"Night, honey."

The next morning Fin hadn't worked out what to say to Ryan so she left for work before both he and Jake were up. She tried ringing Ian when she arrived at her desk, but he didn't answer. Keeping her head down, she worked solidly through the day, and when she got home later that night only Jake was at home.

She tossed her keys and files on the desk in her room and met Jake in the kitchen. "Where's Ryan?"

"Training exercise," he replied, stirring something on the stove.

"Oh? I thought you both had time off."

"We do."

So Ryan and Ian were both avoiding her. Great. "You cooking me dinner?"

Jake turned around, pointing the spoon at her. "I am, and you're gonna like it this time or you'll be wearing it."

"Just like the last time you cooked and I wore your pasta all down my favourite shirt?"

He grinned. "You shouldn't have complained that it tasted like shit."

Fin poked her tongue out. "It did taste like shit."

"Interesting."

"What is?"

Jake smirked. "That you know what shit tastes like."

Fin gagged a little and he laughed. "Don't be gross."

"You said it, not me."

She walked over to the stove and peered into the saucepan. It looked like some kind of red sauce with odd shaped lumps of meat. "What is that anyway?"

Jake stuck the spoon back in the pan, and sauce splattered up the tiles as he gave it a messy stir. "Go away or I won't cook anymore."

She grinned. "Is that a threat or a promise?"

Jake swiped at her with the tea towel, and she danced out of his reach. "Go. Get out of my kitchen!"

It wasn't until three nights later, with Ryan yet to return from his exercise, that Ian called her back.

"Fin," he muttered when she answered the phone.

Fin put her head in her hand. "Ian. I'm so sorry."

"I'm sorry too." After a pause, he said, "We need to talk."

"I know," she agreed softly.

"My place?" Ian shared an apartment closer to the city with his co-worker, Evan. "Evan's not here," he added.

"Okay. I'll be over soon," she promised.

After hanging up, Fin changed out of her work clothes and into a pair of petite tailored shorts and the pretty pink knitted top that Ian had once said looked good on her. Grabbing her keys and sandals from the wardrobe, she called out, "Jake? I'm going out."

"Where?" he yelled from his sprawled position on the couch.

She opened the front door and over her shoulder said, "Ian's place."

He started to get up. "Fin, you can't—"

She shut the door quickly behind her. As much as she loved her brother, he needed to realise that Ian would never hurt her.

Arriving at his apartment, she knocked softly on the door. Ian opened it, his shuttered eyes roaming the length of her before he stepped aside.

"Come in."

"Thanks," she murmured.

She set her bag on the dining table and walked into the living room, sitting down on the wide, navy leather couch.

He scratched at the back of his head. "Drink?"

Fin nodded. "Please."

After a moment he came out of the kitchen with a wine for her and a beer for himself and sat down beside her.

"So dinner was a bit of a fail," he said, looking at her.

She nodded at that understatement. "I'm sorry, Ian. It got out of hand very quickly, and ended badly."

Ian sighed deeply. "I'm not sure where we go from here, Fin. You've resisted me every step of the way. Maybe it's time I cut you loose."

"Cut me loose? What am I? A horse?" She set her wine on the glass coffee table with an angry clatter.

"Christ." He ran a hand through his hair. "If you don't want me, just say so. Stop dragging this out. I'm over it. I'm over ..."

"Over me?"

His blue eyes searched her face. "I don't think I ever really had you. Not all of you. There's always been something missing."

"Is this about work?"

"Part of it," he conceded. "You're always working. Always away on some excursion or some research expedition. What do you want from me, Fin? To sit around and wait for you for another six months?"

"Six months isn't that long!" she burst out.

"But that's what you said last time. And when you're back, then what? You're off to wherever to start on your thesis. Where do I fit in with all of that?"

Fin picked at the hem of her shorts. "I'm not ready to settle down. We're both so young. We've got our whole lives ahead of us to do all that stuff."

After a deep swallow of his drink, Ian set it down next to her wine. "Come here."

He grabbed her hand and pulled her towards him. Fin shifted on the couch until she was straddling his lap, and his hands came around to rest on her ass, his thumbs hooking into the waistband of her shorts.

"What do we do?"

She swallowed. "I don't know."

Resignation swept across Ian's face and he closed his eyes. "I'll wait. Six months, Fin. You come back and we'll see how we feel then." He opened his eyes. "You told me you loved me."

"I did," she whispered.

Ian leaned in, his lips a breath away from hers. "Then show me."

It was after midnight when Ryan let himself through the front door of the little cottage. Seeing both Fin and Jake's doors closed, he shuffled quietly down the hallway and tossed his bag on the bed. In the bathroom, he peeled off his army fatigues and stood under a hot shower.

Resting both hands against the cool tiles, he bent his head, letting the steaming water pound over his neck and back.

He'd had a shitload of rage to work out of his system. The training exercise couldn't have come along at a better time. Ryan always, *always*, had control of his emotions, except when it came to Fin.

Every day he trained—how to crash a car properly, using explosives, climbing, roping, diving, parachuting, tracking. He could speak three different languages. He was taught how to save lives and taught how to kill at the same time. He could take a man out, quickly and silently, with his bare hands. He learned how to lock his emotions down, but when it came to Fin, none of it mattered. Seeing Ian get violent towards her had him losing control in a split-second.

Dead on his feet, he switched the shower off and stepped out, towelling himself dry half-heartedly. Tugging on a pair of sweatpants, he wandered into the kitchen, opened the fridge, and reached for a beer.

"You're back."

Ryan tried to smile but his heart wasn't in it. Over his shoulder he offered a beer to Jake. "Yep."

Jake took it and he grabbed another. Twisting the top off, he took a deep swallow as he shut the fridge door.

"Fin's gone."

He drew the beer away from his mouth. "What?" His voice was sharp. "Gone where?"

Jake moved to the couch and sat down. "Ian's."

"Motherfucker," he breathed. "Christ, Tanner. He threw a goddamn glass at her."

"She says he didn't—that he threw it at the cupboard."

Ryan sat down in the armchair opposite and hung his head in his hand. "It was close enough. It could've hit her. He's a goddamn cunt for treating her the way he does."

"Agreed."

They sat quietly for a long moment until Jake's voice cut

through the silence. "How long have you been in love with my sister?"

Ryan's head whipped up sharply, suddenly breathless. Jake's elbows rested on his knees as he looked at Ryan with steady, green eyes.

He swallowed. "Since as long as I can remember," he admitted.

Jake nodded and set his empty bottle on the table. Ryan tilted his head as Jake stood up.

"Maybe one day you'll pull your finger out," he said and walked quietly back to his room.

"Fuck," Ryan muttered.

He must have sat there for hours, his stomach twisted in knots. When the sound of a key came at the front door, the early light of dawn was just starting to break over the sky.

Ryan stirred, his eyes burning dully as Crookshanks leaped off his lap and trotted down the hallway.

Fin came through the door, dishevelled and utterly delectable. With the cat winding around her feet, she stumbled, scowling as she banged her knuckles into the side table.

Ryan bit his lip at the clumsy and endearing behaviour. He watched as she fumbled her way towards the bathroom and shut the door with a soft click. The shower ran for a solid half hour, and he closed his eyes, imagining every naked inch of her, warm and wet, as she stood beneath the pounding water.

When she came out belting her cotton robe, thick clouds of steam trailed behind her.

He cleared his throat and she looked towards the living room, her eyes wide.

"Ryan. You're home."

He liked how that sounded. Home.

"So are you," he replied as she walked towards him.

Fin brushed her fingers through her damp hair. "I uh ... went to talk to Ian."

"Until five in the morning?"

"I don't have to explain myself to you," she ground out, her hands falling to her sides.

"Maybe you don't, but I don't get it. He was violent towards you."

She huffed, her exasperation clear. "He wasn't. We had an argument. You *punched* him."

Ryan nodded, drawing in a deep breath of satisfaction. "I did, and I won't apologise. Not for that, because I'd do it again."

She stood in front of the armchair Jake vacated earlier that evening and sank into it. "We're just going around in circles," she muttered wearily.

He looked at her, drowning in the desolate green depths of her eyes. "I want you, Fin," he finally admitted. "So damn much I can't sleep from it. I lie in bed at night and I dream of my lips on yours, my mouth tasting every inch you. I want to fuck you until I go blind from it and even then I don't think it would ever be enough."

Fin scrambled out of the chair she'd just sat down in.

"I'm sorry," he added hoarsely. "I want to say I'm trying not to want you, and I did. I tried, but I don't know if I can any longer."

"Stop," she said shakily.

Anxiety rolled off her in waves. He stood up and walked towards her. She held out a hand as though to ward him off. "Ian and I ... we worked things out."

Ryan blocked out her words. Instead, he grabbed hold of her hands and yanked her towards him. The sweet smell of her surrounded him until he couldn't breathe from it.

Leaning in, he whispered in her ear, "Don't tell me. Please."

Ryan grew hard thinking of her in the shower, but having her close like this had him throbbing painfully. With his teeth, he tugged on her earlobe and felt the moan deep in her chest. Grabbing her hips, he pulled her flush against his body, needing her to feel just how much he wanted her.

He licked a path along her neck, letting his tongue swirl maddeningly over her skin. God, she tasted better than he even dreamed she would.

"Ryan," she moaned, and the sound of his name on her lips set him on fire. "Stop."

He wound his arms around her body, his hands gripping her ass before her words registered and he froze.

"We can't do this. Ian's going to wait for me, Ryan."

Ryan closed his eyes and buried his head in her neck. Her arms came around him, holding him close. He blinked away the tears that burned his eyes, not wanting her to see them.

Taking a deep breath, he drew back and her arms fell away. Reaching up, he wiped at the tears spilling down her cheeks. "Don't cry, baby. I'm sorry."

She pressed her lips together.

"Smile, okay? You'll be gone in a little over a week and you can do that moving on thing," he whispered thickly.

Fin nodded through her tears and his heart ached.

"Now smile. For me," he ordered.

Her lips curved upwards but sadness lingered in her eyes. He tickled her ribs, digging his fingers in until he forced a laugh out of her.

"That's better," he murmured and cupped her face with his palm. "I'd give almost anything to wake up to that every morning."

He hated the words that came out of his mouth. It hurt like a bitch knowing her beautiful smile belonged to another man.

"Almost anything." She backed up a step. "That's always been our problem, hasn't it?"

Chapter Six

Five days had passed since that morning with Ryan. They were long ones because every time Fin closed her eyes, he was sitting on her couch, his dark eyes searing and intense, and he was telling her how much he wanted her. God. He didn't need to tell her. When she'd been yanked against that rock hard chest, she could *feel* it.

Time with Ian had been spent at his place until emotions cooled down. She had good reason to believe his reception at the cottage wouldn't be a welcoming one right now. With her farewell party being held in two days, she was thinking it was going to be spent with Ian on one side of the room and her family on the other.

With a sigh, she kicked off her work shoes in the direction of her wardrobe and reached for her phone when it rang.

She unzipped her skirt, answering the call as she wriggled out of it.

"Fin, God. Please don't hate me," Rachael moaned in her ear. "I already hate myself."

Fin laughed. "Are you having a hate party and forgot to invite me? Hang on." She set the phone down, and after peeling off her top, picked it back up again. "Sorry. Getting changed. I swear I'm not running late. We have ages until the movie starts."

A loud sigh came through the phone. "I can't make it."

"Oh." Disappointment welled up in her chest. "Well. You suck. Just for the record."

"So noted. Sorry, Fin. End of month is killing me. Who ever thought being an accountant was a stellar career choice? I should have been a smarty-pants scientist like you."

Fin sat on the edge of the bed and flopped onto her back, her hair fanning out behind her. "You're just jealous because you think all the geeky guys I work with are hot."

"I do. Smart guys *are* hot—except for accountants. Why can't I find a hot guy where I work? I have no eye candy here. If they hired hotter guys, then maybe I'd find the motivation to come into work every day."

Fin laughed. "Okay, so that's your bad news out of the way. Do I get any good news?"

"Only that I've got you the best going away present that ever lived. You can thank me properly at your party on Saturday night."

"I'm gonna miss you, Rach."

"Rubbish. You have Ian to miss. And Ryan. And you'll be surrounded by hot Antarctic men who ride snowmobiles and peel off their thick parka's to reveal tanned chiselled abs just for your benefit."

Fin laughed again. "Are you ovulating?"

"How can you tell? Now scoot. Go take that hot brother of yours and his even hotter best friend to the movies with you instead."

"Okay."

"Good. I'll email you tomorrow."

"Rach, no! Stop forwarding me those dirty emails. I can't open those things at work."

"Can't hear you, Fin. Bye!"

The call disconnected before she could reply, and she tossed the phone beside her with a sigh. Pushing up off the bed, she walked towards her wardrobe. Catching movement from the corner of her eye, she turned her head and jolted. Ryan was leaning casually against the doorframe, his arms folded. Licking his lips, he stepped into the room and shut the door behind him.

"Ryan. You scared me." She reached for the top she'd tossed on her corner chair a few minutes ago and gave him her back.

Fin felt him come up behind her and she shivered. He reached around, grabbed the shirt from her hands and tossed it on the floor. Suddenly breathless, she looked at it, then at his hands where they came to rest on her stomach.

He was an asshole for doing this to her, but her door was ajar. When Ryan heard her voice and saw her lying on her bed in nothing but lacy pink underwear, he couldn't stop himself. How did she manage to look so innocent and so sexy all at the same time?

His lids lowered as he looked down over her shoulder, watching his hands as they skimmed up the smooth, taut skin of her belly to cup her breasts firmly.

Her body trembled as he rubbed his thumbs across her nipples. He felt them harden beneath the flimsy lace of her bra.

"Fin," he breathed, running one hand down along the inner edges of her tanned thigh. Fuck. Her legs were smooth and warm, and he wanted them wrapped around him as he sank himself deep inside her.

Burying his head in her neck, Ryan shifted his hand to cup the pretty lace panties between her thighs and took a deep, shuddering breath. God, he shook with the need to taste her.

"Ryan," she moaned.

With his other hand, he fisted the soft strands of her hair and yanked her head back, exposing the line of her throat, and he fell on it—sucking and biting the sweet skin until he was unbearably hard.

A tap came at the bedroom door and they both froze. "Fin? Are you heading out soon or eating here first?" Jake called out.

"I-I'll be right out," she stammered and took a step forward out of Ryan's arms. She turned around, meeting his eyes.

"Okay," Jake called back.

Ryan's blood pulsed so hard it was a roar in his ears as they stared at each other wordlessly. After a beat of silence, she tore her eyes away and opened the wardrobe door.

"Are you happy now?" she hissed as she grabbed a pair of jeans from the shelves.

His eyes on her ass, he muttered, "What?"

She threw the jeans at him and he caught them when they hit him square in the chest. "This. Us. Yes, okay? I want you. Is that what you want to hear? That I dream of you too?" she choked out. "Your hands on me, inside of me, and I ache too."

Ryan took a step towards her.

"Don't." She snatched the jeans out of his hands and tugged them on.

"I'm sorry," he murmured.

Fin turned, rummaging for a top. She pulled one off a hanger and tugged it on furiously. "You're sorry. I'm sorry. Everybody's sorry. Well it's just one sad, fucking sorry situation, isn't it?"

Christ, Fin was a fiery inferno when she was mad, and it had his dick swelling even harder. "Fin, I—"

"Enough!" She jabbed a finger in his chest. "There's hurt in there. I know it. You know it, but you're not going to move on from it until you let that shit out. Whatever you're doing now isn't working. Own it, Ryan. Stop letting it own you." With that she brushed passed him and opened the bedroom door. She looked at him over her shoulder before stalking away.

"Sizzler?" Fin moaned as Jake pulled into the restaurant car park an hour later.

Pulling the key out of the ignition, he turned in his seat and grinned at her. "That's what you get for a last minute date with the two of us, right, Kendall?"

Ryan chuckled from the front passenger seat. "Right."

Fin eyed the two of them flatly and reached for the door handle. She sighed as she opened the car door. "Let's get this over with."

"Don't be like that, Fin," Ryan called out as they got out of the car behind her and Jake beeped the locks. "It's all you can eat. What could be better than that?"

She shivered at the wicked gleam in his eyes and strode briskly towards the restaurant door.

"I'll tell you what's better than that—if it was full of women instead of food," Jake told him. "An all you can eat women buffet."

Ryan said something she didn't catch, and Jake burst out laughing. She rolled her eyes, shoving open the door.

Twenty minutes later Fin sat down at their table with a small pile of salad. Jake and Ryan followed soon after, sitting opposite her with plates piled high. Did they leave any food for anyone else?

She eyed them both in turn and then pointed her fork at their enormous food mountains. "That's a heart attack on a plate."

Ryan laughed and Jake grinned at her. "We work our asses off to eat like this."

"And this is only round one," Ryan told her.

Jake looked down at her modest salad with disgust. "Seriously, Fin. You don't come to an all you can eat restaurant for the rabbit food."

Her stomach flipped over when she met Ryan's eyes. He was looking at her like she was a frosty ice cream and he'd just escaped the burning fires of Hell. She'd be lucky to choke down a piece of lettuce at this rate. "I'm not that hungry," she muttered.

Jake shrugged. "So what movie are we supposed to be seeing?"

Fin finished chewing the dull tasting piece of tomato and after swallowing told him the title of the movie.

He shook his head. "Not happening."

Stabbing at a piece of lettuce, she raised her brows and looked at him. "Fine. You don't have to come."

"It's girly fluff, Fin. At least choose something we can all watch."

Her lips twitching, she tossed a piece of lettuce at him. "What? You don't like girly fluff?"

Jake used his fork to flick away the piece of lettuce contaminating his plate. "Not that kind," he grumbled.

Later that evening, Ryan bought the tickets for the movie and Jake loaded them all down with popcorn.

"Haven't you eaten enough?" she mumbled as the crowds of people swarmed around her. Getting jostled, she clutched the popcorn to her chest, watching some of it spill over and scatter carelessly on the carpeted floor.

Ryan looked down at her. "How can you go to the movies and not get popcorn?"

With Jake in front of her and Ryan behind, they walked up the dark cinema steps as a movie trailer blared wildly on the giant screen. She stumbled and Ryan grabbed her elbow to steady her.

Flustered, she murmured, "Thanks."

Her heart pounded when his large, warm hand reached out and took hold of hers. She should've tugged it free, especially in light of her earlier anger, but the brief contact felt so good. He gave it a squeeze as Jake guided them into a row of seats, and Fin forced herself to let go when they sat down.

As wild gunfire and ominous music exploded in the background, Jake leaned in and grinned. "Now aren't you glad I chose something we can all watch?"

Frankly, she didn't care all that much what they saw. With Ryan sitting next to her, she'd be lucky to remember what the name of the movie was.

Torture. Sitting next to Fin in the dark cinema was complete and utter torture. Since arriving at the cottage, his desire for her had reignited and it had been snowballing ever since, growing wild and out of control until his hands, now fisted on his lap, shook from it.

Eventually the movie finished, and as they stood, he stretched slightly, the pull on his aching muscles from the morning's workout easing some of his tension.

As they made their way back to the car, he hoped like hell Jake didn't talk about the movie on the way home. He couldn't remember any of it.

Jake glanced at Fin in the rear view mirror as he pulled out of the car park and asked her where Ian was tonight. Ryan felt like growling at the mention of his name.

"Long shift tonight at work, but he's taking me out tomorrow night, and then he'll be at the party."

The farewell party. Ryan felt a dull ache pound through his temples as he stared at his reflection in the car window. Two more days of Fin and most of it belonged to Ian.

Whose fault is that, you dumb fuck?

He shook his head. Fin was right. He was still carrying around a load of hurt and he couldn't let go of it. It *did* own him—that deep shaft of guilt, the pain that had caused his family to implode—had him in its grip. And until he owned it, just like she said, he could never be the man she needed—only the man who wanted her with every burning fibre of his body. The only question was how would he let go of the secret he'd kept hidden from the one person who meant more to him than anyone else? His Mum and Dad had turned their back on him and Ryan couldn't blame them. What if Fin did too? He wouldn't survive it.

Her cousin, Laura, sidled up next to Fin and muttered, "Smile, Fin. It's your farewell party, not your funeral."

Fin tore her eyes away from where Ryan stood across the room—so unbelievably handsome in his military dress uniform—and smiled at Laura.

A passing waiter paused in front of her, and she plucked a glass of champagne from his tray with a murmured thank you.

Her previous farewell party had been more of an impromptu barbecue in the backyard, but with both Jake and Ryan at home this time, her mother had gone all out.

Now here they stood under glittering lights, black tie and evening gowns, drinking and eating finger food while her stomach tied itself in knots.

"Fin?"

Fin sipped at her champagne. "Hmm?"

"Where's Ian?"

She thought back to the conversation she had with Ian last night and swallowed the bitterness.

"It's probably a good idea I'm not there," he'd told her.

"But ... it's my farewell party. I'll be gone early the next morning."

He shook his head. *"I don't think I'm up for celebrating you leaving, baby."*

Rachael bumped her shoulder. "Earth to Fin?" She ran her eyes over Fin's low cut, shimmery gold dress with admiration. "Glad you retired the sweatpants for the evening," she joked.

"Ian couldn't make it," she blurted out.

Her champagne glass held aloft, Rachael raised a brow at her. "Why not?"

"Work," Fin lied and tossed back the rest of her drink. The bubbles fizzed going down her throat, and she scrunched her nose.

"That's a bit rich," Rachael muttered.

Taking a deep breath, Fin plastered a smile on her face and nudged Rachael. "So where's this so-called *best present that ever lived?*"

Rachael nodded towards Laura. "It's from the both of us, and Laura's already had Jake put it in the car for you."

"You have to take it with you," Laura told her, smirking in a way that made Fin nervous. "Don't open it until you arrive at Casey Station, okay?"

Fin pressed her lips together, tears blurring her vision as she grabbed blindly for Rachael's hand. She gave it a squeeze. "I'm going to miss you two."

"Group hug!" Rachael cried.

They huddled in together and she saw a flashbulb go off. Then a hand grabbed hold of her arm and Jake was elbowing his way into their huddle.

"Quit hogging my little sister." He looked down at her. "Dance with me?"

Laura burst out laughing at something Rachael said as Jake dragged her away.

One hand on her waist, the other on her shoulder, Jake twirled her around the dance floor. "How many whales are you saving this time, Fin?"

She rolled her eyes at him. "I'm not on a save the whale crusade, Jake."

He grinned down as he spun her around. "Really?"

"We're testing pollutants and the progress of climate change in the Antarctic," she told him snootily. "It's important work."

"Preaching to the choir, honey." His eyes softened on her face. "I'm proud of you."

She nodded, a lump rising in her throat. "I know. These two weeks have gone so fast. I can't believe I'm leaving in the morning."

"Onwards and upwards."

"You'll take care of Crookshanks while I'm gone, won't you?"

"That conceited ball of fluff will be just fine, don't you worry."

As the song started winding down, Ryan cut in. "May I?"

Jake took a step back and looked between Ryan and Fin. He gave a short nod. "Of course."

As she stepped into Ryan's arms, *The Scientist* by Coldplay started threading its bittersweet song around them. Ryan placed both hands on her hips, pulling her close, and she wound her arms around his neck. With his dark eyes locked on hers, the words of the song filtered through and tears blurred her vision.

"Fin," he whispered thickly.

"Smile!" she heard her mum yell. Fin pulled Ryan in close and they both turned, smiling as the flash went off.

They started dancing again when her mum moved off, snapping more photos.

"Ryan, I don't know what to say."

"Don't say anything, Fin. Just … let me hold you, okay?"

Pressed against his chest, she could feel his heart beating heavily and she closed her eyes. As the song slowly faded out, another song kicked in and she was dragged away from Ryan and into the arms of her dad.

"How's my girl?" He beamed down at her, spinning her quickly away as a livelier tune began.

Ryan's eyes held hers until the crowd swallowed him up and she couldn't see him anymore.

Fin rolled over in bed and glared at the clock. Two a.m. glared right back at her. Bunching her pillow, she huffed as she tried to find the peace that eluded her.

Her bedroom door opened so quietly she wouldn't have known

if she hadn't seen the brief flicker of moonlight stream through.

She sat up, brushing tousled waves from her face as it clicked shut. Her eyes fell on Ryan walking silently to her bed. In a pair of sweatpants, his chest was bare. Muscled ridges, tattoos and deep scars greeted her as he reached her bedside.

"Ryan?"

"Shhh," he whispered softly and lifting up the sheet, climbed into bed beside her. He tugged her close.

Fin put her hands between them, splaying them flat on his chest. The heat of him burned her skin. "Ryan ... Ian is—"

"Don't say his name. Tonight you're mine. If Ian wanted you as much as he fucking claims he does, he'd be here right now where I am, dragging out every last minute he could get with you." Ryan's hands slid down the small of her back and underneath the elastic of her panties until his hands gripped her ass. "He'd be the one touching you." He leaned in and bit her earlobe sharply before licking it better and she shivered. "He'd be the one tasting you," he breathed in her ear. "But he's not here. I am. I'm the one touching you. I'm the one holding you, because you've never been his."

Ryan's mouth travelled across her jaw until it hovered over hers.

"Kiss me, Fin," he whispered against her lips. "Please."

Tears burned her eyes at his desperate plea. Hardly daring to breathe, she pressed her lips lightly against his. Ryan groaned at the touch and crushed his mouth down on hers. Fin opened her mouth under his, and when his tongue touched hers, she moaned. Her hands slid from his chest, downwards, until they were tugging at the waistband of his sweatpants. Shuddering, Ryan reached up and fisted her hair, tilting her head as he kissed her hard.

When he pulled back, he was breathing heavy, his lips swollen. "You're so beautiful," he murmured.

Her chest tightened under the intensity of his eyes. "So are you."

Ryan shook his head as he hovered over her in the bed. "I carry scars, Fin, both inside and out."

"Everyone's perception of beauty is different."

"Fin, I—"

She cut him off, kissing him, and he groaned, his body pressing her into the bed. He slid his hand between them, skimming down until he reached the edge of her panties. He broke the kiss, panting hard as he fumbled with the elastic before sliding his hand between her thighs.

Ryan groaned as he touched the slick heat of her.

"Ryan, I can't …" She drew in a deep, shaky breath. "I can't be the person that does this to someone else. I want you so much, but the guilt. I don't know if I can—"

"Stop," he whispered. He slid his hand from her panties and buried his face in her neck. She could feel his hot breath as he shuddered against her, fighting for control.

"I'm sorry," she choked out.

"Please don't be sorry," he mumbled against her skin. "Don't ever be sorry. Guilt is the one thing I can't let you live with, baby. I won't do that to you, even if it kills me."

Fin swallowed the lump in her throat. After a beat of silence, she asked, "Ryan, will you stay?"

Ryan nodded wordlessly and wrapped his arms around her, pulling her close until it was almost difficult to breathe under the heat of his body. She turned, her lips brushing his, and he licked along her bottom lip before kissing her softly.

He closed his eyes briefly. "Be safe out there, Fin."

"You too, Ryan."

Wound tightly together, they drifted off to sleep, and when five a.m. came, Fin got up and dressed quietly. A light tap came at her bedroom door. Picking up her bag, her hand fell on the door handle and she turned, her eyes taking in Ryan where he lay sleeping heavily. He'd rolled onto his stomach, revealing more tattoos and thick muscle. One hand rested beneath the pillow, the other fisted near his face. His dark hair, cut so short when he arrived, was starting to grow. It made him look like the young boy he used to be.

Fin tucked the memory away and opened the bedroom door. Slipping out quietly, she pulled it shut behind her.

"Ready to go?" Jake asked softly.

No. She ached to feel Ryan's eyes on her one last time, see his smile, and feel his lips against hers. He was just metres away from her, yet an ocean already lay between them.

Fin closed her eyes. "Yes," she whispered.

Jake picked up the last of her bags from the hallway and grinned at her.

"Did you pack your Supergirl suit for those special occasions?"

She chuckled through tears. "I love you, Jake."

Slinging his arm around her shoulder, he pulled her in for a hard hug. "Love you too, honey."

Chapter Seven

Six months later

Fremantle, Western Australia

Dusk was falling when Fin fitted the key in the lock and swung the front door wide.

"I'm home!" she called out. Her voice echoed through the empty space as she wheeled her bags through and tossed her keys on the side table. Slamming the door shut behind her, she walked down the hallway. A glance to her left showed Jake's empty room, the bed stripped down. Farther down, a glance inside the guest room where Ryan had slept was just as empty.

She walked in the room and closed her eyes, trailing her fingers over the bare mattress. Nothing was left behind, not even the scent of him to remind her he'd even been there.

The phone rang and with a shake of her head, Fin left the room. Fumbling through her bag, she picked it up and answered.

"Finlay?"

"Mum."

"You're home, honey? Why didn't you ring us to come get you?"

Fin walked into the kitchen and reached up, pulling down a bottle of red from her little wine rack. "It's fine. I just caught a cab."

"Oh," her mum muttered, disappointment obvious. "Well. When do we get to see you?"

Fin poured wine into her glass. "Tomorrow? I'm tired, Mum. It's been a long day."

"Okay. Lunch?"

"Sounds good. How's Crookshanks?"

"Your devil cat is just fine."

Fin sighed as she rested her hip against the kitchen counter. "What's he done now?"

"He's clawed grooves into the whole left side of your father's favourite recliner."

Fin smothered a laugh. "Poor Dad. I don't think Crookshanks likes him."

"That's an understatement," her mother muttered.

"Alright, Mum. I gotta go. I'll see you tomorrow, okay?"

"Bye, honey."

Pushing away from the counter, Fin got to the task of unpacking her suitcase and sorting what needed to be washed. The last thing to come out was the present from Rachael and Laura, buried beneath as many layers of clothes as she could manage. She should have known that the so-called *best present that ever lived* was one that required batteries. Her face still flamed just thinking about the way the security attendant looked her over while her luggage was being X-rayed. He'd followed it up with a suggestive wink after handing over her bags, leaving her baffled until she arrived at Casey Station and opened the gift.

After relegating the box to the bottom drawer of her bedside table, Fin picked up her laptop and carried it to the living room along with her wine.

After sitting it on the coffee table, she switched it on and the desktop photo greeted her: Ryan in his military uniform; Fin's gold dress shimmering under the lights as he held her close. Their smiles were bright for the camera, but she could see the sadness in his eyes.

Tapping at the keyboard, she called up the email Ryan sent six weeks ago. It was the only one she'd received from him since she left.

Fin,

We've been called up early.

Heading back to Afghanistan in two weeks.

To be honest I can't wait. Being here when you're not is like another kind of war because you're everywhere—your face, your smile, the sweet smell of you. Only it's a war I can't seem to fight.

Don't hope for us, Fin. Please. I can't have you wasting your life waiting for someone who might never return, and remember what I told you once before— don't let anyone stop you from being who you need to be.

Be safe.

Ryan

Every time she read over the words, it brought an ache to her chest, and every time she tried to reply, she could never find the words she needed to say.

Jabbing angrily at the keyboard, she closed the email. Instead, she called up the email from Jake that he sent just before they left.

Finny,

I read your last blog post. Nice photos. I wasn't really sure if that was you in a giant, fluoro parka or just a big orange in the snow. I'm voting for orange.

I showed everyone here your photo of the Southern Lights. Kyle thinks you're in the wrong career and should be a photographer for National Geographic, but he's probably just hoping to one day get in your pants so don't let him near you.

I'm honestly hurt that Tanner thinks so low of me. You can trust me, Fin - Kyle.

As I was saying—don't let him near you!

Dad pitched a shit fit when I dropped Crookshanks off at their place. You know they've never seen eye to eye. I can rest happy knowing I've been knocked off the number one position on Dad's shit list. That honour now belongs to you.

Hope you got home safe. Dad was going to mow the lawns for you, but if you've come home to overgrown weeds, you'll know why.

Love you,

Jake.

Picking up her wine, Fin sipped at it as she flicked the television on. With the background noise for company, she tapped out a reply.

Jake,

Home safe. No overgrown weeds noted. Maybe that means when I pick up Crookshanks tomorrow his fur will be shaved off. Mum's just told me he clawed the shit out of Dad's recliner, so the two of us will be lying low for a while.

An orange? I guess I'll have to return the penguin I brought home for you. Better yet, tell Kyle I said the penguin is now his.

It's really quiet without you here. Miss you. How long are you gone for this time?

Love you too and be safe.

Fin xo

A knock came at the door as she hit send. Standing up, she walked down the hallway and swung it open.

"Ian."

He stood there, olive green cargo shorts, black fitted shirt, his blond hair mussed from running his fingers through it. He swallowed, his eyes softening as they roamed over her. "Welcome home, baby."

She stepped aside to let him through. He held her eyes for a moment before walking down the hallway towards the couch she'd just left. As he sat down, he grabbed her hips, yanking her onto his lap.

"Don't let anyone stop you from being who you need to be."

Fin took a deep breath. Her time away made her realise she was trying to force something with Ian that wasn't there. It wasn't possible to change who she was in order to be the person Ian wanted her to be. It was time to let him go.

"Ian—"

"Don't say it." He leaned in, pressing his forehead to hers. "I know." He kissed her, his tongue sweeping wildly into her mouth. His fingers dug into her hips as his lips moved hard and desperate on hers. Tearing his mouth away, they both fought for breath. Tears filled his eyes. "I know," he whispered against her lips.

Fin closed her eyes and remembered the way Ian had looked at her after their very first kiss. His blue eyes wide as he asked breathlessly if he could ring her.

She remembered their first time together, right through to when he'd returned from Sydney, standing in the bar, and her heart had swelled at seeing him again. She *had* missed him. "I still love you, Ian."

He nodded, a tear sliding down his cheek. "Love you too, Fin."

Ian wrapped his arms around her and buried his head in her neck. "Let's not be friends, okay? Not for a while at least. I can't—" his voice cracked.

"Oh God, Ian. I'm sorry. I'm sorry I can't be the person you need me to be," she whispered through tears.

He took a deep breath and pulled back, his eyes red. "I guess this is what they talk about when they say people just grow apart. We can't force something that isn't working, right?"

Fin wiped at the tears on her cheeks. "I'm tired of saying goodbye to people I love."

He stood up, bringing her with him, and set her on her feet. "Then let's not say goodbye. Just …" He paused and pulled car keys from his pocket before meeting her eyes. "See you later, Fin."

She pressed her lips together, her heart aching. "See you later, Ian," she whispered thickly.

His eyes searched her face, then he nodded once and turned. Striding down the hallway, he didn't look back as he opened and shut the door behind him.

She grabbed blindly for her phone off the table where she'd left it and dialled Rachael.

"Hey, Fin!"

A sob broke free.

"Oh shit. What?"

"Ian," she managed to say.

"Do you have wine?"

"Yes," she whispered.

"Good. I'll be right there."

Fin exhaled deeply. "Thanks."

Two weeks later
Camp Holland Military Base
Tarin Kowt, Afghanistan

Ryan stretched out on his bunk and tried to sleep in the late afternoon. They were only two days in on a recuperation period before heading out on another patrol in just over a week, and he was desperate for some quiet.

Jake walked in, throwing himself down in the bunk opposite. A guitar was sitting ominously in his lap.

"Oh hell no, Tanner."

Jake settled his fingers on the strings and strummed a chord that had Ryan grinding his teeth. He looked up, raising his brows innocently. "Did you say something, Kendall?"

"Take that thing outside. Go play it in the shithouse where it belongs."

Jake's fingers fumbled as he struggled to find the note he was looking for. "What are you trying to say? You don't like my playing?"

"I thought we hid that fucking thing from you in Monty's room," Ryan muttered.

Jake strummed another chord and grinned. "I found it, asshole.

Couldn't find my sheet music though, so I'm just gonna have to play by ear."

"You do remember me telling Fin that Crookshanks could play that thing better than you, right?"

Jake strummed the strings in rapid succession, the sound so painful a passing soldier muttered a solid "fuck" as he passed by their bunk.

"So? I'd be able to practice better if you didn't keep bitching me out."

"Jesus. I thought you hid that bloody guitar, Kendall!" came a loud yell from Kyle in the bunk across the hall. "Keep that shit up, Tanner, and I'm gonna come in there and break that thing across your face!"

Jake kept plucking away at the strings.

"I think Brooks was serious," Ryan warned.

Jake set the guitar aside and focused his eyes on Ryan.

"What?"

"I got a couple of emails from Fin," Jake replied.

Lacing his fingers behind his head, he stared at the bunk above him and took a deep breath. "Yeah?"

"The first one says she's home safe."

Ryan closed his eyes for a moment.

"Did she mention me?" Kyle yelled out from across the hall.

"She says she hopes you live a very long and miserable life," Jake called back. "Oh, and she brought you back a penguin."

"Fuck yeah," Ryan heard him say. "I'm in."

Ryan raised a brow at Jake and Jake shook his head, his lips twitching.

"The second?" he prompted him.

Jake's eyes searched Ryan's face. "She split with Ian."

"What? When?" With all hope of sleep gone, Ryan sat up and swung his legs over the bed.

"When she got back."

"Fuck. He didn't—"

"No," Jake cut him off. "I asked the same thing. She says he didn't hurt her."

Ryan rubbed his brow. "Is she okay?"

"You know Fin. Mum says she's buried herself in work."

Ryan stood up and opened the cupboard beside his bed. He yanked out a shirt and tugged it over his head, tucking his tags underneath the thin cotton.

"What are you doing?" Jake asked.

He grabbed his shoes. "Going for a run."

"Thought you were going to have a sleep," he said as Ryan tugged his shoes on.

"Yeah, I can't see that happening right now, Tanner."

"Kendall?" Jake called out as Ryan reached the door.

He paused and looked over his shoulder.

Jake sat there, his eyes steady. "I love the two of you. I just want you both happy, you know what I'm saying, don't you?"

Ryan pressed his lips together and gave him a short nod. "I hear you."

As he walked down the narrow, bomb-proofed hallway of their base, he heard Jake start strumming his guitar again.

Eight days later, after heavy preparation and planning, their team— including the addition of American snipers—was inserted into the mountains by a vehicle-mounted patrol. It was perfect timing: the night black, the sky clear, and the air cool.

Ryan cleared his mind as he leaped to the ground and weighted himself down with his pack. This patrol might solely be reconnaissance, but it was going to be done inside enemy territory. Intelligence told them Taliban fighters near the village of Khaz Uruzgan were planning something big. Ryan's team was going to gather information that would flush those bastards out.

Jim, one of the snipers that sat opposite Ryan on the drive, gave him a short nod as he slid his own pack on. Ryan returned it. He liked the Americans. They were brash and loyal to their allies, which was pretty fucking important when you were caught under heavy fire.

Monty pulled their team together. "All set?"

Ryan gave the thumbs up.

"Right," he said.

Beside him Jake grinned. "Let's go fuck shit up."

Ryan fell into step behind Monty, Jake following behind him, as they began the long climb.

Ten hours later and they were eighty-seven kilometres northwest of their base at Tarin Kowt and high into the mountains.

"Ready for that nanna nap yet, Kendall?"

Fuck. Jake sounded barely winded. Asshole.

Exhausted, Ryan steadied his breath. "Not me, Tanner, but if you're tired just say the word. I'll read you a story and tuck you in."

Jake chuckled as their feet crunched softly over the rocky terrain.

Five minutes later, Ryan heard a soft, warning click from Monty and he froze. The entire team behind him halted and silence reigned to the point you couldn't hear a single breath.

Monty gave the thumb down *danger close* signal, and Ryan felt tension rise thick in the air.

His heart rate climbed rapidly with anticipation. Like flicking a switch, his exhaustion disappeared, his vision narrowing in the fading darkness on a man fifteen metres ahead.

They weren't expecting foreign enemies this high in the hills, yet they spotted a man approaching, full beard, AK-47 raised and ready. Knowing it was the weapon of choice for the Taliban, Monty ordered quickly, "Shoot to kill, Kendall."

His entire team dropped and found immediate cover as Ryan stood alone, heart in his throat, his eyes trained on the enemy.

Ryan raised his assault rifle, his breathing harsh to his own ears, and with narrowed eyes and steady hands, he opened fire.

Enemy fire returned rapidly. Ryan felt the heat of the bullets tear past him, knowing he was seconds away from one ripping into him and bringing him down.

As his bullets found their target, Ryan watched the Taliban fighter jerk, blood exploding outwards as he fell hard, shock the last fleeting image on his face.

"Enemy dead," Ryan roared.

From his corner vision, Ryan caught another Taliban fighter—rocket-propelled grenade in hand—ducking and weaving through the brush ahead.

"Twelve metres full left, one enemy," he yelled.

Instincts kicking in, Ryan dived for cover and moments later a PKM machine gun opened fire on their patrol and the battle was on.

"Fuck," he heard Jake growl beside him as they returned fire.

Fuck was right. Their team had trekked right into a nest of insurgents.

As machine gun fire cracked into the rocks around them, Monty pulled out a map and Tex began radioing their coordinates back to base, calling in an immediate air strike.

The orange light of dawn began its approach, slowly revealing their position to the enemy.

"Jesus fucking Christ. We need to retreat," Ryan growled.

"Cover me," Jake yelled from the other side of the rocks.

With his heart pounding fiercely, Ryan stood and opened full fire. Jake broke cover. Hunching over, he ran for a better position to take out the PKM that was spewing heavy fire.

New shots rained down from above, taking their team by surprise, and as Ryan turned to fire, he saw Jake fall.

"Tanner!" Ryan shouted hoarsely. "Man down!" he yelled at Galloway. "Cover me."

Galloway unhooked his rocket launcher, and as the explosive rounds lit up the sky, Ryan rushed out and skidded to the ground, grabbing Jake in his hard grip and dragging him to cover.

With the PKM no longer heard, Kyle stood guard in front of them, his rifle raised.

With Jake laid out on his back, Ryan crouched over him. His eyes fell on the bullet wounds to his shoulder and neck. Thick, red blood was flowing freely from the neck wound, and as Ryan jammed his fingers on it, it overflowed, spilling over his hands and leaching into the ground.

"Someone get me some goddamn first aid," he shouted, his voice cracking as he put his entire body weight onto the wound.

Scrambling came from behind him.

"Jake," he yelled.

Ryan's jaw clenched when Jake remained unmoving.

Using his other hand, he felt hard for a pulse.

Nothing.

"Damn you, Jake," he rasped as the heat of bullets cracked wildly around them. "Please."

Ryan screwed his eyes shut when Jake didn't move, his heart splintering into a thousand pieces.

"Jake, you asshole! Goddamn you, don't do this!" he shouted

hoarsely. "Don't leave me."

Opening his eyes, hot tears poured down his face. Bandages were thrust at him. Blinking through blurred vision, he grabbed at them. He took his hand off Jake's neck for a split second, the blood a slight trickle before he slammed the bandage down.

It's not real. I'm gonna wake up in a minute and Jake will be there, strumming that shitty guitar and grinning at me.

Monty crouched down on the other side of Jake and felt for a pulse. With his jaw clenched, he looked at Ryan. "Kendall." His eyes were raw with grief. "Jake's gone."

Ryan couldn't breathe, his head spinning from the lack of air.

"No." Ryan shook his head. "He's not gone. He can't be."

Jake was infallible. He was the strongest, the fastest, the best of all of them. Jake was his *brother.*

Leaning over, he buried his head in Jake's stomach, images spinning through him as sobs ripped him wide open.

Jake glancing sideways at him. *"What grade are you in?"*

"Five. You?"

"Same," he replied, grinning.

Jake looking at him from across the table. *"Ghost Recon rematch?"*

Jake standing beside him. *"Don't let this shit beat you, Kendall. Dig deep and show these cunts how it's done."*

"Ryan's lazy," Jake told Fin, his eyes glinting with laughter. *"He falls asleep during all our training exercises."*

Jake's voice cutting through the silence. *"How long have you been in love with my sister?"*

Jake's eyes as Ryan looked at him from over his shoulder. *"I love the two of you. I just want you both happy. You know what I'm saying, don't you?"*

"Christ. Where's our goddamn backup?" Kyle screamed, his voice cutting through Ryan's wild daze.

"Air support two minutes," Monty yelled back as he stood, raising his rifle. Ryan's eyes fell on the blood coating Monty's fingers and his stomach lurched. "Start a retreat."

Kyle jerked as a bullet caught him in his hip and he fell to his knees. "Fuck," he growled.

Galloway rushed over, helping Kyle to his feet, and Ryan turned back to Jake. Hardening his heart, he took a deep breath and hefted Jake's body up and onto his shoulder. Steadying himself, he started behind Monty through heavy cover fire as they headed for a safe pick up zone.

"Sonofabitch," Ryan rasped when relief came moments later in the form of two FA18 jet fighters screaming overhead. "You fucking bastards are five minutes too late."

Ryan turned as they unloaded their bombs, explosions lighting up the dawn and tearing through the thick brush.

"Ryan!" Monty yelled.

Turning back, he picked up his pace as the bombs wiped out the entire nest in a matter of moments.

Soon after a Black Hawk helicopter thundered above them, and when his stomach lurched as they lifted off, there was no laughter or jokes, just the loud beat of the rotors carrying them back to base.

With Jake lying beside him, Ryan held tight to his cold hand. He let silent tears roll down his cheeks as everything inside him systematically shut down, leaving nothing but black.

Chapter Eight

Three months later ...
Fremantle, Western Australia

As dusk settled in a riot of pink and orange, Ryan pulled the black, vintage mustang he'd collected from storage into the driveway. As the car idled powerfully, his eyes, raw and aching, fell on the cottage. In the time he'd been gone, the pretty little cottage remained the same, which felt wrong because everything had changed. Jake was gone. Despite knowing the danger of their job, Ryan had always felt if either of them was to die, it would be him. It *should've* been him. For three months the guilt had eaten him alive from the inside out.

Ryan had barely been holding himself together, and facing Fin? He hadn't been sure he could, but three months of avoiding her like a goddamn coward was enough. If he had to look her in the eye and see the heavy weight of accusation, then he should be man enough to take it.

Pulling his key from the ignition, he opened the door wide and climbed out. Cars drove down the pretty, tree lined street behind him. People were going about their lives—somehow not knowing that someone so remarkable, and so utterly selfless, didn't walk the earth anymore. How could they not see?

Forcing himself to put one foot in front of the other, he walked up the front path to her door. Before he could change his mind, he knocked sharply, and after a pause, turned to stare blindly at the street, an envelope clenched in his fist as he waited.

"Take this, Kendall."

Frowning, Ryan grabbed at the envelope from Jake before it dropped to the floor. *"What is it?"*

"It's for Fin. You know, in case ..." his voice trailed off. *"Anyway, we better get to this briefing."*

"Tanner, wait!" Ryan called out with Jake halfway out the door. Jake paused and Ryan scrambled around in the drawer beside his bunk. He pulled out his own envelope and held it out. Jake looked at it, then at him, and Ryan hated the thought of what it would mean for Jake to be giving that to Fin. *"Me too, okay?"*

They had a service on base in Afghanistan for Jake. The soldiers formed an honour guard to say farewell, saluting him as he was marched to the aircraft and flown home.

With their deployment ending just a week later, his troop returned in time to attend the service held at home. Ryan had carried Jake's envelope inside the jacket of his military uniform at Jake's funeral, but he couldn't force himself to go to Fin.

Mike and himself, along with Kyle, Monty, Galloway, and Tex, had formed the guard of honour that carried Jake's coffin to the chapel. His jaw clenched the entire way, fighting back tears.

They'd buried Jake with full military honours at Karrakatta

cemetery. The service had included the Prime Minister, the Minister for Defence, the Defence Force Chief, the Chief of Army, and hundreds of soldiers, family, and friends. Jake had been loved, revered, and buried as an Australian hero.

Ryan had stood there, in a sea of army green, holding his breath as he watched Fin. She'd been beautiful in a simple black shift dress, her blonde hair tousled and loose as she climbed the chapel stairs. Walking slowly to the front lectern, she stood in front of a thousand people and spoke. His chest ached as her words had people laughing, tears falling, and hearts breaking. Then she finished with the lines that had made him so fucking proud of her.

"Jake was a brother and a son, a grandson, a cousin, and now an Australian hero. I know a lot of people don't understand war and what it means to be a soldier. Jake told me it's not easily explained, but I know that despite him being gone, his sacrifice was made for those out there that are unable to fight for themselves, and for peace. I ask you today to spare a few minutes to feel the peace we enjoy in this place we call 'the lucky country' and know that it's people like Jake, who give of themselves, that enable us to do so. I have a few small words Jake asked me to read in the event he didn't make it home.

To my country, I hope I have done you proud. To my fellow soldiers, I hope I have honoured you in my actions. To my father and mother, thank you for showing me love ..." Fin paused and looked up, her green eyes searching until they landed on Ryan. *"To my brother Ryan, thank you for sharing your life with me, and to my sister Fin ...'*

She faltered at that point and fighting tears, Ryan felt his heart crack wide open. Fuck it, he'd wanted to walk up there, grab hold of her, and never let go. Instead, Mike reached her side and took the bit of paper to finish reading it for her.

'To my sister Fin, who's busy saving the earth one whale at time, don't forget to smile, because when you do it's like seeing the sun.'

Letting out a shaky breath, Ryan turned and rapped hard on the front door again. Hearing music coming from inside, he frowned. Tucking the envelope into his back pocket, he unlatched the side gate and walked down the side of the house to the backyard.

Then he saw her. She was lying on a deck chair in a loose white dress with thin straps, her silky hair trailing over her shoulder. He ran his eyes over her, and tears burned behind his sunglasses. She'd lost weight. Her hipbones were prominent and her face thinner. One bony arm hung listlessly over the side of her chair, the other held a glass of wine she swirled casually in her hand.

Ryan swept his eyes down her legs, his body still aching from wanting her. He swallowed hard and clenched his hands, realising he must have made a sound because she turned her head towards him. He honestly thought he couldn't hurt anymore than he already did until he looked in her eyes. The green and gold depths, usually so passionate and alive, were empty, and he wasn't sure what world she was in at that moment, but it wasn't this one.

"Oh, Fin," he whispered thickly.

Fin watched the man walk towards her through a fog. Her vision cleared slowly, bringing Ryan into focus. Her heart, so dead inside her, gave a strong thump, as though trying to wake up.

He strode towards her wearing a deep blue shirt stretched tight across his wide chest and a pair of soft, dark jeans. Mirrored aviators covered his beautiful, dark eyes, and his hair—longer now—was casually windblown. His powerful presence reminded her so much of Jake that her stomach lurched.

Fin set her wine down and swung her legs over the chair as he reached her side.

He sank down in the chair opposite, his jaw tight. The pain etched in his face had her holding out her hand. He looked down at it, and her skin tingled with warmth when he wrapped it in his large palm.

She forced a smile. "Ryan."

With his free hand, he pulled off his shades and tossed them aside carelessly.

Her breath caught at the haunted look in his eyes when they met hers.

"Fin," he breathed, his chest rising and falling rapidly as he looked at her. "I'm so sorry."

She reached out and cupped his face with her hands. "A man once told me that guilt was the one thing he wouldn't let me live with, yet I can see it on your face. Don't take this on yourself."

Ryan closed his eyes, a tear spilling over and rolling down his cheek. He turned his head, brushing a kiss against her palm.

"I miss him, Ryan," she admitted with a whisper, her hands falling away. He opened his eyes. "So much. Why does God always take the good ones? How do I keep going without him? When I wake up in the morning, everything's okay for a brief moment until I remember, and then I can't breathe knowing he's not out there walking the same earth, seeing the same stars."

"Fin. Look at me," Ryan said firmly.

She lifted her eyes.

"Just one day at a time, okay?"

Reaching behind him, Ryan pulled out an envelope, turning it carefully in his hands. Her name was written on the front, and her heart thundered in her chest when she recognised the handwriting.

He held it towards her. "Jake … wanted you to have this."

Swallowing, she reached out and took it. "Thank you."

He stood abruptly. "I have to get going."

"I … you can't stay?"

"No." He stared blindly out into the yard. "I can't stay, Fin," he whispered.

"Wait!" She scrambled out of her chair and snagged his wrist as he turned to leave. "I have something for you too."

Fin ran inside the house, returning moments later with another envelope. "You have one too."

"Thank you." His voice was hoarse and he cleared his throat as he reached out and took it. He indicated towards the front of the house. "I need to go."

She nodded and he turned, his long-legged stride taking him quickly from view, leaving her emptiness to return.

Sitting down, she swallowed the last of her wine and fingered the edges of the envelope, opening it carefully and unfolding the single sheet of paper.

Fin,

If you're reading this letter, then I'm sorry for leaving you behind. I've not really gone anyway. I'm wedged inside your heart where you can keep me alive, okay?

I hope it's a comfort to you that I haven't regretted a single moment of my life, and that my reasons for leaving are so that others can live a life of freedom.

Fin, you're smart and brave, so know that I'm leaving Ryan in your hands.

He needs you. He's proud and strong, but it's always the strongest that fall the hardest.

Always smile when you think of me, and please, don't be scared to love. It's what makes life what it is.

I love you,

Jake.

P.S. Don't ever retire your Supergirl suit, okay? I want you out there saving those whales so your kids can grow up seeing them in real life, rather than in history books.

Ryan slumped against the door of his car, swallowing the lump in his throat. He'd let Jake die and then for three months he hid from the world. Why hadn't she been angry with him for that? He would've preferred the spark of fury rather than the emptiness in her eyes.

Jake, you goddamn asshole! I want you to come back to life just so I can kill you all over again for leaving us without you.

Opening the car door, he put the envelope on the passenger seat and slammed the door shut. Hearing screams from inside the house, panic flooded his body, leaving him ice cold.

"Fin!" He rushed towards the house. "Fin!" He yanked hard on the front door but it was locked.

Breathless, he ran hard around the side of the house. Wild screams pierced his ears as he stormed through the back door. What he saw almost brought him to his knees.

Fin stood in the living room, her books—the ones she'd treasured reading her entire life—lay shredded on the floor, ripped pages littering every surface. Broken plates and smashed cups joined them. Even as he rushed the room, a plate spun past his head and crashed into the wall behind him.

"Fin!" he shouted as he ducked. "Stop!"

Held in the grip of rage, she didn't hear or see him. She turned back to the side cabinet for more plates, chest heaving, her face twisted in anguish as she threw another.

Ryan came up behind her and locked his arms around her waist, trapping her hands by her sides.

"No!" she shrieked. She kicked her legs up wildly as he spun her around, walking carefully over the broken shards that would have torn her bare feet. "Let me go! Damn you, Ryan, let me go!"

Her cries cut right through his chest as she wrestled free, shoving him off her as they reached the hallway. "Damn you!" she shouted and he flinched. "Fuck you! Fuck Jake. How could he leave me?" She sobbed hard and loud as her back slid down the wall, her legs unable to support her slender weight, and it ripped him apart. "How could he leave me?"

Ryan sank down beside her and pulled her into his lap, rubbing her back as waves of grief split her open.

"He's out there, alone, buried in the ground where it's dark and cold. I'll never look into his beautiful, smiling face again, and I can't stand it, Ryan," she sobbed as she clung to him. "I just want him to come home. I want him home," she choked out.

"Me too, baby." Tears blinded him as he pressed his forehead against hers, powerless to do anything but hold her. "I want him home too."

Ryan wasn't sure how long he sat there rocking her, listening to her sobs fade into small hiccups and eventually a deep slumber. Not wanting to disturb her, he stayed where he was, his arms holding her as night fell around them.

He pressed his face into her neck and breathed her in, allowing his lips to touch her skin. Feeling his blood stir, he closed his eyes, willing it away.

"Ryan?" she whispered hoarsely.

"Shhh," he soothed and kissed her neck, letting his lips trail up her neck to her ear and murmuring, "Just let me hold you."

Ryan took a deep breath as she shuddered against him. He pressed a kiss against her ear. Turning her head, his mouth trailed gently along her cheek.

"Ryan," she breathed.

Twisting in his lap, she cupped his face in her hands. The emptiness in her eyes now sparked with craving, and the blood he felt stirring became a roar in his ears.

"Fuck," he muttered, and ducking his head, took her lips hard. She whimpered under the pressure, her mouth opening to let his tongue thrust inside.

Ryan groaned at the hot, sweet taste of her. With Fin still in his lap, he stood up. Her long, slender legs wrapped around his waist, his biceps bulging as he held onto her, pressing her into the wall as he kissed her until they couldn't breathe.

He tore himself away, rapidly sucking in air. "Fin, we can't."

She slipped her hands beneath his shirt and finding skin, moaned as they travelled up and over his chest. "Please." She leaned in and bit down on his earlobe with her teeth until he shivered. "You once told me you wanted to fuck me until you were blind from it, so do it."

"Not like this," he said, his voice hoarse. "You deserve better than this."

"Fuck me, Ryan. Make me feel."

"No, Fin." He stepped back from the wall and set her on her

feet. "I won't do this."

She shoved at his chest, and he stumbled back. "Fine," she growled. "Then I'll find someone who will."

Halfway into her room, he grabbed her wrist. "You aren't going anywhere."

"After three months, you don't get to tell me what to do!"

Fin tried to shrug out of his hold, and fearful of hurting her, he let go.

"Fine!" he shouted as she stood there, chest heaving, hands fisted by her sides as tears rolled unapologetically down her face. "You want to feel?" Knowing she would fall apart all over again if he was gentle, he took control. "Take off your clothes. Right now."

Ryan folded his arms, hating himself for taking advantage of her grief but he wanted her too desperately to stop now.

Fin's hands fumbled at the buttons on her pretty, white dress. Head bowed, she slowly undid each one with shaky fingers until he could see she wasn't wearing a bra. Finished, she slid the tiny straps off her shoulders. Her dress fell away, pooling at her feet.

His eyes consuming her, Ryan's blood pulsed rapidly, making him hard enough to wince. Her breasts were small and firm, her nipples a pretty pink. As his eyes trailed down, his heart ached. Grief had taken its toll on her. Her ribs were pronounced and her hipbones sharp.

Realising she was waiting, he lifted his chin at her cotton panties. "Those too."

She hooked her fingers in the waistband, her hands still shaking, and peeled them down her legs. Stepping out of them, she stood bare before him.

How many long, painful years had he dreamed to see Fin like this?

"Baby, you're so beautiful," he whispered gruffly. He tugged off his shirt and her eyes fell on his chest. He crooked a finger. "Here. Now."

She walked towards him, not stopping until her breasts pressed against his chest. Ryan moaned deeply at the feel of her smooth, naked skin rubbing against him. He tucked his thumb and forefinger under her chin, tilting her head until she met his eyes. Seeing the need that mirrored his own, he slammed his mouth down on hers. Gasping softly under the onslaught, her lips parted and he took advantage, his tongue thrusting inside to taste her. Wrapping his arms around her, his hands slid down her back and gripped her ass. Pulling her tight against him, Ryan ground his hips into hers.

Fuck. He was going to come in his pants if he didn't calm down.

He broke the kiss. Breathing heavily, he nibbled a path down her neck. Fin's hands grabbed his shoulders, her head falling to the side to accommodate him.

"Sit down on the bed," he commanded.

She stumbled backwards, Ryan following her as she sank to the edge. Nudging her shoulders, she fell on her back and he hovered over her, taking a small pink nipple and sucking it deeply into his mouth.

"Oh God," she moaned, her hands running through his hair.

Ryan shifted his mouth to the other, fighting to control the urge to ram himself inside her and fuck her hard.

Kissing his way down her torso, his tongue delved inside her belly button. Kneeling at the end of the bed, he ran his hands up Fin's thighs and spread her legs, baring her to his gaze.

Taking a deep shuddering breath, Ryan groaned as his tongue

came out and stroked her. She bucked beneath him and he grabbed at her hips. "Hold still," he ordered.

"I don't know if I can," she breathed.

Ryan held onto Fin as he licked her, focusing on making her feel good. He slid a finger inside her and she gasped, her hips moving wildly in time with his tongue and hand.

"Now, Ryan, please," she panted. "Don't make me wait."

"Fuck," he muttered. The taste and smell of her had his dick jerking violently in his pants. With his mouth still busy, he undid his belt with one hand.

She bucked again, whimpering, moaning his name.

Blind with need, he undid his zipper and pulled himself free. Grabbing her thighs, he positioned himself carefully and slammed his way inside her.

She cried out and he stilled, licking his lips, tasting her on his tongue as her body pulsed around him, burning him.

Ryan buried his head in her neck, shuddering at the tight, wet heat enveloping him. The urge to thrust was overwhelming, but he remained unmoving, a sweat breaking across his brow from the effort. "Did I hurt you?" he rasped.

She shook her head and wrapped her legs around his hips, squeezing him. "Fuck me, Ryan."

Ryan drew back and looking into her eyes, slammed in again. "Nothing, Fin …" he breathed.

"Nothing?"

"Nothing …" he slammed in again "… has ever felt more beautiful than you do right now."

Christ. He didn't just love her, he fucking *adored* her. He'd give his life for her if he had to.

He thrust hard into her, over and over, the pleasure intense and out of control. Shuddering, she cried his name, clenching around him, and he let go with a wild groan. Gritting his teeth, he flooded her body, pumping himself into her until there was nothing left.

Hovering above her, Ryan ducked his head and kissed her, tugging her lower lip into his mouth and sucking on it. The taste of Fin was like the purest Heaven and the hottest Hell.

Taking a deep, shaky breath, he started pulling out and she winced.

"You okay?"

Fuck. Tears were pooling in her eyes. They spilled over, rolling down the sides of her face and into her hair.

And there it was—the guilt—swallowing him until he was drowning in it.

"Baby, please don't cry anymore." He looked down as he slid out of her. "Oh fuck," he breathed.

You dumb, stupid fuck.

"What?"

He looked at her. "I didn't use a condom."

Chapter Nine

Ryan hovered above her, his hands pressed into the mattress over her shoulders. His dark eyes were wide with panic when just moments ago they'd been consumed with a fire so intense she'd felt almost branded.

"Fin? I'm sorry." Guilt swept across his face. "I didn't mean t-to—"

Fin shoved him off and rolled over, curling herself into a little ball. Her hands shook as she clutched them to her chest, her shame palpable. What had she done to him?

She'd read the letter from Jake and suddenly the world had turned black, as though his words had blocked out the sun. Anger for the both of them leaving stabbed at her like a sharp blade, but it felt good—the wild rage giving her life. When Ryan grabbed her, the spark flickered out and as she slid down the wall, all the pain she'd buried deep inside had bled out over both of them.

Then she'd done the unthinkable and begged Ryan to take it away. And he had. He'd widened his stance, tattooed muscles bulging as he folded his arms, and ordered her to take off her clothes. His eyes had been bleak, his jaw tight, as though already forgiving her for what she was doing to them.

But his face. Oh God. He'd rammed himself inside her and she watched his hurt transform into beautiful agony. She felt his muscles flexing as her hands roamed down his back, cupping his firm ass as he thrust deep enough, hard enough, to have her gasping for air. He obliterated her pain with each wild stroke, over and over.

Now, after so many years of longing, their first time had been filled with pain and grief, instead of being sweet and special. Had she ruined that between them for one brief moment of feeling something? She didn't want brief moments. She wanted what she'd yearned for right from the start—the very moment she'd tripped up the school steps and lost her heart. But even now, with Ryan lying naked in her bed, he still wasn't hers. The Army, and the war, owned him—body and soul. Fin never stood a chance.

Ryan's palm scraped over her shoulder. "Fin?"

She shrugged it off. "Don't touch me."

"But—"

"I'm clean, okay? I had a medical for my expedition and I haven't been with anyone since."

"That's not—" He paused. "Me too."

She wasn't on the pill though. Not that she'd tell Ryan that. The last thing she needed to see in his eyes was more panic. She'd go to the pharmacy in the morning and sort it out.

Sheets rustled behind her as Ryan shifted. His fingers began trailing their way down her spine, slowly circling each protruding bone until he reached the small of her back.

"Are you hungry?" he asked, concern weighting his voice.

Fin squeezed her eyes shut. "No."

"You should eat something." He shifted in close, his chest brushing against her back and she shivered. "Cold?"

Cold? The heat of him was scorching her skin and she wanted to bury herself in it. She pulled away a little instead. "I'm not anything except tired, Ryan."

"Enough," he growled. He grabbed at her, her body flailing as he stood up and tossed her over his shoulder.

"Oomph." She pushed at his back. "Put me down!"

"No."

"Now, Ryan," she demanded as he stalked out of her bedroom. His hand slid up her leg, squeezing her bare ass, and she gasped.

"No."

He carried her to the bathroom and reaching inside the shower, flicked on the taps while she struggled in his hold. "Ryan, please. I just want to sleep."

Ryan ignored her. Stretching out a hand, he checked the temperature of the water as steam began pouring out. Setting her on her feet, he nodded at the shower. "Get in."

Anger rose in her chest and it felt satisfying. "Stop telling me what to do!"

"Then stop with the cold bitch act. It's not you and I don't like it!" She resisted when he seized her shoulders. "Get in the goddamn shower!" he roared.

"Ryan—"

He picked her up, his arms locking around her, and stepped in the shower with her. Scalding water pounded over them.

"After this, you're going to bloody eat something. You look like you haven't eaten in months."

She stood motionless as Ryan grabbed at the soap and started rubbing it over her body in rough, jerky movements.

"I forced you to have sex with me," she whispered.

He froze.

Straightening his back, he looked down at her, his eyes searching her face. "Is that what you think?"

Fin nodded mutely.

"That's so far from the truth I can't believe you'd even think it. I have a thick skin, baby," he told her, his wide shoulders crowding her back against the cool tiles, "but you're under it. You're buried in there so deep it's like I was born with you in my soul." His eyes slowly ignited as he slid soapy hands over her hips. "When I'm near you I'm consumed by you—your smile, your eyes, your heart. Even though we've never been together, you've always been mine, and even if I never get to keep you, you'll still be mine." Ryan grabbed her hands and put them on his chest, sliding them down the muscled ridges until she circled him with her hands. He was hard again; she could feel the blood pulsing through him. He put a hand over hers. "This is how much I want you, and you didn't force that. I've always wanted you and I'll never stop wanting you."

A bittersweet ache welled in her chest. How was it possible to feel so much heartbreak and so much love at the same time? The warring emotions were a force, slamming into her, tangling together until she was lost. "Ryan, I—"

"Don't say anything." Ducking his head, his lips hovered over hers, waiting.

Breathing quietly against his mouth, she leaned in hesitantly and kissed him. She watched his eyes flutter closed at the soft, delicate touch.

He sucked in a sharp breath as she stroked the hard length of him with both hands. "Is this what you want?" she whispered against his lips.

Ryan kissed her, moaning into her mouth as she stroked him again, up and down, gentle and firm. "Yes," he breathed.

He pressed his hands flat on the tile above her shoulders, his hips moving in time with her hands.

Fin moved her lips down his neck, his body shivering as she continued her fiery path until her knees hit the shower floor. His dark eyes flickered open, watching her intently. Leaning forward, she took him in her mouth, her tongue swirling around him.

"Baby," he choked out. Bracing his forearm against the wall, Ryan buried his face in it, shuddering as her mouth and hands moved over him.

His other hand buried itself in her hair, and too soon, he was tugging at the wet strands. "Stop."

Ryan gripped beneath her shoulders and yanked her up. He kissed her hard, his tongue thrusting wildly into her mouth as he slid a hand between her thighs. "Need you."

"Now," she told him.

"You ready for me?" She clutched at him when he buried his fingers inside her.

"Oh God," she moaned as he slid them out and back in again. Fin pressed her face into his shoulder and bit him softly. Using his free hand, he reached up and pinched her nipple, rolling it in his fingers as his tongue swiped a path along her lips. He was everywhere, his hands, his tongue, his scent. She was drowning in him. "Ryan, please."

He pulled away. "Turn around."

She turned blindly, giving him her back.

"Brace your hands against the wall and lean forward."

"Ryan?"

"You can trust me, Fin."

Fin nodded. She'd never trusted anyone more than she did Ryan. When she did as he asked, he grabbed her hips, yanking her back further. One hand fell away, and then he was there and pushing inside her. A moan broke free and she didn't even know if it was him or her.

With both hands back on her hips, he slid all the way in. "Oh fuck," he breathed. "My beautiful Fin."

She wriggled against him, so he pulled out and pushed back in again.

"You good?"

"Mmm," she moaned. *Better than good.* Ryan brought her alive. "Harder."

Ryan complied until she thought her hands would give out, but when he reached around between her thighs and rubbed hard, it was her entire body that gave out. His name was wrenched from her lips as she gasped for air, and his arm wrapped around her ribs, holding her up.

"Fuck," he shouted hoarsely as he slammed into her one last time, his chest heaving. He ground his hips as he shuddered against her.

Jake turned around and looked at Ryan with narrowed eyes, thick red blood pouring down his neck and soaking his shirt. Raising his arm up, he aimed his gun right at Ryan's heart and said, "It should have been you, Kendall, not me. I had everything to live for. You had nothing." His voice was cold and biting, the smile on his face as he pulled the trigger sending icy shivers through Ryan's body.

Heart thundering in his chest, Ryan woke up sweaty, his body trembling.

"Goddammit," he muttered, swiping a hand across his face. He looked over at Fin, her breathing was deep and even, her cheeks flushed.

He pressed a hand over her heart, feeling the steady thump beneath his fingers, letting it calm him.

Sensing his touch, she rolled over, one long leg sliding out to rest above the sheet. Her ribs stuck out, her collarbone sharp, and it broke his heart. He'd forced her to eat a sandwich last night before they fell into bed, exhausted. Yet despite being wrung dry, Ryan still struggled finding sleep. What was he still doing here? He would only be leaving again soon. He *had* to leave. Now more than ever. Jake didn't die so that Ryan would give up. Was Fin supposed to happily wave him back off to Afghanistan so soon after losing Jake? And what if he didn't come back? Could he do that to her?

Fuck no.

Fin was right. They kept going around in circles, and it was slowly shredding him into tiny pieces. How much longer could they keep doing this?

Swallowing the lump in his throat, he eased his way out of bed in the early light and dressed quietly.

As he left the bedroom, Crookshanks head-butted his leg, growling his hungry demands. With the cat fed, he pulled the front door shut behind him. Even with the soft light, he hid his eyes behind sunglasses as he strode towards the gleaming, black mustang.

Ryan pulled the keys from his pocket.

"Coward," came the soft whisper in his ear.

He froze, icy tendrils curling around his spine.

"Jake?" he croaked.

Ryan spun around but no one was there.

Christ. He was fucking losing it.

He reached for the door handle.

"Is this how you take care of my sister after I leave? Fuck her and sneak out?"

The voice whipped coldly around him, everywhere, but ... nowhere.

Ryan swallowed, his eyes burning. "Fuck. Don't. I can't do this."

He swung the door open as he slid inside. He put the key in the ignition and started the car, hearing it come to life with a deep, throaty growl.

"Look at you. Your hands are shaking."

His eyes fell to the hand that trembled on the gearstick.

"Damn you, Jake. Stop screwing with my head," he said loudly. He shifted into reverse and let out the handbrake.

"You didn't read my letter."

The envelope still sat unopened on the passenger seat, taunting him with its plain white disguise, masking words he knew he couldn't yet read.

Unease rolled through him. "I'm not sure I can."

"Close your eyes, Kendall."

His jaw clenched as he fought back tears, but he closed his eyes anyway.

"Now picture a world without Fin."

"Oh God," he moaned, burying his head against the steering wheel. His stomach lurched at the thought of her gone like Jake was.

"Good. Now where are you in that picture?"

His eyes moved rapidly behind closed lids, searching, but there was nothing but black, empty space. He wasn't there.

"What do you see?"

"Nothing," he whispered hoarsely. "Without her there I'm nothing."

A chuckle echoed softly around the inside of his car. "Bingo."

Blinking sore, gritty eyes, the ceiling came into focus. Rolling over, Fin saw the empty space beside her and she slumped back on the bed. When loud buzzing registered from outside, she clutched the sheet to her chest and stretched up to peer out the window.

Ryan was mowing her lawn. He paused, lifting the hem of his shirt to wipe sweat from his brow, baring taut, tanned skin to her gaze. Scrambling from the bed, Fin tugged on a singlet and panties and made her way from the bedroom.

Her eyes swept the living room. No evidence of her violent outburst from yesterday afternoon remained. A sharp pang swept through her at the empty bookshelves. *Books*, she reminded herself. *They're just books.*

Going to the kitchen, she grabbed a spoon and reached for Crookshanks' breakfast from out of the fridge. Usually he was twining himself around her legs right now—where was he?

Frowning, she turned, her eyes finding him sitting outside in the morning sun, licking the length of his leg as though he'd already eaten.

The front door clicked and Ryan strode down the hallway, bringing the scent of freshly cut grass with him. His eyes were tired, his body sweaty.

Fin narrowed her eyes. "What do you think you're doing?"

His brows flew up. "Excuse me?"

"Mowing my lawn?"

Ryan rubbed his forearm across his brow, wiping away the

sweat. "It was overgrown. It would've died off if you'd left it any longer."

"So what? Everything dies sooner or later, right?"

Oh God, stop.

But she couldn't. It felt like she was standing outside of her body watching a train wreck before her very eyes.

"Feeding me, my cat, cleaning my house, my yard. It's mine. My house." Her voice rose along with her anger. "And you're not my friend. You're Jake's!"

Hurt flashed across his face, and her stomach pitched feverishly, unable to control the venom spewing from her mouth.

He nodded, his jaw tight. "You think I'm trying to take over?"

"I don't know what you're trying to do, Ryan, but whatever it is, don't. I don't need you coming here and thinking you have to take care of me because Jake died. Don't think that you owe it to him."

Ryan's eyes flashed angrily at her words. "That's not why I'm here."

"Then why are you here?" she shouted.

A beat of silence passed as his eyes locked on hers.

He opened his mouth to speak, but nothing came out.

Fin's heart tugged painfully. "I don't need you, Ryan," she said wearily. "And I don't want you here. You should leave."

He stood there, clenching and unclenching his fists. "You want me to leave?"

Damn you, Ryan. I'd take you, Army and all, even knowing you might not come back just like Jake, but you won't let me have you, so yes, I want you to leave.

But she didn't say any of that. She couldn't choke the words out. Instead, she nodded wordlessly.

He turned around and strode back out the door, slamming it

hard behind him. She flinched, and soon after Fin heard the deep rumble of his car start up. Eventually the noise faded, replaced with a silence that had her ears ringing and the red haze of anger lifting.

What did she just do?

Stupid girl!

She rushed to her room, scrambling for her phone on the bedside table. With frantic fingers, she fumbled over the keypad until she found Ryan's name. As the phone rang, she started pacing, one hand pressed to her forehead.

It rang endlessly until his voicemail answered.

Dialling, she tried again.

"No," she whispered, her stomach rolling when it rang out again.

The beep came through loud and clear to leave a message.

"Ryan? I didn't mean it," she choked out. "I'm sorry." She sank to the floor. "I don't know why I'm so angry. Please come back," she whispered hoarsely. "I'm sorry."

She sat on the couch in the living room all day long, but he never returned her call, and he didn't come back.

Chapter Ten

Rachael dragged Fin out of the dressing room and stood her before the mirror. Fin swept her eyes over her reflection as techno music pounded heavily through the store. The short gold skirt, the slinky black top cut so low there was no way a bra could be worn—it wasn't her.

"It's not me," she announced, tugging the top up to cover a bit more of her chest.

Rachael tweaked it so it fell back down and looked at her in the mirror. "Stop fussing with it. Double sided tape will hold it in place. And exactly. It's not you. That's the point. You're living in a bubble of grief. Tonight you can be someone else. You need that, Fin."

She needed Ryan. Nothing else. Just him, but two weeks and she'd heard nothing. It didn't surprise her. He'd told her he'd always wanted her, that he would never stop wanting her, and the next morning she'd thrown it in his face because for one blinding moment she thought he was there as an obligation to Jake, and it had *hurt*. Who could blame him for staying away?

"I'm not sure I can go out tonight, Rach."

Rachael stood in front of Fin, blocking her view of the flimsy outfit as she took hold of her hands. "Jake would be furious with you right now," she said with tears filling her eyes. Blinking them away, she straightened her shoulders. "I'm furious with you right now. This is not living, Fin. You're just existing inside a vacuum and you can't go on like this forever."

"Yes I can."

Rachael let go of her hands and fussed with the gold skirt. "No. You can't."

Frowning, Fin batted her hands away and tugged the skirt down. She sighed when her hipbones came into view. "Send out a search party, Rach. The rest of the skirt is missing."

Rachael folded her arms in reply.

"Fine." She threw up her hands. "Whatever." Shifting backwards, she sat down on the little button leather couch in the dressing room area. "I have all this anger inside me and it keeps spewing out everywhere. I keep hurting people with it."

Rachael paused and looked at her. "You mean you hurt Ryan with it."

"Ryan's hurting enough as it is. He was the one that was there. He was the one that saw ... th-that saw ..." Her fists clenched. "Fuck."

Standing up, Fin strode back to the dressing room, shut the door, and took the clothes off. In just her underwear, she eyed her body critically. She'd always been slender like her mother, but her bones were sharp now, and prominent. Ryan was right. She needed to eat. Jake would hate seeing her this way.

"Fin?" A light tap came at the door as Fin held her jeans out, ready to slip them back on. "Are you okay? You know it's okay to be angry. You have to let it all out."

Her hands went slack as she slumped against the dressing room wall. "I know."

"You're angry because you know he's going back, and that scares you. You and Ryan—you're both like one half of each other. Neither of you will ever really be complete without the other."

Pushing away from the wall, she dressed quickly and opened the door. Rachael met her eyes. "I was a bitch."

"You've just lost your brother, Fin. You're allowed to be an emotional whackjob right now."

"Ryan isn't."

"Men like him are trained to lock that shit down."

Fin frowned. "But then ... where does it all go?"

"My guess would be wherever he goes," she said softly. She snatched the clothes out of Fin's hand and smiled. "Now let's go spend some money."

Fin shook her head. "Rachael."

"Fin," she sing-songed, turning around and heading for the front counter.

The salesgirl gave them both a bright smile as she rang up the purchase. "Do you have Hollywood Tape?"

Fin looked at her. "Do I have what?"

"Boob tape," Rachael said loudly. "And yes, we've got some, thanks."

The salesgirl gave another bright smile as she handed over the bags. Rachael took them, thanking her, and they headed out of the store. Fin looked at Rachael over her shoulder as she walked down the small set of stairs and onto the street. "I can't believe you have me wearing boob tape of all things."

Not watching where she was going, her heel caught on the bottom step and she pitched forward. The hard chest she smacked into stopped her from falling into a heap on the sidewalk.

"Oh shit," she mumbled.

Strong, tanned hands came out to steady her. "Did someone say boobs?"

Her arms caught in a firm grip, Fin looked upwards into rich, hazel eyes that went wide with recognition as they focused on her face.

"Kyle?"

"Fin!" Grief swept briefly across his face before it was wiped away by a broad grin. His arms came around her and he lifted her up, her feet dangling off the ground until she was looking directly in his eyes. "How are you doing?"

Fin held onto his shoulders as she was suspended in his arms. "You know."

His eyes softened. "I do."

"Should you be lifting me?" she asked.

"I'm fine, honey. It was just a scratch."

Tears filled her eyes. "I'm glad you're okay." She blinked them away as Kyle looked at Rachael standing to her left. "You remember Rachael, don't you?"

He gave Rachael a wink. "How could I forget?"

High colour hit Rachael's cheekbones, and Fin smothered a laugh. Clearing her throat, she looked pointedly down at the ground.

Kyle ignored the silent demand to put her down. Instead, a cheeky glint lit his eyes as he arched a brow at her. "Where's my penguin?"

Laughter bubbled out of her. "Are you serious?"

"You're holding out on me, honey. I've never seen a penguin before. I was looking forward to having one of my own."

"I don't believe you. You haven't been to Penguin Island?"

"That depends."

She raised a brow. "On what?"

"Are you going to take me?"

Fin chuckled and pushed at his chest. "You can put me down now."

She slid slowly down his body as he let her go. Reaching for her hand, he grabbed hold. "What are we doing today, ladies?" He looked at the bags Rachael clutched in her hands. "Shopping?"

"Brooks!"

Kyle turned and Fin peered around him, seeing a car parked farther down the road. One guy was leaning his back against the passenger window, another was resting his forearms over the open car door on the driver's side. Both were looking at them.

He waved them off and turned back to look at Fin and Rachael.

"We're taking Fin out tonight, so we needed to get her something to wear," Rachael said in answer to his question.

He looked at Fin, the bright midday sun shining through his golden brown hair. "Out, huh?"

"Maybe," she mumbled.

"We're going," Rachael said firmly. "Fin needs to get out."

"Where are you off to?"

Fin sighed as Rachael told him.

"Hurry up, mate!" came another shout from the car.

Letting go of Fin's hand, Kyle turned around and waved off their impatience. "Gotta get going," he told them and took Fin's chin softly in his hand until she was looking at him. "Take care of yourself, honey."

"Of course," she murmured.

He nodded at Rachael and walked off.

"Oh, Fin?" he called out. Rachael and Fin, already walking off in the other direction, stopped and turned. "I'll call you, okay?" he shouted, walking backwards. "You can take me out to Penguin

Island like you promised."

She shook her head, fighting a smile. "I didn't promise you anything," she shouted back.

Kyle grinned. "Are you sure about that?"

Reaching the car, he swung open the door as his friends hopped inside the car. He gave a brief wave before disappearing.

"Kyle's huge," Rachael announced. "And hot," she added.

Fin looked at her. "Don't go lusting after a soldier, Rachael. They're not good for your health, particularly that one. I hear his package is footloose and fancy free."

Rachael grinned and linked her arm with Fin's. "Of course it is. *Now.* But that's only because he's waiting for the love of his life to just happen along."

They started walking down the street. "And that's you?"

"Well … yes," she conceded. "Though by the way he was looking you over, it could possibly be you. Don't be greedy. You have Ryan and he's the hottest of the hot."

"I don't have Ryan," she pointed out.

Rachael stopped them both and looked at her. "What are you talking about? You've always had Ryan."

"I haven't. The Army has."

"Fin." Exhaling irritably, Rachael looked away for a moment before meeting her eyes. "You're his heart. You. That's his sacrifice for whatever demons he's carrying around inside him. But he needs to wake up and realise that it doesn't matter where he is, or what he does, you'll still make being together work, because both of you share something that is so far beyond love it won't ever die."

"What about in here?" Kyle said.

Ryan stopped in front of the open deck nightclub he was walking past with Kyle, Tex, and Galloway. He was already unsteady on his feet. Alcohol had done its promised job tonight, and he was almost numb. He just needed one night without having to feel anything.

Putting his hands in his pockets to keep himself balanced, he looked at Kyle. "This place?" he shouted over the loud music. From the street outside, the beat was already thumping through his system. "Are you high?"

Kyle gave the club a once over. "If I was, I wouldn't be here with you girls."

"Yeah? Where would you be?" Galloway asked.

Kyle paused and looked at him. "Fucking of course. That's my high."

"Fucking anything that moves," Tex muttered.

Kyle raised a brow, insulted. "Just women, asshole. Tall ones, short ones, slim ones, curvy ones." He licked his lips and grinned.

A group of girls sat on the deck talking and laughing. One of them broke the huddle and glanced their way. She winked as she brought a glass to her mouth.

"Jesus," Kyle muttered. "Yep. This is the place." He nodded towards the entrance. "Time's wasting."

Galloway followed Kyle's line of sight and frowned. "Hey, isn't that Laura?"

"Laura?"

"Yeah, you know … Jake's cousin."

Goddammit. The numb haze floated away at the mention of Jake's name, ruining all the effort he'd put into drinking so he could forget. Laura's eyes widened when he looked her way. She glanced quickly towards the bar and following her movement, he froze.

Fin stood there looking like nothing he'd ever seen before. His breath lodged in his throat as his eyes wandered over her. She was wearing a skirt that shimmered under the bright lights of the bar. Her beautiful long legs—the ones that felt like heaven when they wrapped around him and squeezed—were on display to the world, and her top? *Fuck.* Was it a top? Whatever the fuck it was, it exposed a long V of her chest that made him hard instantly. He wanted to drag her away, lick his way down that tantalising display, and then rip that thing in two.

Tex said something that had Kyle and Galloway laughing, but he couldn't drag his eyes away.

"… right, Kendall?"

Kyle elbowed him.

"Huh?" he muttered.

"Nothing," Kyle said with a roll of his eyes.

When the guy standing next to Fin at the bar leaned in and trailed his finger seductively over the line of her collarbone, blood roared in his ears. He was saying something to Fin that had her leaning close to hear.

"Fuck," he growled.

His face grim, Ryan ignored his friends and started for the door.

"Looks like we're going in!" Kyle shouted.

"Good one, dick. Look at the bar. Fin's here," Tex told him.

"I know," Kyle replied, smug. "I had it on good authority she would be."

"So look at the guy she's standing next to. Don't you recognise him?"

His brows flew up. "Should I?"

"He's in all the photos we saw of Fin."

"Christ, Galloway. I'm busy looking at *her* in the photos, not raking my eyes over whatever asshole is standing next to her."

"That's *Ian*," Galloway growled.

Kyle's eyes flew to the bar. "Oh fuck," he breathed.

Ryan winced as the lights strobed painfully, but he kept his eyes on Fin as he pushed through the crowd of people.

Ian noticed him first. Glancing over Fin's shoulder, he gave Ryan the once over and his jaw ticked. Ignoring him, Ian smiled down at Fin and Ryan wanted to punch it off his face.

"Fin."

She turned slightly and her eyes, having done something that made them smoky and sexy, widened when she saw him standing there.

"Can we talk?"

Fin blinked. "Now? *Now* you want to talk?"

He nodded at the clarification. Yes, he wanted to talk.

Ian took hold of her bicep, the gesture a possessive one, and smirked at Ryan. "Not really the best time for talking, is it, Kendall?"

Ryan gave him a murderous glare. Did the man have a fucking death wish?

"Ryan." Hearing Fin's sweet voice, he wiped the anger from his face before he looked at her. She shook her head at him. "There's nothing to talk about. I get it. Really, I do. But I apologised. I asked you to come back and after two weeks, you see me standing with Ian and *you* decide we can talk now?"

"Yes, dammit. You needed time to cool off."

"Fin." Ian's eyes narrowed as he stepped closer, crowding her. "What are you talking about?"

Fin shrugged off his hold. "Nothing, Ian."

Ryan looked between the both of them. Ian's body was tense, jealousy obvious in his flushed cheeks. Hell, Ryan was just as bad. His hands had curled into fists. He all but cracked his knuckles and growled at the guy.

"Are you two back together now?" Ryan asked Fin.

"No," she said firmly.

"Maybe," Ian said over the top of her.

With the noise at the bar getting louder, Ryan only caught Ian's response. He flinched, hurt welling inside him. "Really? After what happened between us, you're just running back to him?"

Ian's nostrils flared. "Wait. You *fucked* him?"

Fin pressed her lips together.

"Don't you speak to her like that!" Ryan snarled, jabbing his finger angrily.

Fin focused her gaze over his shoulder. "Hi, Kyle." Her attempts at forcing a smile fell flat because it didn't reach her eyes.

"How long have you been fucking him for?" Ian ground out. "All those times he was staying over at your house when we were still at school—were you fucking him the same time as me?"

With vision blurred by rage, Ryan heard Kyle mutter, "Oh shit," as he cocked back his fist and slammed it in Ian's face. It hit with a hard, satisfying crack, and Ryan growled with pleasure as Ian staggered backwards.

"Kyle, do something," he heard Fin plead.

"Fuck no. Didn't you just hear what that asshole said to you? I'm taking a turn next."

Ian rushed forward, fisting Ryan's black shirt in his hands. "You bastard!" he yelled in his face. "Stop doing this to her. Can't you see? When she sees you, all she sees is Jake and it's fucking killing her! You hanging around is just a lousy reminder of what happened to him. Leave her the fuck alone or she'll never get over it. Let her move on, for fuck's sake!"

Ian shoved him away and Ryan staggered backwards, shock stealing his breath. *Fuck.* Ian was right. The asshole was fucking *right.* He had to let her go. Let her heal. Live without her. Alone. He was always so goddamn alone.

His heart squeezed painfully, like it would rupture in his chest at any moment. Shoving away from the security that arrived after the commotion, he turned and blindly stumbled his way out of the bar.

Tex caught up with him and shoved a bottle of beer in his face. "Here. Think you need this."

In full agreement, he grabbed it from Tex and swallowed half of it down in one go. Seeing a second sitting in Tex's hand, he grabbed it too.

"Hey! Kendall—"

"Fuck off," he growled. Putting a hand on his chest, Ryan slammed Tex into the wall and stalked away. Rounding the corner, he found himself in an alley as he downed the last of the first bottle. Christ. Fucking beer. He needed something harder. Something to annihilate the Hell he couldn't claw his way out of. Hooking his arm, he smashed the empty bottle against the red brick wall. It shattered with a loud echo through the empty alley, glass shards scattering carelessly along the concrete pavement.

"Jake!" he shouted, his chest aching and raw. "Where are your fucking words of wisdom now?'

Stumbling, Ryan leaned against the wall and finished the next beer.

"Asshole," he mumbled when the voices inside his head remained quiet.

Sliding his back down the wall, Ryan drew his knees to his chest, laughter bubbling out of him at his stupidity. Fin had it right. Ryan *had* been trying to take care of her. It was the only thing that kept him going—that she needed him. But she didn't need him at all. Where did he go from here? He was so fucking lost. He buried his head against his knees, gasping with laughter. Hadn't he always been lost? Jake should've told him to buy a damn compass and get the fuck over himself.

"Ryan?" came Fin's sweet voice.

Oh no. Was he hearing Fin's voice now too? He was tired of hearing voices. It was too much.

"Go away," he moaned at the voice, his laughter vanishing as loud, keening sobs broke from his chest. He couldn't breathe when wave after wave of them crashed over him, dragging him beneath the surface.

"I want to sleep," he cried hoarsely. "And I don't ever want to wake up."

"Please, Ryan. Don't do this."

Fin placed a hand on his shoulder, and Ryan screwed his eyes shut, realising that she was really there and he wasn't hearing things.

"I'm so tired," he whispered to her, his voice muffled against his knees. Hot tears fell thick and fast down his face and nothing could hold them back. He didn't even have the energy right then to hide them from her. "So tired of living with so much pain."

"Please get up," she choked out. Her voice held a world of hurt as she tugged at his arm, but he couldn't move.

"It's my fault," he sobbed, holding his head in his hands. "It should've been me."

"You can't take the blame, Ryan. God. It will kill you."

"You weren't there!" he shouted, looking up and finding her kneeling before him. "You have no idea what happened!"

"So tell me!" Fin yelled back, her chest heaving as she knelt before him, her green eyes glaring. She looked away for a moment, and when she looked back, her beautiful eyes were wide with grief. "Tell me," she whispered. "I need to know."

Ryan took a deep shaky breath. "Was he right? Am I just a lousy reminder that's holding you back?"

"No!" she cried desperately. "Don't listen to Ian. I had no idea he'd be here tonight. I'm not ... we're not getting back together. I promise."

"You don't owe me promises."

"It's not about owing anyone anything, it's—"

"It is," he cut her off. "I owe Jake. I *owe* him. More now than ever."

Fin pressed her lips together, fighting tears. "I can't live without you, Ryan."

He nodded, his heart burning with so much love for her he ached with it. "I can't live without you either," he whispered, tears rolling down his cheeks, "but I'm going back. You know that, right? I have to finish what Jake and I started together. This war ... I need to see it through for the both us. If I don't it'll just feel like he died for nothing, and I can't accept that."

Fin reached out and cupped his face in her hands, wiping away his tears with her thumbs. "I know," she whispered.

"Kendall? Fin?" Kyle called out.

They both turned towards the alley entrance. Kyle stood there, peering into the darkness.

Ryan cleared his throat. "Down here, mate."

As Ian stepped around the corner behind Kyle, Fin pushed herself angrily away from Ryan, anger burning brightly in her eyes as she stood up and strode determinedly towards Ian. Ryan staggered to his feet as Kyle reached out to grab her and missed.

"Goddamn you, Ian! How dare you?" she shrieked and launched herself at his chest, her tiny fists pummelling him. "Stop making everything worse. We're not together anymore!"

He stumbled back, grabbing her wrists with enough force that she jerked violently in his hold. "Fin—"

Kyle wrapped his arms around her waist, yanking her away before Ryan could reach her. "Hands off of her, asshole!" he snarled.

"You've done your damage," Fin whispered wearily at Ian. "Just go."

Reaching her side, Ryan took hold of her, pulling her towards him. She buried her face in his chest. "Please take me home, Ryan."

Ignoring Ian, he wound his arms tightly around her. Leaning in, he pressed a kiss against her ear and whispered softly, "You got it, baby."

Chapter Eleven

Ryan's heart thumped heavily as they sat in the back of the cab heading home. He wanted to pull Fin over to him, sit her on his lap and hang on forever. Instead he settled for reaching out and tucking her hand in his. Linking their fingers, he rested them on his thigh as he stared out the window into the night.

Fin squeezed his hand, as though drawing strength from the touch. Had he done the right thing? He'd told Fin he couldn't live without her. There was no taking that back. He always thought he'd been strong—his mind, his body, his heart—but he wasn't strong enough to fight without Fin anymore.

The Army and the SAS had been his dream—his chance to be somebody, save lives, show his parents he was worth something. But after years of what he thought was dealing with his past, the unkind bitch that was retrospect told him he'd just been running from it. Being a soldier had been his escape, his flight from the demons that bound him, and Fin had been the only one who could stop him from running forever. As long as she was here, he could run as far and as fast as he wanted, but for her he would always return.

"Ryan. Are you okay?"

He stared out the window, unable to face her. "I'm not sure I've been okay for a long time, Fin."

"Will you ever tell me?"

He watched the streets pass by rapidly as the cab drove them towards Fin's house. "My past is catching up with me," he said eventually.

"And?"

Ryan turned and looked at her, letting out a deep shaky breath. "My family fell apart when I was seven and that was because of me. You, Julie, Mike. You're the only family I have and I don't want to lose that."

"What happened when you were seven, Ryan?"

Returning his gaze to the window, he swallowed, closing his eyes against the fear and guilt. "I can't talk about it."

The cab pulled up in front of the cottage, and he let go of her hand, reaching for his wallet from the back pocket of his jeans. When Fin started handing over notes to the cab driver, he snagged her wrist. "I got this, baby."

"But Ryan—"

He looked at her and she paused. Satisfied, he paid the driver and slid out of the car. Reaching back in, he held out his hand to Fin. She took it and climbed out behind him. The cab's bright red tail lights disappeared into the distance as they walked up the path towards the cottage.

Fin buried her hand inside her purse, rummaging around for the key to the front door.

"Crap," she muttered when her bag fell to the ground.

They both bent over at the same time to retrieve it, and Fin cracked her nose on his forehead.

"Ow!" she wailed.

Straightening up and taking her purse in his hand, Ryan grabbed hold of her elbow, steadying her as he checked the damage. "Dammit, I can't see. Why didn't you leave the porch light on?"

"Because I like a bit of a challenge," she retorted. "Trying to fit keys in locks in the dark while drunk is the ultimate test of agility."

Ryan repressed a smile in an effort to look stern, not that she could probably see in the dark anyway. "Well you failed, smartass."

"I *am* a smartass. Don't you like nerds, Ryan?"

"Only drunk ones," he teased as he rummaged around in her purse. "Jesus, Fin. How do you find anything in here?"

Fin tugged on it. "Give it here. You're having a man's look."

"Well you can't do much better. You're blind," he pointed out.

She paused to glare at him. "I only need glasses to read."

He waved a hand in front of her face. "Can you see this?"

Laughter bubbled out of her as she snatched the purse out of his hands. "Fine. We can just camp out here. Wait for dawn so we can see properly."

"I'm not sleeping on the fucking porch."

"Why not? I'm sure you've slept in worse places."

He had. Many nights had been spent camped out on the dirt during an exercise or patrol. Interrogation training had been the worst. He'd slept bound—hands tied behind his back and ankles shackled—and after being dragged naked through mud and worse, ice cold water had been tossed over him every half an hour to keep him awake. But fuck, he wasn't training, or at war. He was with Fin. That deserved a cosy bed and warm, naked skin.

Ryan's eyes dropped to her mouth. Visions of picking her up, slamming her back into the wall and kissing those lush lips hit him hard. He sucked in a quick breath when all the blood in his body headed south. Suddenly getting inside was becoming more urgent. He snatched at her purse at the same time she tugged it backwards, and it went flying across the lawn, the contents scattering in what felt like slow motion to all four corners of Hell. Somewhere out there in the dark was the key, and he needed inside, and not just the house.

"Well, now you've done it," Fin announced.

"Fuck." Ryan peered out onto the front lawn. "Don't you have a spare hidden somewhere?"

Fin fisted her hands on her hips. "I used to put a key above the door ledge until Jake found out." She took a deep breath and let it out. "He flipped out and threatened to shave off Crookshanks' fur if I did it again. I guess he was worried about someone finding it and getting inside while he wasn't around. I guess it wasn't the best spot to hide a key, but I never got around to finding another spot."

"No shit it wasn't the best spot," he mumbled before striding over to where her purse landed and getting down on his knees, started the search. "I bet he's laughing at us right now."

Fin knelt beside him, her thigh brushing against his. "You think so?" she asked softly.

"Of course. I hear him laughing at me all the time." He stopped grabbing at the random objects Fin obviously felt were necessary for a night out and looked at her, his chest aching. "I'm sure I even hear him talking to me."

"You too?"

Ryan licked his lips. "You ... I'm not the only one going crazy then?"

"Well ..." she drawled.

He chuckled softly, shaking his head. "What does he say to you, Fin?"

Fin picked up a blade of grass and began shredding it carefully. "Okay, um ... the other day I was backing out of the car park at work and almost got side swiped by a delivery truck. Then it was like

Jake was sitting in the passenger seat, yelling at me to get rid of my little quote-unquote 'earth saving little buzz box and buy a goddamn 4WD with bullbars.'"

"Well, that does sound like Jake, and he does have a point. You're not the best driver. You'd be safer driving a bigger car."

"Well," she muttered, leaning over and running her hands over the lawn searching for the key. "I'm not telling you what else he says then."

"Oh yeah?" Ryan launched himself at her, tackling her around the waist. He landed on his back with a thud, Fin falling on top of him. She scrambled back, straddling him. "I know ways to make you talk."

Fin raised a brow at him, and he trailed his finger down the V of her top, careful to make sure it traced teasingly over the delicious swell of her breast.

She whipped her head around, peering up and down the street. "Ryan, we're on the front lawn."

"Whose fault is that?"

"Yours," she moaned when he cupped both breasts in his hands, rubbing his thumbs over her nipples.

"Fuck," he muttered, desire coiling tight in his belly. He ran his hands down the flimsy edges of her top. "I want to rip this thing off you."

"Oh God. Don't. You'll shred my skin."

He looked at her, aghast. "What have you done? Glued the thing to your boobs?"

"No!" She huddled down on top of him, and he bit back a groan at the warm weight of her chest pressing against his. "It's taped on."

"Really? So I get to unwrap you like a present?" Ryan ground his hips into her, liking the idea.

"Ryan!"

"Are you blushing, baby? Because your face looks bright enough to light up the entire lawn. We might just find the key after all."

Leaning up a little, he caught her bottom lip in his teeth and nibbled lightly. He heard her breath catch before her mouth opened beneath his and her tongue slid inside.

Ryan groaned, his hand sliding up to fist her hair as she kissed him wildly. Breathless, he broke it off and pushed her away. "We need that fucking key."

After what he was sure was a lifetime of frantic searching, Fin jumped to her feet with a squeal, holding up the little silver key in triumph.

He stood and grabbed her hand. "Inside. Now."

"No." Fin started yanking him towards the side of the house.

"Where are we going?"

"The yard," she told him, unlatching the gate and tugging him along behind her.

"Fin—"

"Shush."

Their feet crunched softly against the sandstone pavers as Fin led him along the side of the house and around the low set timber decking.

When they reached the middle of the lush thick lawn, she pulled him in close. Breathing softly, Fin pointed upwards. Wrapping his arms around her waist, Ryan looked up into the black sky. "What?"

"The stars, Ryan." She tilted her head, exposing the long sweet line of her throat as she looked up. "Do you know why they shine?"

He quirked a brow at her. "Am I getting a science lesson?"

"If you're lucky."

"I can think of other ways to get lucky right now," he told her.

Fin rolled her eyes. "That was terrible."

He chuckled softly. "I know."

"Look up," she said, sounding impatient.

Ryan did as he was told, his eyes falling on the twinkling stars.

"Have you heard the term *a star is born*? It's not as romantic as it sounds, but it's a process called nuclear fusion. You would get that, with it being the same process used inside weapons."

He nodded and looked at her, but her face was still tilted upwards, absorbed in the night sky as she spoke. "And they shine because they have huge fusion reactors in their cores that release enormous amounts of energy. Did you know it can take a single photon up to a hundred thousand years to get from the core of the star to its surface? And the sun, which is the closest star to earth, takes eight minutes for its light to reach us? That means when you're looking at the sun, you're seeing it as of eight minutes ago. So these stars you're looking at now ..." She looked at him and frowned. "Look up, Ryan."

Ryan tore his eyes from hers and focused once again on the sky. "We're seeing those stars as they were centuries, or even thousands of years ago. It'll take billions of years for one of them to die, yet Jake was gone in only twenty-seven of those."

Ryan swallowed the lump in his throat her words caused. "What are trying to say, Fin?"

Fin looked at him, her eyes filling with tears. "That it doesn't matter if you live a billion years, or just a short handful like Jake. It's how bright you burn while living them that really matters, and Jake burned so bright it hurt my eyes."

Overwhelmed, Ryan buried his face in her neck, breathing her in. "You're so beautiful," he whispered hoarsely. Pulling back, he cupped her face in his hands and looked at her fiercely. "You burn just as bright, sweetheart."

Her eyes were wide and so full of love it made his heart ache. "So do you, Ryan," she replied softly.

Lowering her gaze, Fin carefully peeled her top away from her skin and pulled it over her head. She took a step back as she shimmied out of her skirt, leaving him breathless as she stood in nothing but a scrap of black lace. "I want you out here, under the stars."

"Fin," he breathed.

She stepped out of her shoes and moved towards him, reaching for the hem of his shirt.

She grinned. "Arms up."

He held his arms up as she tugged his shirt off and dropped it on the grass beside their feet.

Ryan kicked off his shoes as her fingers reached for his belt buckle. The light touch of her fingers against the bare skin of his stomach had him throbbing painfully.

"No making too much noise like you usually do," she teased.

He leaned over, peeling off his socks. Straightening, he looked down into her eyes. "Baby, I'll have you screaming my name so loud, your face will be what's burning brightly every time your neighbours wave hello with a smirk."

"Yeah?" She tugged hard at his belt before undoing the button of his jeans and sliding the zipper down. He sucked in a breath as her fingers trailed the hard length of him along the way. "Well they're your neighbours now too, Ryan."

Ryan froze, his heart thundering in his chest. "What?"

Fin yanked his jeans down and he stepped out of them. Instead of straightening up, she knelt on the soft grass and ran her hands up the outsides of his thighs. "Move in with me, Ryan?"

She tugged at his boxer briefs, sliding her fingers tantalisingly close to him. Leaning in, Fin let her breasts rub softly against him as she slid her hands around his legs and beneath his underwear. She loved looking at his rough, hard body, but feeling it was even better. She heard his shaky exhale as she peeled the boxer briefs down his legs. Was it a dirty trick asking that of Ryan while she was on her knees before him? Fin slid her hands up the back of his legs, and gripping his ass in her hands, she leaned forward and licked the length of him slowly, from base to tip. Ryan let out a loud groan. It probably was, but she was tired of sitting back and letting him leave her to go do what he needed to do. If he had to go back to Afghanistan, then she was going to damn well get every minute with him she could before he did.

"That depends," he moaned when she wrapped her hands around him and swirled her tongue around the tip enticingly.

Pulling back, she looked up at him from beneath her lashes as she continued to move her hand over him in slow, even strokes. "On what?"

"On whether you're going to kick me out the moment I mow the lawn," he mumbled.

Fin tugged on him firmly and he groaned. "Oh, you like that?" she muttered. "Anything else?"

"Am I allowed to feed the cat and help with the housework

without you thinking I'm trying to run your life?"

Fin pulled back, resting back on her haunches as she folded her arms.

"Don't stop." He grinned down at her. "I promise I won't do a thing around the house to help you."

"Ryan!" She pressed her lips together, trying to fight the smile. "Now who's being the smartass."

Ryan chuckled softly before his face sobered. "I can't live without you, remember? Of course I'll move in." He must have seen the wild emotion in her eyes because he gave her a mock glare and folded his own arms. "Now finish what you started."

Straightening up, she took him back in her mouth, teasing him with her hands and tongue until she could feel him fighting for control.

"Stop now," he moaned.

"No."

"Fin, I'll come," he warned hoarsely.

"And that's a bad thing?"

"Yes," he ground out, breathing heavily. "I want to be inside you where I damn well belong."

Ryan stepped out of her reach and grabbed his shirt from the ground. He tossed it on the grass. "Lie down," he ordered.

"You're so bossy."

"You like it."

"Only with you, Ryan," she told him. The grass crunched softly beneath his shirt as she lay over it. "Well now that you've got me here," she told him as he knelt down between her legs and hovered himself above her, "what are you going to do with me?"

His dark eyes flashed heatedly into hers. "Wicked, wicked things, baby."

Her heart lodged in her throat. "Ryan," she whispered thickly and reached up, cupping his beautiful face in her hand. "I love you so much."

Ducking his head, Ryan took her lips hard, his tongue thrusting inside her mouth and tasting her wildly. Tearing away, he looked at her for a long moment, his chest rising and falling heavily against her own. "I want to say I love you too, but it doesn't seem enough."

With a shaky hand, she brushed away the silky strands of hair that caressed his forehead. "Say it anyway," she whispered.

"I love you, Fin. I've always loved you. Right from the moment you walked up those steps at school, you tripped your way right into my heart. I won't ever stop. I'll love you longer than the stars that live in the sky."

"Okay," she replied, the vision of him blurring behind more tears as she smiled up at him. "That seems like enough."

He leaned in and nibbled softly on her earlobe. "Now can I please have my wicked way with you?"

"By all means," she murmured, heat coursing through her body as his hands stroked over her breasts.

Damn the man, he was right, because soon after Ryan's mouth licked and kissed every inch of her body, and he was moving hard and fast inside her, she was moaning and shouting his name hoarsely. It would take weeks for the wild flushes to calm down every time she looked her neighbours in the eye.

Ryan looked up where she sat straddled above him. His body held a light sheen of sweat as he took several deep breaths to recover. "Now that you've managed to wear me out, can we go inside now?" he said, his voice slightly breathless.

Fin's eyes went wide. "Oh crap."

His brows flew up. "What?"

"I don't know what I did with the key!" she wailed.

Ryan's shout of laughter echoed loudly around the yard in the quiet, early hours of the morning.

Chapter Twelve

The late morning sun swirled lazily through the window when Fin rolled over and blinked her eyes open. Ryan was beside her, lying on his stomach with his face pressed into the pillow. He looked so beautiful, but even in sleep he appeared exhausted.

"I'll love you longer than the stars that live in the sky."

The words had broken her heart and somehow put it back together again all at the same time. Ryan loved her. He was here. With *her*. That was all she needed. A smile started to creep over her face until the painful reminder that Jake was gone slammed into her. It happened every morning, yet this time when her eyes burned, she reached for Ryan instead. She trailed her fingers lightly over his scarred, tanned back.

His reaction was instant. With eyes wild and intense, Ryan rolled over and grabbed hold of her throat, his fingers squeezing with aggressive strength.

"Ryan," she wheezed, clawing at his hand.

He blinked.

"Hurts," she choked out.

His eyes widened with horror, and he snatched his hand away. "Fin. Oh God."

Fin drew deep breaths into her burning lungs and rubbed a shaky hand over her throat. "I'm sorry," she whispered. "I shouldn't have—"

"No." Ryan rolled over and hovered above her, moving her hand out of the way. He frowned and touched the skin of her neck gently. "*I'm* sorry. Are you okay?" Leaning in, Ryan peppered soft kisses where it hurt. "Baby …" His eyes searched her face. "I shouldn't be here," he mumbled. Pushing quickly off the bed, he got to his feet.

"No!" she shouted hoarsely and he froze. "You live here now. You don't get to run away. You have to stay." Her bottom lip trembled. "You stay and you talk to me."

Ryan rubbed a hand over his eyes and sank down on the edge of the bed. Leaning over, he rested his elbows on his knees and stared at the floor.

"Did you sleep?"

He breathed out heavily. "Not so much."

"Are you—"

"Fin." Ryan turned sideways on the bed to face her and reached out, scraping his palm slowly down her bare chest. Cupping her breast, he looked at her from beneath thick, dark lashes. "How am I supposed to sleep with you lying naked next to me?" he growled playfully.

Fin's heart thumped when she looked into his eyes and saw the pain he was trying to mask so carefully.

"Ryan," she whispered and placed a hand on his thigh.

She held her words inside because she was scared. What if love wasn't enough for them? Would it heal the deep lacerations life had placed on his heart, or would he always be so completely broken that he would never fully be hers?

Her phone rang and Ryan reached over to pick it up from her bedside table. He looked at the display before handing it over. "It's your mum."

Fin took the phone from his hand and answered the call.

"Finlay, honey." She cleared her throat. "How did your night go last night?"

"That's a long story."

"Oh ... Well, you can tell me about it tonight. Are you still coming for dinner?"

"Yes, of course I'll be there."

Ryan raised his eyebrows in question at her.

"In fact," she said, looking at him, "you'll need to set another place at the table."

Ryan shook his head swiftly. "Fin," he mouthed. "No."

"Oh?"

"Ryan's coming too," she told her mother.

She heard him curse softly, and she rolled over in the bed, giving him her back.

"He hasn't been around," Julie said, her voice a mere whisper. "It's almost like we've lost two sons."

Fin swallowed the lump in her throat when her mother choked on a sob.

"Mum," she whispered.

"I'm okay." Julie cleared her throat. "I'm okay," she repeated, but Fin knew she wasn't.

"How's Dad?" Fin asked in an effort to distract her.

"Your father's fine."

"Mum—"

"So, we'll see you tonight," Julie said over the top of her. "And ... thanks Fin, for getting Ryan to come."

After finishing the phone call, Fin hung up the phone and set it quietly and carefully back on her bedside table.

"I'm not going, Fin."

The warning tone in his voice was clear, yet Fin was silent. Staring down at her hands, she picked at a torn fingernail from her efforts at searching for the house key last night.

"They want to see you," she said eventually.

"I'm not going through this now." Ryan stood and walked towards the door.

"Ryan?" she called out.

He paused without turning around.

"You ..." Fin paused, suddenly hesitant, and licked her lips. "You're still moving in aren't you?"

Turning, Ryan grinned crookedly, but it didn't wipe the sadness from his eyes. "Of course. Everything I've ever said to you has been the truth, Fin. Don't ever doubt me."

She almost flinched at his words because if everything he said was true, did he really hurt so much that he didn't want to wake up? Not even for her?

"Okay." Shifting to the edge of the bed, she planted her feet on the floor and stood. "Oh God," she moaned when blackness swallowed her vision—as though all the light had been sucked swiftly away. She stumbled and went down hard on her hands and knees.

"Fin!" Ryan shouted.

Fin blinked, trying to see. Arms came around her and she was lifted up.

"Christ, baby, you hardly weigh a thing," he muttered.

Her vision cleared, bringing the concern in his eyes into focus. "Ryan." She fought against the brief flood of panic and forced a smile. "I tripped getting out of bed. I'm okay. You can put me down."

"I don't want to put you down."

"Well ..." She tilted her head. "I do have legs, but if you want to carry me around forever, then I'd let you."

"Are you sure you just tripped?"

Fin nodded. The last thing he needed weighing him down was worry for her. She probably just needed to eat something.

Ryan looked down at her.

"Yes, I'm sure!" she added. "Do you seriously doubt I would trip over my own feet?"

"True," he muttered.

Cradled to his chest, he carried her out the door. "Where are you taking me? We haven't got any clothes on."

Reaching the couch in the living room, he set her down and planted a swift kiss on her lips. "I'll get you your robe," he said. She peered over the couch, her eyes falling to his ass as he walked away. "Then I'm making you breakfast, and after you eat a pile of food, you're mine all day."

Her stomach rolled at the idea of food. "Good. I'm starving!" she called out.

As promised, Ryan made a breakfast big enough that even he admitted to being unable to eat it all. That had involved a quick drive to the store because apparently all Fin was existing on was oranges and old cheese.

She had a shower while he'd been gone. Her damp tousled hair hung over her shoulders, and she dressed in a white tank top and sweatpants. Despite looking like the Angel of Sin had dressed her last night, he liked her this way. She had a natural beauty that didn't need fuss. He hadn't known the girl he'd seen in the bar last night, but this one? This was the one he knew. This was the one that had his heart thumping and his hands itching to touch.

Fin took a bite of toast, and his eyes fell to her mouth as she licked crumbs from her lips.

"What?"

Ryan met her eyes from where they sat opposite each other at the little breakfast table.

"You don't have to watch me. I *am* eating."

He nodded. She was. But it looked forced. He made a note to keep an eye on what went in her mouth.

"So how much stuff do you have?" she asked as he chewed and swallowed.

"Not much. Just what's on base. The only thing I really spent money on was my car." He picked up his coffee. "Monday we can go open a joint bank account. I'll have the Army put all my wages in there. You take that money to pay bills, okay?"

Fin frowned. "Ryan, I have my own money. I was going to transfer Jake's half of the house to you."

"Fin." He reached out and took her hand in his. "We'll do this right. Get a valuation. I'll give you half of what the house is worth. I don't care what you do with the money. Invest it somewhere."

She looked at him. "Ryan, I don't need it. You don't have to do this."

Ryan rubbed his jaw, wondering how to phrase the words so they wouldn't hurt, but he didn't think he could. "You're my next of kin, baby. If anything ever happened to me, you'd get it all anyway. That's how I want it."

Fin slammed her fork down, anger and hurt warring in her eyes. "Okay," she said, her voice firm. "If anything ever happened to me, you get everything of mine."

He looked at her sharply, swallowing fear. His need for her was so deep and so utterly consuming nothing could ever take her from him. He wouldn't allow it. "Nothing's ever gonna happen to you."

"Of course it won't," she agreed quickly, her eyes falling to her plate.

The words weren't enough. He needed to see it in her eyes. "Look at me, Fin."

She looked up.

"Promise me. No matter what you do, you'll keep yourself safe. For me."

"I'll promise it if you do."

"Dammit," he growled, his chest filling with unmitigated anger. His chair flew back as he stood. Asking him to be safe was asking him to give up everything he ever was in order to keep that promise. "You know I can't promise you that."

Fin stood up, her eyes sparking fire as she faced him. "You speak to me of love, yet you'll walk away from me so easily to go and put your life on the line! Do you know how hard that is for me?"

He didn't answer because he knew how hard it was. If he had to sit back and let her put her own life in the same danger it would kill him.

"Do you?" she shouted.

"I'm sorry," was his answer, and he watched her suddenly deflate.

"I won't ask you to promise," she said wearily. "I just want you to know that having to watch you leave is going to be one of the hardest things I ever have to do."

Ryan pulled her around the table and into the circle of his arms. "Every piece of me is in here." He placed his palm flat on her chest, feeling her heart beat hard and steady beneath his fingers. He closed his eyes briefly at the beauty of it. "My breath, my heart, my life. I won't ever leave you if you keep that safe inside of you."

"Damn you, Ryan," she whispered fiercely.

His eyes flew open as she twined her arms around his neck and pulled him down to her lips. "What?" he breathed.

"I want to be angry with you, but you make it difficult."

Growling, Ryan picked her up in his arms. Carrying her into the living room, he leaned down and placed her on the couch. His heart hammering, he looked down at the woman he'd loved for as long as he could remember. Fin was so extraordinary, so smart, so utterly sweet, he could hardly believe that she was his as much as he was hers. She owned him. Whenever he breathed her in, she took away his pain. No one else could ever do that.

"Am I enough, Ryan?"

Spreading her legs, Ryan knelt between them and put his hands on her thighs. "What do you mean?"

Her eyes were big, bottomless pools of green as she met his gaze. "For you to want to wake up in the morning?"

His body tensed.

"You told me you always spoke the truth to me," she continued.

Ryan dragged his hands up her thighs and squeezed. "I thought I'd lost you, Fin. What Ian said made sense to me. That I'm a reminder of what happened to Jake and that I should leave you alone. The very idea of having to let you go for you to get over losing Jake … that was how it felt. Just a big, black empty space."

"You believed me, didn't you? When I told you it wasn't true. This morning, when I rolled over and you were right there beside me—"

"Don't remind me of what I did."

"Okay," she replied simply. "But you being there takes away so much of the hurt. I need you with me. Mum and Dad need you too."

How could he face Mike and Julie and knowing they would have preferred it was him that died rather than Jake? What if they blamed him? He couldn't live through that again.

Ryan shook his head. "Not tonight, Fin. I'll go get my things while you're at dinner, okay? Today I have you all to myself." His gaze dropped to her mouth. "So what are we going to do?"

She gave up pressuring Ryan about seeing her parents. For now. Instead, she pretended to give serious thought to his question. "Well," she drawled. "The lawn needs mowing and my veggie garden needs weeding. You could do that while I do some work."

Ryan sat back on his heels, his brows raised.

"And Jake promised he'd repaint the fence at some stage too, so that needs to be done. Maybe I should write a list?"

He stood up and started walking away.

"Hey!" she called out. "Where are you going?"

Ryan turned and smirking, slowly peeled his zipper downwards. Fin's eyes dropped, her breath catching as he reached in and fisted himself in his hand. "Seems you have a lot of work you need me to do. I'll just quickly go take care of this so I can get started."

"Ryan!"

He moved swiftly into the bathroom and shut the door behind

him.

"Damn the man," she muttered. Scooting off the couch, she got up and raced after him. Grabbing the handle, she flung the door wide open and gasped.

Ryan was already naked and standing there facing her. His arms were folded and a smirk still lingered on his face. "Took you long enough."

Fin pursed her lips to fight the grin. "Oh sorry, Ryan. I didn't realise you were in here." She peeled off her top and shimmied out of her sweatpants and panties, leaving her as bare as he was. His eyes ignited as they roamed over her. "I just came in to brush my teeth, but I'll come back when bathroom rush hour is over."

She turned and barely took a step before Ryan wrapped his arms around her and yanked her into him. The hard length of him pressed into her spine when he leaned into her ear and whispered, "Where do you think you're going? Don't you have to brush your teeth?"

Fin licked her lips. "Maybe."

Ryan picked her up and set her in front of the sink. She met his eyes in the mirror as he trailed his hand down her spine and over the curve of her ass. "Don't let me stop you."

She said something in reply, but she wasn't sure what. It came out a jumbled mess as her body slumped against him.

"Fin?"

Ryan's arms wrapped around her ribs, holding her up.

"Baby?"

Fin blinked, her pulse racing as the world faded out again.

Chapter Thirteen

Ryan pulled his car to a stop outside the single-story red brick home and stared, his face impassive. Inside, his stomach was churning from the memories of a house and a family he hadn't seen for ten years. It hadn't changed. It just looked a little older and a little sadder than what he remembered.

"Why are you here?" came the soft cool whisper in his ear.

"Maybe 'why are *you* here?' is probably the better question, Jake. Get out of my head."

Jake's chuckle reverberated around the confined space. "I can't, Kendall. You won't let me go."

Tears swam in his eyes, but he wouldn't let them fall. "Why do I have to do that?"

"You're kidding, right—me in your head for the rest of your life? Do you *want* to be batshit crazy?"

"You mean as batshit crazy as you were?"

"There's the Ryan I know."

Ryan stared hard at the house. The white trim needed painting, the gardens tending, yet it was neat and tidy. "Well, I'm glad someone knows who he is."

Pulling the key from the ignition, Ryan slid from the car and forced his feet to move towards the front door. He drew strength from thoughts of Fin while he waited for someone to answer his knock. Unable to bear waking her, he'd left her sleeping. Instead, he wrote a note on her pillow telling her he had things to do and would be back later that day. He was worried if he told her where he was going this morning she would insist on coming, and he had such a hard time saying no to her, even in this.

He'd been living at the cottage for two weeks now, and for every one of those days he'd been watching her carefully. She swore that day in the bathroom she'd just got a head spin from moving too quickly. After an emotional few months, and such rapid weight loss, it was a wonder her health was as good as it was. Her eating in the last week had been improving steadily, and after forcing a promise from her to go to the doctor if it happened again, he let it go reluctantly.

Ryan rapped smartly again and when the door flew open, his hand dropped to his side.

"Ryan!"

He nodded impassively. "Mum." His eyes fell to where her hand shook on the doorknob before they rose to her face. He felt so different, so removed from her. It was like knowing her was another lifetime ago. "Can I come in?"

She stood out of the way, her hand fluttering to her hair to smooth the dark brown strands. He remembered it as long, glossy waves, but now it was to her shoulders, and smooth.

"I wasn't expecting you."

Huh. After all these years, this was the best she could come up with? "Well, I wasn't expecting an invitation."

She frowned. "You left."

"Why do you think I did that?"

Annoyed already, he stepped inside the house. Most of the furniture he ran his eyes over was new. No. Not new, just different, changed. The photos still plagued the walls like some sad, godforsaken shrine. Ryan ran his eyes over them, his heart aching.

"Would you like some of the photos, Ryan?" his mother asked softly.

Ryan only had the one in his wallet. It was faded and worn from use. He took it out all the time and stared at it, wondering what his life would have been like if she were still alive. Always fucking wondering. He couldn't let it go, and it made him so damn tired.

He swallowed. "Please."

"You can choose them. Can I get you a drink ... or something?"

"No." He turned to face her. She was hugging herself, rubbing her hands up and down her arms. "Where's Dad?"

She sighed. "We divorced a long time ago, Ryan. I haven't seen your father in years."

His brows flew up. "Oh. Was it ..."

"Some people, when they lose a child, they never really recover. Your father couldn't let it go. It was killing us, and then how he was with you, how *I* was with you. We lost you too, that's on us, I know, but I'm—"

"Mum," he cut her off and she froze, her fluttering hands halting mid-air.

Ryan drew a deep breath and let it out. Why couldn't he hate her? He wanted to but it was such a useless emotion. There was no room left in his heart for hate, but for his mother there was no room for love either. He looked at her, really looked at her. She seemed tiny and faded somehow, just a transparent version of the person she used to be. His heart softened. "Maybe I'll have that drink after all."

She flushed. "O-of course. Um ... coffee?"

"Black, no sugar."

"I'll go make it. Why don't you go choose some photos while you're waiting?"

Ryan nodded, moving towards the wall of photos when she stepped out of the room. He ran his eyes carefully over each and every one of them. His sister's bright happy face stared back at him in all of them. Closing his eyes, the day she died burst vividly in his mind.

"Mum!" he yelled loudly, grabbing the football as he flew out the front door. *"Going outside to kick the footy around."*

"Don't go far," she called out from the kitchen. *"Dinner won't be long!"*

"Can I come too, Ryan?" his little sister called out.

"No, Kass. You can't catch properly. You're all thumbs."

Ryan gasped, pushing the memory away. It hurt too much. It should have faded over time, but it still taunted him with the brightest clarity.

His little sister had followed him everywhere with those puppy dog eyes. Ryan had always been such a jerk, telling her to leave him alone. The day she died was the one day, *one fucking day*, when he'd given in.

In his young mind, Kassidy had been just a dumb annoying girl, always stumbling over something. So clumsy, just like Fin was. Despite their different colouring, meeting Fin that first day at school, seeing her trip up the stairs, God, it was like seeing his sister all over again. From that day on he watched over Fin, scared that something would happen to her just like it did his sister.

"It wasn't your fault, Ryan," came his mother's soft voice behind him.

He opened his eyes, swallowing the sudden rush of fury.

Turning, he looked at her, his jaw tight. Ryan had lived with the blame, the pain, the beatings, their hate; he breathed it into his lungs with every step he took, every single day.

"Twenty years," he ground out. "I lived with that and I had to come to you for you to say four little words that back then might have changed my entire world."

She sank down into the pale, cushioned couch behind her and set his coffee on the little side table with shaky hands. When she let go of the cup, she gripped her hands together, her knuckles white. "I'm sorry."

He opened his mouth to speak, but she continued before he could say anything.

"I know words are meaningless, but when Kassidy died … I couldn't come back from it. It was like I was lost, standing outside of myself, for years. Your father … he'd always been quick to rage, but he … oh God," she moaned, wiping at the tears that rolled down her face. "How he would beat you for the smallest things, and I was so lost I did nothing. Then one day, you were just never home anymore and I was glad. I was so glad," she said fiercely.

The words stung. "You never wanted me around anymore."

"No, I didn't. I wasn't strong enough to stand up to your father, Ryan. I wanted you away from him. You had Mike and Julie looking after you, and that was so much better than being in the poison of our house."

Ryan's mouth fell open. "You knew where I was?"

She choked on a sob. "I did."

He went and sat down on the chair beside her. "You never said."

"I watched you. Sometimes I would sit in my car and watch you play rugby with Jake. Mike would be there helping you with your bags, Julie would be cheering you on, and their daughter, Finlay, was always there with either her nose stuck in a book or watching you. Living on the sidelines of your life hurt so much, but that was all I deserved. You were thriving with the Tanners, Ryan. You were smiling and laughing, so I would leave and go back to your father and dread the nights you returned. Though as you got older, and taller, your father couldn't be less bothered with you at all and just drank more." She ran her eyes over him. "You're so big now, so much more than I ever hoped you would be. Seeing you now makes me wonder how Kassidy would've turned out."

Ryan looked down at his hands. Time and again he wondered the same thing. Fin and Kassidy would have been fast friends if her life hadn't been cut so short. "She would have been beautiful."

His mother sighed heavily in the silence.

"Jake died," he blurted out.

Her bottom lip trembled. "I know. It was on the news. Every time I heard of a soldier's death in Afghanistan I would hold my breath and pray. And one day there was your Jake on the news. I'm so sorry."

Why the hell did he bring that up? Ryan stood abruptly. "I should go."

"Oh ... but you didn't drink your coffee."

The walls were closing in on him and she was talking about coffee? *Fuck.* He needed to get outside and draw air into his lungs. "Another time maybe."

Ryan strode towards the door, and his mother started grabbing randomly at some of the photos on the wall. She piled them in his arms, fussing when one started to fall. He clutched it before it fell and turned to leave. Hesitating, he stopped and met her eyes. "Mum. For what it's worth, I'm glad you kicked Dad out."

"Ryan," she whispered and reached for his hand. She gave it a squeeze. "You have this quiet, inner strength about you, and I have no idea where it came from. I'm not like you. I'm weak and tired, never strong enough to deal with your father, let alone kick him out. He just left."

He nodded. His mother was right. She wasn't strong, but the type of people his parents were only made him work twice as hard to be everything they weren't. "Are you happier?"

"I'm not sure I'll ever be that, but I'm better. What about you?"

His mind went immediately to Fin, his pulse racing at the knowledge she was tucked safely in his heart. He smiled at his mother. "I'm getting there."

Ryan strode out the door.

"Ryan!" she called out, and his chest tightened at the memory of that voice calling him inside when he was little. He turned. "Call me sometime. If you want to. My number's listed."

He nodded and gave her a casual salute before getting in his car.

"Well that went well."

Ryan started the car and wiped the light sheen of sweat from his brow. "You think, Jake?"

"I don't think. I'm just a voice in your head, remember?"

"Is this you reminding me about letting you go or risk being a looney tune again?"

"Just read my letter, Kendall."

"Why? So I have to say goodbye to you forever?"

"There are no goodbyes in life. Only see you later."

Ryan followed the coastline as he drove from the northside of the city back to Fremantle. His eyes fell on Mettams Beach where Mike and Julie always took them on the weekends.

"Stop here, Kendall."

Ryan pulled into the car park and switched off the ignition. Sitting back in his car, he gazed out to the horizon.

"Remember that day we snuck off with Dad's paint and immortalised ourselves in stone?"

He did. They'd only been thirteen and had snuck the paint inside their bag of towels. When Mike and Julie had taken Fin to go snorkelling, they ran off down the beach and used Mike's good brushes and house paint to plaster their names over the rocks. After getting caught, they were both supposed to come back and scrub it off but never did.

"Do you think it's still there, Tanner?"

"Go look."

Swinging the door open, he got out of the car and breathed in the fresh, salty air. Reaching back in, he grabbed Jake's letter out of the glove box. After taking off his shoes and putting them in the car, he rolled up the legs of his jeans and trudged along the sand towards the rocks where he and Jake had spent hours plotting their future missions as soldiers.

It took him awhile to remember where their names were, but he found them. Swallowing the lump in this throat, he ran his fingers over the worn paint.

"What are you putting, Kendall?"

Ryan turned and grinned at Jake, the harsh sun beating down on his bare chest. He held the paintbrush aloft, white flecks speckling the rocks they were crouched over. *"Ryan rocks!"*

Jake guffawed loudly. *"You're a dick."*

"At least mine's a big one. What are you putting?"

"I'm already finished."

Ryan stood up, balancing across the rocks to peer over Jake's shoulders. He read it silently. *Jake Tanner. Who Dares Wins.'*

His mouth fell open as he looked at Jake. *"You put the SAS soldier motto."*

Jake grinned down at him. His blond hair was tousled from the sea and sand, his green eyes flashing with excitement. *"Yep. You don't think I'm letting you do this alone, do you?"*

Ryan swallowed hard at the memory. "Fuck you, Jake," he whispered as the breeze fluttered his hair. "You went and left and now I'm doing it alone after all." He waited for an answer, but he didn't hear anything except the sound of waves crashing against the rocks.

As the sun slipped across the sky, he eventually slid his finger under the opening of the envelope and pulled out the sheet of paper. Tears blurred his vision as he unfolded the single page. He waited for them to pass before his eyes fell on the words.

Kendall,

Sleeping during training was bad enough, but leaving you alone to finish what we started together is probably taking it a bit far, huh?

I'm sorry.

Despite what you always said, out of the both of us it was you that was the strongest. The only difference was that I smiled a little easier, but we both know why that is. You and Fin have each other now. Take care of her for me. She has such a big heart and most of it is filled with you. Remember when she was fourteen and trying to learn the clarinet? We both wanted to jab hot pokers in our ears to make it stop. I know that's how you felt when I played my guitar, but that's what you get for putting those baked beans down my pants. Yeah, I knew that was you.

I want you to give my guitar to Fin. She doesn't know how to play it, but she'll learn. She can carry on the Tanner tradition of playing good music badly and annoy the shit out of you in my place.

Remember the day we sliced our palms open with mum's kitchen knife and shook hands? Do you remember what I said?

Ryan closed his eyes and pulled the memory from his mind. It was only weeks after the paint incident at the beach and night time. The full moon had washed the backyard with pale light as they sat cross legged opposite each other in the grass.

"Jake? What are you doing?" Fin called out from the back patio door.

"Nothing, Fin. Go away!" Jake yelled back, a frown marring his face.

"I saw you come out with that knife. You better not be doing anything bad with it or I'll tell Mum."

"Mind your own business!"

"It's nothing bad, Fin," Ryan called, his eyes seeking her out in the soft light. *"Promise."*

Her eyes were wide as she nodded at him. *"Okay, Ryan,"* she replied, and with a brief look at Jake, she went back inside.

Jake raised a brow at him. *"She always listens to you."*

Ryan grinned. *"That's because I'm the voice of authority."*

Jake reached over and shoved his shoulder, laughing when Ryan flew back into the grass. *"Maybe in your own mind, asshole. Now give me the knife. I want to go first."*

With a shrug, Ryan sat up, brushing grass from his hair as he handed it over. He watched Jake fist the sharp paring knife in his left hand and slice deeply into the thick flesh of his right palm.

"Fuck, Jake. I don't think it's supposed to be that deep."

He grinned at Ryan as blood dripped down his palm. *"No pain, no gain. Your turn."*

Jake handed over the knife and Ryan took it. A sharp searing burn rolled through his stomach as it cut through his skin. Dropping the knife to the ground, Ryan looked up, his dark eyes locking on Jake's green ones, and held out his hand. *"Brothers until the end."*

Jake took hold, his grip firm, and squeezed Ryan's hand hard enough for a trickle of blood to travel the length of his forearm. *"There is no end. Brothers forever."*

"Brothers forever," Ryan said out loud. Despite his heart aching, he smiled at the memory and went back to the letter.

Don't ever forget those words.
I love you, brother.
Jake.

"Jake, you saved my life," he muttered gruffly. Where would Ryan have been without Jake in his life? Jake had given him a past filled with happy memories and a reason to keep breathing. "You saved my life and you didn't even know it."

"How did he do that?"

Ryan jolted at the sound of Fin's voice from behind him. He twisted around, shielding his eyes in the sun as he looked up at her. She was wearing a thin, yellow dress with tiny straps that were slipping off her bony shoulders. A pair of brown sandals dangled from her right hand as she focused her eyes on the letter clutched in his fingers.

"I love the two of you. I just want you both happy, you know what I'm saying, don't you?"

"He gave me you," Ryan said softly. He folded the letter carefully and returned it to the envelope, trying not to notice how his hands shook slightly with the action.

"You've always had me," she said simply as he tucked it into his back pocket.

"Come here," he told her, patting the rock surface between his legs.

Fin walked gingerly over to the rocks and settled herself between his legs. He urged her back until she relaxed against his chest, her forearms resting on his thighs.

"How did you know I was here?"

Fin's head fell back, resting in the crook of his neck. "Rach rang. She saw your car and thought we were at the beach. I came down because I was worried about you," she admitted.

"I'm okay."

"Then why are you sitting here alone?"

Ryan tilted his head and pressed a kiss against her temple. "Because I went to see my parents today."

"Oh, Ryan." Her fingers dug into his legs. "Tell me?"

"My sister died when I was seven," Ryan told her, tired of keeping it to himself. For too long the loss had weighed him down.

"What?" she breathed. She tried to turn, but he locked his arms around her so she couldn't move.

"Just ... let me get this out."

She nodded mutely against him.

"There were only two years between us, but she annoyed the crap out of me. She'd take my toys and draw on them in bright coloured texta and it wouldn't come off. Everything of mine she touched, she would break. Not purposely. She was just careless and clumsy. She was so much like you, Fin, with her big eyes and sweet smile. She would have been your age now, but she didn't make it past five years old."

"It sounds like she spent a lot of time trying to get your attention. She looked up to you, just like I do, Ryan."

"She did look up to me," Ryan whispered thickly. "It's so easy to see that now."

"What was her name?"

"Kassidy."

"Kassidy Kendall," Fin repeated.

His sister's name sounded so beautiful coming from Fin's lips, as though it somehow brought Kass back to life.

"What happened to her?"

He closed his eyes and told her.

"Mum!" he yelled loudly, grabbing the football as he flew out the front door. *"Going outside to kick the footy around."*

"Don't go far," she called out from the kitchen. *"Dinner won't be long!"*

"Can I come too, Ryan?" Kassidy hollered.

"No, Kass. You can't catch properly. You're all thumbs."

"Mum!" Kassidy wailed. *"Ryan won't let me play."*

"Ryan," she replied, the warning evident in her tone. *"Let your sister join in or you can go straight to your room."*

"Fine!" he shouted angrily.

Seconds later Kassidy came flying out the front door with a big grin on her face.

"Keep an eye on her, Ryan," his mum yelled.

Ryan kicked the ball hard and laughed when she fumbled and it dropped to the ground. *"Good catch."*

Kassidy pursed her lips and grabbing the ball, she kicked it back hard and Ryan's mouth fell open. *"Hey, that wasn't a bad kick."* Instead of ditching her like he planned, Ryan returned the ball back to her,

179

more gently this time. *"Let's see you do that again."*

Kassidy did it again, and again.

"Wait!" Ryan told her when she went to kick it back. *"Let's see who can kick it the farthest."*

"Okay." Kassidy grinned, glowing under the attention. *"Watch this, Ryan!"*

She lined up the ball and stepped back a few paces. She looked at Ryan and smiled happily before running at the ball, putting her boot hard into the underside. It flew wide, out over the lawn. Ryan's eyes watched as it curved and fell down with a loud *thwack* onto the street.

He turned to Kassidy. *"Wait here, I'll go get it."* But he was talking to air. *"Kass! No!"* he called out when he saw her little legs pumping hard towards the street to retrieve the ball. *"Kassidy!"* he screamed.

His pulse racing, he took off after his sister, hearing the squeal of tyres and the sickening thud of her body slamming hard into the ground before he saw it.

Ryan's legs flew across the thick grass, barely noticing the stones cutting into his feet. His heart lodged in his throat when he knelt by her twisted body. She was covered with so much blood it hurt just to look at her.

She blinked her eyes open. *"Ryan? I don't feel so good."*

Someone was shouting behind him, but the loud roar in his ears blocked it all out. He looked into her big brown eyes. *"You're gonna be okay, Kass."*

She tried nodding and winced. *"Did you see my kick?"* she whispered.

"I did," he replied, tears falling thick and fast down his face. *"You kick a ball better than I do."*

She coughed and flecks of blood spattered his shirt.

"Oh God," he moaned as he heard the wail of sirens in the distance.

Kassidy swallowed. *"Ryan? Are there kittens in Heaven? Daddy never let me have one and it's the only thing I ever wanted."*

He sniffed messily and wiped his face with his sleeve. *"There are kittens in Heaven, but you're not going there, you're staying here. Stay here with me, Kass. I'll get you a kitten, I promise."*

Fin's chest heaved with sobs as she turned and grabbed him in her arms.

"She died before the ambulance arrived. That was the day I lost my entire family. My mother didn't come out of her room for weeks and Dad blamed me for all of it. I let him. I wanted to take her place, just like I did with Jake." He wrapped his arms around Fin and buried his face in her neck as the guilt flooded to the surface. "If I could take his place, I'd do it in a heartbeat. I would, Fin. Jake wasn't meant to die. It should have been me." His voice broke and he let the tears fall down his face and drip into her soft hair as he held her tightly. "It should have been me," he whispered hoarsely.

Fin pushed him away and he forced himself to meet her eyes. They flashed with anger. "Don't say that," she ordered, her voice fierce. "Don't you say that. It shouldn't have been either of you … but you came home, Ryan," she choked out. "You came home and God help me, I'm so relieved you're here that it burns me from the inside out."

His heart beat wildly at her words and grabbing her face in both hands, he crushed his lips against hers. She responded frantically, clutching at his shoulders as he pulled her against him. Ryan squeezed his eyes shut at the sweet agony of holding her in his arms. He kept kissing her until he thought he'd pass out, knowing even then it would never be enough.

She broke away, breathless, and rested her forehead against his. "I love you so much, Ryan."

"I love you too."

"Will you come home now?"

Ryan wiped her tears away with his thumbs and nodded. "Of course."

He held Fin's hand in his as they walked towards the car park, and as he opened his car door, he paused to watch her.

She opened her own car door and turned. "Ryan?"

"Yeah?"

"Do you have any photos of Kassidy?"

He nodded. "I have one I carry with me, but Mum gave me some today."

"Maybe we could put them up on the living room wall next to Jake?"

Warmth flooded his body. "That would be nice."

Fin gave him a brief wave and slid into her car, and as he pulled out of the car park behind her and onto the main road, a soft deep sigh breathed cool air through his body. He shivered because it almost felt like Jake was sitting right there in the passenger seat.

"Brothers forever, right, Kendall?"

Ryan grinned. "Brothers forever, Tanner."

Chapter Fourteen

"Baby, I'm home."

Despite sounding tired and gruff, a thrill of excitement at his words gave Fin goose bumps. Four weeks of having Ryan in her house and it still felt shiny and new. How easy it was to see now that her reason for pushing Ian away was because *this* was the dream she had buried deep inside her heart.

Hearing Crookshanks greet him in the hallway, Fin scrambled madly through the mess on the kitchen bench. Grabbing the tin she'd just filled, she flung open the oven door and tossed it recklessly in the direction of the wire rack.

"What are you doing?"

The words came from so close behind her she shrieked and jumped. Her pulse racing, she slammed the oven door shut and spun around to stand in front of it. Ryan was leaning casually against the entrance to the kitchen in his army fatigues, his arms folded and brow arched as he watched her.

"Nothing," she lied, blinking her eyes wide in an attempt to salvage the surprise.

Fin meant to have all this done before Ryan got home, but she got held up at work. *That's what happens when you tell people you're leaving*

183

work early, she thought crabbily. *Suddenly everything becomes urgent.*

Ryan looked over her shoulder at the disaster zone, and she shifted a little to the left. Her movement exposed the oven door, and he immediately turned and pointed at it, accusation making his eyes sharp. "You're baking a cake."

Fin tilted her head and shrugged. "Well, you know, it's for Crookshanks."

Her breath caught when a grin spread slowly across Ryan's face and lit up his dark eyes. He lifted his chin at her. "Come here."

Needing no further invitation, Fin launched herself at him. She twined her arms around his neck, and when he picked her up, she wrapped her legs around his hips and kissed him.

His fingers dug into her legs, a deep groan rising from his chest when she stroked her tongue against his. She broke the kiss when she couldn't breathe. As her head fell back, he licked a pathway down her exposed throat and bit down on the tender skin of her neck where it met her shoulder.

"Oh," she moaned, rubbing her hips against him.

"God I needed that," he muttered, his voice muffled as he nibbled and licked his way back up. "Needed you. Been thinking about fucking you all day."

Ryan's eyes were heavy-lidded and hot when she looked into them and smiled. "Happy birthday, Ryan."

"You remembered," he murmured.

"I've never forgotten. I baked a cake for your birthday every year you were gone."

He rested his forehead against hers and whispered softly, "Baby."

Fin closed her eyes. "I didn't know where you were, or what you were doing, but even if you weren't here, I wanted to make sure you had a cake."

She opened her eyes, seeing him arch a brow.

"And who got to eat my cake?"

"I did." She grinned. "And Crookshanks. And if there was any left, I'd take it into work."

Ryan ran his eyes along the length of the kitchen bench until they fell on the bowl she had tucked in the corner. He strode towards it and sat her down on the bench. Standing between her thighs, he dipped his finger in the thick, cream cheese frosting. A shudder of heat flooded her body as she watched him lick it slowly from his finger.

"Mmm, baby. This is good."

His hand reached for the bowl again, and she smacked it. "Leave some for the cake."

Ryan smirked as he scooped up some more. "It's my cake."

He smeared the frosting over the swell of her breasts, and she gasped. "What are you doing?"

Leaning down, he began licking it off her skin.

"Oh God," she breathed, fisting his hair in her hands and shivering at the wet heat of his tongue stroking her skin.

"I'm making up for all those years of missed cake."

The idea of baking Ryan a cake every day for the rest of her life suddenly held enormous appeal.

He slipped his hands underneath the hem of her pretty pink dress and spreading his fingers wide, ran them up her bare thighs. "You taste so good," he moaned.

Loud thumping came from the front door and he froze, his muscles tensing as his grip on her tightened. "Tell me you didn't."

"Open the door before we bust it down," Kyle yelled.

Ryan groaned, his head falling onto her shoulder.

185

"I did." Fin sighed and he took a step back, letting her slide off the bench. "I'll get it."

"Hey," he said, and she looked up at him. "Thank you. For doing this."

"I'm just glad you're here so I can."

"Me too," Ryan agreed, his lips curving softly. He wiped at a smear of frosting on her cheek. "I'll get the door," he told her and disappeared up the hallway.

Moments later, Kyle filled the little kitchen followed by Tex, Monty, and Galloway. She was greeted with kisses on the cheek and moved to the side as they filled the fridge with beer and rummaged through her cupboards, grabbing bowls and filling them with chips.

The television was flicked on and the sound of football flooded the living room as Kyle shoved the second beer in his hand at Ryan.

Ryan took it as Kyle slung his arm around Fin's shoulders and grinned down at her. "How's my girl?"

Ryan cleared his throat pointedly.

"Hey, I got a penguin from Antarctica." Kyle smirked. "What did you get?"

"I got Fin," Ryan replied smugly as he folded his arms.

"You win," Kyle muttered. His eyes dropped to her chest and amusement flashed in his hazel eyes. "Fin? You've got a bit of something on your boob."

Fin flushed wildly when she looked down at her cleavage and saw the blob of frosting.

"What is that anyway?" Kyle asked. His arm fell away from her shoulders as she spun around and grabbed for the cloth from the sink.

"That's my birthday cake," Ryan retorted, "which I was enjoying until you all so rudely barged your way into our house."

"Ryan!" she wailed through the laughter and catcalls. He joined in the laughter and she glared. "You won't get your present later."

He sobered. "Later? Why can't I have it now?"

Fin flushed all over again. "Because."

"That's gotta be something good," Tex said around a mouthful of chips as he launched himself into the armchair, his eyes glued to the television.

"Christ, Ryan." Kyle slapped him on the back as he passed by into the living room. "You lucky bastard."

"Excuse us," Ryan said to the room. He grabbed her hand and despite her resistance, dragged her effortlessly up the hallway.

"Ryan. What are you doing?"

"I want my present."

Another loud thump came from the front door, but it flew open before they could do anything. Rachael came through, followed by Fin's cousin Laura and Jess, another friend from Fin's years at university.

Without pausing, Ryan nodded towards the living room. "They're all in there."

Fin shrugged helplessly at the wide eyes and raised brows before she was shoved inside the bedroom and the door slammed shut behind her.

She spun around and folded her arms. "Well, that was rude."

"I don't care. I'm the birthday boy. I can do what I want."

She shivered and he grinned, knowing full well how much she loved his controlling behaviour in the bedroom.

"I'll remember this when it's my birthday."

"Good. I'll look forward to it. Now take off your dress."

"Ryan! No. We have guests, and I have a cake in the oven."

"So we'll be quick." He folded his arms and leaned back against the closed door as the muffled sound of loud talking interspersed with laughter filtered through. "Take it off or I'll rip it off."

Fin closed her eyes, throbbing at the heat in his words.

"You'd like that, wouldn't you? Me ripping off your dress."

Determination darkening his eyes, he strode towards her and her breath caught in her throat. Grasping the hem of her dress in her fingers, she pulled it off with hurried, jerky movements.

Ryan's eyes roamed over the tiny pink creation of lace that barely held her breasts together. "You know pink is my favourite colour on you," he muttered hoarsely. His eyes lowered further and he froze. "What the fuck is that?"

"That's your present," she whispered.

"Get on the bed, baby, and lie down," he ordered.

Fin felt his eyes on her as he stepped towards the bed. Climbing over the soft, cool sheets, she lay down and rolled onto her back. Ryan was right behind her. Leaning over her body, she watched as he hooked his thumbs in her pink lace panties and peeled them down a fraction. With hands that shook slightly, Ryan reached for the rectangular bandage that covered the hollow below her right hipbone. With gentle fingers, he peeled the tape from her skin and folded the bandage over.

"Fin," he breathed. "I …" He swallowed as he stared at the tattoo of his name in swirling black script. The initial was an oversized flourish and at the end sat a tiny little pink heart. His eyes flew to hers. "It's beautiful."

Her eyes swam at the love so bright in his eyes. "Someone once said to me that I've always been his, and that even if he never got to keep me, I'd still be his. Well I'm yours, Ryan, and even if you have to leave me, I'll always be yours."

Ryan crawled up over her and ducked his head, his lips hovering close to hers. "It's perfect. You're perfect."

"Fin!" Rachael shouted from somewhere down the hall. "The oven is screaming. Make it stop!"

"Dammit," Fin mumbled.

Chuckling, Ryan stood and taking her hands in his, helped her off the bed. He reached for her dress and it held it out to her. "We better get out there and rescue my cake."

Fin took the dress from his hands and slipped it over her head. "I thought we were going to be quick?"

Ryan shook his head as he stepped towards her. His hand slid around her neck, untucking her hair from the dress until it tumbled down her back. "I can't be quick after seeing that. I need slow. I need to fall asleep with your thighs wrapped around me and the taste of you on my lips. That's worth waiting a little longer for."

Ryan returned to the living room as Fin raced in the other direction, heading for the kitchen to switch off the timer and rescue the cake. Tex handed him another beer after he kissed Rachael and Laura on the cheek in greeting.

"You remember Jess from Fin's farewell party, don't you?"

He nodded at her with a polite smile. He never forgot a face. "I do. It's nice to see you again."

Tex and Monty roared at the television as someone took a dive over the line with the football. Kyle peeled his eyes away and looked at him. "So don't leave us hanging, asshole. What was the present?"

Ryan grabbed a handful of chips from the bowl on the coffee table and grinned. "None of your business."

The tattoo was completely unexpected and utterly beautiful. Her creamy, flawless skin was now marked with his name. A possessive wave of heat rolled through him just picturing it in his mind.

"Were you showing Ryan your present?" Rachael called out to Fin while she took the cake out of the tin to cool on a wire rack.

"Did she get it done?" Laura said to Rachael as Ryan took a deep pull of his beer.

"Yes I did," Fin called back.

Rachael winked at Ryan. "Did you like it?"

He raised a brow. "You've seen it?"

"Seen what, dammit?" Kyle interrupted.

Everyone paused their chatter and looked at Fin. Wiping her hands on a tea towel, she shrugged as she walked into the living room. "It's just a tattoo."

Ryan frowned at Fin as she perched herself on his knee. "It's not *just* a tattoo."

"It's Ryan's name," Rachael announced to the room. "In a private spot," she added. "I took her to get it done today on her lunch hour."

Ryan's mouth fell open. "You just went on out and got a tattoo during the middle of work?" He felt a sudden urge to thank the guy who did it and punch him at the same time for having his hands where they didn't belong.

Fin twisted and looked down at him. "Well … yeah. When else was I supposed to get it done? Is there some special decree that says you can only get a tattoo on a weekend or something?"

"Smartass."

She winked at him and his heart tripped over. "Nerds are cool."

"That's hot," Kyle announced. Ryan didn't like the way he was looking at Fin like she was naked. "Show us."

"You're not getting your eyes on it," Ryan told him.

Kyle smirked at Ryan. "You'll show me, won't you, Fin?"

"I will," she replied, and Ryan's entire body tightened, "if Ryan says it's okay."

"No," Ryan replied without hesitation.

Kyle grinned at him. "Sharing is caring."

Wine in hand, Jess sat down in a cross-legged position on the fluffy, cream rug. Tiny with black hair and blue eyes, Ryan remembered her from Fin's party. She was an accountant and had been commiserating with Rachael about the lack of male eye candy in the office.

He'd mentioned that the Army recruited accountants and maybe they should try their luck there, laughing when both their mouths fell open.

"Really?" Jess had asked, her eyes narrowing as she searched for Fin through the crowd of people. "How come Fin never told us this?"

"Maybe because you'd have to move across the other side of the country," he pointed out.

Jess excused herself at that point when someone called her name. "I'll be back in a minute. Hold that conversation."

"Not keen on getting off your ass and joining the Army, Rachael?" he teased as they watched Jess disappear into the crowd.

"And break a nail?"

He raised a brow sardonically. "That's your priority?"

"No," she'd said softly, her eyes on Fin. "My friends and family are." Rachael turned and ran her eyes over him in his military uniform. "What's your priority, Ryan?"

His eyes had immediately fallen to Fin, his stomach in knots at the thought of her leaving for Antarctica the next morning.

"Someone better get the barbecue started before I chew a hole in the couch," Jess shouted over the conversation.

He was thankful they hadn't gone anywhere. In the next few weeks, he was going to need Fin to be their priority when he left.

Ryan stood up, setting Fin on her feet. "I'll do it."

"No, it's okay, Ryan. I organised the party."

He pushed her towards the seat he just vacated. "No. Sit down, spend some time with your friends."

As the guys vacated the room with him, he heard Laura say, "Well that got them out of the room, Jess. You can show us your tattoo now, Fin."

Kyle spun around and Ryan reached behind him, grabbing a fistful of his shirt. "You go outside and start the barbecue," he ordered, shoving him towards the direction of the back deck while he headed into the kitchen.

The four girls were laughing loud at something when he peered at them over the fridge door. "What am I cooking, baby?"

She looked up at him. "There should be some chicken and veggie kebabs in there on a platter and some steak I marinated this morning."

He inspected the contents of the fridge, not seeing anything that resembled what she just said.

"It's probably hidden behind all the beer," she called out.

Crouching down, he shuffled a few bottles around. "Got it!" His hands full, he joined the guys on the back deck as Kyle lit the barbecue. Setting everything down on the nearby table, he took the beer that Monty held out. Twisting the cap off, he joined the circle as they saluted him with their bottles and wished him a happy birthday.

Ryan nodded as he stared at the ground. He didn't want them to see his eyes burning because his best friend wasn't there. It felt wrong getting older without Jake aging alongside him. Jake would never grow old, he would never have another birthday, he would simply stay twenty-seven forever. It made his stomach churn. Would the ache ever get easier to live with?

"Jesus," Kyle breathed.

His head snapped up and followed Kyle's line of sight to the group of girls inside. Fin's dress was hiked up, her panties pushed down the side of her hip slightly as the girls crowded around for a closer look at the tattoo.

"Fuck me," he heard Monty breathe beside him.

Ryan rapped on the glass French doors with his bottle of beer, and they all looked up.

Kyle cleared his throat. "Well. That's one hell of a birthday present, Kendall," he said, the girls laughing while Fin snapped her clothes back into place.

Ryan raised a brow. "And that's as close as you'll ever get to it, yeah?"

"Stand down, Kendall," he replied with a grin. "I love you both like family."

"Shut up, asshole, and check if the grill is hot enough yet."

Kyle returned to the barbecue. With his beer in one hand, he used the other to scrape the stainless steel spatula over the hotplate.

"Have you told Fin yet?" Monty asked.

His chest tightened. "Not yet."

Kyle looked over his shoulder at him, grief flashing briefly across his face. "You better do it soon. The next four weeks are gonna fly."

Ryan looked through the doors again at Fin. He hadn't seen her this happy since … he couldn't remember. "Soon," he muttered.

"I need to ice this cake, girls," he heard her call out as she stood.

He frowned when she paused, her eyes going vacant for a moment.

"Fin?" Rachael called out.

She turned to look at Rachael, a distant smile on her face as she said something and waved her hand in casual dismissal.

Had she eaten anything at all today? Was not eating her way of controlling her grief? Maybe he needed to ask someone.

"Back in a minute," he said and walked inside to where she was now standing in the kitchen, bowl in hand.

"Have you got some sort of inbuilt frosting beacon?" she teased.

His brows drew together. "You okay?"

Fin paused, the spatula hovering over the cake. "Of course." She looked at him, her eyes wide. "Why?"

Ryan took a deep breath. "No reason."

She dipped her finger into the frosting and held it out to him, her eyes closing when he leaned forward and licked it off.

He swallowed the sticky, sweet sugar, getting hard as he imagined licking it off her entire body. "Can we send everyone home yet?"

Fin laughed, the sound husky on her lips, and he grabbed her hips, yanking her towards him. "Soon."

"Good," he breathed against her mouth before he kissed her long and slow.

Chapter Fifteen

Fin turned the key in the ignition and Ryan's car came to life with a deep, throaty growl. Pleasure shot through her body, fizzing her blood with excitement at the sound. Putting her hands on the steering wheel, she looked at Ryan, grinning as he opened the passenger door.

Ducking his head, he met her eyes. "I can't believe I'm letting you do this."

"It's only a fifteen minute drive to Mum and Dad's place," Fin pointed out.

There was no way he was getting out of letting her drive this car. For a brief moment of joy, she was going to ignore the gas guzzling pollution and feel the brute force of Ryan's car move beneath her touch. She rolled down the window, knowing the feel of the wind blowing carelessly through her hair would only heighten the experience. Fin returned her hands to their tight grip on the steering wheel and a light sweat of anticipation broke over her palms.

"You're sure about me driving your car, right?" She didn't know why she asked that. It didn't matter because she was driving this car whether he was sure or not.

Ryan shook his head as he slid inside the car. "No. I'm not sure at all. I'm only letting you drive it on one condition."

Her fingers tapped impatiently as she watched him shut his door. "This is the first time I've heard anything about a condition being attached. What is it?"

He grinned at her. "I'm not saying what it is. You just have to agree to it, and when I do eventually tell you, you're not allowed to say no."

"Alright," she replied, knowing she'd agree to almost anything in that moment just to drive his car.

Ryan put his seatbelt on, her first attempt at an apple pie wobbling on his lap as he clicked it into place. Finished, he looked at her. "Remember when you first learned how to drive?"

Laughter bubbled out of her at the memory. Fin's dad had sat in the passenger seat. His voice had taken on that scarily patient tone—the one where you just knew he was holding it together by the skin of his teeth. She would've preferred the shouting because the alternative made her more nervous. What made it worse was that Jake and Ryan were sitting in the back seat, Jake having insisted on getting front row tickets to her misery. Ryan had sat there, his lips suppressing a smile. Jake wasn't so polite—he was already laughing before she even backed the car out of the driveway. How was she to know that the balance of the clutch and the acceleration pedal was an exact science? Dad and Jake, and even Ryan for that matter, made it look so effortless.

After Fin stalled her way across town, she made sure to do a lap around the car park at the beach where Jake and Ryan's friends hung out. It had been a beautiful day—there were no clouds lining the sky and the heat of the sun burned hot and bright, making the beach a busy place that particular morning. She'd giggled as the car bunny hopped wildly around the entire length with Jake hunched over in the back, hiding as he begged Dad to make her stop.

"I'm not sure you've improved," Ryan told her.

Fin arched her brow at the seriousness of his tone. "You're not *nervous* are you?" she teased as he ran his fingers through his silky hair.

Ryan turned to look at her. The heated pink of the sunset reflected brightly in his dark eyes, and her breath caught at their beauty. "It's not your driving I'm nervous about, baby."

He was worried about seeing her parents, but he didn't need to be. They didn't deal with their own heartache by taking it out on others—not like his father. He was solely to blame for the tension making Ryan's shoulders tight. "Ryan … I don't know your dad, but I do know it's possible to hate someone you've never met."

"Don't, Fin." He reached out and grabbed her hand. Rather than the usual warmth, his touch was cold and damp. "Don't hate. I don't want that inside you."

"It's too late for that," she told him.

The anger had taken hold of her the moment she saw the bruises marking his body when he was young. How could someone hurt the very person they were supposed to protect?

"It's all in the past, Fin."

"It's not. It doesn't matter what you've seen and done in your life, Ryan, because everywhere you've gone, your past has followed you. You haven't let it go because it's still here, wedged between us. You're still trying to escape it, and I hate that after everything you're still letting it hurt you."

Ryan squeezed her hand in his. "Remember the night not long after you turned sixteen and your father said you couldn't date?"

Fin nodded, remembering the feeling of calm that settled over her when her dad laid down the law. She'd only wanted Ryan and it had been the perfect excuse to use every time a boy asked her out.

"I was so relieved. I didn't want anyone to have you. Even before then I thought of you as mine. It was that night, when I followed you outside, that I realised you knew about my father. I didn't want you to know. I didn't want you to see me that way—as someone weak and helpless, someone to be pitied."

"Ryan." She frowned. "I would never think—"

"Who was it that told you? Was it Jake or was it Mike and Julie?"

Her mouth fell open. "Mum and Dad knew?" Fury rose swiftly inside her, warring with the confusion. "Why didn't they do anything?" she cried out.

"Don't be angry with them. They tried, believe me, they really did, but ..." he trailed off, his brows drawn.

"But what?"

Ryan sighed deeply. "We argued. It ended with me telling them I'd run away if they said anything. I was young and desperate, and they were scared of what would happen to me if I ended up on the streets. At least this way they could make sure I was okay—that they were there if I needed them."

Fin shook her head. "Why would you do that—not let them help you? I don't understand."

Ryan rubbed a hand over his jaw. "You don't need to understand, Fin."

"Why can't you tell me why you put yourself through it? You could have had a better life somewhere else, you ..."

Oh God. *Somewhere else.* Away from her. If he went into the system it was possible she might never have seen him again. Her chest started rising and falling a little harder.

"Look at me, Ryan." Ryan looked up and the pleading she saw

in his eyes had her heart pounding so hard she thought she was going to be sick.

"Oh no," she whispered, denial flooding her hard. "No, no, no. No!" she shrieked, scrambling for the door handle, desperate to escape what she saw in his eyes. He stayed for *her*.

"Fin!"

He made a grab for her, but the car door was open and she was already running. Her feet pounded hard and fast along the road, panic careening wildly through her system as the night air washed over her face.

"Fin!" Ryan yelled.

Fin ignored him, focusing on outrunning the pain that was weighing heavily in her gut. Her arm was seized in an unbreakable grip, Ryan yanking at her bicep until she was forced to a stop. "Let me go!"

"I'm sorry," he said, breathless. He wrapped his arms around her, and when her legs gave out, they sank to the ground on the side of the road.

Fin buried her face in his chest, her fingers curling into his shirt. "Why would you do that?"

"I couldn't leave you. Not then. If Mike and Julie spoke up, I'd have lost you, and you were the only thing in my life that kept me going." He rubbed her back as she cried, the tears tasting salty and bitter on her lips. "Breathe, baby."

She inhaled his warm, male scent deep into her lungs. "Every time he hit you, every time he made you bleed, you let him because of me."

"Oh God," he moaned into her hair. "Don't. You don't understand. I told Kassidy to kick that ball. I was the one that was supposed to be looking out for her. I let him hurt me because that was my punishment for her dying. I was supposed to be her brother, and I let her down. Then you were there, so bright and happy just like she was, and I couldn't let you go."

"But you did. Eventually you let me go and you didn't look back."

His arms tightened around her. "Because I grew up and realised that someone as smart as you, with a heart as deep and as wide as the ocean, deserved someone who wasn't broken to love you. I'm still broken, Fin, and I don't know if that will ever change."

Why couldn't he see how worthy he was? Fin pulled away and looked at him. His eyes were dull and tired, filled with so much regret. *I wasn't enough for him.* She shuddered as a chill swept through her veins. "I love you, Ryan," she whispered, desperation edging her voice.

"I love you too," he replied hoarsely.

Ryan kissed her. His lips were warm, his mouth hot. She could feel his heart hammering in his chest as she pressed against him. When headlights from a car flashed in the distance, she realised it was dark, and they were sitting in the gutter.

Ryan stood, bringing her with him. He brushed his hand down her dress, removing bits of dirt and grass that clung to her clothes. Even now, after everything he'd been through, he was still taking care of her, putting her above everything else—even himself. "Stop."

Ryan stopped. "Are you okay?"

No. Her hands trembled. How could she ever be okay as long as Ryan wasn't? He was standing there, patiently waiting for her to answer, his concern palpable.

Fin nodded, knowing that was what he needed to see.

Ryan trailed his thumb along her bottom lip, heat following its path. "We should go," he told her, his eyes on her lips.

"We should," she murmured, but Fin didn't want to go to

dinner now. She wanted to stay home. She wanted to feel Ryan hard and aching, feel his heart—his blood—pulsing deeply inside her.

"If you keep looking at me like that, we won't be going anywhere except inside where I can fuck you hard enough to block out the entire world."

Fin's mouth went dry. The soft streetlight cast Ryan half in shadow, adding a dark intensity to the hard planes of his face. His wide shoulders and the tanned muscles roping his arms and chest were illuminated flawlessly. Her eyes fell to the waistband of his jeans, and her hands, now on his hips, eased the hem up slightly on his fitted shirt, baring a small sliver of skin. She skimmed her hand across his warm, taut stomach, letting her hand slide around his torso and glide up and over his back.

Fin looked up at him from beneath her lashes as Ryan shuddered beneath her touch. "I want you."

He exhaled audibly, dipping his head and sweeping her lips up in his, their pressure hard and wild as her heart thumped madly. She dug her fingers into his bare skin and he groaned. "I want you too. All the damn time."

Ryan grabbed her hand and dragged her back towards the car. Fin scrambled to keep up with his rapid pace. The driver's door was still wide open, the interior light shining brightly in the dark. Without missing a beat, he slammed the door shut and continued around the hood of the car. His free hand dug into the pocket of his jeans as he strode purposefully towards the front door. Pulling out a set of keys, he twisted and tossed them towards her. She caught them by sheer luck.

"Open the door," he ordered, his chest rising and falling rapidly.

With shaky hands, Fin turned towards the door. Standing behind her, Ryan bunched up the hem of her dress, his warm, calloused palms scraping along her thighs. She fumbled the keys as he settled his hands on her hips, pressing his hard length against her ass. Heat flushed her body when he leaned in and bit her earlobe. "Hurry up," he breathed.

How was she supposed to hurry when she could barely stand? Finally getting the key to slide into the lock, she turned it, hearing the bolt slide free with relief. Ryan reached around her and shoved the door open, pushing her inside as he followed close behind.

She was slammed into from behind and pushed against the wall, Ryan burying his head in her neck as he licked and bit at her skin. "Don't wait, Ryan. Please," she moaned and dragged in a deep breath. "Need you inside me. Now."

Ryan spun her around and taking hold of her panties, dipped down as he yanked them off. She stepped out of them, and as he stood, she reached for his belt buckle. He slapped his palms against the wall above her shoulders, his mouth finding hers in a kiss that was hot and desperate. Fin dragged his zipper down, and Ryan groaned as she reached inside his boxer briefs and freed him, gripping him tightly as she stroked. He was so hard she could feel his blood hot and pulsing in her palms.

One of his hands came off the wall as he tore free from their kiss, finding its way between her legs. His mouth trailed hungrily down her neck as he slid a finger roughly inside her.

"Ryan!" she cried out, pleasure pooling hotly in her belly.

"Baby," he moaned, slipping in another finger and twisting forcefully. He nipped her skin with his teeth and then licked it better. "I can never get enough of you."

Ryan slid his fingers away, and she whimpered at the loss.

"Need you," she rasped.

"You'll get me," he replied roughly. He dug both hands into the backs of her thighs and yanked her upwards. She squeezed both her arms around his neck, feeling his muscles flex effortlessly as he pressed her into the wall. "Fuck," he growled, looking down.

"What?" she breathed as she rubbed up against him.

"Your dress. I want to see myself sliding in and out of you, but it's in the way."

Untangling herself from his hard body, she shoved him back. He stood, breathing heavy, as she wrenched her dress up over her head and tossed it towards the floor. Her bra followed soon after. Seconds ticked by as he stared at her. She shivered under the craving in his eyes.

"Ryan," she pleaded.

"Jesus, baby." He reached down and stroked himself.

Her mouth dry, she swallowed. "What?"

"I could come just standing here looking at you—that golden skin of yours all flushed and begging for me." Ryan's hand kept rubbing and tugging as his eyes took her in. "Come here."

Fin moved towards him, instinct taking full control of her body. Ryan reached for her, picking her up in his arms. His rough clothing scratched at her sensitive skin as she rolled her hips against him. He walked her towards the couch and sank down into it, leaving her straddling him.

"Now," he commanded through gritted teeth, his voice strained.

Kneeling above him, she slid down on his hard length, moaning as he filled her.

"Oh *fuck*," he groaned, his eyes watching their connection with lowered lids.

"Ryan," she breathed as she moved over him. He was inside her, and right now, she needed nothing else except for him to stay there.

"Mmm?" His eyes locked on hers.

"Harder," she moaned. She wanted it to hurt. She wanted to never stop feeling him, even when he wasn't there.

His hips snapped up at her command and she cried out, her fingers digging into his shoulders. With one hand gripping her hip hard, Ryan splayed the other across her belly. He rubbed, moving upwards until he rolled her nipple sharply in her fingers. Fin's head fell back when he leaned in and took the other in his mouth, sucking deeply.

Oh God, what this man made her feel. Even as her legs trembled, aching from their straddled position over his hips, Fin felt she could keep moving like that forever.

Ryan scraped his teeth over her skin, biting the tender skin before pulling free. Both hands now on her hips, he slammed inside her, her body jolting with the force as pleasure shattered her apart.

"Fuck," she heard him mutter as her body clenched around him. Her eyes fluttered open to find him watching her intently. His lips were parted, his cheeks flushed, and when he came, all his muscles pulled tight as he ground his body inside her, growling her name wildly.

Fear rising swiftly, Fin buried her face into his neck. She wanted him like this forever, wrapped around her like she was all that mattered. But his words came back to haunt her.

"I'm still broken, Fin, and I don't know if that will ever change."

Peeling herself away, she knew that no matter how much love pulsed between them, she wasn't enough and it was possible she never would be.

"We should probably go now," she told him.

"If you say so." Ryan's lips curled and life sparked in his eyes, making her heart ache unbearably.

Chapter Sixteen

After a quick shower, Fin and Ryan arrived at her parents' house. His heart had been in his throat the entire drive as Fin crunched and ground the gears of his beloved car. He didn't yell once, and if that wasn't love, he didn't know what was.

Fin had a tendency to get far too distracted with scenery rather than keeping her eyes peeled to the road. Usually he found her sweet inattention endearing, but not when it involved driving his car. Even the relief he felt when Fin pulled into the driveway wasn't enough to take his mind from the nerves seeing Mike and Julie evoked.

Julie had cried the moment he stepped through the front door and leaned up to fold him in her arms. He had to hand the pie off to Mike in order to hug her back. Mike had stood there, fighting his own tears, and it hurt to see his tough exterior worn down with so much grief.

The dinner that followed had felt almost normal—as long as he kept his eyes from the empty place where Jake used to sit.

"You're part of the family, Ryan," Mike told him later that night as they both sat on the back patio after dinner. "To us you were simply another son."

"Thank you, Mike," he murmured.

"Your mum and dad, they were never your parents, we were. We still are. Don't stay away anymore," he ordered. Picking up his beer and holding it in both hands, Mike cleared his throat. "Now tell me what happened."

After setting his drink on the table, Ryan leaned forward, resting his elbows on his knees and focusing his eyes on the cream coloured pavers he'd helped Jake and Mike lay so many years ago. "It was a nest of insurgents, sir," he began, his stomach pitching at having to relive the memory. "We were dropped near the mountains for a patrol that was going to take us inside enemy territory. They weren't supposed to be there. We were quiet and careful, but they must have seen us coming from miles away. By the time our patrol was deep in the mountains with dawn approaching, we were surrounded. It didn't look good so we radioed for support, but they came too late. Jake ran for a clear spot to take out a PKM that was stopping us from retreating when someone high up on a ridge fired down on him." Ryan swallowed, the image of Jake falling vivid in his mind. "I was supposed to cover him," he whispered. "I ran out into open fire and dragged him back, but he was already gone. It happened so quickly."

God. The blood. He could still smell it. The metallic tang of it had been thick in the air as it flooded over his hands and soaked into the ground. He rubbed a hand across his face, but the smell, the fear, the hollow ache—it all lived inside him and was something that would never be wiped away.

"Ryan."

He looked up in surprise. Mike was standing in front of him, holding out his hand, and he hadn't even heard him move. As he stood up and took hold, Mike wrapped him in a hug.

"I'm so sorry, sir. I carried him back to the chopper and I didn't let go."

Mike pushed him back to look at him. "You put yourself on the line to get to him," he said gruffly. "He was never alone. Thank you, son."

Ryan nodded, hoping that one day he could accept Mike's words and move on. Returning to Afghanistan without Jake wasn't going to be the same. This time he'd be going *for* Jake rather than with him, and it was going to hurt like a goddamn motherfucker.

"I'm going back," he told Mike.

Mike took a deep breath. "When?"

"Two weeks."

They both spun around at the sound of a plate shattering. Fin stood there looking at him, pale and mute as a tea towel hung carelessly from her fingers.

Fuck. He should have told her sooner but he hadn't wanted anything to spoil the beautiful spark of happiness in her eyes. Now it was gone, and who knew when and if he would ever see it again.

"Oh, Fin, honey, what happened?" Julie called out. She came running over, a dust pan and brush in her hands.

"Just a broken plate, Mum," she told Julie without looking away from him. "I'll clean up the mess."

Julie crouched at her feet. "No, I've got it. Just step away a bit so I can get it all."

Fin took a step back. "Actually, if you'll … I just need to use the bathroom. I'll be right back."

"Fin!" he called out, watching helplessly as she fled inside and disappeared upstairs.

"She didn't know," Mike muttered.

"I …" Christ. Ryan ran fingers through his hair. "No."

Mike nodded towards the bathroom. "Better go talk to her."

Ryan opened the bathroom door without knocking. Fin was

sitting on the edge of the bath, staring down at her hands. Shutting the door behind him, he walked over to her and knelt between her legs.

She looked at him and smiled, but it was forced because it didn't reach her eyes. "You don't need to explain anything, Ryan. I just want to go home. Take me home, okay?"

"Okay," he agreed.

Ryan was quiet the entire drive back to the cottage. Why did everyone always paint love as pretty rainbows and happily ever afters? It wasn't any of that. To love was to feel the greatest of agony, burn in the hottest fires of Hell, and fail the only people who ever mattered.

"I'm going to have a shower," Fin mumbled when they walked through the front door.

Ryan let her go without a word and headed for the kitchen. Reaching into the top cupboard, he grabbed the bottle of scotch and a glass. As he slammed the door shut, a piece of paper fluttered down from above the cupboards and landed on the floor. Picking it up, he sat it on the bench as he poured out a glass and tossed back the contents. It burned his throat going down, and warmth spread across his chest. As he poured another, his eyes fell to the slip of paper. Sipping at his drink, Ryan snatched it up and unfolded it. He scanned the page quickly, and before he sat down to read it again, this time more carefully, he tossed back the second drink and poured another.

By the time Fin padded softly into the kitchen in a simple singlet and panties, her damp hair falling over her shoulders, he hadn't moved. She looked at him and then at the bit of paper in his hands.

"What's that?"

Ryan handed it over wordlessly.

"Oh," she murmured and folded it back up as though it meant nothing.

"Please tell me you accepted it."

"Of course I didn't."

Ryan slammed his glass down hard on the breakfast table, anger flashing in his eyes. "This is your dream," he ground out. "An opportunity to do your PhD at the Climate Change Research Centre. This is years of work, Fin. A chance to complete your thesis and be able to carry out your own original research. This is everything you've ever worked for!"

The bit of paper crumpled in her clenched fist. "Don't tell me what it is. I already know."

"Then why aren't you going?"

"Because it's four goddamn years on the other side of the country!" she yelled. "I'm not leaving you!"

"You are," he roared back as he stood up. "Because I'm already going and when I come back—"

"I'll be right here, waiting for you," she shouted over the top of him. "It's a thesis for God's sake, Ryan. You're my life! Every moment with you is one I won't give up for anything, or anyone."

"I can't be your goddamn life! What happens to you if I'm not here?"

She froze, her body still as her heart splintered into pieces at the very thought. "The same thing that happens to you if I'm not."

"No." He jabbed his finger in her chest. "You can't say shit like that."

"I'm not leaving!" she shouted.

"You're acting like you have a choice, but you don't!" he roared back. "You're going. I won't let you put your life on hold for me."

"Ryan—"

He cut her off. "You'll accept the research program. If you can't go for yourself, go for Jake."

"That's not fair!" she yelled, her eyes burning with tears.

"When it comes to this, I can't fight fair, baby."

Ryan strode towards the couch, grabbing his jacket from where he'd flung it so casually when they walked through the front door.

"What are you doing?"

"I'm going out."

"Fine!" she yelled. "Go!"

Ignoring her, he picked up his keys and strode down the hallway. She stood there, her chest heaving with so much anger she couldn't see straight. Why couldn't he see how much more important he was to her right now? Her thesis could wait, it wasn't going anywhere. She needed to be here.

As he opened the door, he looked over his shoulder. "When I come back from Afghanistan, I don't want you here. I don't ..." He paused and took a deep breath. "I've always said to you not to let anyone stop you from being who you need to be, and that includes me."

The door slammed hard behind him.

"Damn you, Ryan!" she shrieked. She grabbed his glass of scotch and threw it hard down the hall. As it shattered against the back of the front door, the world started to fade out.

"Oh please," she whispered. "No. Not again."

Lurching backwards, she reached out to hang onto something, but her hands only grabbed air. Her head cracked hard against the table as she went down; the bright burst of pain was the last thing she felt before blackness overwhelmed her.

Ryan stood on the front porch dragging air deep into his lungs. There was something uncontrollable inside him that wanted to beg her not to go. If he'd stayed in there a second longer he would have. He wanted her right here waiting for him when he returned, and all that did was make him a selfish, fucked up asshole. Asking her to stay was something he wouldn't allow himself to do.

Why was it so hard to be normal? He was so tired of trying to pretend he could be the man she deserved. Ryan ran both hands over his face, fighting with all his strength not to open that door and plead for her to never, ever leave him.

Fin needed to be able to see that *now*, while she was young, was the time to grab this opportunity with both hands. He wasn't going to stand in the way of that. She was smart. One day she'd realise what she'd let slip through her fingers and resentment would set in.

Putting his hands in his pockets, he looked up at the stars. Would they only ever have those fleeting moments—the ones where you lived the briefest, loved the hardest, and burned like the devil had set fire to your very soul? They were the only moments in his life that had been worth a damn.

"I'm yours, Ryan, and even if you have to leave me, I'll always be yours."

Who knew that in the end, it would be her leaving him? With his head still tipped to the night sky, Ryan closed his eyes against the stars that glittered brightly. Fin was slipping right through his fingers and standing there watching it happen was unbearable.

Tugging his phone from his pocket, Ryan dialled as he strode towards his car.

"Kendall," Kyle answered.

Ryan opened the car door wide and slipped inside. "Up for a drink, mate?"

"Fuck yeah."

"Good. I'll swing by base, pick you up."

"See you soon."

Ryan hung up, tossing his phone carelessly on the passenger seat. It skidded across the leather, falling down the other side and underneath with a loud clunk as Ryan backed out of the drive.

An hour later he was leaning up against the wall of the rowdy bar, tipping back his second scotch, fourth if he bothered to count the two he'd had at home earlier. *Fuck.* Not home. Fin's cottage. He couldn't think of it that way anymore. He wouldn't live there without her. That would be too painful.

His eyes fell to where Kyle was taking a year of his life to line up a shot at the pool table. They were playing opposite a couple of other SAS soldiers, Nathan and Davis. Both were new to the Regiment, if you counted just over two years *new*. They'd only seen one season of deployment, but that would change. Ryan would be on his fourth soon and their deployment rotations kept coming around so thick and fast it was almost making him dizzy trying to keep up with two separate worlds.

Ryan waved his empty glass, and Kyle's eyes tilted upwards from where he leaned over the table, pool cue in his hands. "Another drink?" Ryan shouted.

Kyle gave a nod and went back to dicking around with the angle of his shot.

"Hurry the fuck up, Brooks," Nathan complained where he

stood by the pool table. Nathan was a big guy—tall and built—so him weaving a little unsteadily told Ryan he must have been drinking since the early afternoon. "You wearing your Grandma's panties tonight?"

Davis smirked, beer in hand as he leaned against the same wall as Ryan. "He's just waiting for some guy to pin him on the table and drill his ass."

Kyle grinned as he finally lined up the shot, refusing to rise to the bait. "Have you seen my ass? Anyone would want to tap that."

Ryan would've laughed if he didn't feel so sick inside. Kyle met his eyes for a brief moment before taking his shot. The red ball sank hard and fast into the corner pocket as Ryan walked around the table towards the bar.

When he returned with a new round, Kyle moved to his side. "Christ, Kendall. Could you be any less tense?" he said instead of throwing slurs to distract Nathan as he watched him line up his shot. "What the hell is up with you?"

Ryan tossed back the scotch in his hand and picked up the beer chaser. "Fin and I are over."

Kyle didn't give anything away except his knuckles whitening around his bottle. "You wanna tell me why?"

"Not really," Ryan muttered.

"So tell me anyway."

Ryan swallowed, watching Nathan drop a green ball into the pocket with a loud *whoop* and point his finger victoriously at the two of them. Kyle ignored him as he waited for Ryan to speak.

"Fin's been accepted into a research program with the Climate Change Research Centre."

Kyle arched a brow. "Well that's fucking awesome, right?"

Ryan nodded, letting pride make its way to the surface.

Goddamn, but his girl was going to get her PhD and wage her own war. The work she would do would give her a voice in the world, and for her, people would stop to listen. "It is."

"So what's the problem?"

"It's four years."

They watched Nathan sink another shot and high five Davis before taking a swig of beer and returning to the table. "Well, nothing worthwhile is ever easy."

"It's in Sydney."

"Oh fuck," Kyle breathed.

Nathan's next shot rebounded hard, and the ball coasted into the middle of the table. "You're up!" he yelled at Ryan over the loud noise of the bar.

"In a minute," Kyle told Nathan.

"You're kidding, right? Just hurry up and take the damn shot, Kendall!"

"In a goddamn, fucking minute," Kyle growled angrily.

Nathan blanched at Kyle's sudden fury. Kyle was difficult to rile. Everything rolled off his back with an effortless grin, making him a hot commodity to have in your team, just like Jake had been.

Ryan put a hand on Kyle's arm. "I'll take the shot, Brooks."

Shifting around the table, he rapidly sank their last two balls, followed it with the black, and won the round in five minutes.

"Fuck," Davis moaned. "Who suggested we play you two bastards?"

Kyle rubbed his thumb over his fingers with a grin. "Pay up, losers."

They both slid notes across the table. "Let's play again. Double or nothing."

Davis growled at Nathan. "Are you stupid?"

"That's likely," he replied with a laugh.

Ryan nodded. The pool and the alcohol were busy making everything numb, and he needed that right now. "We'll give you a head start by letting you break," Ryan told them. "You'll need it."

Kyle and Ryan returned to their tall bar table by the wall as Nathan and Davis set up the next round of play.

"Four years is a long time, but like I said before, nothing worthwhile is ever easy."

"Nothing's ever been easy for Fin and I," he replied, his chest burning at the admission. "I guess some things aren't meant to be. I mean, how the fuck long is this war going to drag on for? It could be years before the Government decides to pull our troops out. That would mean what—I'd see Fin a total of eight weeks over the next four years with her living in Sydney?" He ground his jaw as he tried not to think about it. "I won't have her putting her life on hold because I can't be there with her and ..."

Kyle downed the last of his beer and set the empty bottle on the table. "And what?"

"And I can't ask her to stay."

"No you can't," Kyle agreed, "but—"

"You're up, Brooks," Davis called out after breaking and dropping two balls.

Glaring at the interruption, Kyle picked up the pool cue and twisted it in his hands. "Does she want to stay?"

Ryan nodded once, the movement abrupt.

"Well then."

"She has to go."

Disbelief made Kyle's eyes wide. "You can't make the decision for her."

"I can." Ryan folded his arms. "This is everything she's ever worked for. If you think I'm going to let her throw that away on me, then you've got more than one screw loose."

"No talk of screwing while I'm stuck in this bar with you and those two meatheads," he said, waving a hand over at Nathan and Davis. He took a step towards the pool table and looked at Ryan over his shoulder. "So what now?"

"Now I'm back on base for the next two weeks and after that ..." Ryan swallowed down the ache in his throat "... she'll be gone."

Chapter Seventeen

Fin woke to sunlight streaming through her room and an empty bed. She jolted upright as the events of last night flooded through her. Turning on her side, she grabbed for her phone off the bedside table. She dialled Ryan's number but when it went straight to message, anxiety clouded every other emotion. *He was avoiding her?*

She sank into bed, rubbing gently at the tender bump on the back of her head. The fall had scared her. Fin had no clue how long she'd been out for, but when she came to, Ryan hadn't returned. Feeling like her head was splitting open, she barely managed to tidy up the broken glass and drag herself to bed.

Picking up her phone again, she flicked through her contacts and dialled.

"Dr. Jensen's office, Trudy speaking."

"Trudy, it's Fin."

"Fin, honey!" Fin could hear the wide smile in Trudy's voice. She'd worked reception for Fin's family doctor for as long as she could remember. "How you doin', girl?"

"Oh, you know." Fin waved her hand airily before she slumped into the soft covers.

"No, I don't know, honey, so tell me."

"Just busy working."

"How's that hot man of yours?"

"You know about Ryan?"

"Of course I do. I ran into Julie down at the supermarket last week and she may have mentioned something in passing."

Fin shook her head, knowing that Trudy would have drilled her mother for every last detail and her mother would have happily complied. "Well, anyway, I need to make an appointment."

"Sure thing." Fin heard tapping at the computer before Trudy spoke again. "She's not free for another three days. How does Thursday morning suit?"

Fin sighed, rubbing at her brow. She'd have to shuffle things around at work and she had a report due. "That's fine."

Trudy rattled off the exact date and time, and after committing it to memory, Fin hung up the phone and tossed it carelessly across the bed.

She lifted up onto her elbow and peeked out the blinds of the front window. His car was still gone. *Did Ryan go back to base?*

Sitting up, a wave of nausea rocked her and she leaned over, moaning. *Shit.* She grabbed at her phone again with a sigh and rang in at work to let them know she wouldn't be in. Now what? Was she supposed to sit idly around in bed and wait for Ryan to call? Thumbing through her contacts, she dialled again.

"Fin," came the breathless reply.

"What are you doing?" she asked Rachael.

"Fuck, shit, dammit," Rachael replied, exasperation making her voice sharp.

"What?"

"I've just ripped a hole in my spare pair of stockings, and when I ironed my skirt this morning, it left a long brown stain down the back. I think I need a new iron. And a new skirt," she added.

"Okay."

"So what are you doing ringing me on a Monday morning. Been at the office for hours already and finished for the day?"

"No, I'm not working today."

"Day off?" Fin heard stomping. "Dammit. I'm out of milk. Why did I get out of bed this morning? Remind me."

"Because you have an obscene love of foreign tax that does wild things to your girly bits?"

Rachael snorted. "Yeah, sure."

"Actually, I don't feel so good. Taking a sick day today."

Fin could almost hear Rachael's jaw dropping open as the sound of a fridge door slamming shut came through the line. "But ... you never take a sick day. Remember that time when you spent the morning vomiting in your recycling bin and they forced me to come collect you? That was gross. Don't do that again."

"I don't plan on it."

"So what's wrong?"

"I just feel sick. I don't know."

"Well tell Ryan to make you a nice cup of umm ... what tea is good for when you feel sick?"

"He's not here."

"Training exercise again? Christ, they do a lot of those."

"No," she mumbled. "We had a fight last night and he left."

"What do you mean *he left*? Is he coming back?"

"I'm not sure." Fin tried to be pissed off, but it wasn't happening. She just felt tired. "Go to work, Rachael. I'll talk to you a bit later, okay?"

"Ring me later," she demanded.

Fin hung up the phone with another sigh and dragged herself out of bed to feed Crookshanks.

Ryan groaned as the alarm beside the bed screamed wildly. He was going to smash the bloody thing and bury it in the backyard behind Fin's veggie patch. Only half awake, he rolled over and planted his fist in it hard. The shrieking increased, bringing him fully awake. He took in the small room at the barracks and remembered why he was here and not in bed with Fin, running his hands over her smooth, bare skin, letting the warmth of it seep into his bones and take the chill of his nightmares away.

Yesterday morning seemed like a lifetime ago.

"What's the time?" Fin whispered, her voice husky as her eyes fluttered open, the bright green glimmering in the morning light.

Ryan grinned sleepily. *"Mr. Wolf."*

She chuckled softly and his heart tugged at the sound.

He reached out and ran the tip of his finger slowly down her nose, his eyes following the gentle touch before he met her eyes. *"It's not quite dinnertime, but I can still have you for breakfast."*

Ryan rolled her over, pinning her arms to the bed, loving how she squirmed beneath him.

Getting to his feet, he ripped the cord from the socket and threw the clock across the room with a growl. Fists clenched and chest heaving, he watched it smash apart against the wall.

"Hey!" someone shouted and pounded back on the other side of the wall.

"Fuck," he moaned and rubbed a hand over his eyes as a brisk knock came at his door.

"Enter."

The door swung open and Monty appeared, his eyes taking in the shattered clock without a flicker of emotion. "Brooks said you were here."

Ryan rolled his shoulders, wincing at all the knots that lived there. "He been flapping his mouth off?"

Monty's brows drew together as he folded his arms. "You know he wouldn't do that."

"Shit," Ryan muttered, running his fingers through his hair. "I need some clothes."

"I'll have some sent in, so get yourself organised. It's Monday morning PT then we're off to the rifle range."

Monty disappeared and Ryan searched the room for his phone, having no idea when he last saw it. He was on his hands and knees, peering under the bed when he heard a thump from above. He looked up and saw Kyle dumping a set of clothes on his bed.

He smirked at Ryan. "You can look all you like, but you'll never find your balls under there."

"Har har." Ryan got to his feet. "Have you seen my phone? I can't find the fucker."

"Nope."

"Shit," he muttered. "I need to ring Fin."

"What for? You need to remind her you're a stubborn asshole in case she forgot?"

Ryan scratched at the back of his pounding head. "No, I need to tell her where ..."

"Where you are?" Kyle's hands fisted by his sides. "Sonofabitch. I could fucking punch you right now."

"You don't get it."

Just hearing her voice would set off that uncontrollable urge to ask her not to leave. If Ryan let that slip out, he would never forgive himself.

"I don't need to get it. Fin does." Kyle tugged his phone out of his pocket and slapped it hard into Ryan's palm. "Here. And hurry the fuck up. We're leaving in five and I want to start off hard. I've got money on today's session, so I need to show those lazy cunts I mean business. I'll wait outside."

Christ. How was he supposed to say everything in five minutes? Ryan sank onto the bed and held his head in his hand as he dialled her number. He put the phone to his ear and waited but it went to message. He cleared his throat.

"Ba—Fin. I'm sorry. I'm on Kyle's phone because I can't find mine. I'm … I stayed on base last night. I just … I can't …" Ryan closed his eyes, feeling like a pathetic asshole. "I'll call you later, okay?"

After hanging up the phone, he got dressed for their eight kilometre soft-sand run and headed out into the bright light of the morning.

"Did you ring Fin?" Kyle puffed softly as they jogged slowly towards the range sentry gate.

"Yeah," he muttered. Today was the first day of the rest of his life without her. He was off to a shitty start because he already ached to hear her voice and feel her warm body rubbing against his own. The feeling was almost desperate and downright unbearable, like he wanted to claw his way out of his own skin.

"And?"

Frustrated, Ryan clenched his jaw. He was hoping the jog would help him switch his mind off, and Kyle was making damn sure that wasn't happening. "And I left a message because she didn't answer." A dumbass message that made him sound like an idiot rather than assertive and cool so she would understand where he stood.

Where do you stand, idiot?

Ryan swiped a hand across his face. All he knew was that Fin was willing to throw her dreams away to be with him and he couldn't do the same. How could he expect of her what he couldn't of himself? He owed Jake to see this through, and there was no seeing past that.

They reached the gate and started stretching, the fifteen odd soldiers quiet as they focused on the strenuous and challenging run ahead.

Later that afternoon, the loud clamour of magazines, sliding bolts, and the loud shout of Monty yelling to commence fire wiped everything else from his mind. Fixated on his target, sweat rolled down Ryan's back and chest in the heat as he squeezed the trigger. The mass sound of rifles firing cracked along the range like a fast approaching thunderstorm as he carefully adjusted his sights and shot round after round, finding his target again and again. Adrenaline pumped through his body and satisfaction curled his lips at the familiarity of holding a rifle in his hands—the smell of gunfire, like charred wood, clung to his clothes, creating a soothing balm on his raw and aching heart.

"Cease fire," Monty roared.

The cracks of gunfire ceased immediately, followed by the sounds of magazines being removed and the discharge of chambered rounds.

In the eerie silence, Ryan felt like he couldn't breathe. The ease of familiarity was dying off as he stepped back from the firing line. His heartbeat surged as he wiped sweat from his brow with his shirtsleeve.

Monty reached his side as he focused on trying to control his breathing. "Nice job, Kendall. Now pull it the fuck together."

Ryan gave a sharp nod, not trusting his voice. The sooner he was in Afghanistan where he could live and breathe this shit, the better. He'd lived with a single-minded determination for so long he couldn't stop now. He could still be that way. He hadn't changed, *dammit.*

Reloading his chamber, Ryan stepped up to the plate, the weight of the rifle heavy in his hands, and waited for Monty's command.

Finally exhausted, both mentally and physically, Ryan arrived back at base and showered off the sweat and grime of a hard day's training. Throwing on the jeans and shirt he wore last night, Ryan grabbed his shoes and sat down on the edge of the bed to slip them on.

Galloway appeared in the doorway. "Mess is open. You coming?"

"Nah. Got shit to do."

He tipped his chin. "See you tomorrow then?"

"I'll be back later." Finished with putting on his shoes, Ryan stood up.

Galloway shook his head. "You do what you gotta do, mate."

The trouble with doing what he had to do was that it involved saying goodbye to the one person he couldn't live without. He would never come back from this. Never.

How did people take sick days? Sitting around while the rest of the world got on with their day to day life left Fin twitchy. By lunchtime she was feeling better and made the trek into the office. She spent most of the afternoon fielding emails from Rachael, typing up a report that made no sense and checking her phone for missed calls from Ryan. A missed call earlier from Kyle's phone had left her panicked, fearing something happened to Ryan, until Ryan himself left a message. The resignation in his voice told her more than what his words could—that his stance on the whole thesis subject hadn't changed.

By the time Fin arrived home in the dark, she was tired and not looking forward to a lonely night. Her little car purred softly when she pulled into the driveway, her headlights bringing Ryan into focus. He was leaning against the door of his car, hands tucked casually in his pockets despite his body being tense and his eyes hard.

Taking a deep breath, Fin stepped out of the car and forced her feet to move towards him. His eyes tracked her until she reached his side.

Seconds ticked by as they stared at each other wordlessly.

"You're leaving," she said eventually.

Ryan nodded.

"I can't … I don't know what to say," Fin managed, inhaling deeply as numbness wrapped her in its cold blanket. She could almost feel the life fading right out of her. "Maybe there isn't anything to say. You should probably just go."

"Fin, I …" His voice cracked but she let it wash right over her.

He looked away, pressing his lips together as though he was fighting against what he wanted to say. "I don't want you to go," he whispered, closing his eyes.

Fin stepped back, creating distance. "It's too late. I've already emailed the acceptance. It was lodged immediately."

Fin didn't know why she lied but *fuck it*. After everything it had taken for them to finally be together, he was leaving her. She didn't need him knowing how much it hurt.

His eyes flew open and she could see both relief and anguish swirling in their depths. "Good."

"You have your things?" she asked, her voice sounding cold to her own ears.

"I do. I left the keys on the kitchen bench … When are you leaving for Sydney?"

"Soon," she told him. She was really going to do this. Leave everything and everyone behind. Maybe Sydney might be a fresh start, a new life, uncomplicated and easy.

"Give me your hand." She stiffened, knowing touching him wasn't going to make this easier, yet she offered her hand anyway. His fingers closed over it, turning it palm up. She watched his finger trace gently along the lines. "You have a long, beautiful life ahead of you, Fin." Tears swam in his eyes as he looked at her. "Go and make Jake proud."

Ryan gave her hand a squeeze, his eyes memorising her face before letting it go, leaving her cold and empty. Lifting his chin, he gave her a quick nod and turned, moving around the back of the car to the driver's side. He opened the door and slid inside, shutting the door behind him.

"Ryan!" She took a step towards the car, and he rolled down the window but she couldn't see him through her tears. "Be safe," she whispered brokenly.

Ryan nodded, wiping at a tear that spilled over and rolled down his cheek. "You too, baby."

Feeling herself die a little inside, Fin turned and walked towards the house. Without looking back, she unlocked the front door, stepped inside, and closed it shut behind her.

Chapter Eighteen

"You're pregnant."

Fin flinched, her body jerking visibly in the small chair where she sat opposite Doctor Jensen. After her initial appointment on Thursday and another week's wait for blood test results, she finally had her answer. She'd been thinking an iron deficiency or some lingering virus, but this ...

"Can you ..." Fin shook her head. Maybe she heard wrong. "Did you just say what I think you said?"

Her doctor nodded, her glossy, dark ponytail swishing with the movement as her lips curved softly. "It's a positive, Finlay. You're having a baby."

Fin stood abruptly, her chair scraping noisily on the thick, gleaming floorboards. "I can't ... you ..." Her hand, cold and shaky, moved to rest on her forehead. "Are you sure?"

"Of course I'm sure." Doctor Jensen half-stood from her chair, her brows drawing together. "Are you okay?"

"I don't know." Fin's eyes collided wildly with her doctor's. "Am I? You're the doctor here!"

Doctor Jensen reached her side and gently gripped her elbow, guiding her back to the chair. Unsteady on her feet, Fin sank back down into the slightly uncomfortable cushioned seat. Her doctor shuffled backwards until she rested up against the edge of her desk. "Finlay, look at me."

Fin looked up, meeting her doctor's concerned brown eyes.

"Are you doing this on your own?"

"What?" she whipped out more sharply than she intended. "You think ... I didn't do this on my own!"

"Finlay." Her doctor's voice was calm, as though soothing a wild animal. "When you came in over a week ago, you gave the impression that you and Ryan were no longer together. That's what I meant."

"We aren't," she said, "so I guess that's a yes. I am doing this on my own." Fin's eyes shifted to the window. The slats in the blinds were half-open letting the midday sunshine wash through. Birds chirped noisily in the tree just outside, oblivious to her turmoil. She turned back to face her doctor, unable to process the shock. "How far?"

"You're three and a half months along. You haven't noticed your expanding waistline?"

She looked down, focusing on the slight curve of her belly. "There's a baby in there? I didn't ..." Fin didn't know what she'd noticed except maybe some bloating. She couldn't even recall what happened yesterday, let alone a week ago. Panic curdled her stomach as her eyes returned to her doctor's. "Wait! Over three months? I can't ... you ... But I've been on the pill since Ryan and I started seeing each other."

Doctor Jensen shrugged. "These things happen. The pill isn't entirely effective. Did you have unprotected sex at any time?"

"No! I would never do that!"

Wait! She did do just that. How could she forget Ryan's eyes, wide and panicked as he told her he forgot to use a condom? That day had been a riot of emotion with protection the last thing on their minds.

She'd meant to sort it out, but instead she'd blocked the entire day from her memory, the reminder of Jake's letter and her subsequent breakdown far too painful to think about.

"We should do an ultrasound." Her doctor waved towards a small machine in the corner with an attached screen. "Do you want to meet your baby?"

Oh God. Ryan was going to be a daddy.

Fin shook her head. "No. I don't. I can't. Not without Ryan. I can't do this without Ryan."

Doctor Jensen tilted her head, her eyes calm and focused. "You can. You're going to be surprised at just how much strength you can find when you become a parent. You have family and friends and my door is always open for you." Her heels clicked solidly on the floor as she shifted towards the slim hospital bed in the corner. "Now come on over here and let's have a look at what's growing in there."

Fin pressed a hand to her belly as she stood, feeling nothing at all. No kicks or flutters or lazy rolls. No evidence at all that part of Ryan existed inside her.

Half an hour later, Fin sat in her car, a photo of their baby clutched in her trembling fingers. She couldn't take her eyes off it, not even registering the joy that was unfurling in her chest. In that moment, nothing else mattered except her need to see Ryan.

Sliding the key into the ignition, her little car came to life at the same time her phone rang. Reaching into her bag, Fin plucked it out, seeing her mum's name on the display.

"Mum!" she answered rapidly. "I can't talk right now, I have to see—"

Julie cut her off. "Honey, where are you?"

She frowned. "I'm just leaving an appointment. I'll ring you later because I have to—"

"Leaving an appointment? I don't understand, Finlay. You need to hurry up!"

Tucking the phone between her ear and shoulder, Fin slipped the photo carefully in her purse. "Hurry up? Mum, what are you talking about?"

Pressing the speaker button, Fin put the phone down and backed out of the little car park. A muffled sound came through the phone as she inched her car into traffic. Her mother's voice began cutting in and out.

"Mum, can I ring you back a bit later?" she called loudly. "I can't hear you!"

Fin checked her mirrors and blind spot carefully before changing lanes.

"Ryan ... base ...." came through.

"What?" Her pulse sped up. How did her mother know where she was going? "Mum? I'm on way to see Ryan now, is that what you mean?"

More crackling.

"Dammit," Fin muttered as she slowed down for a red light. "Mum, are you there? Where are you?"

"We're at the base," came through loud and clear.

"At the barracks? What are you doing there?"

She heard the slam of a car door. "Oh wait, Mike," her mother said, "I just need to get those cards out of the car."

"Mum!"

The car behind Fin tooted and she looked up, realising the light was green. She waved her hand in apology and accelerated, almost growling with frustration when her mother's voice began to crackle again.

"Mum, I'm going to hang up now, okay? I'm on my way to see Ryan and then I have to get back to work. I'll speak to you tonight."

"Honey. We're at Base Pearce."

All the blood drained from Fin's face until she felt faint. "What?" she whispered. "You're at the airfield? Mum? Why …" She licked her lips. "Why are you there?"

Her mother's indrawn breath came through clearly. "Finlay."

"I thought they weren't leaving for another two days."

"The troops are flying out today. Now."

"A-are you sure?"

"Yes, honey. We received word of the date and time of their deployment through the DFA support group. I'm sorry. I thought you would have already known."

Fin's knuckles went white on the steering wheel. Ryan was getting on the same plane that took her brother away, and he was going *right now*. She wasn't ready. He couldn't leave. Not yet. She needed to see him. He couldn't leave without her seeing him.

Fin took a right turn and put her foot down on the accelerator, for the first time wishing her little environmentally friendly car knew how to move.

"Mum, how long do I have?"

"A little over an hour."

Her heart sank. She wasn't going to make it. "I don't think I'll get there in time."

"Oh, honey."

"Mum," she choked out. If Ryan wanted her there, he would have rung her, wouldn't he?

"You know Ryan well enough to know the answer to that

232

question, Finny," came a familiar voice in her ear.

"What did you say, Mum?" she asked, chills snaking down her spine as she entered Roe Highway, her little car weaving wildly into traffic.

"I didn't say anything, Finlay."

Fin rolled her shoulders, feeling a cold sweat break out on her brow. Reaching towards her dashboard, she turned the air conditioning down.

"I'm on my way, okay?"

"Alright, sweetheart. See you soon."

Fin's hands shook on the steering wheel as the speedometer climbed, her little car—unused to travelling at such high speed—shuddering wildly beneath her.

"Slow down, Finny."

"Stop it, Jake!" she shouted. "You're not really here. Don't do this now!"

Ryan, don't leave. I'm coming. Please don't leave before I get there.

The RAAF base airport was crowded with soldiers and family, but Ryan stood alone, not wanting to intrude.

"I don't want you to go."

His fists clenched by his sides. The words had slipped out of their own accord. Ryan was supposed to be strong enough for the both of them, yet Fin was the one who stepped back, her spine straight as she told him it was too late.

"Ryan!" His head turned swiftly. "Ryan!"

Julie was waving as she and Mike made their way through the

crowd towards him. His eyes were frantic as he searched behind them, his heart leaping as he looked for Fin, but he didn't see her bright, tousled blonde waves anywhere in the sea of army green. *Idiot,* he thought, swallowing disappointment. *She didn't even know you were leaving today. Why would you expect her to miraculously appear and happily wave you off?*

Julie reached his side and he leaned down as she wrapped him up in a hug. He buried his head briefly in the motherly embrace before he stepped away.

He turned to Mike's outstretched hand and took it in his own. Mike tugged and soon he was wrapped in a solid hug by the only man that had ever been a real father to him. Mike slapped him on the back before pulling away.

"You didn't let us know you were leaving, son."

What was he supposed to say? I've left your daughter, but hey, I'm heading back to war, so come see me off? He would be lucky if Mike didn't turn around and punch him in the damn nose.

"I wasn't sure ..." He rubbed a hand across his brow. "Fin and I ..."

Tears filled Julie's eyes and Ryan sighed heavily.

"We know," she told him and his jaw locked tight. "Fin told us about the program, about how adamant you were for her to accept it. It just shows us how much you love her to put her future above everything else like this. We can't tell you both what the right thing to do is, but Ryan, honey, we just want you happy. Don't you think you finally deserve some happiness for yourself?"

"I am happy," he told them and mustered a smile. "I love being in the Army. I don't think I could ever do anything else but this."

"That's not the kind of happiness I was talking about," Julie muttered.

"Leave him be," Mike told Julie gruffly and looked at Ryan. "How about a coffee?"

Ryan nodded. "Sure."

As the three of them sat down, Julie rummaged through her bag and handed over a bunch of cards. "These are for you."

Ryan thanked her and sifted through them quickly. There was one from Mike's parents and Julie's mother, Jake and Fin's cousins and family friends. He tucked them away carefully when they finished their coffee, and adrenaline spiked through his system when the announcement came for their flight to board.

As the three of them stood, Julie grabbed at his hand, panic flaring in her wide eyes. "You can't leave yet."

He looked at her. "What?"

"It's Fin."

Ryan's brows drew together. "What about Fin?"

"She's on her way here." Julie checked her watch before meeting his eyes. "She should have been here by now."

"She knows I'm leaving today?"

Mike nodded. "She does now. Julie spoke to her just after we arrived and told her."

Julie already had her phone out and dialling as Mike spoke. "She told me she was already on her way to see you when I rang."

God. He needed to see her, bury his head in her hair and breathe her in. Nothing had ever soothed him and at the same time set him on fire the way she did.

"She's not answering," Julie told them after leaving a message.

The flight announcement came again. All around him, family clung to their loved ones and tears were wiped away.

"I can't ..." Ryan turned to face the both of them. "I have to go."

Once again he was wrapped in warm hugs. "I'm sorry. Tell her I'm sorry. Tell her ..." His chest tightened until he could barely speak.

Julie gripped his hand firmly and squeezed. "It's okay, Ryan. I'll tell her."

He looked to Mike and lifted his chin. "Sir."

Mike nodded. "Son."

With one last search over the crowds, Ryan turned and strode towards his troop. Glancing over his shoulder, he caught Julie, her face buried in Mike's chest, her shoulders shaking. His eyes burned as he kept walking, disappearing from their view.

Chatter was loud and boisterous, emotions running hot and high as the long line of soldiers congregated on the tarmac. Monty stood in front of Ryan and Kyle stood behind him, where Jake would normally stand, talking the loudest of all.

Pressing his lips together, Ryan closed his eyes and Fin filled his vision.

"Come here." Ryan ran his hand over her bare hip and the curve of her ass as she tucked herself against him. *"Kiss me, baby."*

When her lips met his, he rolled her over, pressing her into the bed and kissing her so deeply it made him breathless. Fin's hands circled the hard length of him, stroking him firmly and he groaned into her mouth.

"Ryan," she breathed against his lips.

Ryan buried his head in her neck, growling deeply as he rocked himself slowly in her hands. Slowly, Ryan tasted her skin, inching his way down her body until he reached where his name was etched so beautifully into her skin. He traced over the mark with his tongue.

Fin giggled softly. *"If you keep doing that, it'll wear away."*

Ryan looked up at her from beneath his lashes to catch the smile on her face. *"I don't think it's going anywhere anytime soon."*

"...shoot any straighter, Kendall?"

Ryan turned to face a smirking Kyle. "Huh?"

"Jesus." Kyle rolled his eyes. "I said," he enunciated loudly, grinning, "do you think that letting your hair grow any longer is gonna make you shoot any straighter?"

Ryan ran a hand over the back of his head. He'd loved feeling Fin's hands pulling and tugging at his hair when he was buried between her thighs—the harder she pulled, the hotter he got.

"Fuck you, Brooks," he retorted. "You couldn't lift a rifle past that fat gut of yours and hit a goddamn elephant standing two metres away."

"Oh my God, you think I'm ... *fat?*" Kyle widened his eyes in mock horror, splaying a hand over the well-defined muscles of his abdomen. "It's the army fatigues isn't it?" He twisted his head, looking down over his shoulder as though trying to check out his own ass. "They make me look podgy."

"Fuck podgy," Galloway called out. "You look like the Marshmallow Man from *Ghostbusters*, only greener."

"And dumber," Tex added, laughing as he shuffled forward in the line, in step with everyone else.

Ryan tuned the banter out and took one final, searching look towards the airport windows for Fin.

Not seeing her, he turned back and following behind Monty, stepped up and onto the plane.

Chapter Nineteen

With her heart racing, Fin pulled quickly into the parking lot at Base Pearce and parked the car at a wild angle. Yanking her keys out, she grabbed her bag and flung the car door open. Toeing off her heels, she tossed them at the passenger seat and with a slam of the door, ran towards the entrance. Elbowing her way through the crowd, Fin made it towards the large windows in time to see the plane taxi down the runway and lift off into the sky.

"No," she moaned breathlessly.

Dropping her bag, she pressed both hands against the glass as she watched Ryan disappear until there was nothing left to see but bright blue sky and fluffy clouds. *She hadn't made it.* Closing her eyes, Fin rested her forehead against the glass, her breath puffing softly against the gleaming window. She would be holding this baby in her arms before he even returned. Ryan would never run his hands over her pregnant belly with love; he would never feel the joy of their baby's first kick or see their baby born into the world. She wouldn't be sharing any of it with him.

Goddamn you, Ryan. Anger cut a deep slash through the hurt, leaving her breathless. *You talk about how other countries depend on people like you to fight in their corner, but what about me? I need you too.*

"Fin!"

Fin spun around at the sound of her mother's voice. Her parents were pushing their way towards her through the current of people beginning their slow exit of the building. She lifted her chin. "He's gone."

Her father nodded gravely.

"Well then." Grabbing her bag from its abandoned spot on the floor, she jerked it over her shoulder. "No point in hanging around is there."

"Finlay." Her mother placed a hand on her arm.

Fin halted at the gentle touch, fighting to hold onto the anger that was helping keep her shit together. "Don't, Mum. I'm fine. I need to get back to work."

"We spoke to him before he left," her mother said.

"Oh how nice," she replied icily. "I don't even get a phone call when he's leaving, but you two get time to see him and wave him off. Did he look happy?" Her father frowned, his mouth open to reply. "Don't answer that. I bet he did. I bet you couldn't wipe the smile from his face at the thought of fucking off back to war, the only place he's ever wanted to be." Her mum reached for her again, but Fin slapped her hand away, feeling the cracks forming in her heart. "I hate him," she hissed. With tears blurring her vision, she looked at her mum and dad in turn. "I fucking hate him and I don't want to ever hear his name again."

Spinning on bare feet, Fin strode blindly towards the entrance of the airport and out into the midday heat. What had she been thinking chasing after him like that anyway? Obviously she hadn't been. Ryan had more important things to focus on than waving goodbye to someone he didn't want anymore.

Fin growled audibly as she beeped the locks on her car, hating herself just as much for the useless pity party she was getting swept away in.

"Finlay," her father called out, his voice firm and loud.

Fin spun around, seeing him stalk towards her. "What?" she replied tersely.

"Don't you take that tone with me, miss. I know you're upset but—"

"Upset? I'm more than upset!" she yelled, cutting him off as she rummaged through her bag. Finding the photo that had been tucked so carefully in her purse, she ripped it out and thrust it at him.

He took it, frowning at her before looking down at the photo. Her chest rose and fell rapidly while she waited for her father to speak, her body growing tenser by the second.

"That sonofabitch," he eventually growled, his nostrils flaring wide as comprehension dawned in his eyes. Peeling his eyes from the photo, they flickered to her belly before lifting to her face. "He ended a relationship with my daughter when she's having his baby? I had nothing but respect and love for that boy, but this ..." Her father started to crumple the photo in his hand, cursing loudly.

"Dad! That wasn't how it happened."

He pointed at her, fire in his eyes. "You're defending him now? He has a lot to goddamn answer for."

Seeing her father's anger made her own deflate. She didn't like seeing him assume the worst. Not of Ryan. "He didn't know, Dad. *I* didn't know, not until this morning. I tried to get here in time to tell him, but I was too late."

"Shit." Her father rubbed his jaw, expelling a heavy sigh as his shoulders slumped. "I hear you, love. I shouldn't have thought the worst. It's just ... you're my little girl."

"Well I won't be little for much longer," she tried to joke but her heart wasn't in it.

He pulled her close for a hug. "You'll always be my little girl."

Fin took a deep breath. "Thanks, Dad."

"It's going to be hard for both of you, being apart for this."

"I know. Maybe it's not such a good idea to tell him about the baby right now."

Letting go, he looked down at her, his expression stern. "You need to tell him."

Fin leaned up against the car and looked at her dad. "Do you remember the day I found that dead bird in the yard?"

She'd been almost ten when she'd stumbled upon the pretty rosella, its colourful feathers fluttering wildly across the lawn and into the sky. Seeing something so carefree and beautiful so sad and lifeless was the first time she'd ever felt a crack in her heart. Hearing a noise, Fin had spun around and shielding her eyes against the sun, looked up. Slingshot in hand, she caught Jake slamming his window shut.

"Remember how I shouted for you and you came out and took care of it?"

She'd watched for a brief moment—her wounded heart satisfied her father was doing the right thing when he cradled the bird gently in his hand—before storming inside and up the stairs.

Reaching Jake's room, she'd flung open the door. Both Jake and Ryan jerked as it banged loudly against the wall.

"How could you?" she shrieked at Jake, balling her small fists with fury. "That little bird did nothing to you, you big stupid jerk!"

Jake paled. She'd never seen him so pale, and it threw her anger off course. Pushing his way past her and out of his room, she heard the bathroom door slam. When the muffled sound of retching filtered down the hall, Fin met Ryan's eyes.

"What's going on in here?" her father said, the sharp tone of warning evident in his voice.

"Mike." Ryan swallowed visibly and grabbed the slingshot off the desk. "Sir. I was just uh … I didn't really think I'd hit it, the bird that is. I'm s-sorry."

Ryan flinched when her dad strode into the room and held out his hand, indicating for Ryan to give him the slingshot. At the time, she didn't understand the flinch, or the fear in Ryan's dark eyes, but looking back now made it clear.

"Ryan never killed that bird, Dad. It was Jake. I saw him from the window. I didn't understand why Ryan took the blame, but I can see now. He was protecting Jake from you. He thought you would lay into Jake for what he did."

Her dad frowned. "I would never—"

"I know that," she cut him off. "But don't you see? Ryan's always protecting everyone else and putting them before himself. Even as a kid. He'll take the blame for this; for me not being able to do the research program and having this baby when he can't be there for us. I can't let him do that. I can't let him be distracted when he needs to focus. He has to come home safe, Dad. I couldn't bear it if …" Her throat constricted and her father took her hand and squeezed.

"You're right, love. It's possible Ryan *will* take the blame, but you have to trust that he knows what he's doing over there. He's going to be a father. No matter what happens, I think he deserves to know that, don't you?"

"I need to think," Fin admitted. "I'm all over the place right now."

"Don't think too hard. You might hurt yourself."

"Dad!" Her lips curved at her father's attempt to lighten the situation. "That was a lame joke."

"Hey. I'm going to be a Grandpa. Lame jokes are my job." Her father smiled down at her, and his eyes sparked with a light that had been missing for too long.

Fin tried returning the smile and faltered. "How am I going to do this without him?"

Four days later
Bagram Airfield, Afghanistan

The C130 Hercules circled Bagram Airbase in the dark of night. Weather conditions were shit. Turbulence was knocking the plane around wildly as they waited for clearance to land.

Last time this happened they got sent back to the Arabian peninsula to wait out another night. Ryan just wanted to get this deployment the hell under way. The sooner he could focus on something other than Fin the better.

The load masters turned, and giving the thumbs up, yelled, "We're going in!"

Ryan exhaled, closing his eyes in relief as the talk of fifty troopers around him became loud and boisterous.

"Ryan?"

"Hmmm?"

Monty elbowed him in the ribs and waved a bottle of water in his face. "Drink?"

Ryan scratched at his head and yawned. "Yeah, thanks."

"You alright, mate?" he asked as Ryan took the water from his outstretched hand.

Fuck, no. This would be his first tour without Jake and it burned. "Nothing I can't handle."

Monty assessed him carefully and lifted his chin. "Good."

"You're kidding, right?" Kyle called from two seats across as Ryan cracked the lid on his water bottle and took a sip. "Kendall doesn't even know how to handle his own dick."

Water spewed out Ryan's nose, laughs ringing out as he choked. "Sonofabitch," he rasped with watery eyes and wiped at his face. "You handle yours so much it's worn down to a stub."

Kyle responded with a wink, but it was no joke. Sexual frustration after months of deployment on the front line was a bitch. They would all be suffering soon enough. All Ryan had to do was close his eyes and remember the taste of Fin and his dick didn't just twitch, it flooded so hard it was almost painful.

He cursed silently. There was no getting her out of his system, not even here, and that was dangerous. Afghanistan was a hot zone of IEDs and enemy fire. He couldn't afford to lose focus.

"Alright, troopers," Monty yelled. "Move out."

Kyle clapped him on the back as they both stood, and Ryan met his eyes. They glimmered with a fierce eagerness to get outdoors and into the thick of the action. "Let's go do what Jake would want us to do."

Ryan gave a short nod and then grinned. "Let's fuck shit up."

After waiting for everyone else to head out ahead of him, Ryan shifted the heavy pack onto his back and moved down the ramp of the Hercules. He took a deep breath as his feet hit the ground, taking the dry air into his lungs and feeling a bittersweet excitement climb his throat at what the next few months had in store.

The next day Ryan's patrol was already shipping out into the frontier of Eastern Afghanistan. Monty gathered them together and issued detailed verbal orders for the reconnaissance mission. Ryan's eyes slid towards the new man on their team with a heavy heart. Their squadron commander had personally selected Nathan for this patrol, showing a high level of trust in the man's abilities. Ryan knew Nathan well enough. He was young and cocky, but that was off the field. He'd witnessed Nathan's fitness levels first-hand, and his self-discipline, honour, and reliability as a team player were intense—he wasn't a weak link.

When the operation was completed successfully, they returned to Bagram Airbase and settled into a familiar rhythm of training. It wasn't until a little over two months after arriving in Afghanistan when Ryan's deployment began a steady decline into a steaming pile of shit.

In the late afternoon, Ryan made his way to the computer room to check his emails. Mike and Julie corresponded regularly, along with some of Ryan's friends, but it was seeing an email from *Finlay Tanner* in his inbox that had him breaking out in a cold sweat.

Ryan stared at the email, feeling it taunting him with feigned innocence. It was bolded with no subject line, giving no hint to its contents. His hand hovered over the mouse. *Shit.* Reading that email would be a crappy idea. He closed his eyes for a moment. How much longer did he think he could keep doing this to himself? Why couldn't he be selfish and have her any which way, regardless of the cost? He wanted to fight everything that stood in the way of keeping her with him, but he would only lose, because he couldn't fight himself.

"Did the big, bad soldiers tucker poor little Kendall out?"

Ryan's fingers jolted on the mouse. Opening his eyes, he found

Kyle smirking in the doorway. Turning to face the computer, he shut his email down in hurried, jerky movements and logged out. "I *could* do with some sleep," Ryan replied as he got to his feet. "No one gets any rest bunking with you, asshole. You snore like a wounded elephant in heat."

"How would you know what a wounded elephant in heat sounds like?"

"Easy. It sounds like you."

Kyle tipped his chin towards the computer. "Heard from Fin?"

Ryan raised his brows. "Why do you ask that?"

"You just got that look on your face."

"What look?"

"The look you get whenever you're around her or when someone mentions her name. You know—the puppy eyes."

"Puppy eyes!" Ryan shoved Kyle into the doorway as he walked through to leave. Being a rock solid bastard, Kyle barely budged an inch, which for some reason only irritated him further. *Puppy eyes* his fucking ass. "Fuck off, Brooks. You don't know what you're talking about."

Kyle choked with laughter as Ryan stalked away. Usually the normal banter between his patrol mates slid right off his back, but the mention of Fin made him an easy target.

"Hey!" Ryan turned at Kyle's shout. Kyle was leaning casually against the doorframe, a smirk still playing on his lips. "I wasn't here to stalk your ass. Monty called a briefing at 1900 hours."

A briefing meant an operation was on the horizon, and they were all itching to get out into the field. "Good," he muttered, and cracking his knuckles loudly, Ryan left to grab something to eat.

Two days later found them scoping the back of the mountains behind a suspect village for evidence of enemy presence. Their task was not to engage fire, but gather intelligence. Either way, an incident occurring was highly probable.

As Ryan crested a small rise, he came across what looked like a weapons pit. Crouching down, he examined the man-made rock structure. The ground had been flattened and an etching into the rocks gave no doubt enemies were occupying the area. Standing, Ryan signalled to both Nathan and Kyle to come over and document the site. Just as he was putting down his machine gun to grab his binoculars and scope further down, a bullet zinged passed his head, flying over the top of Nathan and Kyle and slamming into the tree above.

"Sonofabitch," Ryan growled.

Snatching his weapon, Ryan folded himself behind the thick barrier of rock and assumed a firing position, his mind racing. *Were they under attack?* He was lucky that bastard was a bad shot.

Nathan reached his side, crouching down to assume defensive fire. A shot rang out as Kyle joined them, and Ryan's heart thundered in his chest when he heard Kyle suck in a sharp breath.

"Fuck," Kyle groaned with clenched teeth. "I'm fucking hit."

Ryan's stomach rolled, his vision tunnelling when Nathan turned towards Monty and barked, "Man down."

Pull your fucking shit together, Kendall.

With clammy skin and sweat pouring down his face, Ryan shuffled over to Kyle as Galloway appeared with first aid. Kyle's face was red, his lungs drawing in short, sharp gasps of air.

"Where?"

"Right arm," he panted. "It's my goddamn elbow."

He could already smell the blood, the same metallic tang that hung so thick in the air when Jake died. When Ryan closed his eyes he could still see it pouring out, Jake's life slowly seeping into the ground.

Ryan shook his head, blinking hard and gingerly took hold of Kyle's arm. Bone and muscle tissue were exposed. It looked messed up, but this was no life-threatening injury. "Suck it up, Brooks," he ribbed, relief lightening his tone as he reached for gauze and bandages. "It's just a scratch."

Kyle tried to laugh but the sound came out choked. "Fuck you, Kendall," he mumbled, his eyes scrunched shut from the pain.

"I'd appreciate if you didn't." Chuckling, Ryan met his eyes as he numbed the area and began to patch the injury. "Your firing arm is gonna be out of action for a little while."

They locked eyes, a silent acknowledgement of what this would mean. Not just surgery to piece the bone and muscle back together, but likely months of physiotherapy to get him back to the standard of fitness the Regiment expected. Kyle was going home.

"Fucking hell, Kendall," he muttered with quiet frustration. He closed his eyes, tilting his head to the sky. After several deep breaths, he re-opened them, the pain and disappointment shuttered—tucked away for what was probably a more private moment. "I'm gonna have to learn how to use my left hand to jack off now," he said loudly for the team's benefit.

Unable to work up a smile, Ryan focused on putting together a sling, the team falling silent and keeping watch as Tex set up satellite communications. With a major attack appearing unlikely, and with Kyle patched up, they were informed the request for casualty evacuation had been granted.

Monty inched towards Ryan. "We don't know what the fuck we're dealing with out there. Could be one or two rogues, but from the intelligence we've gathered so far, which isn't much, it could be fucking hundreds. Let's retreat to a pick up position for Brooks, and then we can formulate a plan."

"Fuck this shit," Kyle growled.

Ryan slapped him on the back in sympathy, knowing it wasn't the pain making Kyle pissed—it was having to leave his team in the middle of an operation. They trained hard for these missions, living and breathing it every day. Being rendered useless to your team and missing out on the action would be a goddamn motherfucker.

Moments before Kyle was evacuated, he lifted his chin at Ryan, the action saying more than any words could.

Ryan nodded back, and after their team received a response from Squadron Headquarters, they moved further up into the mountains in order to gather further intelligence.

Gripping his weapon tight, Ryan looked up at the ridge as darkness fell and repressed a shiver when cool air collided with his sweat dampened skin. They were one man down and heading directly into a region yet to be occupied by Coalition forces. In essence, they were quite possibly climbing their way right into Hell.

Chapter Twenty

Seven weeks later
Fremantle, Western Australia

"Honey, you can't eat that."

With narrowed eyes, Fin watched her mother reach into the supermarket trolley and take out the packet of smoked salmon she'd just tossed in there.

Then she listened to her mum sigh with enough exasperation to make Fin feel like she was ten years old again.

"Didn't you read the pamphlet I gave you on what you could and couldn't eat?"

Fin rolled her eyes at Laura who was rounding out today's contingent of the female Tanner shopping expedition. Laura smirked in reply.

Fin had taken one look at the pamphlet and tossed it on her desk for another day. The list of what she supposedly couldn't eat was at least a mile long. If she paid it any attention, she may as well give up eating altogether. She wanted sushi and her favourite sandwich—smoked salmon, cream cheese, and rocket; or turkey with cranberry sauce, camembert, alfalfa, and avocado.

"I looked at it," Fin told her mum as her stomach growled angrily. *Dammit.* Was food all she could think about anymore? *Better than thinking about Ryan.*

Her mother rolled her eyes before striking up a conversation with the lady over the deli counter and ordering a half kilo of ham. Sliced deli meat was one thing she remembered skimming her eye over. "If I hadn't, I wouldn't know right now that I'm not allowed to eat that ham," she pointed out.

"It's for your father," her mum murmured distractedly.

Intent on using the distraction to her advantage, Fin gripped her hands firmly to the trolley and made a rapid escape from the pair of them. Breathing a sigh of relief at seeing the next aisle empty of people, Fin gave up the pretence of trying to walk like a normal person. Her feet, encased in plain black flip flops, were literally going to kill her. She was only just past six months along—were they supposed to be that swollen already? *God.* She just wanted to be at home lying on the couch, her feet elevated on the arm rest as soothing music wafted through the room. She could rest her hands on her belly and imagine they were Ryan's, but she was only kidding herself and the pretence just made her feel worse.

Moving farther up the aisle, Fin halted in front of the cereals and hitched up her bright purple yoga pants. "I really need to buy some maternity clothes," she muttered as they slid back down, the soft, elasticised waistband folding back underneath her tummy— enough to expose the very tips of her tattoo.

Sighing, Fin tried to tug her tank top down instead. It didn't quite reach the waistband of her pants, leaving a sliver of exposed skin.

"You may as well just bite the bullet, Finlay Tanner," she told herself as she adjusted her clothes without success, "you're doing this on your own. Putting off buying maternity clothes isn't helping anyone, especially the public who right now have to bear witness to your fat stomach."

Grabbing at both a packet of Weet-bix and Coco Pops, Fin held them aloft as she examined the contents. She had to have the milky chocolate crunch or someone would pay, but Weet-bix was the healthy option, wasn't it? Maybe she should get both. *Why was choosing a cereal so hard?* A tear slid down her cheek, and then another, until clutching both boxes of cereal to her swollen belly, Fin began to sob openly, not even caring that she was crying in the middle of a supermarket. She was pregnant, *dammit*. She could get away with all kinds of emotional outbursts. It wasn't like the supermarket was full of people anyway, and even if it was, she was sure most would be giving her a wide berth. They would have to anyway, what with her giant belly being in the way and all.

"Hey now, what's wrong, sweetheart?"

Fin spun around at the familiar voice and came face to face with Kyle's cheeky hazel eyes. What was he doing here? She looked frantically up and down the aisle for Ryan, but she didn't see him. Was he here somewhere too?

Kyle reached out and cupped her face, using his thumbs to wipe her tears away. He pressed a kiss to her forehead before taking a step back and looking down at her, waiting for some kind of response.

Flustered, Fin glanced down at the cereal boxes crushed against her. "I can't choose what cereal to buy," she choked out.

Kyle's eyebrows flew up. "Okay," he drawled. Using his left arm, he reached out for one of the boxes in her arms, and she jerked back. He cleared his throat. "Well, you seem kinda attached to both of them. Maybe you should just buy both."

"Right," Fin muttered, in no hurry to toss the cereal into her trolley and expose her supersized form. It was then that her eyes fell on his right arm. It was bandaged heavily and bound tight to his body with a heavy duty sling. Alarmed, she met his eyes. "Your arm!"

Kyle shrugged. "It's nothing. Just a scratch. They sent me home a little early."

Fin's eyes widened. "They sent you home for a scratch?"

She watched Kyle cringe a little and rub awkwardly at the back of his neck. "Yeah. I got scratched by a bullet."

"A bullet?" Dizziness engulfed her, and the boxes in her arms went a little lax. "So really, you were shot. Are you … Is Ryan …"

"Ryan's fine!" Kyle replied quickly. Fin let out the breath she didn't realise she was holding. "It wasn't even an attack, just some bastard who pinged off a shot and got lucky."

"Kyle," she muttered. Why did they keep going back there? How many people had to get hurt or die?

"I'm okay," he replied and amusement filled his eyes. "As good as I can be. I really miss using my right hand." Fin flushed wildly at the implication, and he burst out laughing. "You're so easy."

Knowing her mother would soon be catching up, Fin cleared her throat. "Well, I should get going. Maybe you can stop by the cottage for dinner one night," she threw out.

He nodded. "Okay, what night are you free?"

Oh shit. Fin was only being polite. She never thought he would take her up on the offer. "Umm … well, let me think …"

Kyle arched a brow. "If you don't want me to come over, that's okay. I know, what with … Jake and now Ryan … Well, me being around might not be the best thing, but it might be nice to catch up, you know?" His eyes searched her face.

"Of course it would," Fin agreed. "It's not that I don't want to—"

"Let me get those." He reached again for the cereal, and she flinched backwards, hitting the shelving with a wince.

Kyle frowned. "Fin?"

Fin aimed for a laugh but the sound came out strangled and high pitched.

With just his left hand, Kyle somehow scooped both boxes from her arms and tossed them in the trolley. "There. Now back to why you were crying over a bunch of cereal." His eyes fell, widening when they latched onto the chest that had expanded considerably. *Crap.* She really needed some new bras too. "Holy shit, Fin. Wow. You sure got …" Kyle trailed off as his eyes lowered, his mouth dropping open as he stared at her belly. "That's … you … you're pregnant."

Fin nodded casually, her eyes finding something interesting behind his shoulder. "Well, these things happen. Anyway, um … I should go."

"He doesn't know," came Kyle's flat voice.

She averted her eyes, hurt pooling in her stomach as she focused on the painfully swollen sausages that were masquerading as her toes. "I emailed him. I asked him to give me a call, but you know, he's obviously busy saving a whole bunch of people and whatnot so yes, you're right. He doesn't know."

"Fuck," Kyle growled.

Fin placed a hand on his good arm. "Don't. Just let it go. I have," she lied. "I can do this on my own. I don't have a choice anyway, so there's no point in getting angry or whatever. Life is what it is." And it sure as shit wasn't turning out anything like she expected it would.

Kyle nodded, but his body remained tense.

"Please don't say anything to Ryan. He needs to hear it from me, but I've made the first move. It's on him now."

Taking a step back, Kyle's eyes slid down the end of the aisle to where her mother and Laura were making their way towards them. Laura's arms were piled high, Fin's mum scouring the shelves and adding more to the pile as they made their way towards them. "Well, how's Friday night for dinner then?"

"Are you serious? Friday nights are for drinking and pretty girls, not a crazy pregnant woman with moods that change faster than you can flick channels on the TV."

Kyle laughed. "I've been in Afghanistan in case you forgot. I'm sure I've faced enough crazy to handle whatever you can throw at me."

Fin tugged on her tank top again. Kyle's eyes followed the movement and she flushed, lamenting the fact that she hadn't bothered to choose her outfit more carefully before leaving the house. "Then you're the one who's nuts."

"Hey." Kyle grinned. "You're the one standing on your own in the supermarket aisle, crying because you can't decide what cereal to buy." Putting his left hand in his pocket, she heard the jingle of car keys. "Anyway, I better get going. Got physio. Does seven work for you?"

"Probably not, unless you don't mind me falling asleep on you." Staying awake past eight p.m. these days was like swimming against the current, and Fin was slowly learning to pick her battles.

"Six then," he replied as Fin aimed for another furtive tug upwards of her yoga pants. "You look ..." Kyle swallowed, high colour hitting his cheeks as he met her eyes. "You're beautiful. Pregnancy suits you." With that he turned, offering a brief nod and a "Mrs. Tanner" and a "Laura," to her mum and cousin before disappearing from the aisle.

"What's Kyle doing back home?" her mother asked.

Items tumbled from Laura's arms and into the trolley. "And did I just hear him call you beautiful?"

"Laura! Honestly. He was injured, but he's okay." Fin brushed at a rogue wave that had escaped her messy knot of hair. With her swollen body and ill-fitting clothes, she'd never looked or felt more unattractive in her entire life. "Besides, he was just being polite. I'm pregnant for God's sake."

"So what if you are?" Laura winked. "That doesn't mean you can't have sex."

"Laura," Fin hissed and once again, took possession of the trolley to make for another escape.

"I didn't say to have a relationship with him, Fin."

Fin gasped. "You did not just say that! He's one of Ryan's best friends. This conversation is getting out of control. Can we just get this shopping over and done with? What I need is to park my bum on something cushioned and eat. What I don't need is to stand in the supermarket aisle while six months pregnant, talking about having sex just because a man was polite enough to call me beautiful when I look like complete ass!" She finished her rant by sucking in a deep lungful of air. All the added weight to her chest and belly had her breaking a sweat just by breathing.

With another irritable tug at her pants and an audible growl, Fin pushed the trolley along rapidly, and the faster she moved, the more she felt herself beginning to waddle.

"Coco Pops? Really?"

Glancing sideways, Fin realised her mother was keeping pace beside her. "Yes. You got a problem with that?"

Her mother shrugged. "Not really. My thing when pregnant with you was double cheeseburgers. I haven't been able to eat another one since." She shuddered before stopping in front of the vitamins. "Oh, when we're done here, we should go pick out some maternity clothes. You're busting out of those pants, honey."

Pressing her lips together, Fin focused with wild desperation on getting out of the supermarket alive.

Two days later
FOB Khost
Eastern Afghanistan

"How's life at the barracks, Brooks?"

"Fucking boring," came the moan in his ear, "and I'm busy pissing everyone off just to keep myself entertained because there's nothing else to do. Although they do have a bunch of new recruits due in over the next two weeks. Giving them shit will keep me occupied until my arm heals."

With elbows resting on his knees and phone to his ear, Ryan laughed. "How *is* the arm anyway?"

"It's fine, but if one more asshole makes a joke about my inability to jack off, I'm going to shoot them. I could load and fire a rifle with my left hand while blindfolded and hit a moving target in the time it would take them to find their own dicks."

Ryan chuckled. "Careful, Brooks. You're sounding a bit frustrated there."

Kyle cleared his throat.

"So is that why you're ringing me at, what time is it there—three a.m.? To talk to me about your sexual frustration?"

"Bet it's nowhere near as bad as yours is."

Ryan's entire body tensed, and it was Kyle's turn to laugh. "Actually, there is something I'm ringing you about."

"Yeah?" Tucking the phone between his ear and shoulder, Ryan clenched and unclenched his fists. "What?"

Silence.

"You there?"

"Yeah, I'm here." Another pause. "It's Fin."

His fingers tightened on the phone. "Is she okay?"

"She's fine, Kendall," Kyle replied. "I, uh, ran into her at the supermarket the other day. She was there with Julie and Laura."

"How is she?"

"Well, maybe that's something you could ask her yourself, you know?"

Getting to his feet, Ryan started pacing in short spurts, back and forth, back and forth. Stopping, he scratched idly at the beard forming on his face from their patrol. He hated not shaving, but it wasn't a high priority in the middle of a life and death operation. "Probably not a good idea."

Kyle's growl of anger came through the line.

"Brooks ..."

"She told me she emailed you."

Ryan closed his eyes. *Finlay Tanner.* The bold words. The empty subject line. It still taunted him.

"Have you even read it?"

His brows drew together in a sharp frown. "Why are you suddenly making this your business?" Ryan deflected angrily.

"Christ, Kendall. I wouldn't have expected you of all people to forget how short life is."

"Exactly. That's why she's moving to Sydney and studying at the Research Centre."

"Hmmm."

"*Hmmm* what? Fin is still going, isn't she? She told me she accepted their invitation and that it was all set."

"Look, Kendall. I'm not being the go between for the two of you. If you want to know anything about what she's doing, you can bloody well ask her yourself."

Ryan pinched the bridge of nose with his thumb and forefinger. Kyle was right. That was a shit thing to do. "Sorry," he muttered and checked his watch. He was due for debrief in thirty minutes. "Look, I gotta go. Have a beer for me tonight, will you?"

There was zero alcohol tolerance for all soldiers on deployment. Knowing it was Friday morning there, Kyle would no doubt be hitting the piss that night.

"Will do," Kyle murmured.

After hanging up the phone, Ryan turned to the computer. Switching it on, he logged into his email and stared at it again. *Fuck, Kendall. Just grow some fucking balls and open the email already.*

Hovering the mouse over her name, Ryan double clicked before he could think about it any further.

Ryan,

It feels like I've started this email a thousand times because it's so hard to know what to say.

Remember before you left, you told me to "go and make Jake proud"? I hope you are doing the same thing.

I miss you. So very much.

Exhaling deeply, Ryan tilted his head upwards, his eyes burning. God, he missed her too.

I know you have certain expectations about what I should be doing with my life, but you should know that life always gets in the way of plans.

Sorry. It's not my intention to be cryptic, but I need to talk to you and some things are better discussed over the phone rather than email.

Ring me when you can. Please.

Love always,

Fin.

Pressing his lips together, Ryan hit delete on the email and started the process of logging out and shutting the computer down.

I need to talk to you ...

The soft whir of the computer wound down until silence filled the room, and still he sat there staring at the screen.

Ring me when you can.

Getting to his feet, Ryan strode determinedly towards the door and swung it open.

Please ...

Pausing with his hand on the door, he turned and looked at the phone. Who was he kidding? Fin would never have emailed him— not after he stormed out, got drunk, disappeared, and showed up the next day to tell her it was over—unless it was important. *Christ, did he really do that?* What a fucking asshole.

Moving back into the room, Ryan picked up the phone and began dialling.

Chapter Twenty-One

Buried under the sheets, dawn fighting its way inside the bedroom, Fin growled irritably after another night of rough sleep. She hated, *hated*, sleeping on her back, but she was stuck with it like some beached whale. Jake would've got a great laugh out of this, no doubt suggesting a rescue from Greenpeace to push her into safe waters or something. Her baby was going to miss out on having the best uncle a kid could ask for.

Realising there would be no more sleep for her this morning, she reached for her phone off the bedside table, intent on turning off the alarm before it began shrieking. Grasping it with an awkwardness that would have been embarrassing if anyone was watching, her fingers shook at seeing the missed call just after three in the morning from a blocked number. She quickly checked her messages but there were none. Had it been Ryan? What if he was hurt? Without care at the early hour, she called up her list of contacts and dialled.

Kyle answered sleepily with an "am I being ditched for a better offer already?"

"No!" Fin rolled to her side and grabbing the mattress, pulled herself to an awkward sitting position, a groan slipping out in the process. The baby performed a lazy roll, obviously annoyed at Fin's rearrangement. Fin rubbed her tummy soothingly and sucked in a sharp breath after getting booted for the gesture.

"Holy shit!" Kyle suddenly sounded wide awake. "Are you in labour? Shouldn't you be ringing your labour buddy? Who the fuck is your labour buddy anyway? Christ, it's not me, is it? Because if it is, you really should have told me. I've never trained for this kind of—"

Fin would've laughed if she wasn't busy having her own panic attack. "Kyle! I'm not in labour," she informed him.

There was a pause and then, "Thank God."

"I thought you said you could handle crazy?"

"Labour's not crazy. It's savage and disturbing on too many levels and has no place in my life."

Fin arched a brow. This man had seen war and having a baby was savage and disturbing? "Because you're a man?"

"Hell yeah."

"Careful, Kyle. The dark ages called. They want their caveman back."

His laughter boomed into the phone. "I've never been around a pregnant woman before. You're kinda scary now."

"*I'm* scary?"

"Uh huh."

Fin heard the sound of sheets rustling, reminding her of the early hour. "I uh, didn't wake you, did I?"

"Nope. I don't sleep much."

"Oh," she murmured.

"Just one of the hazards of the job, you know?"

Fin did know. It was rare to catch Ryan in sleep. When she did, she took full advantage, studying features that looked almost boyish in slumber—from the strong jaw to his straight nose and thick, dark lashes that brushed softly against his cheeks.

The image of Ryan reminded Fin of the reason for her call. "Um, Kyle? If Ryan was hurt, would someone ring me?"

There was a pause. "Why do you ask that?"

"I missed a call this morning just after three from a blocked number. When Jake died ..." Her chest tightened. Saying that would never come easy. "It was Mum who told me, so I don't really ... I'm scared that something will happen and I'll never know." There was a pause, so clearing her throat, she added, "I'm sorry."

"Don't ever be sorry," he replied, his voice husky.

Frowning at how much he sounded like Ryan, Fin pushed up off the bed. "I should get going."

"No."

Her brows flew up as she stumbled over the top of Crookshanks' twining form. "No I shouldn't?"

"No, they wouldn't ring you if something happened to Ryan. If you were next of kin, they would tell you in person."

"Oh." Ryan hadn't mentioned it before leaving, but it was highly unlikely she was his next of kin. Not now.

"I spoke to Ryan early this morning, Fin. It was probably him ringing you like you asked him to in your email."

"You didn't say anything, did you?"

"Of course I didn't," he replied. "I'm sure he'll ring back so don't get yourself upset."

"You worried I might go into labour tonight while you're here?" she teased as she made her way towards the kitchen, Crookshanks making a rapid trek in front of her with hungry anticipation.

"Fuck yeah," he mumbled with a laugh.

"Well don't. I have months to go yet."

"Really?"

His voice took on a high pitched sound of disbelief that made her laugh. "Shut up!" Tucking the phone into her shoulder, she began spooning out Crookshanks' breakfast while he sat there growling impatiently. "I do not look like I'm ready to pop!"

"If you say so."

"So does baked beans on toast sound good for dinner?"

"I was only teasing," he said quickly.

"Sure you were." She placed the bowl of food on the floor for her cat and with a flick of the kettle, headed back towards her room. "I have to go get ready for work."

"Shouldn't you be on maternity leave by now?"

"Kyle!"

His laughter was loud. "Okay, okay. See you tonight."

"See you then."

"Oh, Fin? You can ring me anytime, okay?"

"Thanks, Kyle."

Hanging up, Fin tossed the phone at her bed. How long had it been since she'd sent that email to Ryan? If it *was* him that rang, why had he waited so damn long?

Later that night, Fin answered the door to a grinning Kyle and a tub of ice cream. "Pregnant women eat everything in sight, right? So I figured ice cream would taste better than a bunch of flowers."

Fin snorted and then covered her mouth, flushing with embarrassment as she let him in.

"Did you just snort?"

"No."

"You so did."

Fin reached for the ice cream, but he held it aloft in his good arm as he stepped inside. "I so did not."

Kyle arched a brow at her. "Admit it or you get no ice cream."

She pressed her lips together, fighting a laugh. "Don't ever get between a pregnant woman and food."

His eyes widened with alarm, dropping to her belly when she clutched it with a groan. When Kyle reached for her, she snatched the ice cream out of his arm and did a waddle type run for the kitchen.

Following behind, he pointed at her, his eyes narrowing. "You played me!"

Fin dug through the kitchen drawer for a spoon and waved it triumphantly. "I warned you."

Spooning out a mouthful, Fin sighed with pleasure before tucking the ice cream into the freezer and getting Kyle a drink.

As they sat talking and laughing through dinner, Fin couldn't remember the last time she felt so relaxed. Kyle reminded her so much of Jake that when he was around, it was almost like Jake had never left.

"Oh, I almost forgot," she told him from where they were both splayed out the couch, trying to decide on what movie to watch. "I got you a present."

Kyle's eyes lit up like a kid at Christmas. "Really?"

"Oh, it's just a little thing," she muttered, grabbing hold of the armrest to lever herself out of the seat. She'd been walking past a small row of shops when it caught her eye, tucked into the window of the tiny gift store, begging to be taken home.

Picking up the gift bag from her dresser, she carried it out and handed it over as she sat back down.

Kyle let out a shout of laughter as he peeked into the bag. He pulled out the cute, furry penguin she couldn't resist buying and shook his head, still grinning.

"You have to give him a name now," she said.

"Percy of course. Percy Penguin."

Fin rolled her eyes. "Of course."

"Fuck," he muttered, and putting the stuffed toy to the side, reached out and took both her hands in his. Fin looked at him, surprised at the hint of anger in his eyes. "Ryan's an idiot."

Her mouth fell open. "What does that have to do with anything?"

"Because he's a stubborn asshole who let you go."

A wild kick forced the air from Fin's lungs. Gasping, she closed her eyes.

"Christ, you're not—"

"Kyle!"

"Jesus, Fin. It didn't help any with you faking a labour thingy just to get ice cream."

"They're called contractions."

"That's more than I needed to know."

Her brows flew up with surprise. "I feel sorry for the mother of your future children. It was just the baby kicking."

Kyle eyed her belly with deep suspicion.

"I promise."

"It's not a real promise unless you cross your heart."

Pressing her lips together, Fin crossed her heart. "Feels like I'm back at school when I'm around you."

Kyle nodded knowingly. "I make you feel young again. I get that a lot."

Fin laughed, rubbing her hands over her belly in a gesture that was becoming familiar.

"Can I ..." He looked at her before glancing down to where her hands now rested comfortably, hesitating. "Is it okay if I ..."

"Sure. Everyone does. Most don't even ask."

With gentle hands, Kyle raised the soft cotton of her stretchy tank top and placed both hands over her huge stomach. Fin closed her eyes, shivering at the warm scrape of his palms on her skin. Her heart ached for Ryan and what he was missing.

The baby kicked hard as though understanding her feelings, and Kyle let out a shout. "Holy shit! There's a real baby in there."

"Umm ... so I'm not going to ask what you thought was in there," she replied.

Her phone rang from where it sat on the bench in the kitchen, and Kyle removed his hands, yanking her top down haphazardly. He stood up. "I'll get it for you."

Pressing the answer button for her, he held it out. She answered absentmindedly as Kyle flopped back down on the couch beside her.

"Fin?"

The air left her lungs in a whoosh. "Ryan?"

"Yeah, it's me."

Fin burst into tears at the deep, familiar voice. How did she think she could ever get past loving Ryan? Hearing his voice had the entire world fading out, as though nothing existed but him.

The phone was taken from her as tears ran down her face. The more she tried to control them, the faster they fell. She could hear Kyle murmuring softly while his other hand began rubbing her back in warm, soothing circles. Sniffling quietly, she heard Kyle say that maybe Ryan should ring back.

"No!" she blurted out and snatched the phone from Kyle before Ryan could hang up.

Looking at her, he mouthed, "Should I go?"

Fin shook her head. "Stay," she mouthed back. She had no idea how Ryan would react to her news, and she was scared of being alone right now. Getting up, Fin left Kyle on the couch and went outside. With the phone clutched to her ear, Fin rested her elbows on the railing of the deck and looked up at the stars.

"Sorry. I'm here."

Ryan leaned against the wall as he rubbed at his brow. He hated hearing her upset and being unable to do anything about it. "Are you okay?"

"I'm fine," she replied, sounding anything but. "How are you?"

He wanted to tell her he wasn't doing so great, that he missed her more than anything. She was the only one he could talk to, the only one who knew him like no one else and still loved him anyway. "Doing okay." He cleared his throat. "So, I thought you would've left by now. When do you go?"

There was a pause. "I'm not."

"Not what?"

"Not going."

"Dammit, Fin," he ground out, his body tense with anger. He'd walked away from her so she could have this opportunity. Ryan tried to rein in his anger. She wasn't supposed to be pissing it away. "Not going is not an option."

"Stop," she whispered. "Don't be angry. There's just ... something you need to know."

"What? What in hell could be so damn important for you to give up everything you've ever worked for? Tell me because right now I just don't understand."

"I'm pregnant."

Ryan's heart raced in the deafening silence. "You ... you're having my baby?"

"Yes."

His anger deflated, rapidly replaced with shock. "You ... I'm ..."

There was more silence on the other end as he processed the words and realised what they meant. Moving to the other side of the country for a four year research program was hard enough. Doing it alone and pregnant was impossible. How could he have managed in one brief moment to do the one thing he'd tried to avoid from the moment they met?

"I fucked up," he growled, furious with himself. "Baby," he whispered thickly. Turning around, he pressed his forehead against the wall as agony tore him in two. "You've had to give up your future because I couldn't keep my fucking hands off you!"

"No!" she cried out. "Don't. Please. Our whole lives you've pushed aside your own feelings to always do what you thought was best for me. You think that if you can give me the future Kassidy never had, then maybe you can forgive yourself for what happened, but it doesn't work that way. You keep forgetting about yourself. You have to stop doing that, Ryan. Stop fighting what's in your heart. Maybe if you do, you'll realise there's nothing to forgive."

"There's everything to forgive! Don't you see? I keep letting down the people I love. Somehow I keep doing it and I don't know how to stop. I don't know how ..." Dragging in a breath, he banged his forehead against the wall.

"Ryan," Fin said, her voice thick with tears. "You haven't let me down. You haven't let anyone down. This baby, our baby, it's not the future that was planned, but I want this so much. I know it's a shock, believe me I know, but you're going to be a daddy in three months and—"

"Three months?" he cut her off. Doing the calculations in his head, he said, "That means your six months pregnant, Fin."

"I know," she replied and he could hear the smile in her voice.

"When did you find out?"

"The day you left," she said softly.

The realisation hit him like a punch to the gut. "You were coming to tell me, weren't you?"

"Yes. I didn't want to tell you over the phone, or have you hear it through someone else. Ryan ..." She exhaled deeply. "I'm going to be having this baby before you're home, so telling you this way, there was no other choice."

"I waited for you," he whispered, remembering the need to see her one last time before he left. "I kept looking for you until the moment I stepped on the plane."

"You didn't tell me when you were leaving."

"I thought it was best. I didn't want you upset. Since Jake ..." He swallowed, his throat tight. "There's been so many tears. I hate seeing you upset, and I hate that I can't do anything about it. I'm so far away and I don't know what to do."

"Ryan," she breathed.

He closed his eyes, wanting her in his arms, so much that he said, "I miss you," with a tremble in his voice. "Are you okay? I mean ... healthy? You and the baby?"

"We're fine. It's scary and lonely, but it's exciting, Ryan, and amazing feeling a life growing inside you. It's so hard to explain."

Pain ripped through his chest. Fin was his fucking heart and he'd left her scared and alone. "I'm glad you're both okay," he choked out, tears burning his eyes.

"Don't be upset. Be happy, please? You're going to be a daddy, Ryan."

"I'm going to be a daddy," he repeated, the words yet to sink in.

Fin chuckled softly and his grip tightened on the phone at the sound. "Hang on," she told him. He heard her say something softly to Kyle before coming back on the phone. "Sorry."

"I should go."

"Ryan ... I need to know you're okay."

"This isn't about me right now. You need to think of yourself, and our baby."

"I worry about you."

Hearing the fear in her voice was killing him. "You don't need to be doing that, okay? Just ... keep in touch. Tell me how you're doing, how our baby is doing. Be safe."

"You too, Ryan."

Hanging up the phone, Ryan slid down the wall, buried his head in his hands and cried.

Chapter Twenty-Two

A light tap came at the door. Ryan looked up, blinking hard. Monty stood in the doorway, freshly showered and rubbing a towel over the back of his head. Ryan grimaced. He needed a shower himself. After a hard day's training he was covered in dirt and dried sweat.

"You okay?" Monty asked, brows furrowed.

Ryan swiped a hand across his face, and it came away with a layer of grime. "I don't know."

Monty tossed the towel in the direction of the desk as he walked into the room. Taking a seat across from where Ryan sat on the floor, Monty rested his elbows on his knees and looked at him. "What's going on?"

"Fin's having a baby." He couldn't stop the smile that began to spread wide across his face. "I'm going to be a dad."

Monty's eyes lit up as he sprang out of the chair. Grabbing Ryan's hand, he launched him upwards and into a brief, hard hug. "Shit, mate. Congrats." The smile still on his lips, Monty pulled back and tilted his head in question. "I didn't realise that you two were … uh …"

"Hell." Ryan ran fingers through his hair as he started to pace. "We weren't. It wasn't planned. She was supposed to be taking on a four year research program in Sydney, but now she's not." He stopped and looked Monty in the eye. "I fucked that up for her."

Monty grabbed Ryan's bicep when he resumed pacing, and Ryan stilled. "How the fuck do you figure that?"

"Ever since we were little I've always protected her. I wanted the best for her. I made sure that nothing, namely me, stood in the way of that, and look how good a job I did of that!"

Monty jabbed his finger towards the chair. "Sit down."

His stomach in knots, Ryan instinctively followed Monty's order and sat.

Monty stood in front of him, looking down. "I think you're lying to yourself."

"What?"

"You heard me."

Ryan's breathing quickened as he sat back in the chair. "Lying about what?"

"About being scared," he replied.

"Scared?" Ryan growled, his nostrils flaring dangerously. First it was *he couldn't forgive himself for Kassidy* and now he was *scared?* Who else was going to take their turn at psychoanalysing him today?

"We're a team. You know that. We all know that. There's nothing we don't know about how each other operates. Our lives depend on that knowledge, on being able to interpret each other's emotions at a glance. I can see it, Kendall. Just admit it to yourself and maybe you can get over it and move on."

"That's bullshit, Monty. You know—"

"I know you need to man the fuck up, Kendall!" Monty shouted, pointing his finger at him in sharp, angry jabs. "Stop being so fucking scared about not being good enough for her. Who the hell did this goddamn number on you anyway?"

Ryan stood up, right in Monty's face. "I killed my sister!" He dragged in a deep breath, his chest heaving with emotion. "I killed her."

Monty flinched.

"It was my fault. Kassidy was only five years old when she ran out on the road and got hit by a car. I was supposed to be watching out for her. Fin is so much like her. So much that I want her to have what was taken from my little sister. I want her to have every opportunity. Why is that so damn wrong?" he yelled.

"Because you're not thinking about what *she* wants."

"I am! She's always wanted this!"

"More than she's wanted you? More than she needs you?" Monty shook his head, disappointment obvious in his eyes. Ryan hated seeing that. "Think about it," he was told before Monty strode out of the room, the silence he left behind suddenly eerie as it rang loud in his ears.

Shit. Just ... *fucking shit.*

Was he really just scared?

No. Of course he wasn't. Ryan was a goddamn SAS soldier. He was trained to be one of the toughest sonofabitches in the military. He didn't *do* scared. Scared was for little boys who couldn't stand up to their fathers—who took the beatings and then cried under the cover of darkness. That wasn't him. Not anymore.

Standing up, Ryan shrugged the thought off and put the chair back underneath the desk.

Two months later
Eastern Afghanistan

His adrenaline pumping, Ryan left the briefing with determination and narrow-eyed focus. Shit was heating up, back-up was being called, and he was about to be heading right into the thick of it.

Monty clapped him on the back as they moved fast towards their respective bunks. "Let's suit up and get the fuck out there."

Exhaling steadily, Ryan gave a short nod. Reaching his bunk, he stripped down with short, sharp movements. Tugging down a fitted white shirt, he tucked his tags underneath. Next, he slid on his green and brown pants. Sweat already lining his brow, he did up his belt and pulled on his shirt, working his way down the buttons and tucking it in. Over that went his standard issue Tiered Body Armour System, and after adjusting it in place, Ryan did a final check of his ammunition and equipment pouches. Satisfied everything was where it was supposed to be, he sat on the edge of the bed and pulled on thick socks and boots.

Knowing he had a few minutes, he stood and opened his locker. A sheaf of papers sat inside. He pulled them out and sat back down, running his fingers over Fin's handwriting.

He skimmed over each one, the phrases that meant the most catching his eye as he went.

I'm glad you couldn't keep your hands off me. When I close my eyes at night I feel them running over my bare skin as though you're still here. I feel your hand resting on my chest at night like you used to do, and I know it's because you like to feel the beat of my heart beneath your fingers. Did you know that you always sleep deeper that way? Some nights you cry out in your sleep, and it hurts just hearing it, but then your hand will eventually settle over my heart and your breathing evens out.

Ryan flicked to the next page.

I miss you. Each day hurts a little more than the last.

He flicked again.

You're the strongest person I've ever known, but someone smart and brave once told me that it's always the strongest that fall the hardest. You can trust me, Ryan. Let go. I'll be here to catch you. I'll always be here.

Ryan's hands shook.

I've attached an ultrasound image of our baby and a list of names in order of my favourites, but it would be nice to have your input—if you'd like to.

Ryan had emailed her back, telling her the name at the very top of the list was perfect. She'd also attached a photo of herself and he couldn't stop himself from telling her that *she* was perfect too. And their baby.

Monty had been right. Having it yelled right in his face forced Ryan to finally admit it to himself. He was scared. He'd panicked— his entire chest tight with anxiety at the thought of her choosing him over everything else. How could he live up to that and be worth the sacrifice? It was a risk he'd been too scared to take. But now?

Ryan ran trembling fingers over the photos and swallowed hard before tucking them carefully into his shirt pocket and doing up the button.

Now?

She was his, and just like Monty said, it was time to man the fuck up and take the damn risk. Picking up his weapons, Ryan wrapped up all the beautiful memories in his mind and tucked them deep inside. He had to focus. There was an entire unit of soldiers out there in trouble, and right now they deserved everything he had to give.

Ryan stepped outside, taking a deep breath of the thick warm air in the fading dusk. He joined his team as they made their way to the waiting Black Hawks. The rotors were already thumping, the engines warming.

Monty slapped him on the back. "Ready?"

"Never been more ready." He looked sideways at Monty and grinned. Soon—just a few weeks from now—Ryan would be home. He was going to take Fin out under those stars, right in the very spot he told her how much he loved her and ask her to be his forever. "I'm going to ask Fin to marry me."

Monty returned his grin. "'Bout fucking time, Kendall."

His heart lifted as they kicked up their pace into a jog, leaping into the chopper with excitement. Soon they would be in the thick of battle, and their entire team was pumped to get in on the action.

Ryan gripped Nathan's arm as he leaped up behind him, and when they were all on board, Monty twirled his finger, his eyes hard and serious. "Let's move out!" he yelled.

"Don't give up on me, Fin," Ryan whispered softly in the fading light as the chopper lifted.

Same time

Fremantle, Western Australia

"Ugh," Fin muttered as she set the glass of fresh vegetable juice back on the breakfast table. She was trialling the recipe her mum had given her and made a mental note to tell her it was disgusting.

Sitting beside her, Rachael began gagging.

Fin's eyes widened with horror as her own stomach began heaving in sympathy. "Don't you dare throw that up!"

"You should ..." gag "... give that recipe to Ryan. He could ..." gag "... use that as some form of torture device on the enemy."

Grabbing both glasses off the table, Fin stood and walked to the sink, dumping the contents down the drain with relish. "You tell that to Mum," she said, rinsing them out under the tap. "She keeps foisting all this over-the-top health crap on me, and it's driving me daft. At least I can be honest and say I tried it, but that's enough. From now on, I'm going to enjoy these last four weeks of pregnancy by eating whatever the hell I want." Turning around, Fin tried folding her arms, but her belly was sitting so high, her arms rested somewhere up near her face.

A knock came at the door and Rachael clapped excitedly. "That'll be the cavalry."

Fin shook her head, laughing. "You're more excited about doing up this nursery than *I* am!"

Later that morning, with her dad and Rachael hard at work painting the nursery, Fin sat on the couch, banned from being near any paint fumes. Deciding to check her emails, she found a reply from *Ryan Kendall* sitting in her inbox. The beginnings of a smile formed on her face as she clicked it open.

"Fin, love!" her dad called out. "When's the furniture being delivered?"

"Next week some time!" she shouted back from the couch, her computer wobbling precariously on her rapidly decreasing lap space.

He walked out of the nursery, paintbrush in hand, his brow creased. "You don't know what day?"

Exhausted, Fin waved at the pile of … receipts her mum had laid out over the dining table after their mammoth shopping expedition. "We went to a few stores," she admitted. "So I guess they're delivering on a whole bunch of different days."

Her eyes returned to the computer.

Fin,

I never saw this for us—creating a family together. Not because I never wanted it, but because it never seemed possible so I put it from my mind.

"Fin," her dad said sternly as he walked over to the table and eyed the pile of receipts. "That's not very organised of you."

"Dad!"

"Don't take that tone with me, miss."

"I'm trying to work," she lied, desperate to get back to her email.

Her dad let out a loud *hmmphf* and disappeared back to his painting.

I can't believe I'm not there for any of it—that when I come home, I'll be coming home to a son or daughter. Honestly? I can't wait. I want to hold both of you in my arms and tell you I love you. Tell you I'm sorry—that I was scared of not being good enough.

Please forgive me.

I don't want you to think I'm saying this because we're having a baby. Maybe it might have taken me a bit longer to work it out in my head, but I would have eventually.

I miss you, baby. So much it hurts, but I'll be home soon.

Please take good care of the both of you for me.

Love,

Ryan.

P.S. I've transferred money to your bank account. Please use it for whatever you or the baby needs.

Not good enough for her? That couldn't be any further from the truth, and her heart felt lighter knowing he finally worked it out. He would be coming home soon and she would be where she wanted to be all along, waiting for him.

"Please come home safe, Ryan," she whispered softly, trailing her fingers down the photo of the two of them on her computer.

How long ago it seemed now, the both of them smiling at her farewell party. That had been the last night she'd ever spent with Jake, and it couldn't have been more bittersweet, or more perfect.

Out of curiosity, Fin signed into her internet banking and checked her bank account.

"Holy shit!" she shouted.

The laptop gave up its fight for space and crashed loudly to the floor. Rachael and her dad both came running out, their eyes wild, brushes held aloft as paint flew everywhere.

"Is it the baby?" Rachael burst out, almost breathless with panic.

"Fin?" her dad questioned.

Fin levered herself from the couch and made a grab for the laptop that laid overturned on the ground. "No." She waved her hand at the computer. "It just fell off my lap, that's all."

Rachael sagged visibly with relief. "You're supposed to be resting. Stop freaking us out! You keep faking your little labour pains to get your own way and it's sending us all into gibbering lunatics."

"I didn't do it deliberately," Fin pointed out as she huffed about on the floor, trying to bend over with no success. "A little help?" she panted.

Her dad grabbed her arm, none too gently, and assisted her back to the couch. His efforts left a big smear of creamy yellow paint up her forearm. "Awesome. Thanks, Dad," she muttered as Rachael picked up her computer and set it down on the coffee table.

"Holy shit!" Rachael shouted as her eyes caught Fin's bank account information spread out on the screen for all to see.

"Would you two ladies stop swearing at the top of your lungs? You'll send an old man deaf," her dad muttered.

Ignoring him, Fin waved her hand at the screen. "It's from Ryan to ... you know ... help out with stuff for the baby."

Rachael's eyes took on a manic gleam as her dad squinted at the screen. "Does he think cots automatically come gold-plated and prams need mag wheels?" Those eyes narrowed as they focused on Fin. "Is this guilt money?"

"No! He emailed me." Fin had no intention of sharing that email with anyone. It was private. It had all the love she felt for him swelling so big and so bright, she couldn't breathe from it. "It's going to be okay." She grinned. "We're going to be okay."

Chapter Twenty-Three

Half an hour later
Eastern Afghanistan

The Black Hawk thundered heavily through the sky, three more following on their tail as Monty gave an update.

"We're heading right into a hotbed of enemy fire," he shouted. He looked Nathan in the eye and reinforced words they'd heard during their briefing. "You're up first. Run low and hard for position. Signal when you're ready for cover fire."

Ryan ran his mind over the details. A patrol had been scoping out a village of potential enemy fighters, keeping watch and tracking details of possible militant activity. They'd taken images, analysed them, noted details and forwarded the information back to base, but during the operation, a soldier had been forced to initiate contact with the enemy and gunfire had escalated into a full scale fight.

Thanks to the intelligence gathered, the briefing Ryan attended encompassed enough detail on the village for them to be able to plan their approach.

"We enter in the western end of the village," Monty continued, his voice forceful and commanding, "and make our way towards the northern end. No splitting up unless you're caught under heavy fire and it's absolutely necessary. We enter as a team, we leave as a team."

Short nods were given in response as tension ran thick.

Ryan was calm on the outside—eyes focused, hands steady, body locked tight—but inside his blood was simmering, ready to bubble through his veins the minute they reached their destination.

"Kendall."

Redirecting his gaze from the horizon ahead, Ryan looked to his teammates—Monty, Galloway, Tex, Nathan and Simon, the man temporarily replacing Kyle—but no one was looking his way. His brows drew together. "Did you say something, Monty?"

Monty shook his head.

Shrugging it off, Ryan glanced around the inside of the chopper once more before looking back to the horizon. Almost there. He could just make out brief tufts of smoke ahead. His breath caught when a big explosion imploded an entire building in a thick plume of orange and grey.

"Motherfucker!" Nathan shouted. "Did you see that?"

With his back facing what lay ahead, Monty met Ryan's eyes. Ryan tipped his chin to the skyline and Monty turned. "Fuckers have got the rocket launchers out."

"We can't get too close," the pilot shouted, tilting his head as he gave Monty a quick glance. "We need you out fast!"

From his peripheral vision he saw the choppers behind them peel off in different directions—aiming for alternate insertion points to enable a full-scale attack.

"ETA five minutes," the pilot yelled.

With his heart thundering in his chest, Ryan wished he could take Fin's photo out of his pocket for one last glance, but there was no time.

Instead, he closed his eyes and saw her instantly. Her blonde locks in a wild tangle, her eyes sleepy, her lips curled as she woke up in bed next to him. That's how he liked to remember her best because she would snuggle into his side, and all that warm, naked flesh would press up against him. Nothing felt better. Even now—his heart pounding fiercely—didn't compare to how it felt waking up beside her in the morning. Ryan remembered telling her just that the morning after the impromptu birthday party Fin had pulled together for him.

"What?" she'd muttered sleepily, pushing hair from her face as she blinked and focused her pretty green eyes his way.

"You."

Her finger trailed a torturously slow path down his chest, her lips curving lazily when he shuddered with pleasure. *"What about me?"*

"You're my heart," he replied softly.

Tucking his hands behind his head, Ryan focused his gaze on the ceiling of Fin's bedroom to give his pulse a chance to slow down. *"Not much compares to the rush of adrenaline when you're in the middle of heavy fire, or when you're screaming off inside a Hercules, or how a Black Hawk makes your stomach drop as it lurches hard in the sky. Except for you. None of it makes my heart beat the way you do."* He tilted his head to meet her eyes and the rush of love he saw in their green depths made him feel ten feet tall. *"It's like it's beating just for you."*

"Kendall."

Ryan's eyes flew open and once again he looked to the Black Hawk occupants, but no one was looking his way. His brows drew together. It couldn't have been Jake. Reading his letter had been like a final goodbye. Since then, the voices inside his head—Jake's voice—had stopped. *Why was he here? Why now?*

Ryan resisted the urge to roll his eyes at himself. *Idiot.* Jake wasn't *here.* Sometimes he felt like he really *was* losing his mind.

Shaking his head to clear it, Ryan forced everything from his mind.

"ETA one minute!" the pilot called out.

The Black Hawk doors were locked open, ready for a fast rope insertion. Nathan was up first. Ryan would follow directly after. Looking to Nathan, Ryan gave him a short nod. After a hard swallow and a swipe of his palms down the length of his thighs, Nathan returned it.

Unclipping his harness, Nathan stood up. At that exact moment, the chopper pitched wildly, and Ryan saw nothing but ground as the bird tilted hard right.

"Motherfucking sonofabitch," the pilot yelled as Nathan stumbled and grabbed hold of the rope above to steady himself. "They're aiming their rocket launchers right at us!" After a brief burst of chatter on the radio to base, the Black Hawk slowed until they were hovering a hundred feet above ground. "We're not going in any further. You guys have to get out here."

The thick, heavy rope went over the edge, unravelling rapidly until it hit the ground below. In what felt like slow motion, Ryan removed his harness and stood. The wind rushing through the open doors was thick and hot. Ryan rolled his shoulders, his dark eyes turning flat and hard as sweat travelled a line down the length of his back.

"Go, go go!" Monty roared over the loud, heavy thumping of the Black Hawk's hovering rotors.

At Monty's command, Nathan flew out the door and into the sky. Stepping up to the edge, Ryan peered downwards to watch him. Nathan's legs and arms were locked around the rope as he slid down with ease. The ground below was hazy with thick, swirling dust—Nathan making his way right into the middle of it. With one big leap, he landed on terra firma and right into incoming fire.

"Christ," he muttered. Nathan was getting surrounded. He needed to get out there.

With instincts firing and years of training kicking in, Ryan locked his body around the rope and launched himself out the door. Nothing else held his focus except the urgent need to hit the ground and get to his teammate.

Glancing to the horizon, he saw a rocket heading right for their Black Hawk and paused on the rope. "Incoming!" he roared, looking up to where Monty stood at the open doors.

The Black Hawk lurched upwards, tilting to the left and the rope Ryan was still attached to jerked wildly.

"We have to pull out!" the pilot called out.

"No!" Monty shouted.

For the first time, Ryan caught a slip of panic in Monty's calm demeanour. At that exact moment, a searing pain burned through Ryan's shoulder. *They were shooting at him!*

"Sonofabitch," he growled, his stomach rolling as pain engulfed his entire body.

Another burst of sharp agony hit his leg, and then another, until he lost count of how many bullets were slamming into him. His grip slackened on the rope.

"Kendall!" he heard Monty roar from above.

Fuck. Time was running out. He needed off this rope before his entire team was shot down.

Ryan looked up, breathing hard as he met Monty's eyes for a split second that stretched for an eternity.

"Don't you fucking dare let go!" came a furious growl right in his ear.

"Jake?" he whispered.

His grip slackened further as the edges of his vision began to blur. He could feel the blood pumping out of his body. It was seeping through his clothes and dripping down his arms and legs.

"We have to get out of here!" the pilot screamed.

"Damn you, Kendall," came a deep growl—Jake's growl—in his ear. "Don't you let go."

With hands slick from sweat, Ryan slid further down the rope. His muscles burned and his mind screamed at him to hold on, but his body wouldn't obey. "I can't," he gasped.

His body was weakening with every breath he drew in, and Ryan knew he couldn't possibly survive this. He wouldn't be going home—not alive. He would never see Fin again, never hold his son or daughter, and the agony had him crying out.

"I'm sorry, Fin." Taking a deep breath, Ryan felt tears burn his eyes and he lost all focus. "I'm so sorry."

Four hours later
Fremantle, Western Australia

Fin stood in the middle of the freshly painted nursery, eyeing the walls with satisfaction. The creamy lemon colour she'd chosen contrasted prettily with the white trim around the windows. She'd bought a set of sheer lace curtains that would sit over a set of white timber blinds. Fin could already see the window open, the lace billowing in the warm summer breeze.

"Alright. Time to leave and let the paint dry," her dad ordered and began shooing her out of the room.

His efforts at getting her away from the thick, caustic fumes irritated the excitement right out of her. *Wait for the paint to dry! Was he serious?* She wanted to curl up on the floor—right in the middle of the room—and imagine Ryan was there with her. She could see him laughing at her as he worked at putting their baby's cot together, or hanging blinds, his brow furrowing as he concentrated.

To her surprise, two deliveries had already arrived a couple of hours ago. The minute her dad and Rachael took off, she was going to start putting together as much as she could.

Fin winced when her belly twinged. It was a painful reminder that she wasn't supposed to be doing anything except resting in bed. The maternity leave from her Government job started four weeks ago, but she hadn't made the reason for her early departure public knowledge.

It hadn't been long past the seventh month mark, just four weeks ago really, that her doctor sat her down and explained the problem.

"You have preeclampsia."

Fin's brows flew up. "Pre *what?*"

"Preeclampsia," her doctor repeated.

"Uh, can you explain what that is?"

"It's serious, Fin. If you hadn't missed your last two appointments, we would have detected this earlier. You—"

"I didn't mean to miss them," she cut in, anxiety creeping into her voice. "It was work. They know I'm leaving and I swear they've loaded me under until I can't breathe. How serious are we talking? Do I have to take a couple of days off?"

"Fin." Her doctor arched a brow in stern disapproval. "You're done with work. As of right now. You're on strict rest until your baby arrives."

"But ..."

"Your blood pressure is extremely high."

"It's stress. I just feel so anxious all the time. I can't relax. Not until Ryan's home."

"According to your urine test today, the high levels of protein are telling us it's not just stress."

"So if I just lie around for a bit, it'll go away?"

Unfortunately it wasn't that simple, and now the birthing plan she had mapped out—from the music, to the levels of pain relief, to who she wanted with her—was all moot. Her baby's growth level was starting to drop off, and the twinges in her belly were becoming more frequent.

"We're booking you in for a caesarean, Fin. Two weeks before your due date."

Honestly? She felt robbed. Denied the right, and the experience, of a natural labour in favour of something so much more cold and clinical. It was something she would have to email Ryan about, but she'd been putting it off. In a previous email he'd mentioned he could be there on Skype during the labour, if she wanted him there, that was. She did, but it seemed her body had other plans.

"Dammit," Fin muttered as she shuffled her way over to the couch and splayed herself out with more than a little effort.

Rachael followed behind, leaning down to wrap her in a hug. She squeezed a little before pulling back. "See you tomorrow."

Fin's brows drew together. "Tomorrow's Monday."

"Yeah, I know." Rachael grinned. "But someone has to keep an eye on you."

Fin didn't relish the idea of being placed under a microscope. Still, it served her right, she supposed. All those mock labour pains done in jest to get her way were coming back to bite her. "Don't you have deadlines or something?"

"Or something," Rachael replied, quirking her brow. "Besides, Kyle's always over here checking on you. I'm starting to worry I'm losing my bff status. Why else do you think I'd be spending my Sunday rolling paint all over your walls?"

"Oh, I see," Fin muttered and snagged a cushion. Panting from the effort, she wedged it behind her head.

"What do you see?"

"It's not really about me at all. You're just worried Kyle's going to get more time with the little baby in here." Fin patted her huge belly for effect.

"I'm supposed to be the cool Aunt Rach." Rachael picked up her bag off the coffee table and flung it over her shoulder. "He's not coming in at the last stretch and stealing that baby away with all his 'cool Uncle Kyle' shit," she air-quoted.

After Rachael plucked her keys from her bag, Fin reached out and snagged her hand. "Thank you."

Rachael's brows flew up as she looked at Fin. "For what? Being a jealous twat?"

Fin laughed. "No. For being the best friend a girl could ever ask for."

Looking a little glassy-eyed, Rachael gave her hand a quick squeeze. "Just don't expect it all the time."

Her dad walked out of the laundry and Fin let go of Rachael.

"Well that's the brushes and paint trays all clean," he announced and leaned over the back of the couch to press a quick kiss to Fin's forehead. "Your mum will be over in a couple of hours, love."

Fin didn't complain as she waved them out the door. She was suddenly exhausted and needed her mum. Her legs ached and her belly was cramping enough for her to gasp. Were they those ghosty pains they were talking about in birthing class? What were they called? Braxton Hicks. What the hell kind of a name was that anyway? Maybe it might be a good idea to call her doctor in the morning. With the decision made to do just that, Fin drifted off into a quiet doze.

An hour later she was startled awake by a knock at the door. Blinking, she called out, "Just a minute!"

Using the arm of the couch as a lever, she pushed herself to a standing position. One step towards the door and she found herself doubled over, her belly tightening with a pain that couldn't be normal. Breathless, she wiped at her clammy brow as she moved towards the door.

"Oh God," she moaned as another pain overtook her. "Mum if you've lost your key ..." she flung the door wide open "... there's going to be ..."

Behind the screen door stood three men. They were all attired in official Australian Army uniform and wearing grave expressions.

Her heart lurched to her throat.

"Ma'am?" Fin focused her eyes on the man who spoke. "Finlay Louise Tanner?"

She nodded mutely as her entire body began trembling.

"I'm Officer Gavin Reed." He indicated to the older man standing by his left. "This is Australian Army Chaplain Bryce Wethers." Then he gestured towards Kyle. "And I believe you know

Trooper Kyle Brooks."

Fin searched Kyle's pained hazel eyes before her gaze dropped to where he was turning a plain white envelope in his hands with care. She watched his fingers run along the edges of it before turning it over and repeating the process.

Her eyes flew back up to meet his. "No," she whispered, her vision blurring as tears came thick and fast.

"Ma'am? May we come in?" asked Officer Reed.

Fin gritted her teeth as another sharp pain stole her breath.

"Fin? Sweetheart?" Without waiting for an invitation, Kyle grabbed the handle of the screen door and yanked it open.

"Can't breathe," she gasped when he took hold of her arms, holding her up when her knees gave out. "Everything hurts. Oh God, Kyle, it *hurts.*"

"Where?" Wild panic filled his eyes as he looked at her. "Where does it hurt?"

Feeling bile rise in her throat, Fin swallowed it down, but it wasn't going anywhere. Leaning over, she coughed and blood filled her mouth. "Oh no," she moaned, wiping at her face.

"Oh *fuck,*" Kyle breathed, his eyes going wide as they fell on the blood she couldn't keep down. "Fin!" He turned to the men behind him. "Call a goddamn ambulance!"

Chapter Twenty-Four

"Finlay. Can you hear me? Miss Tanner?"

Fin tried responding to the urgent voice she could barely hear, but agony was crushing her. She was drowning in it, feeling it take her under, holding her there until she feared it would break her apart.

"Fin!"

Fin blinked her eyes open for a brief second. She was being wheeled inside an ambulance. Kyle had hold of her hand. His grip was firm and soothing. It kept her from being pulled beneath the surface.

"Are you the baby's father?" she heard someone ask.

Kyle met her eyes for a brief flash.

"Don't let go," she whispered weakly.

He nodded at her as she was wheeled swiftly inside the open back doors.

"I am," she heard him say.

"Get in," he was told.

Relief swept through her until he let go of her hand. Unable to stay afloat without it, Fin gave in to the pull and began slipping under.

"Priority one!" someone yelled.

The loud wail of sirens filled her ears.

She didn't want to live without Ryan by her side, but she couldn't bear the thought of her baby dying too. Fighting oblivion, Fin reached out blindly for Kyle's hand again and he took hold, his grip tight as he leaned in. "Don't let my baby die."

Kyle cupped the side of her face, his thumb stroking her cheek. "You're both going to be fine," he reassured her, but the fear in his eyes was obvious enough to tell her she wasn't fine. Not at all.

"Kyle." Fin licked her lips. "You ..." She moaned and drew a sharp breath into her lungs. "You and Rachael ... Godparents. Please, take care of our baby for us."

Kyle choked down a sob. "Ryan—"

"Promise me," she demanded furiously, cutting him off. Her trembling body felt ice cold, like being back in Antarctica, only a thousand times worse.

"Fin. You're going to ..." His voice trailed off as her vision greyed. Something was placed over her mouth and then blackness took her.

What felt like only moments later, Fin was blinking her eyes open. Ryan was standing in her field of vision. She turned her head, unable to see anything else but him. He was so beautiful it made her ache.

"Ryan."

"I'm here, baby," he said softly.

She ran her eyes over him. The bright light was hitting his dark eyes, turning them the colour of liquid scotch. He smiled. "I missed you. So much."

Why was he standing so far away? "Come closer. Please."

Ryan took a step towards her.

"I love you," she told him.

His gaze on her softened. "I want to say I love you too, but it doesn't seem enough."

"Say it anyway," she whispered.

Ryan took another step towards her, and her brows drew together. Something wasn't right. "Ryan?"

"I love you, Fin. I won't ever stop. I'll love you longer than the stars that live in the sky."

Light's flickered above and she blinked. "Ryan. Why aren't you—" She broke off at the crushing weight on her chest.

Ryan frowned, tilting his head as he watched her. "Are you okay, baby?"

"No!" she gasped, fighting desperately for air. He was walking towards her, but it was like he wasn't moving at all. "Why aren't you getting any closer?"

Confusion clouded his eyes and he looked down, watching the ground move beneath his feet. "Fin, I … I don't understand."

"You're not real," she whispered, cold chills snaking down her spine.

His head whipped up, hurt shadowing his eyes. "How could you say that?"

"You're dead. You died!" she cried out. "You left me. You weren't supposed to die, Ryan. I can't live without you. I don't want to. Please take me with you. Please," she begged, tears spilling over and slipping down her cheeks.

Ryan held his hand out towards her and smiled. "I'm here, baby. I didn't leave you. I'll always be here. I won't ever leave you."

Fin reached for his hand, but no matter how far she stretched her arm towards him, he remained out of reach. "Ryan," she gasped.

Ryan paused after taking another step and frowned. "Fin? Why can't I …" He took another step, and another, but he wasn't getting any closer.

She tried to stand but something inside was ripping her apart. Fear had her pulse racing when he started disappearing before her very eyes. "No!" she yelled.

Ryan looked around frantically as though he couldn't see her anymore and suddenly he was gone.

"Don't go!"

A warm hand circled hers, rough and calloused. It squeezed tight, soothing her fear. "I won't go," the voice said.

The bright light burned her eyes as she blinked them open and focused on the man hovering above her. "Kyle? Where did Ryan go? Please tell me he didn't die. I can't ... I can't ..." Fin moaned.

"We're losing her!" someone shouted.

You can't lose me. I'm right here, she tried to say, but the words wouldn't come out.

Ryan had been seventeen when Fin asked him about life after death. It was something he thought about all the time. After losing Kassidy, it was *all* he thought about. Was her soul still alive somewhere, or had she ceased to exist entirely? The memory of talking to Fin that day had stuck in his mind.

It had been just another hot Saturday spent at the beach. Ryan and Jake, along with five of their close mates, had been thundering through the dry sand on the beach, sweat pouring off them as they played a friendly game of rugby in the heat of the day. *Friendly* was really a loose term. They were all competitive; tackles came hard and fast, and swift elbows were planted in ribs as laughter rang out. Sure that shit hurt, but fuck, it was fun. Playing rugby—whether it was for his club or just on the beach—made him feel alive and free of the heavy weight he always carried with him.

Having Fin there made the day that much brighter. Along with Rachael, they were both spread out on enormous beach towels wearing flimsy bikinis that no girl their age had any right to be wearing. Not that he minded running his eyes over every inch of Fin's exposed skin—he just didn't want anyone else to.

Every day it was getting harder to ignore her, especially when she was wearing next to nothing. That particular day he'd been so focused on her rather than playing rugby he found himself getting hard. He had to force the ball to go wide—right into the cold surf—so he could chase after it and cool off.

Ten minutes later, one of his mates and major flirt, Corey, kicked it right in Fin's direction with impressive finesse. Ryan's eyes narrowed to slits at the deliberate manoeuvre, even as he yelled, "Heads!"

Both girls squealed, arms flying up to cover their heads as Corey flew after the ball. Sand was kicked everywhere as he ploughed right through the middle of them to pick up the ball.

"Ladies." Corey grinned as he stood and turned. Ryan stalked over, his eyes on Fin as she sat up and brushed at the sand Corey had flicked over them so carelessly.

Ignoring Corey, she looked up, her green eyes locking on Ryan as he reached the little group of three. His heart fluttered at her focus, making him frown irritably.

Hands on his hips, Ryan raised his brows at Corey. "You about done here?"

Corey gave him a mock salute, and after a casual, "Later, girls," thrown over his shoulder with a wink, he headed back into the thick of the game. Satisfied no harm had come to Fin, Ryan followed.

"Ryan! Wait!" she called out.

Ryan paused and turned around.

Fin stood up, the movement not overly graceful as she stumbled in the sand.

He hid a quick grin and asked, "What's up?"

Ryan was glad the words sounded casual because his pulse was racing as she tripped her way towards him, brushing sand off her ass as she did so. He swallowed a groan, fighting the urge to offer to do it for her.

Fin reached his side. "You okay?"

Ryan wiped the sweat from his brow with his forearm. "Yeah, sure. Why?"

"You just looked a bit funny for a minute, that's all."

Yeah, that's probably because my dick really likes the idea of my hands on your ass. Ryan cleared his throat. "I'm fine. So what's up?" he repeated, anxious to extricate himself from her company just as much as he wanted to stay right where he was.

"I was uh, hoping that maybe you could teach me to body surf?"

Ryan's eyes slid over her near naked form and his dick jerked. *Shit. Pervert.* He forced his eyes over to where Jake was taking Corey down in a hard tackle. Satisfaction curled his lips when he saw Corey eat a mouthful of sand. "You can't get your brother to teach you? He's better at it than I am."

Turning back, Ryan caught the brief flash of hurt in Fin's eyes before it was hidden. "He *is* better," she replied, grinning, and *fuck* he loved how she was losing her shyness and gaining confidence in herself. "But ..." She bit her lip as she reached for his hand. The gesture was sweet and her touch sent shivers of heat down his spine. Unable to fight against it, he curled his hand around hers, linking their fingers as she tugged him towards the shoreline. "You're more patient with me, and you don't make fun of me when I do stupid things."

"That's because you're cute when you do stupid things," Ryan blurted out as he let her drag him behind her. *Shit.* Did he really say that? He needed to take his eyes off her ass before he said something more damning.

Fin stopped abruptly and he almost smacked into her back. She turned, her mouth open. "You think I'm cute?"

"Umm ..."

"Where are you two going?" Jake yelled over his shoulder.

Ryan owed Jake big time for that save, otherwise he might have admitted to just how hot he thought she really was, and encouraging anything between them wouldn't be right.

"Swimming," Fin yelled back.

Jake tipped his chin at Ryan, the gesture telling Ryan to *look after my little sister.*

He gave Jake a brief salute before they continued their path. When the cool, salty water rushed over their toes, Ryan stopped. Fin stepped up beside him so they were both looking out towards the horizon.

Ryan pointed over to the left. "Don't go in there, okay?" His brows furrowed. "See the darker channels? That's a huge rip. And over there..." he pointed further off to his right "...see how the waves aren't breaking consistently there? That's another one. You should avoid that side of the ..." he trailed off, feeling her eyes on him rather than where he was pointing.

"What?" he asked, looking at Fin. Her eyes were clouded and suddenly sad. "What's wrong?"

"I know how to spot the rips." She looked down at the water

rushing over her toes. "When Rachael was little, her dad got caught in one and died."

Ryan turned to face her, taking both her hands in his. "I'm sorry."

"Oh, you … it's okay. I mean, I didn't know him. Rachael barely knew him. It's just …" Fin bit her lip and looked up, her hair fluttering in the soft, warm breeze as she met his eyes. "I don't know what I'd do without my dad … Oh, Ryan, I'm sorry, I didn't mean—"

He squeezed her hands. "No, don't. It's okay. I'm pretty sure I don't know what I'd do without your dad either."

"Do you ever wonder what happens when you die?"

Kassidy's face swam in his mind, and Ryan swallowed the ache. "Sometimes," he replied. "I guess it's normal to think about it, isn't it?"

"It's just … I think if I ever lost a parent I'd wonder if they were still there, hovering somewhere on the edges and watching out for me. I'm scared that when you die that's it. There's nothing after that, like the entire life you lived really *is* all gone in the blink of an eye."

Ryan's stomach rolled at the thought of Fin dying. It wasn't ever going to happen—at least not while he was alive to see it. "I don't know what happens after you die, Fin, but if there really is just nothing, I guess it makes that whole *make the most of your life, you only live once* thing that much more compelling."

"I googled it," she admitted.

"You googled life after death?" Ryan fought a smile. How typical of her to get to the facts of the matter.

"I did. Did you know that when you die, your brain keeps working for thirty seconds after blood flow stops? Then it just switches off. I guess science can't tell you much more beyond that point."

"What do you think happens?"

"I think believing in life after death is a coping mechanism—a way for death not to overwhelm the mind with its finality. Does it make me stupid for still wanting to believe in it anyway?"

"Stupid?" Ryan allowed his hands to rest on her hips, loving the feel of her smooth skin. He tugged her closer and she shivered beneath his touch. "You're the smartest person I know." Then he winked at her. "Besides me of course."

Fin's eyes lit up with laughter, and his lungs expanded at her beauty, at being the one to make her laugh.

"Are you two idiots going swimming, or are you just gonna stand there making cow eyes at each other?" Jake yelled.

"Cow eyes?" Ryan yelled back in the most disbelieving tone he could muster.

Jake laughed as a pretty flush climbed Fin's neck.

"Come on." Ryan grabbed her hand and started leading her into the water. "Let's get this body surfing lesson under way."

"Ryan."

Ryan turned, but Fin wasn't there. *How could she have just disappeared in an instant?* Breathless with fear, his eyes searched for Jake, but he was gone too. The entire beach was empty—the only sound was the waves crashing in the ocean. Ryan stood alone, icy water swirling around his ankles as the day turned dark and cold. Was this the thirty seconds that Fin talked about? Was this all he had left before blackness stole all the beauty away?

"Ryan!"

Irritated, Ryan ignored the voice. Something was wrong. He needed to get back to the beach and find Fin.

"Damn you, Kendall. Wake the fuck up! Fin needs you."

Ryan's eyes blinked open. "What?" he croaked. He tried focusing. Someone was hovering over him. He could see light, but it was hazy, like a film of white was covering his eyes.

"You have to leave now. He needs rest," came a firm voice from somewhere to his right.

"You really have no idea what he needs, lady," Monty growled from somewhere on his right.

"That's Doctor Lady to you," came the firm voice again, albeit a bit more snippy this time.

Ryan blinked rapidly and turned his head to focus on Monty. Why did he feel so damn sluggish and sore? "What the hell happened out there, Monty?"

Monty's brows drew together. "You don't remember?"

Ryan's head fell back against the pillow and he closed his eyes. "The rope ... They were shooting at me ..."

"They got you, Kendall. Once in the shoulder, arm, and the leg. I came down the rope. Managed to grab you just before you fell. They winched us both up and we we you got you the fuck out of there."

"How long have I been out?"

"Twelve hours from the start of surgery 'til now. Kendall ... Kyle rang through. He's—"

His eyes flew open. "Nathan?"

Monty shook his head, the movement short and impatient. "Another team grabbed him and radioed it in. Shot like you but he's fine. Look, Kendall, something's happened to Fin."

"To Fin?" Ryan's hands started to shake and he fisted them. "Monty?"

Monty stepped closer to the bed, rubbing his jaw. "Fin's at the hospital. The doctors are saying she's got something called eclampsia. They're doing an emergency caesarean right now. She's lost a lot of blood. It's … Ryan …" Monty held his eyes. "She's not doing so good. It sounds like her organs might be starting to shut down."

Ryan shook his head. "No." What Monty was telling him couldn't possibly be real. Not his Fin. No. Just … no.

"Kendall. We have to—"

Leaning up on what he recognised as a hospital bed inside Bagram Airbase with no idea how he got there, Ryan fisted Monty's shirt in his hands. "No! Please," he cried weakly, shaking his head over and over, swallowing desperately against an enormous wave of fear. "No."

Monty's lips pressed together, visibly fighting back tears. "I'm sorry."

"Fuck sorry!" he roared. He shoved Monty back hard enough for him to stumble and swung his legs over the bed. Pain screamed through his body like a freight train. "I have to get home," he panted, sweat popping along his brow. "Now. I need to get out of here." He met Monty's eyes. "Help me," he begged hoarsely. "Please."

Monty nodded. "Whatever you need me to do."

The doctor came racing over with a cart, her jaw set determinedly. "You're not going anywhere. You need time to heal and rest."

Ignoring the doctor, Monty helped Ryan to his feet, and he cried out as his stitches started tearing. Red patches were blooming on the bandages winding around his shoulder, left bicep, and leg.

The doctor pushed her way through, and a deep, burning rage gave him the strength to shove her cart out of the way. It careened wildly across the floor, hitting the wall opposite with a loud clatter before tipping over.

"You're not listening!" he yelled, breathing heavily. "I have to get out of here!"

"You're busting all your stitches!" she shouted back.

"I. Don't. Care," he growled, his clenched fists trembling where they rested by his sides. Ryan looked to Monty. "Monty?"

"Already arranged your leave. Got your bags packed. Flight's waiting for you."

Swaying, Ryan closed his eyes for a brief moment. "Thank you," he whispered.

Chapter Twenty-Five

After being rushed through Australian Customs, Ryan left the airport. The automatic doors opened at his approach, and he stepped out. The sky was dark, the air cool, and the stars blinked vibrantly. Closing his eyes for a brief moment, Ryan tilted his head, breathing deep.

Home.

Yet it had never felt less welcoming.

Searching for Kyle's car, he found it idling by the kerb, Kyle at the wheel. Seeing Ryan, he went to step out of the car but Ryan waved him off. The young soldier following behind Ryan stowed his bag in the boot, and after thanking him with a brief salute, Ryan opened the passenger door and slid inside.

A sharp pain stabbed his shoulder as he reached for the seatbelt and he hissed. "Shit." Giving up, he rested his head against the seat, cold sweat popping out on his brow. "How is she?"

Checking his mirrors, Kyle accelerated into the street. "Kendall ..."

God. Ryan could hear a thousand emotions in that one, solitary word. He closed his eyes and braced himself for the worst. "Tell me."

"Fin went into cardiac arrest." Kyle's voice cracked. "She's slipped into a coma."

"Fuck," Ryan moaned, swallowing the tears that burned his throat. "I can't lose her, Kyle. I can't." Opening his eyes, he stared out into the night. Buildings, cars, trees—they were all a blur as Kyle raced them towards the hospital. "What happened?"

"I spoke to Monty. He told me Fin was listed as your next of kin. You were shot, Kendall. You know with those sorts of injuries they notify next of kin personally, especially since the media got involved. He thought—we both thought—it would be a good idea if I went too."

"I didn't think." Ryan swiped a hand across his face. "I should have changed her from next of kin."

"No." Kyle glanced at him, meeting his eyes for a brief second before returning his focus to the road. "You shouldn't have. She's the one who has the right to know first."

Ryan nodded, swallowing. Even though it wasn't fair to put that on Fin's shoulders, Kyle was right, but at what cost? "Was that why ... did she ..."

"According to the ER doctor, Fin was already in trouble and it went downhill from there. She used to fake labour pains." Kyle huffed, shaking his head. "She'd get this little furrow in her brow and would groan and shit—do the whole belly clutch thing just so she could get her way. She got me with it every time, and for a split second it would scare the shit out of me..." Kyle paused, checking his mirrors before changing lanes "...but when we knocked on the door, she was already pale, breathing heavy and hunched over like it hurt just to stand. As stupid as it sounds, I think if you hadn't got hurt, we wouldn't have been there when we were, and it might've been too late."

Ryan stared out the window. "I owe you for being there."

Kyle's lips pressed in a thin line as he changed gears. "You don't owe me shit. It's life. That's all. Just life. What we do isn't easy, and it's not just us that live it—the people we leave behind do too. War is a cold, selfish bitch, Kendall. It changes you. It makes you hard, and it makes you hurt, yet somehow, we keep going back for more."

"Because we're soldiers," Ryan told him, feeling hollow. "It's not just our job. It's who we are."

How many people had he seen die in his lifetime? Kyle was right. It did make you hurt. While people were moving on, living their lives, a deep pulsating hurt lived in him from what he'd seen, and what he'd done, and it would never leave him alone—it was there to stay—and it should have crippled him a thousand times over, but he was hanging on by his fingernails because of Fin. If he lost her, he wouldn't be able to hang on anymore. Already, he could feel himself slipping.

"You're not just a soldier anymore, Kendall. You're a father now too." Kyle glanced over at him, his eyes brightening for a brief moment. "And he looks just like you."

"A son?" Ryan sucked in a sharp breath. He had a son? How was he supposed to be the father he always wanted to be without Fin alongside him? And what did he know about babies? Nothing. Absolutely nothing. Tears blurred his vision when he realised there *was* one thing he did know—*his* son would be loved, and he would never have cause to doubt it.

"Ryan!" Julie called out to him, as though somehow he would miss where she and Mike stood at the end of the hospital hallway. How could he not see the only real family he'd ever known, or miss the devastation written in their eyes? The slump of Mike's broad shoulders told him there was only so much a parent could survive, and losing Fin would surely break him.

Ryan kept his eyes focused on them, forcing himself to take one step after another. How was it they raised two of the most remarkable people ever to grace the earth and it was him that was still standing? How was that fair? Ryan wanted to throw a punch at something. He wanted to yell. He wanted to wake up from the horror. Instead, he shoved his hands in his pockets, ignoring the dull throbbing of his injuries.

Julie threw herself into his arms, and Ryan's bottom lip trembled so hard he had to clench his jaw. If he could go back in time would he have ever left? Would everything be different now? Would Jake still be here, and would Fin be living her bright future instead of fighting for her life?

"You're leaving."

"I'm sorry. You understand don't you, Fin, why I have to do this? You have such a big future ahead of you. You're going to do big things with your life. Don't let anyone stop you from being who you need to be, okay?"

That right there had been the fork in his road. The path he'd chosen had given him his biggest heartbreak, and his deepest grief; it had taken his brother, it had given him a son, and showed him the brightest love he had ever known.

Choking on a sob, Ryan tugged his hands from his pockets and wrapped them around Julie, burying his face in her neck. She brushed her hand over the back of his head in comfort, holding him tight.

"How is she?" he asked, his voice hoarse as he drew away.

Julie shook her head and Ryan looked to Mike. He put a hand on Ryan's uninjured shoulder and squeezed lightly. "She's a fighter." Mike nodded towards the doorway. "Go in, son. She'll fight harder knowing you're there with her." Mike's hand slid away as Ryan moved, taking a step towards the room. "I'll send a doctor your way to look you over when you're ready."

About to tell Mike he was fine, Ryan glanced over his shoulder and paused at the frustration on Mike's face. It was obvious he needed to do something to keep his mind occupied. "Thanks, Mike," he said instead. "I'd appreciate that."

Mike nodded and Ryan caught the flash of relief.

"We'll be down the hall if you need us," Julie told him. "Take your time."

They walked away and when Ryan stepped inside the room he was slammed with a blinding rush of pain. Nothing, *nothing*, had ever hurt more than seeing Fin's slight frame, machines breathing for her, keeping her alive.

Stepping up to the bed, Ryan reached out with a trembling hand and brushed the backs of his fingers over her pale cheek. He trailed his index finger down her nose, across her eyebrows, and over her bottom lip as the machine beside her forced her lungs to inflate, in and out, over and over.

When Ryan smiled at Fin, her eyes would light up for him. When he touched her, her body came alive. Now she felt cold and lifeless, and it broke his heart.

"I'm scared that when you die that's it. There's nothing after that, like the entire life you lived really is all gone in the blink of an eye."

"You can't leave me," he whispered thickly, fumbling blindly for her hand and taking it in his. "Can you hear me? You can't. I won't allow it. I need you." Ryan drew in a deep, shaky breath, tears filling

309

his eyes and spilling down his cheeks. "I need you," he choked out. How did he manage to convince himself he was better off alone for so many years? Fuck that. *Fuck* that. If she died, so would he.

Sitting down before his legs gave out beneath him, Ryan rested his forehead on the edge of the bed, not letting go of her hand. He drew in a deep breath, and let it out slowly. "I have this image of you in my head when you were fourteen," he told her. "Jake and I were teaching you and Rachael how to play soccer in the backyard of your parents' house. It was late afternoon, the sun about an hour away from disappearing over the horizon. It was Jake and Rach against you and me, and we were getting our asses handed to us because sport was never your thing. It was like you had these slender limbs that were so long you couldn't quite work out how to use them. That never really changed. Anyway, I was dribbling that ball up the side, and Jake was running at me. You called out, 'Over here, Ryan,' and glancing sideways *I* was the one that almost tripped over the damn ball." Ryan shook his head at the memory, lifting his head to look at her still form. "You see, the sun had made this golden halo out of your long, pretty hair, and your eyes were so bright and alive as you ran alongside me. You were smiling at me like I was the only person in the whole world." Ryan's voice broke, but he had to keep talking. "My heart skipped a beat because it was right then, in that simple, carefree moment, when I realised I *wanted* to be your whole world. That everything would be okay as long as you kept looking at me like that. That's how I remember you. But you're not looking at me like that now, and I need you to do that. I need you to wake up and smile at me like I'm your everything, because without you, I'm not anyone's anything."

Ryan wiped away tears from his face, and for another hour he sat there—talking, waiting, and hoping—but Fin never stirred.

With a hard sigh, he stood and walked to the window. He stared outside, not really seeing anything. His muscles ached and even under the heavy painkillers, his injuries robbed him of breath at every movement.

Hearing a noise at the door, Ryan turned his head and his fists clenched automatically. He closed his eyes, but when he opened them again, Ian still stood frozen in the doorway like an unwanted illusion.

"Ryan," he said, giving him a nod as he stepped inside the room.

Ryan bit down the urge to tell him to get the hell out. He didn't want Ian here, witnessing him falling apart, reminding him of what Ian and Fin had shared.

"I saw her once, while you were away," Ian told him. "Did she tell you that?"

Ryan shook his head mutely, not trusting himself to speak.

"She was walking down the street in this long, flowing summer dress. I caught the flash of blonde hair and called out. When she turned around it was like I'd been punched." He stepped closer to the bed, towards Fin, his eyes running the length of her, taking in the machines, the tubes, the deep bruising under her eyes. "I felt so cheated," he whispered—almost as though he was telling Fin and not Ryan—until Ian paused, his strained eyes finding their way to his. "She gave you what I always wanted." Ian looked back to Fin. "Maybe I *was* an asshole, but you were the one that abandoned her. I've loved her since forever, and you …"

Don't say it, Ian. Don't fucking say it.

"You broke her," Ian told him hoarsely.

A rush of anger crashed into Ryan, so overwhelming it left him dizzy. "Don't talk about shit you know nothing about," he growled, his chest rising and falling rapidly as he struggled to rein himself in.

"You left her!" came Ian's cry of accusation. "I heard what you did. I *wanted* her. I would have given her everything, but all she ever wanted was …"

"Me," Ryan replied when Ian trailed off, and all Ryan ever wanted was a better life for her. What a fucking mess he'd made of everything.

"You don't deserve her," Ian ground out. The bitterness edging his voice had Ryan gritting his teeth. "You never did."

"Who do you think you are to talk about what I do or don't deserve? You know nothing about my life and you know nothing about Fin's!" Jealous rage leaked wildly into his system, and he couldn't fight against it; he was too worn out, and his heart too broken. "She might have loved you once, but she was never yours. She always belonged to me!"

"That's your fault!" Ian cried out, jabbing his finger as he took a step towards Ryan. "You were always there! Even after you left, you were always there between the two of us. God knows I tried, but you had your fucking hold on her and she couldn't—"

"Will you both stop!" Julie cried out, appearing in the doorway pale and shaken. "Now is not the time or the place. Ian, if you came here to start a fight, you can leave right now. Come back when you've cooled off. And Ryan…" Julie turned to look at him, disappointment clouding her eyes "…I thought better of you than this."

Ryan flinched, her words a whiplash.

"Julie." Ian gave a short nod. "I'll come back later," he told her and with a final, bitter glance at Ryan, he turned and strode from the room.

"I'm sorry," Ryan murmured.

"Don't. I shouldn't … You're not yourself. I get that."

"That guy always brings out the worst in me."

Julie walked over to Fin's bed. She brushed gently at Fin's soft hair, tucking it behind her ears with so much love in her eyes it hurt to watch. "And Fin always brought out the best in you."

After hesitating, he said, "Sometimes I wish that I had—"

"I know what you're going to say, Ryan, and don't. You both had your own growing to do, you especially." Julie stopped stroking Fin's hair to look at him. "Neither of you were ready for what everyone could see between the two of you. You did what you thought was best at the time by leaving. You needed to do that, for yourself, but then you did it again, Ryan, and that didn't just hurt Fin, okay?"

"Julie, I'm sorry."

"Stop apologising. That's not why I'm telling you this."

"Then why?"

"Because you've always been our son. We've always loved you. You see how much you want the best for Fin, how you want her to have everything? We want that for her too, but we feel the same way about you. We want that for you as well." Julie's eyes were firm, her jaw set determinedly as though expecting him to deny her words. "Stop trying to be a hero all the time. You're so busy saving everyone else you forget about yourself."

Turning to look back out the window, Ryan tucked his hands into his pockets. "Saving people is my job."

Julie sighed loudly. "That's not what I meant."

Ryan stared at his reflection. He looked like hell. Fitting, considering that's where he was. "I know what you meant. Leaving Fin was a mistake. I know that now."

After his wounds were re-bandaged and more pain meds administered, Ryan found himself in the neonatal unit, staring down at his son. At just five pound six ounces, his boy was tiny, but "a real fighter," the nearby nurse told him with a happy grin.

"His mother is too," Ryan murmured softly, his eyes taking in every inch of the soft skin, huge brown eyes, and thick, silky cap of dark hair.

The nurse came over to his side, looking between the two of them. "He's all you."

Ryan tried to smile up at her, but he couldn't force his eyes away. "Poor little guy."

"Oh, I don't know about that," she said as she picked up a chart and began scribbling. "Besides, he's probably his mother on the inside."

Ryan looked up swiftly then, his eyes wide as they focused on her. "You think so?"

"Of course," she replied firmly. "This one is a real sweetie. We all fight over who gets to hold him." She smiled again, full force, before tucking the chart away and pressing a button on the crib. "You ready to hold him?"

He panicked at the thought. What if he got all tangled in the tubes and dropped him? "I ..." Ryan hesitated. "What's that tube through his nose? Is that ... can I ..."

She waved a hand at him casually, brushing off his question. "That's just the feeding tube. It'll come out in a few days. He's just in here until we know he's going to be safe against infection, that's all.

He's doing just fine."

She slid her hands beneath his son's neck and bottom, lifting him with practiced ease. Ryan watched her hold his son out towards him, and he took hold, his movements awkward and hesitant. Eventually settled in his arms and the nurse satisfied Ryan wasn't going to panic, she walked away, other tiny little patients demanding her attention.

"You know," she said, pausing as she reached another stirring little baby nearby, "we only know him as Baby Tanner. Does your little guy have a name?"

Trailing a finger down an unbelievably soft cheek, Ryan watched his little boy yawn, his tiny fists clenching as he shifted about in his father's arms. "Jacob. Jacob Kassidy Kendall," he murmured. Jacob would be a Kendall, not a Tanner. Fin would pull through this, she had to, and when she did, she would be a Kendall too.

"Such a pretty name," she replied, moving further away.

"He's named after his Aunt and Uncle," Ryan told her with pride. How he wished Jake was here right now. He ached for it so much.

"Ahhh," the nurse replied, picking up a chart and scribbling absentmindedly. "So he's got big shoes to fill huh?" she called out with a quick wink before turning away.

Ryan blinked back tears as he clutched Jacob to his chest. "You have no idea," he whispered so softly the nurse didn't hear him.

"Kendall!"

With Jacob tucked warm and tight in his arms, Ryan spun around at Kyle's shout. His eyes were red and full of tears. Slivers of fear wound their way through Ryan's body, leaving him ice cold.

"It's Fin," Kyle breathed.

Feeling his heart stutter, he hugged Jacob tighter.

"She's waking up," he told Ryan.

Chapter Twenty-Six

Seven months later...

Ryan stared out the kitchen window of the cottage and into the backyard. He'd mowed the lawn that morning, and now the sweet smell of fresh cut grass lingered in the warm afternoon sun. Pretty flowers fluttered from a light breeze that drifted across the garden Fin maintained with such care.

Fin was lying on her side in the shade of the tree, a brightly coloured blanket spread out beneath her. Her head was propped in her hand, laughter in her eyes as she watched Jacob fidget wildly as he learned how to move his little body.

He watched as Fin shifted to a sitting position and clapped her hands at a giggling Jacob. He was busy impressing his mother by displaying his new rolling technique, and she was lapping it up—encouraging him like he was the first child in the history of the world to perform the feat.

With Fin by his side, it was his chance to finally be free of his demons, but seven months later he realised they would never truly leave him. Maybe they would remain dormant, but they were buried in his soul, just like Fin was.

I can live with that, he thought, his eyes opening to fall on his family. *As long as I have Fin and Jacob, I can live with anything.*

Ryan closed his eyes at the sound of their muted laughter, remembering back to when he almost lost her.

"She's waking up," Kyle had told him, and Ryan had trembled with relief.

Twenty-four hours after Fin stirred for the first time, they'd taken the tubes out and she began breathing on her own. He wanted to weep as he watched her eyes flutter open.

"Ryan," she rasped, her first word throaty and just a bare whisper on her lips.

"I'm here, baby," he replied, brushing her hair off her forehead with the flat of his palm.

"Can't see you," she mumbled.

Ryan was hovering above Fin, looking right at her; but her eyes were blank and unfocused, staring at the ceiling like empty pools. He buzzed for the doctor immediately, fumbling the button in his panic.

"Ryan?" she called out, her voice cracking on the word.

He squeezed her hand. *"Shhh, sweetheart. I'm right here."*

Her eyelids closed and she drifted back under again when the nurse came in.

"She says she can't see," he told her.

Frowning, the nurse left abruptly, returning ten minutes later with Doctor Lee, the man who'd been working around the clock since Ryan had arrived at the hospital. He went straight to Fin's bedside, lifting her eyelids and waving his bright penlight back and forth.

"Why can't she see?" Ryan demanded to know.

"How was her speech?" the doctor asked him, ignoring Ryan's question. *"Was it slurred? Did she know who you were?"*

"It was fine. Scratchy, from the tube, but otherwise okay, and yes, she called me by name, why?"

Fin's doctor moved to the end of the bed, picking up her chart. *"We're going to have to send her upstairs for testing. If you can return to the waiting room, we'll come get you when she comes back down."*

"Tests for what?"

Dr. Lee conferred quietly with the nurse. She left the room and he looked at Ryan as he tucked the chart away. *"It looks like Fin might have suffered a minor stroke while she was in a coma."*

Ryan's brows drew together. *"A stroke?"*

"It's common for this to happen," Dr. Lee told him. *"Her body's been under a lot of stress, along with her heart. When blood flow—"*

"I know what a stroke is, but her sight? Is that permanent?"

"I can't give you any guarantees right now, but if it was a stroke, then it was only mild. Loss of vision can be one of the symptoms, but in mild cases, it usually returns within twenty-four hours."

And it had. Fin had overcome the twenty per cent chance they'd given her of surviving. They all watched the light slowly return to her eyes every day, until four weeks later, she returned home for the first time.

After months of physiotherapy, Fin could walk without effort, but her body had suffered. The cardiac arrest had damaged her heart permanently. She would be on medication for life and was now living with twice the odds of having a heart attack later in life, or a stroke. It was something they wouldn't think of. Whatever the odds were for their future, they would overcome them, just like they had for everything else.

Kyle stepped up beside him in the kitchen, having just arrived for their late afternoon barbecue. "You ready to do it all over again?"

Ryan shook his head. "No. Not this time."

He was clapped hard on the back and caught Kyle's grin. "Well, last time you came home to a baby. Who knows what you'll come home to after the next deployment, huh?"

Ryan smiled slowly. "A wedding," he murmured, taking satisfaction in seeing Kyle's grin getting smacked off his face from surprise.

"No shit?" Kyle peered out through the window, looking to the ring finger on Fin's left hand. No doubt he was catching the giant sparkler right now. It was hard to miss. Rachael adored that ring more than Fin did. Fin *did* love it, but she was always scratching Jacob with it, or whacking it on something. She was worried the stone was going to fall out, but it was insured for God's sake. It was easily replaced if that happened.

"But it's not the same," she'd insisted, pouting until Ryan leaned in and nibbled her bottom lip with his teeth. *"It would be a replacement. It wouldn't have the same soul."*

Ryan laughed. *"Baby, that's mumbo jumbo hippy talk right there."*

"Maybe it is, but I'm all about saving the earth, aren't I? I'm supposed to be hippyish."

"Hippyish?"

"It's a word."

"Jesus Christ," Kyle said, bringing him back to the present. "That ring would pay off the national debt."

"Probably," Ryan agreed with a laugh, bringing the beer in his hand to his lips and tipping it back for a long swallow.

"When did you ask her?"

"A few nights ago," he replied, his eyes falling to Rachael and Julie as they returned to the blanket, both fighting over who was next in smothering his son.

Ryan had been impatient to ask her. He waited months for her to heal properly, but when the right moment came, he was suddenly nervous. Waiting until Jacob had been sleeping, he'd made love to her first, so slowly he thought he'd go out of his mind.

Afterwards, with her tucked in his arms, he'd told her to close her eyes.

"Why?"

"No questions. Just do it."

And she did.

"Ryan?" she called out when his weight left the bed to rummage quietly in the drawer of his bedside table. Finding the ring, Ryan took it from the box, his hands trembling so hard he almost dropped it on the floor. He shook his head at himself. He could lock everything down in the middle of a war, but over this he had no control?

Holding it in his fist, he said, *"You can open your eyes now."*

They flew open, finding him standing naked beside the bed. *"Come with me,"* he commanded, holding his other hand out towards her.

Putting her hand in his, he tugged her from the bed.

"It's cold," she told him, frowning.

Grabbing the sheet and bundling it in her arms, he led her down the hall, and after undoing the locks, he walked her through the French doors and outside.

"Ryan. We haven't got any clothes on!" she hissed, her eyes wide as she pointed out the obvious.

If he had his way, she'd never wear clothes around the house ever again, but she hadn't liked that idea when he told her. *You can't win them all,* he thought, grinning.

"That's what the sheet is for."

Reaching the middle of the lawn, Ryan took the sheet from her and after shaking it out, he wrapped it around the both of them until they were bundled together. Her breasts rubbed against his chest, and he tried not to get hard all over again. He had a proposal to get to, not lawn sex, though that one time after they'd lost the house key in the grass was hot. Maybe after.

"What are we doing out here?" she whispered, looking up at him, the cool air swirling harmlessly around them as they shared body heat.

"Look up," he told her.

A smile spread slowly across her face, but Fin did as he asked. She tilted her head upwards, her long tousled waves flowing in the breeze as they fell down her back.

He looked up with her. It was the perfect night. No clouds. Black sky. Clear bright stars.

"I read the other day that our universe contains more than a hundred billion galaxies, and each one of those galaxies has more than a hundred billion stars. Did you know that every single one of those stars is unique? Out of all of them, not a single one is the same."

"I did know that," she murmured, a smile playing on her lips.

"And they're all beautiful," he told her.

"They are," she agreed.

Ryan's heart started pounding a little harder. What if after everything they'd been through, she decided that life with him—a soldier—wasn't something she could deal with anymore? Was love enough? It had to be. He had to take that chance.

He took his eyes off the stars and looked at Fin, the weight of love he felt for her crushing his chest. *"Ask me, Fin, what I see when I look up at all those stars."*

She met his eyes, shifting closer, her smooth skin brushing against his rough, hardened body. *"What do you see?"*

"You," he said simply.

Tears filled her eyes.

"You're all I see. Nothing holds more beauty in my eyes than you do. No one will ever love you the way I do."

"Ryan," she whispered thickly.

"Remember that day I let you drive my car? You had to agree to that one condition, and when I eventually told you what it was, you weren't allowed to say no."

"Uh huh," she murmured. *"But you never told me what it was."*

"Marry me, Fin."

Feeling Ryan's eyes on her, that prickle of awareness tickling her spine, Fin tore her eyes away from her son and looked up.

Ryan was standing at the kitchen window chatting to Kyle, but his eyes were fixed on her. Catching her glance, he winked and her heart fluttered. His eyes dropped to the ring on her finger, turning those flutters to hard thumps at the reminder of him asking her to marry him.

It had been the singularly most beautiful night in all her life.

He'd looked down at her, his eyes dark with love and apprehension and asked, *"Marry me, Fin?"*

She'd had to close her eyes for a brief moment against the waves of emotion that took her on a wild path down memory lane.

The first time she'd met him that connection had been instant, and had never gone away. Growing up, she'd always been aware of him, the love for him growing inside her, falling into an ache that she was too young to recognise as heartbreak when he'd walked away, leaving her and joining the Army, giving *them* the heart that should have been hers all along.

"Six years, Ryan. Do you know how hurt I was, each day passing by and getting nothing—not even a note or an email? Both of you left me, and I was okay with that. I understood that this was what you needed to do, so I moved on. I built a life that doesn't include you … I'd have given you my entire heart if you'd only asked, but it's not yours now. It's not yours."

She hadn't meant the words because she'd already given him her heart. It had only ever been his.

"I hurt too. For six years I fought every day not to think of you, and I lost, because every day you were all I could see."

And now here he was, in her arms, telling her she was still all he could see, and asking her the one thing that would tie them both together forever.

The smile on Fin's face grew wide. *"Yes, Ryan. I'll marry you."*

Jacob's little legs kicked her in the thigh, startling her out of the memory. "Hey, little man," she murmured as she tickled his belly, warmth spreading through her as he giggled. "Beating on your poor old mum already. That's not nice. We're going to have to get daddy to teach you how to treat a lady, huh?"

He babbled noisily, the sound ranging from a sweet, low pitch to a decibel breaking squeal.

"Wow, Fin. Your son is loud," Rachael told her, as if Fin couldn't hear it already. "It feels like a thousand rusty forks are stabbing me in the ears."

She swooped down on the blanket to pluck Jacob into her arms, but her mum snatched him up before Rachael got the chance. Lifting his little white singlet, she blew a noisy raspberry onto his little belly.

Rachael watched on, her eyes flat, hands on her hips, making sure Fin's mum could see she was unimpressed. "Excuse me, Julie, but I believe we agreed it was my turn?"

"We did." Julie paused to nibble on Jacob's fingers. "But it's bath time, isn't it, my little darling?" she said to Jacob.

Fin's mum started walking away, her grandson tucked securely on her hip.

"Well I can do it," Rachael told her, hot on her heels, her voice fading as they trailed inside and left Fin alone.

She sighed, splaying out on her back on the blanket and staring up into the blue sky, feeling a pang at the knowledge this was her last night with Ryan.

Deeming him fit for duty, the Army were deploying him to Afghanistan, so he was trying to do too much, wearing himself out around the house in the need to fit the coming six months into just a few days. Fin tired easily now—her heart too damaged to function normally—and though she never said, she knew he could see her exhaustion, and it only pushed him harder and wore him out faster.

How could they send him back? Hadn't they suffered enough? When would this war torn country be ready to stand on its own two feet and give her back the man she loved? They'd had him long enough, using him up until there was nothing left for the rest of them.

Fin closed her eyes and an icy breeze dusted her skin gently, causing goose bumps to skate down her arms. She shivered.

"Jacob's beautiful, Fin."

"Jake?" she breathed, her heart clutching at the sound of her brother's voice.

"You'll tell him about me, won't you? I want him to know the person who's watching over him."

Her bottom lip trembled. "Every day. I promise," she whispered, her voice cracking. "He looks so much like Ryan but already he reminds me of you. He has your smile, Jake. It hurts Ryan to see it. He still cries your name sometimes in his sleep, but I don't think he knows."

"He knows, Fin. He'll always have scars, but he's accepted them because he has you, and you make his world beautiful."

"You did too, Jake. The world doesn't shine as bright without you in it. I miss you."

"You can't miss what's already in your heart, honey."

The cool breeze chilling her skin began to die off.

"Wait, Jake!" she cried out, choking on a sob. She wanted to see him one last time, but there was nothing tangible to hold on to except empty air.

"Don't be scared. Just remember to smile when you think of me."

The warmth of the sun began shining through, creating dappled sunlight through the trees.

"Jake?"

Nothing but silence greeted her.

"Fin?"

Her eyes flew open. Ryan was hovering above her as the sun set on the horizon. "You've been asleep for over an hour."

"Oh," she murmured, pushing up on her elbows. She rubbed at her eyes, echoes of Jake's voice still lingering in her heart.

"Are you okay?" His brow was furrowed with concern as he reached down and picked her up effortlessly in his arms.

"I'm fine. I *can* walk you know."

"I know that. I remember a girl once telling me that she *did* have legs ..." he told her, hugging her to his chest as he carried her over to the deck table where everyone was starting to sit down. "But if I wanted to carry her around forever, then she'd let me."

"Ryan," she replied softly, reaching up to cup his cheek in her palm. "You could carry me into Hell and I'd go with you."

"I've been to Hell, baby," he replied. "It's the one place I'll never take you."

The next morning with Jacob tucked in her arms, Fin watched Ryan, dressed in his fatigues, walk out on the tarmac towards the plane. She tried blinking rapidly to clear her blurred vision, desperately wanting the last image of him to be perfect, but the tears were spilling out faster than she could control them.

Holding her breath, Fin watched him reach the stairs of the plane. He took the first step, and then the next, until he turned, as though looking right at her. She knew he wouldn't be able see her from outside—the tint on the windows was dark to keep out the glare of the sun—but she pressed her hand flat against the glass anyway.

"I love you," he mouthed silently.

"I love you, too, Ryan," she choked out through tears.

Then he was gone.

Fin watched the plane eventually taxi off the runway and lift into the sky. When she couldn't see it anymore, she turned and walked away, Jacob held tight in her arms, her heart broken, and knowing it would stay broken until he returned.

As she stepped out into the bright, morning sun, she knew the world would never know her brother, or Ryan, or any of the other silent heroes of the SAS. No one would ever hear their story—what they did, what they gave, and how much they lost. But that was okay, because the world hearing their story was never what it was about.

Epilogue

Present day ...

"What is it about, Mummy?" Jacob asked her, placing his chubby hands on her cheeks as she was nearing the end of her story.

"It's about being the best you can be, Jacob," she told him, turning slightly to kiss his palm before taking both his hands in her own and squeezing lightly. "It's about being brave enough to stand up for what you believe is right, giving everything you have to see it through, and finding peace knowing that what you did mattered to someone, somewhere."

"Did Daddy give everything?"

Fin's bottom lip trembled. "He gave so much, sweetie. So much."

She shifted Jacob in her tired arms, trying not to let exhaustion get her down. After years, her body still had not fully recovered. It never would.

"Daddy's heart beat for us, didn't it? Just like he told you it did in the story."

"It did," she murmured softly, trying desperately not to cry in front of her son. "And you know what?"

"What, Mummy?" Jacob's dark eyes, so like his father's, were wide as they peered up at her, waiting.

Fin didn't immediately reply to his question. Instead, she pointed through the crowd at the airport, her broken heart once again finding peace as her gaze fell on the man she loved with every breath in her body.

"It still does, my baby, and it always will."

Following her direction, Jacob's eyes lit up. He wriggled in her arms until she set him on his feet and he ran towards his father.

Ryan's eyes were bright with love, meeting hers across the crowded airport as he lifted their son into his arms and hugged him hard.

Her husband was home, and with Australian troops finally being pulled from the Afghanistan war, maybe she could hold him a little longer this time, and a little harder.

The End

Acknowledgements

To my readers. I write for my heart, but I publish to share these stories, and these characters, with you. Thank you for reading what means the world to me.

To my husband, my daughter, and my son. I've found my happy with you and I'll love you all longer than the stars that live in the sky. Thank you for your never ending support.

My editor Max. You fought for this story. When I was struggling I remembered every word of support, every comment of encouragement, and I remembered that you believed in me. I love your honesty. I love that I can be myself with you, that I can speak freely, that I can laugh, argue, and be stupid, and in the end, pull something together that makes you proud. I love you.

My amazing team of betas and critique partner BJ Harvey. You work behind the story, spending countless hours of your time helping, supporting, and promoting me. Why? Because you believe in me. You help me believe in myself. You are honest, and you care. You put up with me when I drive you crazy, and when I change things and make you read it all over again. I laugh with all of you, and I cry when it gets hard, and when the book is done, it feels just as much yours as it is mine. Thank you Tammy, Kylie, Kim, Trisha,

Barb, Shelley, Natalie, Orchita and Jo.

To Claire, my proofreader and one of my closest friends. I make your job easy! Thank you for being a perfectionist and making sure my words are seamless.

To Keith Fennell, a former Australian SAS soldier, and author of *Warrior Brothers* and *Warrior Training*—stories about his life in the Army. Australian SAS soldiers are notoriously private, and I'm not sure I could have written this story the way it needed to be told without you. Thank you for sharing your stories from your time in the military, and for your words of encouragement.

To the ladies in the Australian Army who beta read this book. You gave your time helping me and answering questions, and there were lots! Thank you.

Thank you to all the bloggers who have supported me. You work tirelessly—reading, reviewing, promoting—and I'm eternally grateful.

Website:

http://katemccarthy.net

Facebook:

https://www.facebook.com/KateMcCarthyAuthor

Twitter:

https://twitter.com/KMacinOz

Titles by Kate McCarthy

Fighting Redemption

The *Give Me* Series
Give Me Love (Book 1)
Give Me Strength (Book 2)
Give Me Grace (Book 3 coming soon)

Turn the page for previews of
Give Me Love
And
Give Me Strength

GIVE ME LOVE

Evie Jamieson, a former wild child, is not only a headstrong, smart-mouthed trouble magnet, she is also a lead singer with a plan. That plan involves relocating her band, including her two best friends guitarist Henry and band manager Mac, to Sydney to kick off their dreams of hitting the big time.

Jared Valentine is the older brother of Evie's best friend Mac and also the man determined to make Evie his. They strike up a long distance friendship which suits Evie because she's determined to avoid the distraction of love, not only because it doesn't fit in with her plan but because twice in the past it has left her for dead. Moving to Sydney however, has put her directly in Jared's path and he has decided it's the perfect opportunity to make his play.

Unfortunately Jared, co-owner in a business that 'consults' in dangerous hostage and kidnapping situations, makes an enemy who's determined to enact revenge. When this enemy puts Evie in his sights, Jared not only has a fight on his hands to make her his own, but also to keep her alive.

Is accepting the love he's so desperate to give worth the risk to both her heart ... and her life?

GIVE ME STRENGTH

Quinn Salisbury doesn't think she's cut out for this whole living thing. Even as a young girl she struggled. Just when she thinks she's found a way to leave her violent past behind her, the only thing that's kept her going is ripped away, leaving her damaged and heartbroken.

Four years later, she is slowly rebuilding her life and lands a job as an assistant band manager to Jamieson, the hot new Australian act climbing their way to the top of the charts. There she meets Travis Valentine, the charismatic older brother of her boss, Mac.

From his commanding charm to his confidence and passion, Travis is everything Quinn believes is too good for her, and despite her apprehension, she finds their attraction undeniable and intense.

When her past resurfaces, it complicates their relationship. Instead of reaching out for help, Quinn pushes Travis away, until a staggering secret is revealed that leaves her fighting for her very life.

Torn between running and opening her heart to the man determined to have her, can Quinn find the strength within herself to fight for her future?

CPSIA information can be obtained at www.ICGtesting.com
Printed in the USA
LVOW10s0029061214

417510LV00018B/1230/P